PRAISE FOR SINCLAIR BROWNING and

THE LAST SONG DOGS

"[A] remarkably assured first mystery. . . .
Uncompromisingly tough . . . Browning is a strong
writer. And if you can read her opening sentence and
then just stop—well, as Bogey said to Mary Astor,
'You're good, Angel. You're real good.'"
—*The Plain Dealer,* Cleveland

"Authentic and believable . . . This is a great read by
one of Southern Arizona's most enjoyable writers."
—*Tucson Weekly*

"The action moves briskly and is boosted by the motley
cast of characters and Browning's inspired descriptions of
the Southwest landscape up to the very end."
—*Publishers Weekly*

"Written with lots of local Arizona ranch flavor, this first
novel is promising. . . . The down-home, humorous,
often humble, back-to-the-land-and-happy-about-that
attitude of the principal character is refreshing."
—*The Drood Review of Mystery*

"The author . . . knows her way around the territory
and her love of the desert is infectious."
—*The Purloined Letter*

Also by Sinclair Browning

THE LAST SONG DOGS

THE SPORTING CLUB

SINCLAIR BROWNING

BANTAM BOOKS
NEW YORK TORONTO LONDON SYDNEY AUCKLAND

THE SPORTING CLUB
A Bantam Crime Line Book / February 2000

ISBN 0-553-57943-6

Published simultaneously in the United States and Canada

Bantam Books are published by Bantam Books, a division of Random
House, Inc. Its trademark, consisting of the words "Bantam Books"
and the portrayal of a rooster, is Registered in U.S. Patent and Trademark Office and in other countries. Marca Registrada. Bantam Books,
1540 Broadway, New York, New York 10036.

PRINTED IN THE UNITED STATES OF AMERICA

OPM   10 9 8 7 6 5 4 3 2 1

For Ben,

A fine writer in his own right, who is also one of
the most color-blind people I know.
Thank God.
I never knew I had a hidden room in my
heart until you came along.
Thank you.

Acknowledgments

The author wishes to thank the following people for contributing their expertise to the writing of this book: Ken Peasley, Deputy Pima County Attorney; Marge Tremblay, Office of Public and Congressional Affairs, Federal Bureau of Investigation; Dr. Walter H. Birkby, forensic anthropologist, Human Identification Laboratory, University of Arizona; Lori Davisson, retired research historian, Arizona Historical Society; Joyce Garcia; Ron Penning, investigator, Pima County Medical Examiner's Office; Cecelia Rios, clerk, Pima County Fiduciary; Tim Helentjaris, Plant Scientist, University of Arizona; Ben Browning; Mark Sitter, horticulturalist, Arizona-Sonora Desert Museum; Officer Natalie Marquez, San Diego Police K-9 Unit; William B. Addison, Jr. and Charles Lane, Evergreen Cemetery; Lance Sinclair; Debby Adair, Adair Funeral Home; Karen Krebbs, Collections Manager of Mammalogy & Ornithology, Arizona-Sonora Desert Museum; George Kalil, Kalil Bottling Company; Frank Kalil; Joyce Garcia; the late Elizabeth Crane for her knowledge of potbellied pigs; Heidi Vanderbilt; Lisa Baget; and finally, Kara Cesare for her ongoing editorial efforts.

THE
SPORTING
CLUB

1

I PROBABLY WOULD HAVE STAYED IN TOWN A LITTLE WHILE longer if I'd known what I was in for when I got back to the Vaca Grande.

My ranch is just outside the little town of La Cienega, which in turn lies about thirty minutes north of Tucson. While some might think the drive an inconvenience, I really don't mind it at all. It gives me a chance to shake out the cobwebs in my head, and some of my best thinking is actually done on these solitary drives. Business had been a little slow—I'm a private investigator—and on the home front fall roundup hadn't started yet. The grass was still good and the calves were gaining, so I didn't have a lot of heavy thinking to do.

Until I got home.

In November we lose our sun early so it was almost dark by the time I pulled into the ranch. The blackened windows of the little adobe where Juan Ortiz lives reminded me that he left yesterday to visit one of his daughters in Sonora. He won't be back until right before Thanksgiving, when he'll help with roundup.

The lights were on in the bunkhouse, though, where Juan's son, Martín, my ranch foreman, lives. While he always feeds all of the ranch horses, tonight he'd also fed Dream and Gray, my personal horses, along with the chickens and the ducks.

Mrs. Fierce and Blue, my two dogs, greeted me

warmly and we all dashed into the house in an effort to escape the evening chill.

The coffee had just finished brewing when there was a knock at the kitchen glass door.

Martín opened it when he saw he had my attention.

"*Chiquita*, got a minute?"

Even if I hadn't had one, I would have said yes just because of the way he looked. His deep brown eyes were rimmed in red, like he'd been crying, or maybe hadn't had much sleep. The last time I'd seen him looking like that was when I was twenty and he'd been eighteen. Instinctively I knew the same thing that had set him off then was rearing its ugly head again.

"Sure."

Taking off his battered cowboy hat as he crossed the threshold, he sat it on the counter, crown down, threw his lined Levi jacket on one of the wall hooks and took a seat at the old scarred wooden table. That table is like a member of the family. It soaked up my tears when I was told about my father's death when he was killed in a head-on collision years ago along with Martín's brother Memo. It sopped up my sorrow when an aneurysm took my mother, who was half Apache, a short time later. It's supported countless small animals for minor surgeries, been pounded on by angry fists, including a monthlong bout years ago before I finally said *adiós* to my cheating ex-husband, and cradled my head when I've fallen asleep late at night doing the ranch books. The old table has held countless meals and, although laden to the point of collapse during numerous parties and roundups, it has never asked for a repair. Judging from Martín's face this evening, I knew the table was about to share yet another burden.

I poured two mugs of sluggish black decaf and set one in front of him before pulling up my own chair. Picking up the mug, I blew on the steaming coffee and looked at Martín, who was studying his callused brown hands.

Neither of us said anything for at least two minutes.

"Cori," he began.

His forearm, clad in an old denim work shirt, swiped at his eyes before he continued.

Whatever it was, I knew it was going to be hard for

him. And, I'd been right, the same problem that plagued him years ago had come back to haunt him.

Haunt him? Hell, she was probably asleep in the bunkhouse.

Martín had taken a well-deserved vacation last spring, spending a month in Mexico. While he had spent a week here and there away from the ranch, he'd never before asked for an entire month. He'd looked tired and haggard before he'd left so I really had no trouble at all encouraging him to take the time off.

But I wouldn't have been nearly so supportive had I known what he was going to bring home.

Corazon Elena Figueroa de la Fuente Orantez.

She was known as Cori Elena and we all knew her. Her father had worked on the Double A Drag up near Oracle and we'd had a joint childhood. While ranch kids always have to find ways to amuse themselves, since their parents are usually too busy to get down on the floor and play Monopoly or other games with them, as the years went by, Martín and Cori Elena had found a new diversion. They'd fallen in love.

All through high school the two of them had gone steady. It was kind of a given that after graduation they'd marry and Cori Elena would come to the Vaca Grande and set up house with Martín.

But it never happened.

Graduation night, Martín had presented his true love with a minuscule diamond ring and his pledge of undying devotion to her.

And Cori Elena had responded with her own pledge of sorts. Ranch life was too tough. She loved him, but she could never, ever see herself as the wife of a dirty-shirt cowboy.

And that was it. She left the Double A Drag and Martín's broken heart behind and went to work for Valley National Bank in Tucson.

Within weeks she met a nightclub owner, Lazaro Orantez from Magdalena, Sonora. With his bright red Cadillac convertible, gold neck chains and gravid wad of cash, he'd immediately turned her head. Very quickly the rest of her body followed, and when she was noticeably pregnant, a lavish wedding had been held at the Señora de Santa Maria de Magdalena Catholic Church in the town of the same name.

None of us had been invited.

For some reason, her husband hadn't wanted us there.

Although Martín and I had always been close, he hadn't said much since he'd brought Cori Elena home. In fact, I hadn't seen much of his houseguest either. Although she'd arrived with a broken leg, courtesy of Señor Orantez, the cast had come off months ago and she'd still been avoiding me. It was, however, apparent from her current residency, that Light Heart and her Mexican husband were having serious marital problems.

Concerned that she would break Martín's heart again, I'd tried to talk to Cori Elena several times, but she was having none of it. She'd only said that she had some things to work out, and then had tried to assure me that she truly loved Martín and would never, ever do anything to hurt him again.

Right.

I'd noticed that she was still wearing her wedding ring. Maybe, in spite of his abuse, she still loved Orantez, or maybe she just didn't want to give up the two-carat sparkler that graced her left hand. Whatever her reason, I didn't view the ring as a good sign. Hell, that was the first thing I'd chucked.

"I don't need to lay this one on you," he said, pushing his mug aside as he rose.

"Sit down, Martín." I knew if he didn't let his problem out tonight it would fester like an old cactus thorn until it finally burst open. "Talk to me."

He dropped back into the chair.

"*Querida*, you know how important you are to me."

This was totally out of character for him. While we'd been raised together and spent most of our grown-up years working long hours on the ranch, he never waxed poetic about our relationship, nor did I. My connection with the entire Ortiz family had always been solid, one of the few things on the ranch that I took for granted. My mind briefly flirted with the possibility that Martín was going to quit.

I searched beyond his red-rimmed eyes and found the

steady pools of brown, flecked with gold, that were so familiar to me.

"Remember that time when Chapo fell on me and broke my leg?"

I nodded. We'd been up in the Catalina Mountains riding a fence line in rough country when a mountain lion had jumped out of the brush, spooking Martín's horse down the hill. The gelding had lost his balance in the rocks and fallen on my foreman. Entangled in the fence, the situation had quickly gone from bad to worse. Every time the horse tried to get up, he fell back down on Martín. Finally, after thirty minutes of explaining things to the horse and cutting the wire, I was able to untangle the two of them. Somehow Martín had gotten back in the saddle and he'd ridden down the mountain without a single word of complaint. His X-rays had disclosed a double compound fracture of his right leg.

"This is kind of like that," he said.

"Entanglement, or the pain?"

"Both." He forced a smile. "And I need the boss lady's advice."

I laughed. Martín and his father Juan made as many decisions as I did on the ranch. But when there was one that we wanted to avoid making, or wanted to put off, our excuses ran from my "I'll check with my foreman," to Martín's "Gotta check with the boss lady." Of course it was all rubbish since the ranch was really under a joint command. The only difference was that I owned the place.

"Cori . . ." Martín started again, "The baby . . ."

Baby? What baby? God, I hadn't thought of that. Martín had just turned forty-one, and I knew she was a few months younger. Had he been that stupid?

Martín's hands clutched his coffee mug so hard I thought it would pop out of them.

"Quinta . . . ," he stammered, "is mine."

"Quinta?"

"Cori Elena's girl."

"Is yours?"

He looked up at me as a smile slowly spread across his tortured face.

"Martín," I began, "are you telling me that when Cori Elena married Lazaro she was pregnant with your baby?"

He nodded.

"Oh shit." I knew there was no way I could pull out the wire cutters and free him this time.

"She usually makes the coffee, but she had a headache last night. I found a letter in the canister from someone named Carmen mentioning Cori Elena's daughter by a man named Martín. Then she admitted it."

Damn her hide. She kept that from him for all these years. Why the confession now? Why this letter?

"Congratulations," I offered, not really knowing what else to say.

"*Chiquita*, she hasn't told the girl."

I did some quick mental calculations. The "girl" had to be at least twenty-two.

His lips hovered over the coffee mug. The bruises and cuts on his face that he'd come home with, along with Cori Elena, had healed months ago.

"I'm a father," he said, as a look of disbelief overtook him. "And I never even knew it."

"Where's Quinta?"

"In Mexico. With him."

Remembering Cori's broken leg, I asked, "Did he . . . ?"

"She says not."

We talked for another thirty minutes. Cori Elena had told him last night about Quinta's paternity and he'd been awake all night thinking of the daughter he never knew he had. The problem was that not only had Cori Elena never told the girl about Martín, she had no intention of ever doing so.

His bloodshot eyes sought mine.

"I don't know what to do."

I had a sick feeling in the pit of my stomach. I knew there was nothing I could suggest that he hadn't already thought of. The sick feeling was soon overtaken by anger. How in the hell could Corazon Elena do this to him? To Martín? *My* Martín? The man I'd grown up with and loved like a brother. The man who had never intentionally hurt anyone or anything in his life, who, even when branding calves, did it with a sure and steady hand, applying the iron only long enough to leave its mark.

Martín was strong and tough. One time he'd had a toothache when he'd been out rounding up cattle, miles from the ranch or a dentist, and he'd pulled his own molar with a pair of pliers.

And now he sat hunched over the old wooden table, his eyes misting as he spoke of the daughter he never knew he had.

By the time he walked slowly out the kitchen door, we had solved nothing. Our lives had just become more complicated, that was all.

2

BY 7:53 THAT EVENING I WAS STUDYING A COCKROACH.

It was crouched under a corner table and when the old woman sitting there moved her dirty Nike it scurried away, skidding into the adobe before disappearing around the bend. My eyes drifted to the Health Department rating proudly displayed on the wall. An A establishment, cockroaches notwithstanding.

I took another sip of my margarita and looked at my watch. My potential new client, Victoria Carpenter, was now twenty-three minutes late.

Although I'd never met her, I knew Carpenter when she came in. She looked like a ghost, dressed top to bottom in white, with a frilly poet's blouse and bleached lace skirt. She was wearing shiny alabaster cowboy boots that looked as though they'd never kicked a road apple. Her long blonde hair was pulled back, which emphasized the pearl earrings and choker that she wore. She was aptly named, for there was a real Victorian look about her. Still, I wondered if it was her real name.

The cowboy boots weren't so unusual. After all, this is Arizona. But the white getup, in early November, was a dead giveaway. Sure, we're sunny in November, sometimes we're even into the eighties. The Tohono O'odham Indians call this month the "moon of the fair-cold." October's heat is past and January's cold is a month away. Still, we can always tell the snowbirds by their tropical attire during the winter months. Some of them are even bold enough to don swimsuits on their pasty white bodies and sit poolside in December. The crazy ones get in the water. By Christmas I'm usually into a sweatshirt.

Carpenter had good radar though. Before I could get up to meet her, she was headed straight for my table.

"Trade Ellis?"

I stood and we shook hands and made small talk until the waitress arrived with two more margaritas.

"Buffy can't say enough good things about you," she began.

I ran my finger around the rim of my glass insuring that it was, in fact, *sin sal*. Buffy Patania, a former client, had called me, so I already knew the drill. Victoria Carpenter had been a good friend of Rebecca De Ville's, the sister of Charlene Williamson, formerly one of Buffy's best friends. Rebecca and Victoria had gone all through school together in Tucson. In later years they also shared the same vocation. Both were successful romance writers. At least Rebecca De Ville had been successful up until she'd gone off with an ecological study group to Norway. She'd had a bad day, which resulted in her providing a Scandinavian polar bear with a hearty American meal.

After we'd emptied the courtesy bowl of tortilla chips and salsa, Carpenter began talking.

"This is so strange, I'm not sure where to begin."

I stayed quiet, knowing she'd find her way.

"It's, um, not a current thing that I want to find out about." She began to twist her paper napkin into a tight spire. "I've, uh, been undergoing some therapy in Chicago and uh, some things have been coming out that I'm not sure about. Things from my childhood."

Inwardly I groaned. I knew the syndrome. We were in an epidemic of uncovering repressed memories. People throughout the country were remembering awful things done to them as children. And blaming the course of their lives on these blocked events. Not that I'm not sympathetic, it just seems that there are times as adults when we need to get on with things, and take responsibility for our own lives. Yesterday isn't a Pinto with an exploding rear end. We can't recall it and take it back and get a functioning one.

"I have a niece, Jasmine, who lives in Chicago. She's the daughter of my younger sister. Jasmine's six now." Carpenter dabbed her eyes with the twisted napkin. "I see a lot of her and she reminds me of myself at that age." She fumbled in her white handbag and withdrew a picture of a skinny, smiling blonde kid who was missing her front teeth.

"Cute," I said, handing the photograph back to her and thinking the next thing I was going to hear was a dismal recollection of child abuse.

"Maybe it's Jasmine's age, I don't know. But about six months ago I started having terrible dreams, nightmares about things that happened when I was a child, when I was growing up here in Tucson. The dreams would come after Jasmine had spent time with me so I knew they were somehow connected to her, had something to do with her." She drained her margarita.

I motioned to the waitress to bring a small pitcher. Somehow I knew we were going to need it.

"Finally it hit me," Carpenter continued. "It was that Jasmine reminded me so much of me at that age. I guess maybe my subconscious started working, maybe she was the catalyst for my memory. I don't know. Pieces of things that happened a long time ago would pop into my mind at odd times during the day. Scary things, Trade."

"How old are you?" I asked.

"Forty-two."

Mentally I calculated. We were almost the same age. The things she was remembering had happened thirty-seven years ago.

"We lived in the country back then," Carpenter said. "In fact, my father still lives in the same house where I was raised."

I waited.

"There were picnics, not at the house, but farther out in the country. Family outings where people would come and bring their kids and fried chicken and their dogs and we'd spend the day."

So far the memories sounded fairly idyllic, not the stuff that sent therapists' kids to private schools.

"Some of them, that's all that happened. But the others . . ." She shuddered and a faraway look drifted into her eyes. It was as though a piece of gauze had settled on her face. "The others were awful."

"Awful?" I prodded and poured her another margarita. "In what way?"

She stared at me with overwhelmingly sad eyes. "They beat them to death."

My hand missed the glass, slopping some of the margarita on the table. I mopped it up with my napkin.

"Beat who, the dogs?" I said, missing her point.

"People, Trade. They sometimes beat people to death."

"You're telling me that you had these picnics, where people brought their kids, and then beat people to death over fried chicken?" Was she kidding? She didn't really expect me to believe this, did she? I made a mental note to check with Buffy on Victoria's mental stability.

"Look, I know it sounds crazy." Her hands were slowly going up and down the stem of her glass. I noticed they weren't shaking. "And some of it's murky in my brain and I can't remember a lot, even though I've been hypnotized three times. But the pieces that do come in are very clear and they scare the hell out of me. I have these visions of men, and their faces are blurred so I don't know who they are, but I think my father's involved. And they're beating people who have gunnysacks over their heads. They're beating them to death."

"Them?" I asked.

"There was usually only one on a picnic day. But I'm haunted by a man and his two little children."

"They killed his kids?"

She nodded. "Little boys. I can remember that some of the men were really mad about it. The man was invited to go hunting with the rest of them and the invitation wasn't clear so he brought his children along. Someone said, 'It's all right, we can take care of them too.' And they did."

I noticed her eyes were dry. Very dry.

"I remember one of the little boys clinging to his father's leg right before they hit him. He knew something bad was going to happen."

"And you were allowed to see all of this?" Although it was grimly fascinating, I was having trouble swallowing any of the story. Not only did it not make much sense, but I've lived near Tucson all my life. Surely I would have remembered newspaper stories covering something this grim.

"That time with the kids, someone, I don't know who, pulled me away. And I think there were other men who were killed at different times, not on the picnics."

Somehow I knew I'd never hear the word *picnic* again without remembering her story, even if it was far-fetched.

"Vicki, if what you're telling me is true, if people were murdered, then you really need to go to the police."

"Oh, I have," she assured me with a wave of the twisted cocktail napkin. "They've put me through the wringer on this. I talked to the county attorney and they even opened a file."

I felt better, knowing it was out of my hands.

"But there's a problem with it."

"What's that?"

"They're reluctant to stir things up since the murders took place so long ago. Some of the names I remember, some of my family friends who may have been at the picnics are dead, others are respectable people now. There's a danger of ruining their reputations."

"I can certainly understand that."

"And so much of my memory is just a blur."

A blur? Or a stretch of a wild imagination? Where did memory end and imagination begin for a writer? Probably a tough call.

"I've been in therapy for years." It was as though she had read my mind. "The police are willing to do a little, to dig a little and see if they can find any verification at all that the murders took place."

"You've told them where to look?"

She shrugged. "I was five years old. I know the general direction, but I can't remember anything really specific."

I thought about this for a minute. We were in an election year and the county attorney, being an *elected* official, understandably was not going to be in a hurry to slander God-fearing citizens of Pima County. He was probably sticking his neck out to even open a file on the damned case, knowing that it would, in all likelihood, remain unsolved.

"I've come back to Arizona to try to resolve this in my mind," Carpenter said. "I'm here for the winter. I can write my next romance novel and at the same time, try to remember what happened so long ago. I want to hire you."

"I don't know what I can do to help your memory," I said, clearly skeptical. "That's not my field."

"But maybe you can find the people who were killed."

I shook my head. "I don't know that I can. From what you've told me, the police are already looking. They're the ones with the resources."

Her hand gripped mine. "They're not going to waste a lot of people on this thing, Trade. I need to know. I need to find out what really happened back then."

While I've handled some crazy cases as a private investigator, this one sounded like it could win the blue ribbon at the county fair. Still, Buffy Patania, who was rich and knew a lot of people, had referred Victoria Carpenter to me. I can always use extra money, and I can't afford to ignore my referrals, either. Rather than flatly turn her down, I took another route.

I decided I could at least start to look into it, although I was pretty sure there'd be nothing there. The whole thing had happened a long time ago and, even if it wasn't a figment of Carpenter's imagination, I doubted whether I would have much luck. Still, I'd probably know fairly quickly how the case was going, so it wasn't like I was going to filch a lot of money out of her. Besides, with her romance books plastered all over the grocery store bestseller racks, she probably wasn't going to sweat paying me for a week or two. That way, at least, Buffy would know that I had tried to help her friend, and would, I hoped, continue to refer people to me.

"I'll see what I can do," I said. "Can you come to my office tomorrow morning and we'll get started on the paperwork?"

She agreed and I gave her directions to the Vaca Grande Ranch.

Carpenter walked out ahead of me and I was fascinated with the back of her hair. Like the rest of her, it too reminded me of something Victorian. She had it swept up on the sides and then free-falling down her back. I recognized what generated the effect. It had to be one of those Topsy Tail things I'd seen advertised on TV. I'd never seen one in real life before.

We walked across the lighted parking lot together before she turned off in the aisle before mine. I had just stuck my key in the lock of Priscilla, my three-quarter-ton Dodge truck, when she remembered something.

"Trade!" She was in the next row of cars but her voice carried across the dry Arizona night. "I forgot to tell you something."

"What's that?" My door was open and I stood on the floor of the truck so I could see her over the row of cars.

"Those men that were killed?"

"Yeah?"

"They were all black."

3

AT HOME LATER THAT NIGHT, AFTER CHANGING INTO SWEATS AND lighting the fire, I made a cup of cocoa and settled into the La-Z-Boy. While I was disturbed about Martín's revelation of a daughter, there wasn't much I could do to help him with his problem. So instead I mulled over my evening with Victoria Carpenter.

Mentally I made a note to get some of her romance books. While they are not my customary reading, I thought that if I picked up a few of them, it might give me a little insight into what made the woman tick. I was frankly having a hard time figuring her out, which is not like me at all. Usually I can nail a person right off, but Carpenter was not an easy read.

I took inventory on what I did know. For starters I gave her points for intelligence. After all, she was a published writer, and that had to take some doing. Also she was articulate. And attractive. Remembering her geeky white outfit, I gave her a demerit for questionable taste.

In spite of her subject matter, she'd been cool, almost chilly. She'd talked about the black kids being murdered and nothing on her had shaken, nothing trembled, no tear threatened to fall, there had been no show of emotion that I could detect.

The one thing I kept coming back to was *writer*. Romance writer. *Fiction* writer. A shortage of imagination would probably not be a problem for her. After all, didn't she make up stories for a living?

And the one she'd told me could certainly make a book.

But why? What motive could she possibly have to make up such an outlandish tale? If the story got out, I couldn't help but believe that it might turn some of her readers off. The Victorian-looking, romance-writing Carpenter on a Stephen King picnic just didn't smack of a good public relations campaign.

If, and it was a very big *if*, the story was true, what had happened to the black families involved? Had they come forward at the time? Did the police investigate? Why had I never heard anything about a conspiracy to kill black people?

I grabbed a copy of the *Western Livestock Journal* that was sitting on the table, flipped it over and began making notes. Even as I did so, I knew that I was hooked. The cases I turn away, I never put pencil to paper. I always work them out mentally and then discard them. Now, I was making a commitment. Even as I wrote, I felt that the whole thing was just too far-fetched to be true. My curiosity was piqued, though, as I wondered what Victoria Carpenter had to gain by telling such a whopper.

After making my notes, I flipped the magazine back over and got into a story about a new national beef ad campaign. Of course I fell asleep reading it and it was after midnight when Mrs. Fierce's cold nose on my hand suggested that it was well past our bedtime.

A shrill wind blew in during the night and by the next morning the trees were bending and swaying in protest. I bundled up before venturing outside.

When I spotted Chapo saddled and tied to the hitching post in front of the bunkhouse, I knew that Martín would be riding out soon. We'd all been checking on the cattle in anticipation of roundup, and I suspected that that was where he was headed this morning. Although we'd never really talked about it, I also suspected that he knew an hour on the back of a horse could beat weeks in a psychiatrist's office.

Dream and Gray whinnied the minute they heard the screened porch door slam. It was their way of encouraging me, for they knew that breakfast was on the way. They're always frisky in the cold mornings and as I came around the barn they were engaged in a grand game of Arabian tag, their tails flipped high over their backs as they snorted and bucked and reared. They got down to serious business though and came trotting in when I threw their feed into the bins.

I walked back across the yard and watched the ducks waddle out of the pond, scolding me for not feeding them first. After throwing a scoop of feed at them I headed in for breakfast.

Martín's daughter was like a tiny grain of sand wearing away at one of the gears in the back of my mind. Just as I knew that he'd probably had another sleepless night, I also knew that the minute he rode out this morning, I was going over to the bunkhouse to have a serious talk with Cori Elena.

None of these ruminations, however, deterred me from thinking about something to eat.

Breakfast is my favorite meal. I like the sound of it for one thing. Break fast. Yes! I fast every day from about ten at night to five in the morning. *And I don't like it.* I like to eat. Everything. Well, almost everything. I'm actually not that fond of liver, sweet potatoes or okra. Everything else is okay.

So, as sick as it seems, one of the highlights of my day is peering into the pantry and the bowels of the refrigerator in a quest for something yummy to stuff in my face first thing in the morning.

Bingo! I had some enchiladas left over. After a brief debate on eating them hot or cold, I zapped them in the microwave and topped them off with sour cream. In deference to moderation, the light variety.

One good thing about living alone is that it doesn't take any time to do the dishes. A quick rinse and you're done. Life is good.

When I looked out the kitchen window shortly after eight, the roan horse was gone. I waited for another ten minutes before bundling up in my down jacket and heading over to the bunkhouse.

In spite of the stiff wind and the complaints of the swaying trees, I heard the jazzy Mexican music when I was halfway across the yard.

A dancing Cori Elena, clad in an oversized sweatshirt over black tights that hugged her finely molded legs, opened the door on the first knock.

"Trade, *pase*, I've been expecting you." She yelled to make herself heard over the loud music. Bebopping in place, she opened the door just wide enough to allow me, and not too much of the cold air, inside.

The fire in the potbellied stove was doing a great job of heating the room and I quickly shed my jacket.

Unlike her boyfriend, Cori Elena looked like she was getting plenty of beauty sleep.

Petite, almost tiny, she'd always been a looker and this morning was no different. Her black hair was cut in what I suppose could be called a stylish bob. She'd obviously taken some time with her makeup, for her lipstick was shiny and fresh and her dark eyes were ringed in black eyeliner.

As she danced over to the counter and turned off the radio the bunkhouse was suddenly silent.

"Coffee?" She flashed me a smile, one of her best features, framed with deep dimples and punctuated with teeth white enough to star in a Colgate commercial. A tiny mole dripped from the left corner of her mouth.

"Thanks, no. I'll be chasing rabbits all day."

"Rabbits?"

"Going to the bathroom."

"Oh."

Cori Elena was cute, but I'd thought on more than one occasion that her skylight leaked a little.

"I knew you'd be coming to see me." She hung her head and raised her eyes like a kid who had been caught misbehaving. I wondered if she'd practiced the effect in the mirror, for she seemed to have it nailed, but it was lost on me.

"What's this about a daughter?" I asked.

"Quinta." Her contrite look disappeared as she lit up like a Cinco de Mayo parade.

"And Martín's her father?"

"Sí, claro." When we'd known Cori Elena before, she only used English. Since her return from Magdalena, she'd taken to combining the two languages.

Briefly I wondered if she could be so sure of her daughter's paternity, but that was a discussion I was willing to let go for the time being.

"Why didn't you tell him before?" I tried hard to keep the anger out of my voice.

"What would that have solved? I married Lazaro, my life was with him."

"But the baby was Martín's. Why'd he have to find that stupid letter?"

She shrugged.

"That was an *accidente.*"

"But the baby was his," I persisted. "Didn't you think he had a right to know? To watch her grow up? To see her ride her first tricycle? And teach her how to ride a horse and be at her *quinceañera?*"

"You knew about that?" Cori Elena's eyes opened wide.

It had been a guess. And not a too far-fetched one, for many wealthy Mexican families gave their daughters lavish coming-out parties on their fifteenth birthdays.

"Tell me why you did it."

"We did it together." She tried to laugh, but couldn't quite pull it off.

"I'm not talking about that."

I was on slick ground here. After all, Martín was in love with this woman, and if I really crossed the line, who knew what power she had over him? Maybe she'd convince him to pull up stakes and leave. That was a loss I didn't want to consider.

"How could I explain all of that to Lazaro? That the baby he thought was his, wasn't? That Martín was going to be in our lives forever? This is not a good thing to explain to your new *esposo.*"

"But it was a good enough secret to keep from your old boyfriend."

She nodded.

"And from your daughter."

"*Sí.*"

"If you're in the mood for confessions, why not tell Quinta?"

She looked at me like I was a crazy woman. "That's not possible, even if I could tell her that her mother was a *chapucera.*"

Interesting, she'd used the word for cheater, not liar.

"What good would that do now?" she asked, but she wasn't looking at me anymore. She was pecking at the gold moon and stars painted on the red polish of a long dragon-lady fingernail on her left hand.

"It would give them a chance to know each other. Let Martín know his daughter, Juan his granddaughter, Manda her niece . . ."

"That won't work, Trade, trust me."

When she looked up from her hand I was surprised to see that her eyes were swimming.

"It's more complicated than that."

"Is it?"

She looked at the ceiling, then at the potbellied stove, massaged her knuckles and rubbed her face before she finally answered.

"There is a problem . . ."

"No baby?" I prodded.

She shook her head.

"I lied to Martín. Quinta does not live at home with her father."

I waited while Cori Elena got up and retrieved a Kleenex from the box on the counter. She patted the end of her upturned nose.

"She lives in a home in Hermosillo, a home for people who are not right. There was an . . . an accident. Her head was injured."

"Her father?" I asked, meaning Lazaro Orantez. After all, he'd apparently had no trouble pounding on Cori Elena.

"No, no. She was in an automobile accident with some kids."

There it was. Martín's daughter was probably incapable of understanding that he was her real father, even if

Cori Elena was willing to share that information with her. Why in the hell had Cori Elena kept that letter?

"Martín would still love her," I said.

"*Sí.*"

"And he would still like to get to know her."

"There is nothing to know." Although she dabbed at her eyes, she couldn't keep the mascara from running down her cheeks.

"You've got to tell him."

"*Sí*, I am going to. That's why I'm telling you this."

She was covering her bases, this one. She knew I'd tell Martín anything she told me anyway. My allegiance was with him, not her. In spite of her screwing up and leaving the letter in the coffee, she wasn't entirely stupid. She knew Martín well enough to know that if he had a daughter on this planet, he'd track her down and find her. She was cutting her losses now by coming clean with Quinta's condition. Before her boyfriend found out on his own and had another strike against her.

I left feeling disgusted with myself. In spite of Cori Elena's being a battered wife, in spite of her having a vegetable for a daughter, I was not feeling charitable toward her.

She had Martín by the *cojones* in the vise grips and I knew that no matter what happened, I was going to have to keep my mouth shut until her little passion play ran out.

4

When I finally got to my office, an old stage stop on the ranch that I'd converted a few years ago, a few cows were milling around outside. Only a mile from the house, the location has worked well for me.

The old schoolhouse clock read nine o'clock as I poured water through the coffee machine and checked my messages.

I reached for a fresh file folder and wrote Carpenter's name on it. This was the beginning of what would become my paper trail. Every supposition, interview, site, telephone call, lead, newspaper story—in short, anything and everything I could unearth, would eventually find its way into this file. That documentation, along with copies of my weekly reports, combined with the final resolution of the case, would be written up in a report and presented to the client when my work was done. In Carpenter's case, I expected this to be a very slim file.

Nevertheless, I retrieved my notes from the back of the *Journal* and neatly transcribed them onto a clean piece of paper which I dropped into the file. Once I finished that, I stamped the front of the folder with my heavy block stamp, wondering what would eventually be written under the resolution line. Win, lose or draw, something was always written on that line.

Then I got caught up on a little housekeeping, shook the dust out of the Navajo rugs and ran a quick dust mop

across the polished cement floors. I debated about empty-
ing the trash can, but decided in favor of stomping on its
contents, thus compacting them into an even tighter mass
that would make it even harder to dump when I finally got
around to it. Procrastination can be a complex thing.

Although it was Saturday, by the time Victoria Carpenter arrived, I was ready to get down to business.

The seasons had changed overnight, judging from her
dress this morning. She was wearing a paisley turtleneck
over a long black tiered skirt with black boots. A tunic-
length jacket completed her ensemble and her hair was
now piled up on top of her head. I was thankful that the
morning wind had made her come to her fashion senses.
Now at least I could take her into Rainbow's, our local
restaurant that fuels the body and, to some extent, the soul,
depending upon the conversation *du jour*, which can range
from *Is our God a benevolent one?* to *Did you see Pete's kick-ass
buck, it will make it into the Boone and Crockett Record Book for
sure!* On weekends, when the bicycle crowd pedals their
shiny butts up to La Cienega, the conversation can extend
into even broader realms.

Victoria Carpenter was carrying a black leather pouch.

I poured each of us a cup of coffee and then we settled
down, me in front of the rolltop desk, Carpenter to the
side.

"I do want to hire you," she said, as though there
might be some mistake.

I groped in the desk drawer for a contract and went
over it with her. If it was left to me, I'd still operate on a
handshake basis, but the company that issues my liability
insurance insists on contracts. Mine was a simple one and
it didn't take long to explain it to her. Once done, I grabbed
the sheet that I had been working on and started down my
list.

We started with her family. Her maiden name was
Brewster and I learned that in addition to the sister in Chicago, she had a brother living in Tucson. Her parents were
divorced and her father had remarried. I got the addresses
and phone numbers of everyone except her mother. We hit
a stall when it came to the subject.

"I'd rather not talk about her," she said.

"Fine," I agreed. "But I'll need to touch base, to see what she remembers."

"My parents will remember nothing," she said flatly.

"They know about this?"

"Yes. My father's not speaking to me."

That didn't surprise me.

"His yard's already been dug up. The county attorney at least did that."

"Do you want to tell me about it?"

She shrugged. "One of the first things I remembered was that my brother and I were playing hide-and-seek and I went to hide in an old Quonset hut we had on the property. We weren't allowed to be in there, but I snuck in and when my brother finally found me, he opened the door and the light came in. It was one of those wide sliding doors so my father could get vehicles in and out. We found a long cardboard box, sort of like what you'd pack a refrigerator in. There was a body in it, a creepy body with white chalky stuff on it."

"A black man?"

She nodded.

"Of course it scared us to death. We went running up to the house screaming our heads off. My parents got into a big argument over it. Later that night I looked out my bedroom window and saw my father digging a big hole in the yard."

"You think he was burying the body you found?"

"Yes. And I thought I knew where it was."

"I guess the county attorney didn't find it?" I knew the answer to my question or she wouldn't be here.

She shook her head.

"And your mother?" I still needed the information.

She reached in her black bag and handed me a card.

While I didn't recognize the name on it, I knew the place. The Arizona State Hospital, on Van Buren in Phoenix. The loony bin.

"How long has she been there?"

She waved a manicured hand. "Years."

Since I was having trouble suspending my disbelief, I was surprised to find myself again asking *if* the story was true. Had the truth driven her mother crazy?

"She won't be any help. She's lost it."

"You've seen her then."

"Sure. But that's all it was, seeing her. She couldn't, or wouldn't, tell me anything."

I had a feeling of *déjà vu*. She sounded a little like Cori Elena talking about Quinta. What had she said? *There is nothing to know.*

"And your father?"

"Furious. Says it never happened. Can't understand why I would say such things." She anticipated my next question. "My sister remembers some things and my brother Hank denies everything."

"That's not going to make it any easier."

"No." She reached into her pouch. "I think this will help." She handed me a sheaf of papers. "I've been recording things as they come to me. I've made you a copy."

I glanced at the pages. They were dated. "Therapy sessions?" I asked.

"Some. Some come from hypnosis, others from dreams. It's like a giant puzzle in here," she tapped her head, "one of those crazy rotational ones that are almost impossible to solve. I keep getting pieces, but I can't seem to find the big picture, the one on the puzzle box."

She motioned to my contract and I handed it back to her. Taking a Mont Blanc fountain pen out of her bag, she began writing on the top sheet. I was pretty impressed. It had been years since I'd seen a real live fountain pen; in fact, I thought the last one had died along with my Scottish grandfather, Duncan MacGregor. I watched as her bold hand flowed effortlessly across the signature line.

"I've rented a guest house in the Tucson Mountains. It's quiet and will be a good place to write my romance novel."

I grinned. "What do women see in that Fabio guy anyway?" The long-haired blond had graced many a romance novel cover.

"Who knows? He's been on three of my books, though, and they've all done well." She handed me back the contract. "Here's the address, telephone and fax numbers."

She capped her fountain pen. "I'm also looking for a therapist. Do you know a good one?"

I shook my head. My own therapy consists of shoveling horse manure and stomping through mud puddles in my Red Ball boots. As for real therapists, I'm generally suspicious of them. Seems to me that most of them are fairly screwed up to begin with and go into the field looking for answers to their own problems. Besides, if any of them were any good, would Woody Allen still be going after all these years?

"I guess I'll go with my doctor's recommendation."

"You may find that our winters agree with you and you won't need one," I offered. I'd read in the paper about all the people in the East who get terribly depressed in the fall when the days are robbed of sunlight. That isn't a problem in Tucson or La Cienega. We only have a couple of rainy months in the summer and we rarely get snow. When we do, we go apeshit and cancel work because we don't know how to drive in the stuff.

"Well, that would be nice."

I gave her the fax number of Darrell's Hardware in La Cienega and then walked her to the door. I watched her get into her car, fighting the stiff wind as she did so. She was driving a white Jaguar with Illinois plates. While I'm not a car buff, it looked like it was an older model. Still, romance had obviously been good to her.

As I watched her dust settle, I couldn't help wondering if she wasn't thinking of switching genres and moving over to horror.

5

I SPENT THE REST OF THE MORNING LOOKING OVER THE STACK OF papers that Vicki had given me. The pages, obviously computer-generated, were easy to read. While some of the sheets only carried a single phrase, others were more like chapters, going on for several pages.

Even giving Carpenter extra credit for being a novelist, she was telling a whale of a story.

The papers were arranged in chronological order and she started with a brief autobiographical sketch. She'd spent her entire childhood living in the same house in the west end of the Avra Valley. Until she left for Flagstaff to attend Northern Arizona University, she'd never left home for any significant period.

Vicki's parents, Phelan and Dorothy Brewster, were, for their times, a fairly traditional couple. Phelan worked at the Arizona Bottling Plant and Dorothy stayed home and raised the kids. They divorced when Carpenter was in college. After putting in his thirty years, Phelan had retired. Victoria, in her notes, reiterated that her father still lived in the same house where he had raised his children. I made a note in the margin. Later, if there was anything to Carpenter's story, I knew this could be important. Seven years ago Phelan Brewster had remarried, a woman named Hazel Love.

Since I knew where Dorothy was living, I clipped the card with her address on it to the file.

Carpenter also listed her siblings. Jessica, her younger sister and mother to Jasmine, was divorced and working as a secretary at the Art Institute of Chicago. Her brother Henry lived in Tucson and worked at the Old Pueblo Cement Plant.

After the brief family history, Victoria Carpenter launched into her story. It started, she thought, when she was very young, but the most substantial pieces of the puzzle that she was uncovering stemmed from the time she was around five years old. She began talking about her family.

She identified her father, one of those hail-fellow-well-met types, as a "man's man." He was into sports. Big-time. Flopped in front of the television set with a cold one in one hand and a bowl of chips in the other as he watched football, basketball, baseball, prizefights, whatever the local affiliates had to offer. In the fall he went hunting for dove, quail, turkey, deer and bear. He put in every year for elk, antelope and bighorn sheep permits. February would find him stalking javelina, while the open season on cottontails, coyotes, fox and bobcats kept him busy in the off-months, for he prided himself on not being a poacher, although buddy hunting was not beneath him.

Phelan Brewster's biggest moment of hunting glory came when he ran across two mountain lions in *flagrante delicto*. Although he had to waste two shots, he was able to kill them both. Unfortunately, his friends were envious.

As I read, I discovered that all of his activities were peppered with male chums. They would drift in and out of the ranch house on weekends and either watch TV with Phelan or jump in their Jeeps and dune buggies and tear off across the virgin desert, leaving a two-track scar in their wake as they went on their quest for something to kill. If they lacked likely targets they resorted to peeling into the first reasonably high sand bank, where they would set up empty beer bottles in soldier-boy formation and proceed to blast them away with whatever guns they happened to bring along for the great event.

They even had a name for themselves.

The Sporting Club.

If it had anything to do with sports, they were in.

Victoria had written extensively about her mother, and as I pored over the pages, I learned a lot about her, too. Dorothy Brewster, if she minded these weekend invasions to her home, said nothing. Seemingly content to raise her children and keep a spotless home, for she was a victim of her German ancestry, she was the model wife. She sewed, patched, scoured, scrubbed, washed, even ironed her husband's T-shirts and underwear, and cooked.

Carpenter remembered huge vats of stews and soups simmering on the stove so when her father and his friends came home from their expeditions, they would not go hungry. Without protest, Dorothy Brewster boiled the wild ducks with slices of celery, onion and apple to thwart the wild-gamey taste before baking them. She pored over her cookbooks in search of finding those recipes which would disguise the raw taste of venison, eventually perfecting venison ragout, smoked venison sausage and venison jerky. Her husband raved about her braised elk chops in mushroom gravy, and her bear mulligan was fit for a company dinner. Homemade bread, cookies and cakes were ever present. The fridge was always stocked with Millers and Bud. Dorothy Brewster's life was clearly entwined with that of her husband.

Daddy never wanted us to go with him, Victoria wrote, *only Henry.* Henry, I learned, was the oldest child and the only boy. Perhaps Phelan Brewster was disappointed when his fine strapping young son was followed by two girls, for he called them Vic and Jess, never resorting to using their full names, but abbreviating them to names that the casual listener might mistake for those belonging to the opposite gender.

Carpenter vaguely remembered overhearing her parents whispering one night and thought the conversation had something to do with Dorothy's reproductive system. Her mother had gone to the hospital. The reason for the visit had never been explained to her, for such things were never discussed in the Brewster family, but after that, there had been no more children.

Victoria wrote about the occasional picnic, sandwiched in between all of the sporting events. Sometimes there would be potluck affairs at one of the members' homes, but more frequently the group would head out to the boondocks, start a fire and have an all-day party where the men would target practice, toss horseshoes, arm wrestle and drink beer and the women would sit, sew and chat.

In reading her account of the picnics, I felt as though I were transported back into the past by a time machine. The segregation of the sexes was so obvious in her telling of it. The men took the active roles, the women content to sit back, visit and watch them have fun. Funny how archaic and stereotypical it all seemed now. But this part, I knew, could have been true.

I continued reading the family history for several pages and before long I came to the black family.

Victoria's notes detailed a picnic on the far east side. There were six or seven families that came to it. She remembered that her father had not driven out to the country with the rest of the family. He had come later, bringing a black man and two small children. She thought that the older one was around her age, five, and the other was a year or two younger. As I read what she had written, the words actually sounded as though they had been written by a five-year-old, not by an accomplished novelist.

When Daddy drove up with the black people I remember that his friends, the other men, were very angry with him. He took the black people to the back of a truck where the food was on the tailgate and told them to eat. Then he came over to where the men were, near our car. I was playing in the dirt with Jerri Osborne's new Barbie doll on the other side of our station wagon. I had taken it from her chair and later she was real mad when she found out I had it. Anyway I was pretending that Barbie was baby-sitting and I remember she came with a little baby.

I heard the men argue with Daddy and ask him why he had brought the black boys. He said, "I invited him hunting, how was I supposed to know that he'd bring his goddamn kids?"

Then one of them, whose face I can't remember, said, "It won't matter, we'll take care of them too."

Although the office was heated, I was suddenly chilled. I had been warned about what was coming next, but even so, I wasn't sure that I wanted to read it.

I was still playing when they left the area of the car. I don't know exactly what happened next, but a little later I was getting thirsty so I went to the truck to get a drink. Far away, in a clearing, Daddy and the men were standing around the black man and his kids. I remember thinking they looked scared and I thought, "How silly, who would be afraid of my daddy?"

I got my drink and went looking for my mommy. She was with the other ladies and they were sitting in folding chairs. Some of them were sewing.

Handwritten in the margin of these notes was *Stella Robinson passed away last year.* I continued reading.

The other girls were there too, but all the boys who came to the picnic were over at the clearing with their daddies.

I walked around the chairs and started to go back to where I had left the doll. I heard someone crying, so right before I got to the car, I headed over to the clearing. I heard my mommy call my name, but I wanted to see who was crying so I pretended I didn't hear her.

As I got closer to the clearing I could see that black man's hands were tied behind his back, and he had something that looked like a pillowcase over his head. I was small and so I was looking through the legs of the men and I could see the black boys clinging to their daddy's legs. One of them was crying a lot.

I didn't see my daddy, but there was a big man with something that looked like a baseball bat. He hit the pillowcase hard and the black man fell down. One of the little boys yelled something and they were still clinging to their daddy and then they fell down too.

I must have made a noise, because the next thing I knew someone scooped me up and ran with me back to my mommy. I don't know who it was, but when I got back to Mommy I looked back and saw my brother Henry holding a baseball bat. I don't know if he hit the man or not.

I stopped reading long enough to catch my breath. Tears threatened my eyes and I wondered about my wisdom in telling Victoria Carpenter that I would help her. While I am naturally curious, there are always things that I do not need to know. The Sporting Club picnics clearly fell into that category. I knew, even though I had barely gotten my feet wet, that the things I was reading, whether they be fact or fiction, would haunt me forever. Was it worth it?

But along with the tears I could feel my blood pressure

rise. If the stories were true, then it meant that the killers had gotten away with it. I decided I could live with the visions if it would help bring the monsters to justice.

I didn't see the black people again. When we left the picnic, Daddy and Henry didn't drive home with us.

Scrawled across the bottom of this page of the printout was a handwritten note. *Trade, I'm pretty sure I was five when this happened which would make it 1963.*

I continued reading through the papers. There were more one-line sentences and phrases, none of which were readily connected to anything. Obviously Victoria Carpenter was remembering snippets of information. It was like an Etch-A-Sketch drawing, but rather than waiting for the entire picture to form, Carpenter was recording the small memory bytes as they came to her.

She remembered three picnics where nothing happened and then I came to a single sheet of paper that read:
"Hitchhiker? Tags?"

Spellbound, I continued reading, but there was nothing more on the hitchhiker. I did learn that the picnic locations were always new, they never returned to a former site.

I jotted on my legal pad. If there were bodies, then there would certainly be a risk in returning to the scene.

Although I'm not a lawyer, I knew enough about the law to know that there was very little to go on. The recollections of a five-year-old child's memory would not be enough to convict anyone, or even indict him.

I wrote the name Jerri Osborne on my pad. Victoria's playmate had been on at least two picnics. Then I continued reading.

Carpenter included a couple of even hazier memories. It was as though a dark cloud lurked in the back of her brain and she couldn't figure out a way to either erase it or let the storm rain down. The problem with all of it was that it was so unclear. Other than the reference to Jerri Osborne, whoever she was, no names were mentioned in the incidents. When I got to the last sheets, she acknowledged this shortcoming.

It is so frustrating to see these pictures but there are no faces. Sometimes when I see them, I think I hear voices that I can identify. Some of them are the voices of my parents' friends, but then I can't connect them to a face. Somehow, I feel if I can get over this hurdle, I will be able to unlock the puzzle.

The hearing of voices didn't exactly cheer me up. Just when I was really getting into the story she had to pop that one on me. It was a classic schizophrenic symptom. After all, hadn't that "Son of Sam" killer in New York testified that his neighbor's dog had told him to kill? A headline blazed across my mind: ROMANCE WRITER HEARS VOICES, MOTHER IN STATE HOSPITAL. A defense lawyer would have a field day with this one in court.

Carpenter then launched into the story of the dead man in the refrigerator box in the Quonset hut. As in her story to me, she related that her parents had argued and that later that night she had seen her father dig a big hole in the yard. I made a note to talk to Abel Messenger, the assistant county attorney who had gotten the warrant to tear up her father's yard.

The wind was really howling now. Although it was just past noon, the sky outside was ashen, and if it were not for the inside lights being on, I would not have been able to continue reading.

Since there wasn't much more I could do on the case on a Saturday afternoon, I put Carpenter's papers back in the file and headed for the door.

As I turned off the lights, the room was cast in a murky pallor. Kind of like Victoria Carpenter's memories, I thought.

As I closed my office door an old nursery rhyme came into my head. *"Ring-a-ring of roses, a pocket full of posies, a-tishoo, a-tishoo, we all fall down."*

The ditty, like many old nursery rhymes, was an allegory. This one, I remembered, had to do with the Great Plague of London during the seventeenth century. The necklace of roses signified the telltale rash, the pocket full of posies represented the herbs that people carried in their pockets to thwart the dreaded disease, and *tishoo* was the final sneeze before death.

When it played again in my head, I knew then that the visions that I hadn't wanted had begun.

Only instead of pestilence victims falling to the

ground, I saw two small children clinging like baby opossums to their father's buckling legs.

What was wrong with this picture—besides everything—was the fact that Victoria made her living making things up. Maybe I could have bought into the whole thing a lot easier if it hadn't been Tucson. How could such horrible things happen here? And if they had, what were the odds of an invisible plague hitting Arizona years ago and we hadn't even known it was there?

6

In spite of what I'd read, as I climbed into Priscilla I realized that I still wasn't convinced. Victoria Carpenter's story was just too wild, too far out for me to buy into it. Why hadn't there been anything in the newspapers? I'd never heard anything about people disappearing. I also couldn't afford to overlook Dorothy Brewster's mental condition. Did insanity run in the family? The whole thing was just too damned preposterous. Why had I even bothered with having Victoria sign a contract?

Feeling guilty because I had, I headed toward La Cienega. It was too windy to get much done outside, so the library was as good a place as any to hang out.

Our branch of the Tucson Public Library isn't very old. Situated in a remodeled home, right off Highway 77, it is probably the single most intellectual addition to our rural community. There are three other business establishments which have made some concession to the arts. The feed store rents videotapes, Darrell's Hardware Store sells a few books and Rainbow's Coffee Cup advertises "and art gallery." This may be stretching it, as she has now gone to those prints that look like forest scenes and snow and boulders but when you really check them out you find that inside the forest is really a pair of Indians on horses but they are all the same color as the forest and therefore blend in. Frankly I find this insulting to the Indians, to the trees, and to the horses.

If we throw aesthetics into La Cienega's cultural pot then I suppose we could acknowledge the barber shop and beauty parlor. Entertainmentwise there's the Old World guitarist who sometimes sits in the Qué Pasó Mexican Restaurant and the pool table up at the La Riata Bar. On any given Saturday night, spontaneous entertainment can vary in scope and intensity at any of La Cienega's watering holes.

An hour later, surrounded by reference books, I was quickly discovering one thing.

The whole issue of recovered memory was tricky beyond belief.

There were a number of articles written by apparently prominent psychologists affirming that the memory of a traumatic event, usually of sexual abuse, could be repressed by a young child. There was some evidence that very high-level traumas could be removed from the conscious and stored as a complete, flawless unit until something triggered the recall. Yet Victoria, if I believed her, was recovering only bits and pieces.

As I mulled this over, I ran across yet more research. This time, it supported Carpenter. Some so-called experts contended that memories aren't neatly stored in filing cabinets or brain Rolodexes, but are scattered about, cluttering our most important organ. Exactly what Victoria Carpenter was telling me.

Unfortunately, the subject itself wasn't that cut and dried. Memory and emotion were closely aligned. While steroid hormones produced during times of emotional or physical stress increased awareness and imprinted indelible memories, I learned that prolonged stress could have the opposite effect—it could really screw up the old memory storage bank.

Faced with this Lady or the Tiger conundrum, I continued reading.

The kind of memory loss that Vicki was professing was psychogenic amnesia, having nothing to do with injury or disease. Her lost memory might or might not be recovered, with or without the help of a psychotherapist. It was all a big crapshoot.

And complicating matters were the articles written by

psychologists chalking recovered memories up to induced delusion, thereby denying the entire subject.

Evolving from this school of thought were still other experts describing the "false memory syndrome," suggesting that some psychotherapists used techniques that implanted false memories in their patients.

I was closing the last book, when a phrase caught my eye: *Recovered memories often seem to emerge with increasing clarity the longer they are pursued*. If Victoria Carpenter was legit, then maybe as long as she was pursuing it, something would come out.

I turned my research to another avenue as I browsed through the library's lone computer terminal, comforted by the whirring as it tried to fulfill my search. Unfortunately I wasn't sure where to even begin. I went through several categories, but found that I was a bit hamstrung without having a little more to go on. Probably what I really needed, in addition to more information, was access to the old Tucson newspapers, which were housed in the main downtown library. Maybe I could find some record of a missing black man and two children. After searching the computer records in vain, I finally settled on identifying some general books on the Ku Klux Klan.

Although I had no evidence of Phelan Brewster's being involved in the Klan, his so-called picnics didn't seem that far-fetched from organized Klan activities. Reading up on the hate organization might give me a better handle on what I might be facing, although I still doubted that the case was going anywhere.

I was pleasantly surprised to find a couple of books on the subject in our tiny library. One was *Klanwatch*, by Stetson Kennedy. I checked it out along with another volume. My guilt thus assuaged, I headed home.

I was still up at midnight, reading the Kennedy book. It was a chilling tale, filled with hatred and violence and death. Kennedy had gone underground in the 1940s and had joined the most violent klavern in the country, the Nathan Bedford Forrest, Klavern No. 1, in Atlanta.

Stetson Kennedy told all about the so-called Invisible Empire. The secret handshakes and passwords, the codes for people, places and mobilization points. His details of the organization included the oath pledging allegiance to white supremacy and the purity of white womanhood, the color-coding of the robes and the hierarchy ranging from the Kleagle, or organizer, right up to the Imperial Wizard.

Some of the official titles sounded like they could have come out of *Boy's Life* magazine—the Night Hawk, the Great Titan, the Exalted Cyclops and the Grand Dragon. In best secret-club tradition, even the Klan language was different, using a simple code which substituted Kl for the letter C.

It would have all sounded silly and harmless if Kennedy had not included the senseless brutal attacks on black people that resulted in their being terrorized, beaten, and in many cases, killed.

Many law enforcement officers had been drawn, for whatever reason, to the Ku Klux Klan. Klan membership rosters were filled with prominent local types, including businessmen, politicians, governors, state attorneys general, and judges, the most distinguished being Hugo Black, who later became a U.S. Supreme Court Justice.

My eyes were starting to droop and I found myself rereading paragraphs when a passage jarred me out of my somnolence. President Warren G. Harding had been inducted into the KKK in the Green Room of the White House. The five-man induction team had apparently been so rattled at enrolling such a notable personage that they had forgotten to bring their Bible. In its absence, the White House Good Book was brought into service. The President had been so pleased with his conscription that he had gifted the team with War Department license tags so they could run red lights with impunity. Reading that reminded me of Victoria's rote. "Hitchhiker? Tags?" Where was her imagination going to take that one?

I read for a while longer before turning out the lights and finally going to bed.

Sleep did not come easily, for I could not readily dismiss the image of the President of the United States swearing allegiance to the Imperial Wizard of the Ku Klux Klan.

If President Harding could take such a tumble from his senses, was it unreasonable to suggest that Phelan Brewster might have done the same?

7

By Sunday morning the wind had quit and the day dawned in the thirties. I spent a leisurely morning entertaining myself with breakfast, a flour tortilla wrapped around eggs scrambled with cream cheese and salsa, and the Sunday newspaper, which Martín had thrown at my door. The Ortiz men have spoiled me, for on Sundays one or the other drives up to the string of mailboxes at the end of the lane, and retrieves the paper. The rest of the week I'm on my own.

As I wallowed through the news sections, I took particular note of two stories. One was the sentencing of a Texas skinhead who had been convicted of a hate-motivated murder of a black man; the other had to do with a Florida A & M professor who was fired over using the phrase "nigger mentality" in an all-black class.

Rereading them stirred my memory.

Vaguely I remembered David Duke's perpetual candidacy. What was it for? Congress? A governor's seat? I couldn't remember. But I did recall reading that a white racist had won election in London not long ago and that a skinhead in Montgomery, Alabama, had killed a homeless man in a drunken celebration of Adolf Hitler's birthday last month.

And hadn't there been something about a black tourist in Florida being doused with gasoline and set on fire? Last week there had been a news story about our national luge team being attacked by skinheads in a small German town.

Had things really changed so much in the last thirty years? Skinheads, neo-Nazis, the Aryan brotherhood, and other white supremacist groups were still alive and well.

Thus discouraged, I decided to go for a ride to cheer myself up. As I walked toward the barn, I spotted Brownie, one of the old ranch horses that had been brought in to the holding pasture near the house. He'd been a great horse for us—we'd had him since he was six—but he was getting a little arthritic and we'd found a new home for him with a twelve-year-old girl who promised she'd only pleasure-ride him. All he needed was his hauling papers, and the brand inspector was coming tomorrow.

At the barn I found Martín under the tractor. What looked like the oil pan was on the dirt next to it.

"That looks suspiciously not good," I said.

He scooted out from under the ancient Massey Ferguson, stood up and grabbed an old towel off the tractor seat and wiped his hands, which were covered with grease.

"I was dragging the pastures when the whole thing went crazy. Noisier than Mexican Independence Day in Mexico City." He grinned.

In spite of the news, I was happy to see that the sad face he'd left me with on Thursday night was gone.

"Looks like it threw a rod," he explained.

"Sounds expensive." The thing about owning a ranch is that there's always something that needs fixing, replacing, washing, greasing, stripping, painting, stacking, raking, weeding, watering, shoeing, dumping, doctoring—the list is endless.

"Nah." He gave me another wide grin. "Just a pain in the ass. I had to take the oil pan off and I'll have to run into Tucson tomorrow for the part."

"Thought I'd go for a ride"—I stated the obvious—"want to come?"

He shook his head. "Cori Elena wants to go to church."

I'll bet she did. Probably to confess her sin of lying to her boyfriend.

"She said you came over."

"Yeah, we had a chat. You're right, it looks like you've got a daughter."

"I'm working on it," he said with a glint in his eye. "She really doesn't have any good reason not to tell Quinta. After all, she's not a little kid anymore."

Damn. Cori Elena had not told him about Quinta's accident. Mentally, I wrestled with it, but I knew if I unloaded such a heavy thing on him it might force him to choose sides, and I sure didn't want him to be on the other side of the team line. And any relationship I would ever have with Cori Elena—not that that was too much of a consideration as far as I was concerned—would definitely be jeopardized.

So I did the logical thing. I went out and caught Gray, saddled him and rode out the back gate.

Riding is excellent therapy. I think it has something to do with releasing endorphins. The one thing I'm pretty sure of, is that my horse is not, as some men would have us believe, my substitute penis. I never could figure out where that came from. Why would we want such a troublesome organ? But I do need a therapist and friend, and Dream and Gray fill the bill on both counts.

I headed Gray up toward Deer Camp. In spite of the crisp day I ran across a gray squirrel who scurried across the trail with careless grace, his long bushy tail an elegant banner heralding his departure. His tail not only gives him a stylish air, it's also handy. In cold weather the gray squirrel will curl up and wrap his plume around his body, much in the way an old woman cloaks herself in a woolen shawl on a chilly morning. If the squirrel finds himself caught in a rain storm, he'll flop his broad flat tail overhead in parasol fashion. These squirrels are the only mammals I know of with a built-in roof. Pretty neat contraption.

After a healthy climb through cactus and brush and rocks we finally arrived at Deer Camp. Ambitious cowboys, years ago, had dragged up some accoutrements to make their overnights gathering cattle on the mountain a bit easier. Early in Deer Camp's history, the accommodations must have been luxurious for an outdoor camp. Now all that remains are two rusted iron beds with steel springs and an old wooden picnic table with benches attached.

I tied Gray to a tree and sat on the table looking at the valley below. Surrounded by natural beauty I could still see civilization, for the table offered a panoramic view.

Below me, development marched northward like a giant cancer. To the south I could see the vast expanse of the Del Webb retirement community; to the north Saddle Brooke, yet another desert scar that had metastasized into a second planned retirement community—this one parented by a Phoenix corporation—which now hosted over eight hundred fifty homes, with another two thousand scheduled. I never could figure out why people would want to be so far from the city center and put up with all of the country inconveniences—scratchy or nonexistent telephone service and closed roads during thunderstorms, scorpions, rattlesnakes and poodle-eating coyotes, exorbitant home-repair service bills, added travel distance, early editions of the morning newspaper—all to live in a subdivision where you are so close to the guy next door that you know what he is throwing on his barbecue grill. The way I figure it is if you can't have land around you, then you might as well go for the city where at least things are convenient. Still, there are great mountain views from both subdivisions and they offer segregated living to those who can afford it.

Thinking of the segregated living brought me once again to Victoria Carpenter. I guess it made sense, even in this small corner of the world, that there would still be hate-filled people ready to crush those who were not like them. While signs of democracy and hope were widespread, as evidenced by the dismantling of the Berlin Wall, the crumbling of the Soviet Union, the nuclear test-ban pacts, the scaling back of the American military, there were also signs of a resurgence of intolerance and hate.

Yet somehow, sitting on top of the picnic table, eating a Granny Smith apple and contemplating the affairs of the world with a dozing horse tied to a tree, Victoria Carpenter's story still seemed surreal. Could those terrible things really have happened in Arizona? In Tucson?

I took my Buck knife out and carved on the table.

Ordinarily I'm not a vandal. But the Deer Camp table has been around a long time and has suffered through countless surgeries. There are names and dates and linked lovers and scratched-out former lovers and designs and drawings scrawled across the tabletop. Curiously, no one who has ever come up here has chosen to be profane. Maybe it's the mountain air, I don't know.

In one corner I scratched half of a small heart. This would be a symbol for me, I decided, in a rare moment of poetic indulgence. If what Victoria said had happened, happened and the Sporting Club was ever convicted, I would come up and complete the heart. It would sort of be like those old necklaces we wore as kids, where each of us would wear half a heart around our neck and our boyfriend would have the matching half. If there was nothing to the case, then the worst thing that had happened was that the table had gained yet another blemish.

It was only after I had given my apple core to Gray and had started back down the mountain that the thought came to me that I really did have to consider the worst-case scenario, that black people had in fact been killed by white supremacists years ago. While this frankly scared the shit out of me, I found the corollary even more frightening. If I chose to ignore it, and it had happened, then the murderers were free and the victims forgotten, perhaps even unknown. Denial has never been one of my strong suits.

By the time I got back to the ranch it was mid-afternoon. I checked my answering machine and found a message from my Aunt Josie inviting me for Cousin Bea's birthday dinner on Wednesday night. I returned the call and accepted the invitation.

Maybe it would still the raging emotions running through my head.

8

SHORTLY AFTER MARTÍN DROVE OUT MONDAY MORNING, THE brand inspector's white truck drove in. He was probably there to inspect Brownie. I started to go out, but when Jake Hatcher pulled in front of the bunkhouse I figured I'd let Cori Elena handle it. Besides, I had to call Abel Messenger.

I knew Mondays were bad—they are in any business endeavor, it seems—and the county attorney's office was no exception. When I finally got through to Messenger's secretary forty minutes later she tried to put me off, said he was busy in court all day with motions and couldn't possibly see me. I let her ramble on about his busy schedule but resisted letting her pencil me in for an appointment later in the week.

"Please have Mr. Messenger call me," I finally said.

She sniffed with that who-are-you-kidding-he-never-will-on-Monday tone but dutifully recorded my vital statistics.

I wasn't too concerned about his return call. I knew I had an ace up my sleeve.

I used to date Abel Messenger. While it hadn't been the love affair of the century, we'd had some good times together and had parted friends. I knew if there was any way he could call me today, he would. Curiosity alone would drive him to it.

When I walked out to Priscilla, I was surprised to see

Hatcher's truck still parked in front of the bunkhouse. Was there a problem with the horse?

I walked out to the corral but found no sign of either Jake or my foreman's girlfriend.

When I knocked at the bunkhouse, Cori Elena opened the door immediately. She seemed rattled.

"Is everything all right?" I asked. I could see Jake sitting at the kitchen table, his tablet of livestock inspection forms beside a coffee mug. While I'd noticed they'd spent a lot of time together at spring roundup, this was beginning to become a habit.

"Hi, Trade." Jake, looking sheepish, retrieved his cowboy hat from the ear of the ladderback chair and came to the door.

"It seemed like you were here for a while and I thought something might have happened with Brownie," I said lamely. It almost sounded like an accusation.

"No, everything's fine. Cori Elena invited me in for coffee and I had a minute so I took her up on it."

"Have you got time for *café?*" she asked sweetly, but I noticed her eyes were trained on Jake.

"No, I'm heading into town."

"I gave the paperwork to her for Martín," Jake said.

"That'll work. I've got to get going."

Jake left the same time I did.

By the time I hit the office there was a call on my answering machine from Messenger. He said he was heading for Superior Court but would be free for an hour for lunch around twelve-fifteen if I wanted to meet him at the El Charro restaurant downtown.

I called his secretary back and accepted his invitation. She had a hard time keeping the disapproval out of her voice.

I spent the morning getting caught up on files. I worked on two insurance company reports detailing investigative work I'd done for them and then neatly worked on their bills, which I was including with the weekly updates.

On my way out I dropped the insurance reports in the mailbox.

I got to El Charro early. I'd gauged a lot more time than

I needed because I frequently get discombobulated when I'm driving downtown, especially on a business day. Parking can be a bear, but today I got lucky and found a two-hour meter on the street not far from the restaurant, which was set in the vintage 1920s Flores home. Since I had beaten the lunch-hour crush, I had my choice of tables.

I followed the waitress across the hardwood floors through the colorful interior, past the lace-curtained windows and sponge-painted orange walls with their paintings of our Lady of Guadalupe, and ended up on the sheltered brick patio with its own colorful mural. I wasn't eager to advertise my business and I assumed that Messenger would also appreciate some discretion, especially if he was going to talk to me about Victoria Carpenter, so I settled into a corner table, not far from the fountain, hoping the water splashing through the sombrero would help drown out our conversation.

Promptly at twelve-fifteen Abel came in, looking terrific. His tie was askew, his long white sleeves rolled up just below his elbow, his hair and beard that soft salt-and-pepper color, which in addition to giving the appearance of wisdom and maturity, is pretty damned sexy.

I stood and we did quick hugs.

Ordering wasn't difficult. We settled on the *carne seca* burritos. The marinated Angus beef is laced with garlic and lime and sun-dried in a huge metal box that hangs from the roof of the restaurant.

Since we both knew we didn't have much time, we wasted little on exchanging pleasantries. That was one of the things I always liked about Messenger, that I didn't have to tiptoe around him or stroke him before I got down to business. He was a very work-oriented guy. He lived, slept, breathed the law and he didn't suffer fools lightly. He couldn't. He'd hit the county attorney's office right out of law school and had been there ever since, rising through the ranks as his ability and talent in the courtroom illuminated him as a star.

While he'd had many lucrative offers from private firms, including two I knew of from major defense practices, he'd turned them all down, preferring to stay in the county attorney's office. This in itself marked him as an unusual lawyer. Oftentimes the youngsters get their feet wet at the public trough and then bolt at the first mention of a decent salary. Abel was one of those rare types who actually enjoyed prosecuting criminals. Pima County was lucky to have him.

He was also loyal. Randy McIntyre was the county attorney, a conservative Democrat who faced the humiliation of running for his office every four years. So far, Randy had vanquished every Republican challenger thrown at him. He'd spent twelve years in the office and by every indication would spend another twelve. Abel would never take up the gauntlet until Randy was through with it. Until then, he was content to be his water boy.

Our cheese crisp arrived and I played with putting more of the green chiles on his side of the huge tin plate.

"I've got a new case I'm working on," I said. "Victoria Carpenter."

He gave me a blank stare. I could tell that he was having trouble placing her, which wasn't unusual considering his mammoth caseload.

I leaned closer to him and dropped my voice. "Dead bodies, dead black bodies?"

"Oh, Brewster," he said in recognition as he broke off a chunk of the cheese crisp. "What in the hell are you doing?"

"She wants me to investigate, try to find out what happened."

"Lots of luck, Lady Love, the best legal minds in Tucson have been stumped on that one. It's too old."

"So what do you think?"

"About what happened?"

I nodded.

He shrugged. "I honestly don't know. Maybe it happened, maybe it didn't. We put a lot of guys on the case and they came up with zippo, zilch, *nada*. Hell, we even dug up the old man's yard, she tell you that?"

"Yeah, and I keep wondering why you'd do that if she was a kook."

"Gut. Instinct. Whatever. You've got to look at every one of them because maybe one out of twenty will be real."

"She was that sincere?"

He laughed. "They're all that sincere, at least they don't think they're lying to you. They really *saw* that spaceship land in the backyard."

"And there was nothing there?"

"That's a tough one. We could have been off two feet. If a body was buried, there's just no telling."

"Can't you use dogs or something? I can't believe with all of our modern technology that there isn't a more scientific way to find buried bodies than with a shovel."

"Ground-penetrating radar. Big city. Sci-fi. This is the real world of budgets and getting by with what we have. Plus we're dealing with a kid's memory. I knew it was a long shot."

The waitress set our plates down, refilled our water glasses and left us alone.

"Victoria gave me a written account of what she remembered."

"We've got one too. It's pretty bizarre."

"Do you believe it?"

"Hell, I don't know. We see and hear a lot of strange stuff in this business, anything's possible." He waved his fork in the air. "But we've got a lot of problems with this one. Number one, it's ancient history. That's tough. It's hard enough getting a conviction around here with something that happened a year ago, much less thirty. We put a team on it. With the stories she told, one thing kept coming back again and again to me."

"The kids."

"Yep. I kept thinking that if a father and his two kids disappeared, someone must have known about it, reported them missing. The kids would have disappeared from school, someone would have had to have noticed. I felt if I could just track down those kids, then maybe I'd have a case. She thinks that guy worked with her father at the bottling plant."

"Then there must be records."

"Buried in dusty basements, and we don't have the manpower to go through them. I concentrated on the kids, sent some guys over to the school district. The problem is, back then, no one seemed to care if a couple of black kids didn't show up for school. The records may be there, but they'll be hidden in tons of paper. No one's got the manpower, it would just take too long."

"There must be a way."

"I haven't been able to find one. The detectives went to the bottling plant, checked records there, but there was damned little from the sixties and nothing that helped. The guy could have been an itinerant worker. Maybe he was hired for a couple of weeks or something. No one seems to remember him, and a lot of the players are dead."

"And you checked with the black community?" I asked.

A troubled look came over his face. "That may be the one loose end. We asked a few questions but didn't get very far. I had the Franklin case then, which didn't make me very popular."

I remembered Jonathan Franklin. He was a handsome black kid who had gotten into some fracas at a local fraternity. In the uproar a university policeman had been killed and Franklin had been nailed. The problem was, a lot of people, black and white alike, had thought him innocent and just a convenient scapegoat. Abel had successfully prosecuted the case and Franklin had gone to jail.

"There's a dual responsibility here. If Victoria Brewster is telling the truth, then I want to nail the sons-a-bitches. On the other hand, what if it's not true? Now it's thirty years later and we go tearing into people's lives. They're in business, responsible people, how do we investigate without harming them? It's ticklish. Plus all she talks about is fuzzy faces."

"Can I get access to the file?"

He reached for the check but I grabbed it out of his hand. After all, this was my idea.

"Nope. It's still open."

"Then you're still investigating it?"

"No, it's just still open. There are a couple of detectives that don't want to let it go. As long as it's an open case, I can't let you have it."

I nodded. Carpenter had not put the names in my file for a reason. I'd have to talk to her.

Messenger stood and I followed suit.

"One more thing, Lady Love."

I looked at him.

"Carpenter's elevator may not go all the way to the top floor."

That didn't make me feel any better.

9

Once I was back in Priscilla I checked Carpenter's file, rummaging through it until I found her address. I remembered her telling me that she had rented a guest house in the Tucson Mountains.

Tucson is nestled in a broad valley, surrounded by four mountain ranges, actually more if you count the ones behind the major highlands. The Tucson Mountains are closest to the downtown area, a nice natural backdrop to the city's few high-rise buildings.

Since I was so close, and needed the answers to some questions, I decided to drive out to Carpenter's. Briefly I thought about stopping to make a call to her, then dismissed the thought. In my business, dropping in can sometimes be rewarding.

So I headed west on Speedway toward Gates Pass. Since I've lived in this area all of my life, I have a pretty good idea of direction and usually have no trouble finding addresses. Carpenter's was no exception.

I found the long string of mailboxes that heralded the Great Rock Ranch. I knew the place. It had belonged to one of the Campbell's soup heirs years ago and had started as a large rock home on a lot of acreage. Over the years the property had mutated and now there was a scattering of small rock houses, all rental units that nestled around the huge main house like chicks around a mother hen. The ranch had a reputation for harboring artistic types—writers, musicians, artists, occasionally an itinerant actor. The ranch had even hosted some people who had gone on to make it big.

Of course not all of them confessed to having been residents, since they were not eager to be tarred with the Great Rock Ranch Rumors. They had run rampant, starting back in the ranch's early history with stories of wild, drunken orgies. As the rumors changed, moving on to skinny-dipping parties, love-ins, pot-planting moonlight rituals, psychedelic birthday cakes, AA picnics and male howlings, the history of the ranch had become a great social commentary of the times, as accurate a barometer as any sociologist's master's thesis.

While from time to time I had known various residents of the ranch, I couldn't recall anyone that I knew who was currently living there.

Victoria had given me the number of her guest house, so I drove slowly through the property. Visitors were apparently common, since none of the mongrel dogs bothered to even give me a bark. In fact, most of them seemed content to stay sprawled out on the dirt as Priscilla's diesel roar drifted by.

I found Number 14 at the rear of the property and was glad to see the white Jaguar in the drive. Like all of the small houses, this one had its privacy. Although the mesquite trees had shed their leaves for the winter, the thick limbs and overhanging canopies still offered ample shade.

Before I even reached the front door I could see Victoria Carpenter through the huge plate-glass window. She was working at what looked like a kitchen table. I rang the wind chimes that served as a doorbell.

She disappeared from my sight and the door opened.

"Trade! What a pleasant surprise!" Carpenter stepped aside, holding the screen door so I could enter the house.

"I was in the area so I thought I'd drop in," I said, aware that my explanation sounded pretty feeble.

"I was just having a cup of tea, won't you join me?"

My eyes drifted to the table. A stack of papers was piled next to a laptop computer along with a cup and saucer set to one side. Books lay scattered across the table and on the floor.

"Excuse the mess," Carpenter said as she turned over two of the books next to the computer, titles down. She kicked the ones on the floor under the table, in an obvious gesture to keep me from reading the titles.

I was disappointed. I thought that as a writer she would have had more respect for books.

Now she was behind the tile counter, pouring tea.

"Peach Spice," she said, handing me a cup.

"Nice place."

"Isn't it though? Small but just right. I've already had several fires." She pointed to the rock fireplace. "I don't have one at home."

She handed me a cup of tea and I followed her into the living room. Victoria curled up on the couch, tucking her feet underneath her, and I chose a worn leather chair.

"Did you find a therapist?"

She wrinkled her nose. "I went with my doctor's recommendation, but I'm not sure about this one. I've seen him once."

"Well," I nodded in the direction of the table, "it looks as though your work is going well."

"It usually does. It's only when I get to the love scenes that I choke up." She sipped on her tea.

"That's not a pun?"

"Unintended."

"So writing the sex isn't the fun part?"

"Not when you've done it year after year, book after book. It's kind of hard to stay either creative or enthusiastic."

I laughed, wishing I could give her some good ideas, but the fact was, I haven't been laid in quite a while, so the only contribution I could make would come either from some dim recess of my mind or from my fantasies. Judging from the success of her books in the supermarket, she wasn't having any trouble with her own imagination.

"My agent's coming out in a few weeks and I'm hoping to be able to give her a large partial on the new manuscript to take back."

"I'd like to read one of your books sometime."

"Really?" She seemed pleased. There was a wicker

basket on the floor next to the sofa. She threw a couple of magazines aside and handed me a paperback book.

"*Love's Finest Hour*," I read. It was a historical romance with a clinch scene on the cover. Fabio hadn't graced this one. Two movie-star-looking people were welded together. Somehow the kneeling hero had managed to bury his face in no-man's-land, just below the heroine's breasts. This worked out all right, allowing her cleavage to bulge upward from her low-cut lace bodice. While in my estimation he didn't seem to be doing anything significant, there was a look of beatific ecstasy on his playmate's face.

"Very nice," I lied as I held the book out to her.

"Keep it. If you like it, I have more."

"How many have you done?"

"I don't know, somewhere around twenty."

The book was heavy in my hand. Twenty of them was a substantial amount of work.

"Soon to be twenty-one," I said, nodding in the direction of the laptop.

A funny look crossed her face, so fleeting that I wondered if I was imagining it.

"Yes."

"What's this one about?"

"What's what about?"

I nodded in the direction of the table. "The book you're working on."

"The usual. Woman meets man, loses man, gets man."

"They can't be that simple." I turned the book over in my hands and glanced at the back cover copy.

"They're not. Just somewhat formulaic."

"But fun to write?"

"I look at it more like work."

"How do you come up with the guys?"

She retrieved one of the magazines she'd pushed aside, flipped through it and held up a car ad with a gorgeous-looking mountain climber looking down on a glamorous woman in a Chrysler Le Baron convertible. "He'll do."

"It can't be that easy." How could a picture become a character?

"It is. This gives me the visual and I run with it."

"So is he the one in this book?"

She gave me another funny look. "I don't really like to talk about my work."

Strange. Most people loved to.

"My subconscious doesn't know the difference between writing something down or telling it. If I talk too much about what I'm writing before I write it, the written material won't be as fresh or as spontaneous." She fidgeted on the couch, clearly uncomfortable.

Was this the same woman who had just chalked her romances up to being formulaic? Who put the burr under her saddle?

I quickly changed the subject.

"I met with Abel Messenger today."

"Does he have anything new?"

"No, although he's still got it as an open case, which won't help me. It seems there are some names missing from the papers you gave me," I said, trying to keep accusation out of my voice.

"No, I did it on purpose. I wanted you to read it without them in it so you wouldn't be influenced by them."

"Influenced in what way?"

She got up and walked out of the room.

I waited.

She returned almost immediately and handed me a single sheet of paper before she sat back down.

I looked at it. There were four names on it and at least a paragraph beside each name.

The first two, Charles Stone and David Robinson, meant nothing to me. The third name was Trevor Osborne, and under his family Victoria had listed Jerri, the same child that she said she had played with on some of the club picnics, the girl who had the great toys, the fantastic plastic horse and rider collection and the brand-new Barbie. Trevor's wife, Libby, had committed suicide years earlier.

But it was the fourth name that threw me.

"Dan Daglio?" I said. "*The* Dan Daglio?"

She nodded.

"He was in the Sporting Club?"

"I don't know. He was on some of the picnics and he

went hunting a lot with Dad. He was a great hunter, you know."

That sounded vaguely familiar.

But Dan Daglio had been known as more than a hunter. He'd been a successful trial attorney and a family man. He loved deep-sea fishing and he played tennis, now regularly winning in the senior division to which he had evolved. He was a tall, handsome man with distinguished gray hair and a ready sense of humor. Popular and well spoken.

And for the past eight years he'd been Tucson's mayor.

10

I STOPPED IN AT THE FEED STORE ON THE WAY HOME AND BOUGHT some food for the dogs and cats. Curly, the proprietor, showed me a cute little Vietnamese potbellied pig that he had for sale. At least the Unpopular War hadn't been totally without lucre.

Potbellied pigs are kind of like English bulldogs. They're so ugly they're cute. The prices are also coming down, as the market has become glutted with them.

"Petunia," Curly said, handing me the pig. "I'll let you have her for fifty dollars."

I nuzzled the little bargain, wishing her coat was not quite so bristly. Petunia was a *ganga*. Just a few years ago the same pig would have cost me five hundred bucks. Still, since I hadn't totally taken leave of my senses, I had to ask myself, did I really need a pig?

Then I remembered Cousin Bea's birthday. She needed a pig. After all, she has everything else. An anchorwoman's salary will do that for you.

So instead of writing a check for thirty-five dollars for the feed, I scripted one for $87.96, including tax.

I had an interesting drive home with the little pig ricocheting around the cab of the truck. There was a momentary scare when she nestled between my leg and the fuel pedal, causing Priscilla to take a giant lurch forward at the four-way stop. Luckily nothing was coming. Halfway home I made the discovery that Petunia was not one of those housebroken Vietnamese potbellied pigs. This time when I said, "Oh shit," I meant it. Briefly I considered returning her, but Bea had a nice little patio at her town house and besides, she was always good with animals. She'd have her housebroken in no time.

Mrs. Fierce and Blue's radar must have been working overtime. By the time I pulled into the driveway they were jumping up and down, mauling the truck, trying to get at the little treasure inside. I cradled the pig in my arms and told the dogs to "get down," which of course in their finely trained fashion, they ignored.

Somehow Petunia and I made it into the house and left the dogs outside, barking and scratching at the door. They knew something big-time was coming down and wanted in on the action.

The phone was ringing so I put Petunia down to answer it. It was Sanders, my closest neighbor, asking when we were going to start the fall gather. We were kindred spirits. Some people get turned on by wedding receptions; we like cows. As we talked, the dogs got into a full-fledged howling, which meant that I had to explain the pig's presence to Sanders, who, of course, thought I'd lost my mind, although in typical cowboy fashion he did not tell me so in so many words.

Petunia, oblivious to the pandemonium she was causing, scurried around the kitchen and living room, with her piggish snout checking things out. After sticking her nose as far under the refrigerator as she could manage, she was now wearing a mélange of lint and cobwebs across her face. She trotted out of the kitchen and as I nervously watched, still enslaved by the telephone, she left a piggish deposit on the Navajo rug in the living room.

After cleaning up her mess I decided that the honeymoon period was over, so I opened the back door and let the pig accompany me on chores. Immediately Blue and Mrs. Fierce came racing around the house to check out the new addition. While there was an initial game of tug-of-war with the pig in the middle, after I had sufficiently refereed it, the players settled down to being reasonably civilized.

I fed the horses and the rest of the animals and then

made Petunia a little bed on the screened porch. I watched her gobble up her food like, well, a pig. Then I scratched her and told her she was a good girl and I left her for the evening.

By nine o'clock I had finished the second Klan book. The fire bombings and killings that had been so wide-spread in the sixties had spared no one, including children. I made a note to call the FBI in the morning to see what information they might give me.

After a quick shower I climbed into bed and read until I fell asleep. The pig, as far as I know, never stirred. Good pig.

I was in the stage stop early the next morning, taking advantage of the time changes to call the FBI. Any time I can call the East, I'm thrilled. If I do it well before eight A.M. I can save a ton of money on my phone bill.

I talked to a Mrs. Walker in the Office of Public and Congressional Affairs, part of the Research Unit of the FBI. After listening to my request she said that there was no information on the KKK in her division, but promised to send me notes on the files that fell under the Freedom of Information Act. She also suggested that I get in touch with the Southern Poverty Law Center in Montgomery, Ala-bama, which had a Klanwatch Intelligence Report.

I called them next and was disappointed to learn that their report began in the early eighties, two decades after the time frame I was interested in.

Thus thwarted, I had little choice but to drive up to my mailbox for my morning newspaper and then go for break-fast at Rainbow's in La Cienega.

It was nudging eight o'clock by the time I got there, which meant the cafe was nearly empty. Rainbow and Darlene, a recently hired waitress, were taking a break, smoking and sipping coffee in the front room.

"Sorry," I said by way of an apology. My presence would send them both scurrying, Darlene to take my order and Rainbow to cook it.

I ordered the Magic Number although it wasn't on the menu.

"Wrong time for avocados," Darlene said.

"Surprise me."

The Magic Number is my creation and since I do a fair amount of business with Rainbow's they are happy to make it for me. Crisp bacon and chopped tomatoes crumbled across an English muffin with slices of avocado, topped with a slice of American cheese, broiled, then topped with sour cream. A cardiologist's dream.

There was nothing too outstanding in the *Arizona Daily Star* until I got to the Metro section. KKK PAMPHLETS LEFT IN MIDTOWN NEIGHBORHOOD, the headline read.

I skimmed the story for a more complete picture. Sometime on Monday evening, pamphlets urging membership in the Ku Klux Klan were dropped in a couple of hundred driveways in Tucson. "Minorities are the root of our crime problem," the script read. "Fight crime! Join the KKK!"

A cold, pasty lump threatened my stomach.

I'm always amazed at how the universe rises to meet our needs. I hadn't heard anything about the Ku Klux Klan in Tucson, or in Arizona, for that matter. Ever. All the stories about the protest marches and burning crosses had occurred elsewhere. *In the East. Or South*. Yet suddenly, on the heels of Victoria Carpenter's far-fetched tale here was a story on the KKK. Sometimes things are so connected it's almost eerie. Coincidence, or had the stories always been there and I was just now noticing them?

As I continued to read, I was heartened to see quotes by many of the KKK brochure recipients, all of whom derided the mailing. Disgusting, archaic and racist were just a few of the comments. That made me feel better.

The Magic Number arrived and tasted better than the ones I make. Seems like other people's cooking always tastes better than my own, and I'm a passable cook.

I worked the crossword puzzle while eating, which made me feel like a genius. The easy ones in the morning newspaper always do that to you. I think it helps their circulation. Of course if this was the *New York Times* they'd get tougher as the week wore on.

"Trade, can I have a minute?" Rainbow stood at the table.

"Sure, sit down."

She brought her coffee cup, but thankfully no cigarette. "I've got something I want to talk to you about."

I groaned to myself. Rainbow's is like one of those big cocktail parties where everyone is doing just fine until they find out you're a lawyer or a dentist or an accountant. Then ZOOM. Suddenly someone corners you with questions about their hysterectomy, their root canal or their IRS audit and you find yourself tied up for thirty minutes with a dullard while you dispense free information. Which is why I frequently do not tell people what I do. Of course it could be argued that I am denying myself business by not advertising.

But there are no secrets in Rainbow's. Everyone knows everyone else's business and if they don't, they make it up. Whatever works. But I've been coming in here since before it was Rainbow's, so what I do is no mystery.

"It's about those things," Rainbow nodded at my empty plate.

"What?" I couldn't believe my ears. Here I thought she would have some clandestine thing for me to look into.

"They're shit," she said solemnly.

"Shit."

"Carcinogenic."

Now we were talking shit. I don't come to Rainbow's to get a health lecture on my nutritional habits.

"The latest," she said, dropping her voice to a whisper as though there were anyone listening who would care what we were talking about, "says that mixing burned bacon and cheese causes a reaction which creates carcinogens, which, when eaten, may cause cancer in the body. I'm not putting them on the menu."

Jesus, Rainbow, get a life, I thought. But I said, "Republican plot."

This cheered her considerably.

"Of course we'll still make them for you, but you might want to be careful."

I studied the yellow nicotine stains around her second and middle fingers and was sorry that I was too full to order a second Magic Number.

We talked a while longer, mostly about politics, which never works out. She's still tied into the Kennedy conspiracy theories and I wanted to share the latest Clinton jokes. Neither one of us thought the other was particularly brilliant this morning, so I dropped my fare plus twenty percent before leaving.

That twenty percent is a thing with me. Years ago I read where waitresses cringe when a group of women walk into a restaurant, for they know they are not going to get a decent tip. Since then I've been using twenty percent as my standard, even though I know I'm overdoing it to make up for the scores of stingy women who have preceded me. Also, probably more truthfully, figuring twenty percent of something is a hell of a lot easier than multiplying by .15. I've hated higher math ever since I learned about it in fifth grade. Thank God division does not have to come into the picture on any of this high-finance stuff or I'd really be stuck.

The Tucson downtown library was bustling by the time I arrived. Lots of people going in and out, including transients who were looking to get in from the cold, use the bathroom and spend the day reading.

I found the periodicals room and asked about the index to the *Arizona Daily Star* for the years 1963 and forward. I must have had the look of someone who does not know her away around a library, for the librarian exited the counter and shuffled ahead of me until we got to the appropriate area, where she pointedly showed me the requested volumes. I noticed she was wearing tennis shoes, which made me feel better, knowing that she had not singled me out for this special treatment.

The indexes were organized by category and month and gave a portion of the headline detailing each story as it appeared in the *Star*. Since Victoria was fairly confident that she'd been five the year she'd witnessed the black family being beaten, 1963 was my focal point. I dug in, starting with categories relating to the civil rights movement. In addition to that topic I covered Discrimination, Employment, Housing and Education, photocopying anything that I thought might be helpful to the case.

I moved on to Missing Persons and Unidentified Bodies. As I went through the books I found a lot of missing persons—winter visitors lost while hiking in the desert, displaced hunters, kids who wandered off from home, missing soldiers from Fort Huachuca, Indians disappearing near Sells, a Boy Scout troop lost in the Santa Ritas, lost wives, husbands, children and assorted kin. But most of the stories had a cheery follow-up headline revealing the missing had been found. In truth, some of the follow-ups were less encouraging. The Boy Scouts froze to death on the mountain and one of the soldiers was found dead in a well.

The Unidentified Bodies were varied. Bodies and parts of bodies were found near the Southern Pacific railroad tracks, extricated from mine shafts, detected floating in irrigation canals, discovered shot in the desert and located in the bottoms of steep mountain canyons. Bones were found near Evergreen Cemetery and one body was even discovered in a boxcar.

While the stories were varied, they all had one thing in common.

No missing man and his two young sons and no bodies matching their limited descriptions had been found.

It was time to call on Phelan Brewster.

11

As I EXITED THE HIGHWAY, INSPIRATION HIT ME IN THE FORM OF A McDonald's. I drove through and ordered six Big Macs and a Diet Coke. My plans for the hamburgers did not include my eating all of them, although I did scarf one down immediately.

Avra Valley is the northern part of the larger Altar Valley. Scores of poor immigrants came here years ago to harvest crops, and the valley still does not evoke prosperity. The laborers were housed in shacks along the highway, and as farming became more mechanical the shacks were eventually replaced with an odd assortment of mobile homes and manufactured housing.

Part of the valley is tucked behind the Tucson Mountains and the rest stretches into a long flat semi-desolate desert prairie. Named by the Papago Indians years ago, before they renamed themselves the Tohono O'odham, Avra means "big plain." The one good thing about the soil here is that it can grow a lot of things, like milo maize, alfalfa and cotton. The warren of irrigation canals, coupled with the milo maize fields, makes the valley a bonanza for dove hunters in the fall.

The season was now past and as I drove along the two-lane road the only things that littered the verge were Budweiser cans, wayward papers and tufts of cotton that had escaped the large caged trailers that take the fiber harvest to the gin for milling.

The valley is known for a few other things. Several roping arenas, a few horse traders, fighting cocks, illegal dogfights and rough Saturday nights that can result in a shooting or a nasty knife fight. On the plus side, a lot of Future Farmers of America live here and there are a few Holy-Roller-type churches, if in fact they can be counted as assets. Avra Valley is also pockmarked with abandoned mines, many of which have been fenced off to protect the hiking public. Unfortunately, a lot of them are still open and exposed.

Many of the original farming families were Chinese and some of their descendants still live here, along with a sizable Hispanic population and a scattering of black people. Given this cultural diversity, I never thought of Avra Valley as being a particular haven for bigots.

But with the vast expanses out here and with many families living on acreage, it didn't take a rich imagination to figure out that it would have been a logical place for the Sporting Club to thrive without interference from the neighbors' prying eyes.

Victoria had given me good directions to the family homestead. After leaving the pavement, I headed down a narrow dirt road called Miller Lane. At the third fork I turned south and drove for another two miles until it ended at a metal farm gate.

I drove Priscilla right up to the gate. The NO TRESPASSING and BEWARE OF DOG signs did little to bolster my confidence, although Vicki had warned me about the dogs. I was alone, and my Lady Smith and Wesson .38 was safely tucked away back at the ranch.

Like many of my fishing expeditions I had intended for this one to be a surprise, so of course I had not called to tell Phelan and Hazel Brewster of my impending visit.

I waited for a minute, my eyes scanning the landscape for the dogs, but there was no sign of them. I couldn't see the house either, for the dusty road behind the gate appeared to top a small hill and disappear down the other side.

I opened the truck door and left it that way to insure my hasty retreat should I need one.

The gate, I was happy to see, was not locked, merely

chained shut. I opened it, swung it ahead of me, climbed back into Priscilla and drove through.

The Code of the West says that you are to leave gates as you find them. This means that if you come upon one that is open, you leave it that way. The converse is also true. The rationale for this is if you mess with a man's gates you are also messing with his livelihood. You may be cutting his cattle off from water or turning them loose to be slaughtered on the highway or to intermix with cattle whose progeny he may not desire.

Although my heart said *leave it open*, in case I wanted to beat it out of there, the years of ranching took over and I dutifully shut the metal farm gate.

Since there was still no sign of the dogs I assumed that the house was some distance off and that they were confined closer to home.

I crested the hill and drove through a sandy gully that gave me some pause as I envisioned getting the three-quarter-ton truck stuck in it. I kept a steady pace through the heavy sand and made it through all right and up yet another hill. From the top of this one I could see the Brewster place below, nestled in a mesquite grove in a small valley. The house looked long and drawn out, as though it had been added onto many times in this incarnation. To the north of it sat an old Quonset hut, its steel doors shut. It was probably the one that Victoria had mentioned in her notes.

When I pulled into the circular driveway the dogs came running out, snarling and snapping. There were three of them, a Doberman, a German shepherd and a rottweiler. I guess Phelan Brewster wasn't taking any chances, for he had one each of probably the scariest breeds on earth, although I've met a few Saint Bernards in my time that I wouldn't want to tangle with.

As the dogs circled Priscilla I rolled down both of my windows a few inches before shutting down the ignition. No one was coming yet, so I quickly unwrapped the Big Macs and tossed two of them out the window, a few feet apart. The Doberman instantly attacked, fending off the other two dogs in a snarling gesture that also included wolfing down the hamburgers.

I leaned over and threw two more hamburgers out the passenger window and gave a low whistle. Instantly the rottweiler and the shepherd were at the sandwiches, each running off with one before the Doberman could take them away. I nudged the remaining Big Mac out my window and the Doberman demolished it in one bite.

She dropped her voice to a low, deep-throated growl, and while her tail wasn't wagging and I can't say she was exactly cordial, at least she was now showing some interest in the vehicle that reflected something other than a passionate desire to dismantle it with her impressive teeth.

"Good girl," I said, which caused her to go into another paroxysm of barking and snapping. The other two, as if on cue, returned to their serenade.

I didn't care. I wasn't leaving the vehicle until someone told me that it was okay to do so. In the meantime I had learned something important.

The trio were not professionally trained protection dogs. If they had been, they wouldn't have taken any food at all.

As if I needed further confirmation that I was in the right place, a collection of assorted antlers and horns forming an archway over a wooden gate in front of the house gave testament that this was a Hunter's Home.

I wadded the empty McDonald's wrappers together and stuffed them back in the bag, placing it in the console between the two front seats. And waited while the dogs barked.

The center of the circular driveway was done in desert landscaping, the plants neatly laid out with bare earth in between. There were two kinds of prickly pear cactus, a few cholla and barrels, some ocotillo, and a desert broom that was shedding fine tufts of white snowflake stuff, which I knew was the plant's way of reproducing itself. Its deliberate presence told me that probably none of the Brewsters was an allergic type.

In the middle of the desert garden was a funny-looking tree that I had never seen before. It had a fat, stubby trunk that tapered narrowly upward. Sparse branches, resembling waving arms, stuck out from the top. Although it was brown, it reminded me of a carrot stuck in the ground upside down. A very ugly carrot.

The dogs' barking had been replaced with the sound of a motor. A heavyset man on a four-wheeler rounded the corner of the Quonset hut and pulled up next to the wire fence in front of the house. He shut the noisy thing down and walked up to the truck.

He was short and stocky and wearing worn Levi's, a red plaid flannel shirt, hiking boots, a bush of white hair and an irritated look. The dogs, now quiet, walked at his heels.

I rolled the truck window all the way down.

"Mr. Brewster?"

"Yes." His eyes, the color of a churning sea, narrowed at this familiarity as he tried to figure out what I was selling.

I handed him a card. "Trade Ellis."

He looked at it but said nothing.

"I'm working with Victoria."

"My daughter."

"Yes, on this memory thing."

"On the pile of crap, you mean."

"May I get out?"

He thought about it, then turned and called to the three dogs, who followed him around the side of the house. When he returned, he was alone.

I got out of the truck and extended my hand. He shook it, but softly, in that way that older men do who are not sure what to do with women who insist on shaking hands.

"I'm sorry to pop in like this, but I had business in Avra Valley," I lied easily.

"Well you might as well come in. The sooner we can get this behind us, the better off this family's gonna be."

He held the wooden gate open for me, then the front door.

A bank of windows on the west side gave the living room a light, airy feeling which was quickly dissipated by the rows of glassy-eyed stares I was receiving from the stuccoed walls. He had almost everything. Deer—both whitetail and mule—javelina, antelope, bighorn sheep, even an elk on the far wall. An adult coyote, stuffed and rather raggedy-looking, was a floor mount; and a black bear rug, complete with mounted head, lay across the carpeted floor. Although these things give me the heebie-jeebies, one of his mounts stood out above the rest. It was a huge mule deer, certainly the largest one I'd ever seen, alive or dead, and as I stared at it, it in turn seemed to be evaluating me.

I looked over the room for some sign of racist leanings—a swastika, a portrait of Adolf Hitler or even the Confederate flag, which I knew was popular with KKK types. There was nothing. A tweed couch with some needlepoint pillows, a few hunting magazines sprawled across the coffee table along with *TV Guide*, and framed photographs of various people who I assumed were family members. A huge wooden cross was hung on the wall above the sofa. The cross sported a great-looking Jesus with really bloody knees. Most of the Jesuses you see are the preppy, Beach Boy versions, but this one looked like he'd really been put through the wringer.

A tall curio case in one corner was filled with Hummel figurines, Tyrolean children walking goats, carrying water, looking up a tree filled with blossoms and stuff like that. While a case could be made that they were Aryan children, I knew that many people who were not racists collected the silly little figures. This collection, I assumed, belonged to the new Mrs. Brewster. There was also a glass-fronted gun case, filled with rifles. Not surprising, given Dad's hunting bent.

As my eyes took it all in, Brewster proudly looked at me as though he was expecting a compliment on his trophies. I said nothing.

"Sit down," he said, motioning to a worn Early American maple table at one end of the living room. It was covered with papers which he shoved aside. He flipped an overhead light, bathing the table in a warm glow. "We might as well get to the bottom of this."

I sat.

"She's told you all the stories?" he asked.

"What she remembers."

"Remembers? Ha. It's lies, all lies. None of it happened." He pulled out a chair, flipped it around and sat on it backwards, resting his massive forearms on the back of the chair. The hair on his arms was thick and white, like that on his head. "She's always had an imagination, I can tell you that."

"Why would she lie?"

"Who knows? She's not alone. It's happening all over. You know there's an organization that's trying to get to the bottom of this."

"The county attorney's office," I said, trying to be helpful.

"No. Not *this*. The lying thing. People are doing it all over the country. Destroying their families, themselves."

He leaned over the table, dragging a heavy clutch of papers to our end. As he rummaged through them, he mumbled, "Where did Hazel put that? You should see it."

After pushing some of the paper to one side he finally found the one he was searching for. "Here. Here it is." He handed a pamphlet to me.

It was from something called the False Memory Syndrome Foundation. I'd never heard of it. While I knew that now was not the time to sit and read the entire pamphlet, I opened it to be polite.

"It's all in there," he said, with all of the conviction of a man armed with knowledge. "All the crap. All the lies that kids are telling about their parents. All this therapy stuff that brings out things that never happened."

"Then there never was a Sporting Club?"

"Of course there was a Sporting Club. But we didn't kill niggers."

He must have seen the revolted look on my face as he struggled to amend himself. "I don't call 'em Negroes and I don't call them Afro-Americans and I don't call them blacks. I grew up in the South, I'm not ashamed of it, but I've called them niggers all of my life and I'm not gonna stop now. But just because I call them niggers doesn't mean I killed any." He leaned over the table, placing his face very close to mine, and in a very strong, low voice, averred, "I've killed a lot of animals in my time, but I never killed a nigger, never killed a man."

While I wanted to ask if he considered them one and the same, I kept my mouth shut.

"I don't know where Vic gets that crap. Why she wants to hurt me and the family. It's not right."

I asked him about Dan Daglio and the rest of the names on Victoria's list and he admitted that he knew all of them.

"Osborne's dead. Stone lives in California and Robinson and I are still good friends. And *they* didn't kill anybody either!" he said. "Haven't seen Dan in years, but he used to hunt with us from time to time." His fist hit the table hard, startling me as I jumped in the straight-backed wooden chair. He took an envelope from the stack of papers, looked at it and then flipped it over. Grabbing a pen from the table, he scribbled on it. "Here's my son Henry's phone number. Checked with him, and Robinson and the others. They'll tell you what they told the county attorney. *It . . . didn't . . . happen.*" While he was staying in control, his face was very, very red, and heavy veins were standing out at his temples. "None of what Vic has said is true."

I noticed he did not offer his daughter Jessica's telephone number.

"Mr. Brewster, were there any black people that worked at the plant?"

He shook his head. "I don't remember any. Back then we didn't hire them."

"So if there had been a black man working there, you would have remembered it?"

"I just said that, didn't I?"

I changed the subject. "Have you seen your daughter?"

He shook his head. "No, and I don't care to. Not until she's gotten this poison out of her system. She's ruining the family, especially her sister." He stood and walked to the gun case. For a moment I was afraid he was going to pull out one of his rifles. Instead he reached to the top of the case and pulled down a carved wooden box. He walked back and handed it to me.

"Open it."

I did, and the contents revulsed me. The box was filled to the brim with rattles. This feature of his anatomy a rattlesnake does not willingly give.

"They can be deadly," he said, reaching into the box and removing one of the larger strings of rattles and shaking it at me. "But they're honest, they let you know they're there. But these lies," he returned the rattle to the box, taking it from me and slamming the lid shut, "you don't know where they're coming from and they can kill you, kill your family, kill your spirit. Right now Vic's a viper, striking and spitting at anything and everything. Deadly."

There was really nothing else to say to him.

"I'll be checking with the others. May I talk to you again?"

"As often as you like," he said, not unkindly. "I just want my family back together again." His eyes looked wet as he handed me the False Memory Syndrome brochure. "You can keep this."

As he walked me to the truck I remembered the funny tree.

"That plant over there, I don't recognize it." We were closer now and I could see that it had tiny little leaves.

"Boojum tree, grows in Baja. That's the only one I know of in Tucson, although the kid I bought it from had a truckload of them to sell."

"Have you had it long?" I was fascinated by its funny, ugly shape and thought it might be fun to plant one at the Vaca Grande.

"Don't know how old it was before it came here, but it's been in that spot for thirty years."

"Well, that's one to look up in the plant books," I said, thanking him again for his time.

He was still standing by his front gate as I circled the driveway and drove down the road.

When I got to the farm gate it was open, and a tall, thin young woman with short blonde hair in a layered cut was standing next to a white Taurus on the other side. Luckily there was a wide area next to it and I pulled up next to the car, rolling my window down.

She walked up to the truck.

"May I help you?" she said, which I thought was funny since I was coming out and she was going in.

"No, I've just finished. You're?"

"Hazel Brewster."

"Trade Ellis," I said, extending my hand. She touched it lightly. "I'm working with your stepdaughter, Victoria."

"Oh." A look of disgust crossed her angular features. "Phelan?"

"I just met with him. Listen," I fumbled in the console for a card and handed it to her. "Would it be possible for me to meet with you sometime?"

She read the card and handed it back. "No, I don't think so. All of that was before my time and I hardly know Victoria. Have a nice day," she said as she returned to her car.

Phelan Brewster had quite a family. So far one was talking too much, and one wasn't talking at all.

But there were two left.

And Momma made three.

12

USING THE PAY PHONE AT MCDONALD'S TO CALL MY ANSWERING machine, I discovered that Victoria had faxed me more material and that it was waiting for me at the hardware store.

After retrieving it, I stopped at the office on the way into the ranch and began reading it. Another memory had come to her. Her communication started with an apology.

Some of this is so sordid that I almost hate to write it down, she began. *But I remember a man, a very large black man. I remember someone saying "hitchhiker" when he came to one of our picnics. Maybe someone picked him up on the highway. I don't know. He was there for a little while and then walked off with some of the men. I never saw him again.*

Years later, before I went to Flagstaff to school, I remember a party that we had at the house. A lot of the Sporting Club men were there. I walked into the Quonset hut where the men were. Dad's back was to me and he said something about the hitchhiker and then he held something up and said a word that I didn't remember.

I noticed that Victoria's recollections this time seemed to be closer to those of an adult, not those of a five-year-old child. I wondered if therapy was maybe helping her.

They all made jokes about it, saying it was from the big buck. I remember being confused because Dad usually only saved the antlers. Mr. Robinson looked up and saw me and said something

*to Dad and he grabbed a wooden box that was on the table and
dropped the thing in it.*

I shuddered, remembering the box of rattles.

*They acted really strange with me then, which of course
aroused my curiosity. Later that night I snuck down to the hut and
looked for the box. I found it in a drawer of the workbench. When
I opened it I found something that looked like leather, it was dark
and split down the middle.*

*Today, in therapy, I remembered the word I heard Dad use.
It was "foreskin."*

Although the lights were on in the office it felt as
though a dark cloud had come over the place. If I was to
believe Victoria Carpenter, Phelan Brewster had kept the
foreskin of a large black man that the Sporting Club had
killed. This was the stuff of which horror movies are made.
Then I remembered all of the glassy eyes staring down at
me from Brewster's living room. He liked heads and hides
and rattles—was it so far-fetched that he would keep such
a trophy?

My stomach roiled at the thought. The fax was so
disturbing I didn't even want to take it with me, it was as
though it might somehow contaminate me. I put it in the
file, turned out the lights and headed home.

As I drove in the driveway I was startled to see three
shapes come running up. Then I remembered the pig, Petunia. Apparently she was now considered one of the girls.
As I got out of the truck all three animals jumped up on me
in greeting. Lovely creatures.

Seeing the combination of the ranch trailer hooked up
to Martín's old pickup and the empty holding pasture told
me that Brownie had obviously been delivered to the
young girl. I smiled, knowing that the old horse had found
a great retirement home.

I got inside the house just before five so I hauled the
telephone book out of the pantry and thumbed through it
until I found the number of the Arizona Bottling Plant. I
called and identified myself and set up an appointment for
the next afternoon with the general manager. After hanging up, I jotted the phone number and address of the bottling plant down on a piece of paper.

When I went out to feed, I found a pair of legs draped in worn Levi's and cowboy boots, sticking out from under the old tractor. A new rod bearing was laying on the ground.

"Martín?" Sometimes I'm a rocket scientist.

His response was a grunt.

"Guess you got that part."

My logic was rewarded with silence. Was that really my foreman under there?

"Uh, is there a wrench in your mouth or something?"

Not likely, especially since I could hear him clanking away.

Something was seriously wrong. I lightly nudged his leg with the tip of my boot.

"Martín, tell me you're alive."

A hand, with the wrench still in it, was flung out from under the tractor's canopy.

"*Chiquita*, why"—there was a catch in his voice—"didn't you tell me?"

Shit. I took a deep breath.

"Cori Elena said she wanted to tell you. I was going to give her a day or two." Was this a test or something? If it was, by honoring her request to tell Martín herself, it looked like I had flunked. Or maybe Cori Elena had wanted me to flunk.

"This is like a very bad dream."

"I know."

What had Cori Elena's confession brought him but sorrow?

"I can't believe this."

"Maybe she could be up here, in a place up here," I suggested.

"He won't go for that."

"Lazaro?"

"Yeah. Cori Elena says that he'll continue paying for her care as long as she stays in Mexico."

I wasn't surprised. After all, Lazaro Orantez thought Quinta was his daughter, so why would he want to send her to Arizona?

"And those places are pretty expensive, from what I hear."

I suppose I should have leapt in and said we could work it out, but truthfully, I didn't have a clue as to what kind of money we were talking. What did one of "those places" run a month? Three thousand dollars? Five?

Martín saved me when he said, "Hand me that bearing, will you?"

I did.

"Those others are probably going to go, so I bought three more, but I'm running out of daylight and I need to move some hay around tomorrow, so I'm just gonna do this one tonight."

"Fine." I guess any heavy conversation we might have had evaporated.

"Martín, if there's anything . . ."

"I know."

And then he was back to banging on the tractor.

When I fed the horses I took an extra couple of minutes just to nuzzle them. I do that from time to time when I have several "inside" days in a row, where I can't get outside with the animals. Sometimes just the horsey smell is enough to keep me going. There was too much rolling around in my head, what with the gruesome fax that Victoria had sent and my conversation with Martín. I needed the therapy. Of course it isn't as good as an honest horseback ride, but some days it's the best I can do. Today had been one of those days.

An hour later, I pulled out a couple of frozen tamales and zapped them in the microwave for dinner, poured myself a glass of merlot and caught the six o'clock news.

After dinner I went to work. I found an old city map and spread it out on the kitchen table. I took a red ballpoint pen and drew a fat red dot in the general location of the Arizona Bottling Plant. After attaching a piece of string to a pencil, I held the point at the plant dot and then drew a generous circle around it, holding the string taut.

I retrieved the telephone book and turned to the Tucson School District listings and went down the list of elementary schools. Some of them I could readily dismiss, knowing that their locations would fall outside the circle I had drawn. Seven schools clearly fell within my boundaries and I had four that I was unsure of.

It wasn't much, but it was something to work on.

Although I was fond of him, I found myself damning Abel Messenger for not being more generous with his files. There had to be more information out there, but I knew he wasn't going to share it as long as the case was still open.

When I let the dogs in for the evening, Petunia came running in with them. She had cleverly forgotten about her cozy little bed on the back porch as she made a beeline for my bedroom, where she made a swinish swan dive into Mrs. Fierce's bed. Mrs. Fierce, of course, took a dim view of this adverse possession and jumped up and down, barking her displeasure as the pig curled up in a ball and promptly went to sleep. Petunia was like a little kid, precious when she slept and a devil the rest of the time. Remembering her presents to me which she had scattered through the house on her last indoor foray, I picked up the sleeping pig and returned her to her own quarters.

Knowing that Bea was going to be thrilled with her new baby, I fell asleep wondering how much I really was going to miss the little porker.

13

THE TEMPERATURE WAS DOWN TO TWENTY DEGREES THE NEXT morning. The cloud cover that had been hovering for a few days and bringing warmer temperatures, was now gone, its exit bringing colder weather. I quickly fed the animals and by the time I hit the screened porch, the phone was ringing.

I caught it just as the answering machine did, and we went through a couple of *hello, hello*'s before the message on the machine finally ended and two real people were on the line. I looked at the clock. It was six A.M.

"Trade?"

I recognized the voice. "Victoria."

"I hope I'm not too early for you."

"Any time after five," I said, and meant it.

"Did you get my fax?"

"Yes, I read it yesterday."

"I tried to call you but all I got was the machine and I didn't want to leave that as a message."

"I can appreciate that. I saw your father yesterday."

There was a pause and then, "Yes?"

"He denies anything happened. Didn't remember a black man at the plant."

"Of course. Was Hazel there?"

"I met her on the road as I was leaving. She's not going to be much help."

"No. Listen, I thought I'd go see Mother Monday and

maybe you'd like to come. It might be easier, because of the confidentiality rules and all."

I thought about it. I had planned on eventually seeing Dorothy Brewster. While I'd never visited anyone in a mental hospital before, I could see where the patients' privacy and identification would be guarded. I agreed that it sounded like a good plan. We made arrangements to meet at Rainbow's on Monday morning and then said goodbye.

By mid-morning the weather had warmed up and since my appointment at the bottling plant wasn't until two, I decided to take a ride.

I saddled Dream and headed down the valley toward Catalina State Park. Since we would soon be gathering cattle, I wanted to see how many of them had drifted south. Technically, the cattle aren't supposed to be in the park. Practically, they're in there all the time, because in open range country it is the responsibility of the person who does not want them on his land to fence them out. The park budget was shot this year and since a long-gone, well-meaning park director had dismantled the old rusting barbed-wire fence that once separated his park from our pasture, there is currently nothing to keep the Vaca Grande cattle out of the public domain.

The cattle love it down here. While the creeks are dry right now since the snow hasn't come to the mountains and melted, there's still lots of water at the equestrian center. If that's too great a distance for these creatures who can travel miles in a single day, then there's always the water spigots in the campground, which obligingly break when pushed against by an eleven-hundred-pound cow. To make the park even more attractive to my bovine charges there's also lots of green grass and even an occasional tourist they can scare the shit out of. Life is good if you're a cow.

So I headed south, figuring that with luck I'd find some cows and push them toward the north tanks and back onto the ranch. That way I might avoid a call from the park personnel about the broken water spigots.

While I started out with a sweatshirt and vest over my lightweight cotton shirt, I shed them the first hour into the ride. By the time I reached the barn at the equestrian center I had run across a lot of fresh tracks, but no cows. I watered Dream and circled around to the Sutherland wash, jumping a huge mule deer buck. He was not as large as the trophy on Phelan Brewster's wall, but a big one nonetheless.

The deer in the park see a lot of traffic, so they don't get as alarmed as the ones in the more remote areas. It helps to be on a horse. The deer are goosier with people on foot. I reined Dream in and watched the buck.

He was a beauty, but for the fact that he had only one antler. He stood watching me, trying to decide whether or not I was a threat.

Mother Nature does a pretty good planning job on her deer friends. The buck loses his antlers early in the year—either together or one at a time—spends the spring growing them back, including the fuzzy-velvet period, rubs the velvet off against trees, ending up with antlers that are big and strong and healthy for the mating season, which is now through Christmas. This apparently impresses the does.

This buck had the full swollen neck characteristic of a buck in rut. Since it wasn't time for him to shed his antlers, he must have met with some unfortunate accident to have lost the one side. As he walked off he had a funny, ambling gait which reminded me of a camel's pace. I chalked his stride up to an inept hunter and rode on.

I checked out the group picnic area where some wild Bermuda grass grows but found no Brahma cows. Zigzagging across the landscape, I checked a few gullies and mesquite thickets but again, had no luck in finding my quarry.

When I topped out on the plateau overlooking the Sutherland I jumped two whitetail does. Like the mule deer buck, they didn't seem all that alarmed to see me as they trotted off with an occasional look over their shoulder. I was surprised to see them at the lower elevation, and not particularly happy about it. Naturally more aggressive than the mule deer, the whitetail have had some success at pushing the larger deer out of their habitat. As I watched the two small does top out on the ridge it seemed hard to believe that I was watching the most dangerous game animal in North America. More people are injured or killed by whitetail deer than by any other wildlife species. And we sweat bears.

As I dropped into the Sutherland I ran across some cattle tracks. They were fresh with crisp dirt walls, made this morning for there was no night sign crossing them, no little leaves or beetle or spider feet that had traipsed across the broad, splayed marks.

I settled Dream into a nice steady lope on the way home, walking him in the last fifteen minutes. By the time I had unsaddled him, brushed him, put him away and taken a shower it was past one o'clock.

Since I was running a bit late, rather than driving my customary five miles over the speed limit, a measurement which usually grants me immunity from the local gendarmes' attention, I pushed Priscilla and was relieved when I arrived at the Arizona Bottling Plant at five until two without a speeding ticket.

A hand-painted mural adorned the long block wall outside the facility. It had been painted years ago by an itinerant artist and was kept up by retouching from time to time. There were scenes of people enjoying the outdoors, having picnics, fishing, hiking, riding horses and swimming. The people all wore happy smiles on their faces and in many of the scenes they were clutching in their hands brightly painted aluminum cans decorated with streaks of hot pink and orange, purple and turquoise. All of the cans carried the smiling sun face which was the logo of Sunny Cola.

As I turned into the lot, something struck me about the mural.

There were no black faces enjoying Sunny Cola.

14

THERE WAS AN EMPTY PARKING SPACE IN FRONT OF THE BRICK building and I drove Priscilla easily into it. While I love my truck, her looks, and powerful Cummins diesel engine, I must confess that sometimes she can be a bear to park. With the longer cab and wheelbase, she does not always fit into those neat little spaces that urban designers designate for parking.

I got out and fumbled in the toolbox, my office on wheels. After a minute, I finally found the appropriate card, this time my real one. I carry a cache of fake cards—well, they're not really fake, they are cards that belong to real people. They're not even pilfered, for I have found that it is a great American phenomenon that almost total strangers will press one of their cards into your open palm, giving you their vitals—what they do, their telephone number, their fax number, their cellular number, their address and suite number, and sometimes even their *home* phone number. Amazing. So I take advantage of these little gifts and have been known, on occasion, to pawn them off on other people.

But today I decided to be myself. There was no advantage I could see to making up an elaborate story. So I took the cleanest Trade Ellis card from the pile nestled in the sliding upper tray of the toolbox. This one had only a tiny smudge of WD-40 on one corner. I dropped it into my purse and headed for the corporate offices of Sunny Cola, a division of the Arizona Bottling Company.

Kevin Lightner was a surprise. I had expected the general manager of Arizona's oldest soft-drink company to be older, but the man before me looked like he hadn't been out of college five years.

After exchanging pleasantries, I got down to business and explained that I was working with Victoria Carpenter.

He nodded. "The police have already been here. I'm afraid I wasn't very helpful, but it's hard after all that time."

"So there wouldn't be any employment records from 1963, no paper trail of any people who were here then?"

"Oh sure, we have records of people who were working back then, but they're still here. Our policy is that we destroy the records ten years after an employee leaves the company. If you're looking for Brewster or that black man we don't have the records."

"But there are still people working here who were working here then?" Thirty-seven years seemed like a long time to work for a bottling company.

He must have seen the amazement in my eyes. "It's not at all unusual in this business. They started when they were very young and their numbers for retirement don't add up yet to the total required." He handed me a list with three names on it. "When the police were here, I gave them the names of these employees. Since your call I've checked with them and they don't mind my giving you their names. You can talk to them."

I thanked him and put the list in my purse. If his cooperation was any indication, Kevin Lightner sure wasn't acting like he had anything to hide.

"But you don't have Phelan Brewster's records?"

He shook his head and reached for a piece of paper on the corner of his desk. "I'll tell you what I told the police and this is from Morrison, he's on your list." He nodded toward my lap. "Brewster started out stacking cases and then got promoted to the production line. Then he drove a truck. When he retired he was the assistant to the salesman supervisor."

I thought about this for a moment. After all those years

at the bottling plant the best Brewster could do was *assistant* to the supervisor of sales? I had another thought. "What kinds of duties would he have had if he were in the sales department?"

Lightner waved a pencil in the air. "The usual. Ride herd on the salesmen, court new accounts, pacify the old ones."

"Would he travel much?"

He checked the piece of paper. "His territory was southern Arizona so he probably pretty much stayed down here. We've always had another management team in the northern part of the state."

Interesting. Southern Arizona meant he'd be covering Cochise and Santa Cruz counties as well as Pima. A lot of rural acreage, which translated into a lot of space for bodies.

The manager turned his chair to the credenza behind his desk and opened a small refrigerator. He held up a Sunny Cola. "Want one?"

I declined and he popped the top and guzzled the soft drink.

"Mr. Lightner, do you ever remember hearing about a black man being hired by Sunny Cola, or anyone disappearing?"

A hard look came into his fresh eyes. "We are a major minority employer in Tucson. In fact, we're color-blind. If a person is black, red, pink or yellow, we don't care as long as they get the job done. Over twenty percent of our employees belong to some minority group. We have fifteen people who are mentally challenged."

I knew I had struck a nerve. "I mean back then. Do you know how many black people were working for Sunny Cola in 1963?"

"No. Those records have also been destroyed." He drained the cola. "But in all truthfulness, I can't believe that we would have had many, if any, black people back then. For one thing, there just weren't that many around."

I knew what he meant. In southern Arizona our largest minority group is Hispanic. Blacks only account for about three percent of the population. From my library research I had noted an article that made a big deal about Goldwater's, a Phoenix department store, hiring its first black employee in 1963. The headline had read NEGRO SALESWOMAN HIRED AT GOLDWATER STORE. And that had come a day after one of the owners had denied that Goldwater's refused to employ Negroes. I imagined that any blacks that had been hired in 1963 at the bottling plant would have been given grunt jobs.

"If you had had black people working then, what kind of jobs would they have had?" I pressed.

"Hmm, probably at the bottom of the barrel, stacking cases or working on the production line, unless they had had special skills."

Cases. Production. The two areas that Brewster started in.

"Did you hire part-time help back then?"

"Sure, still do. Summer help and other part-time people. They're not put on any of the benefit programs and back then probably weren't even on the employment records."

"So hiring a drifter would not be unlikely?"

"On purpose it would be. People drift in and out of here, just like in any company. It's difficult to tell because most people won't admit to it and you don't know the person's a drifter until he leaves."

Thinking of the three people who had worked with Brewster that were still there, I pulled out the paper Lightner had given me. "Do any of them remember a black man working here?"

He shook his head. "Which isn't that unusual. Over the years we've had a lot of black people here, but no one remembers a man with small children."

I was out of questions. I had hoped Lightner would have been more helpful, but it was not to be. "May I talk to those employees?"

"Sure." He stood and arced his soda can into his trash can.

"Two points," I said.

"Nah," he said. "That was an outside shot, three."

We walked downstairs and through a long brick hallway that had offices branching out from it on either side. Finally he stopped at a door marked VENDING SALES. We went in and he introduced me to Clyde Morrison, a tiny gnome-like fellow with a full head of curly gray hair. He could have passed for one of Santa's helpers.

Lightner excused himself and left the two of us alone. Morrison was as friendly as he could be; in fact, at one point in our conversation he placed one of his round, elf-like hands on my knee. I quickly handed him back his hand. He tried to be helpful, but his memory was not that good, he claimed. He remembered a few blacks working on and off over his early years at Sunny Cola but could remember no dates, or names.

"Disappeared?" He snorted when asked. "Disappeared? Hell, yes, I would have remembered a man disappearing. A fellow wouldn't forget something like that," he assured me.

But that was it. He didn't remember anyone not showing up for work.

"Mr. Morrison, do you hunt?" I asked.

"Nope, I'm a fisherman."

Our interview concluded, he took me down the brick hallway to Accounting.

"Joanne here?" he asked an attractive black woman behind the counter.

"Out sick," she said. "That flu thing that's going around."

We walked outside to a huge warehouse, stacked with towers of Sunny Cola. Morrison howdied several workers as we walked through. We climbed some wide metal steps up to an observation deck that served as a porch for a glassed-in office. The sign on the door read SUPERVISOR.

Hector Martinez was the only one in the office. He looked a little older than I was. Doing some quick mental arithmetic, I figured he must have started with the plant as a teenager.

As Lightner had done, Morrison introduced us and then excused himself.

Martinez was the epitome of Sunny Cola. He was very round, with a sunny disposition. He smiled frequently during our conversation and, like Morrison, could remember a few black people who had worked back then, but could not remember their names or what had happened to them.

He didn't recall a black man with two young boys. He also was not a hunter. As I stood to leave, he pressed a six-pack of Sunny Cola on me.

Back at Priscilla I rummaged in the toolbox once more, withdrawing the Tucson phone book. Once inside the cab, I pulled the list that Lightner had given me out of my purse. Joanne Devlin was the third name on the the list. The woman with the flu.

Thumbing through the D's I found a J. Devlin listed on Cortez Road. I checked the city map and headed out.

That I was beginning to get consumed by the Carpenter case was quickly becoming apparent to me. What did it mean? Did I really believe the things that Victoria had said happened, happened?

I didn't know. I just knew that I was like a junkyard dog with a bone in his teeth and I wasn't ready to let this one go yet.

Which meant I was now on my way to roust an old lady out of her sickbed.

Which begged the question.

Who really was the sick one?

15

Twenty minutes later I stood at the front door of a neat tan stucco house. I had rung the bell twice and now waited.

Inside a dog was yapping. It sounded like one of those small alarm types, a miniature poodle or a Chihuahua.

The door had an old-fashioned, small dome window and it soon swung open.

"Yes?" The voice was throaty and raw.

"Mrs. Devlin?"

"Yes?"

I held up a card. "I'm Trade Ellis, a private detective working on the Phelan Brewster thing. I've just come from the bottling plant. May I come in?"

"I'm sick."

"I'm not worried."

There was a fumbling of the locks and finally the door swung open, revealing a stooped old lady holding a nondescript small dog in her bathrobed arms. The dog snapped and snarled at me so I kept my distance.

"Come in," Devlin said, hobbling away from the door. She went to a crystal bowl on a sideboard and retrieved a small Milk Bone, which she handed to me. Her companion still acted as though he wanted to have me for his mid-afternoon snack. "Hand it to him and he'll be all right."

Shit. But he was a small dog and I figured he probably wouldn't even be able to take off a full finger. I held the

Milk Bone out as far as I could, clasping the tip of it with my short fingernails. When the dog saw what it was, he shut up and took the offering. The old lady put him down and I had a tense moment, like playing that kids' game where you freeze as a statue. But to my relief the dog was more interested in chewing on his bone than on me.

"Please sit down."

I took a seat in a Queen Anne chair that had crocheted gizmos on the arms.

"I told the police what I know," she said.

"I'm just looking for anything, anything at all that you may remember from 1963, about any black person who may have worked for Sunny Cola."

The woman took an ironed white handkerchief out of a pocket of her robe and blew her nose. I watched, fascinated. No one I knew even had a handkerchief. Kleenex had taken care of all that. Briefly I wondered if the handkerchief and its contents went into the washing machine with the rest of her clothes. Visions of boogers swirling around with her dinner napkins caused me to move on.

"Any detail, even the smallest, could be helpful."

The woman coughed, covering her mouth as she did so.

"I knew Phelan Brewster, of course. Dreadful man."

"Dreadful in what way?"

"He just wasn't nice. He killed things, animals. Hunted them down. Drove his wife crazy, you know."

"How did he do that, Mrs. Devlin?"

"Oh I don't know how he did it, he just did it." She dabbed at her red-chafed nose with the handkerchief. "Phelan didn't like anyone who was different."

"Different?"

"You know, other races, other nationalities. I always thought he was a Klansman or something like that. He frequently made fun of black people, called them jungle bunnies. I didn't like it but I never said anything. I was afraid of him."

I remembered the five-year-old Victoria Carpenter wondering why anyone would be afraid of her daddy.

"Afraid of him? Why?"

"I don't know. He was just so big, so boisterous. I'd

seen him use his spiteful tongue and I didn't want it to turn on me so I stayed as far away from him as I could."

Joanne Devlin was clearly eager to talk. Now if I could just find the right questions to ask.

"You mentioned that you thought he might belong to the Klan. Did he ever talk about that or any other groups that he may have belonged to?"

"No, but if he had joined it wouldn't surprise me at all. He had nothing good to say about the Negroes or the Chinese or the Mexicans."

"Were there many of them working at the plant?"

"Well, over the years, we've had a number of black people working there. Back then, no, probably not many."

"Did Brewster ever talk about his home life?"

She shook her gray head. "Not with me. I was a woman, after all."

I caught the sting in her voice.

"Did you ever hear him mention a group called the Sporting Club?"

She shook her head and sneezed.

The wretched beast, who had finished his bone by now, jumped up on the overstuffed couch and curled up next to his mistress.

"Mrs. Devlin, I'm trying especially hard to reconstruct what might have happened at the plant in 1963 because I think that year might be very important to this case. My client remembers something from that time frame."

"That was a long time ago," she said wistfully. "You know a person's memory's a fragile thing. Sometimes I can remember things perfectly, and sometimes I can't remember my brother-in-law's name."

And some people couldn't remember traumatic experiences that happened to them in childhood, I thought. Of course, it might be hard to remember things if they'd never happened. If you were a fiction writer who liked to make things up. And got paid for doing so.

Still, as long as I was remotely considering this case as fact, what questions from my bleak research might trigger her memory? I pressed on.

"Do you remember anything significant happening at

Arizona Bottling during that year?" I prodded. "Maybe someone disappearing or being hurt?"

She closed her eyes and leaned her head against the back of the sofa. It also wore a crocheted doily. "No, nothing. We have an excellent safety record, you know."

"Sometimes it's hard to remember that far back," I said gently. "Is there anything special, anything at all, you remember about 1963?'

"Well of course," she sniffed, blowing delicately into the handkerchief. By now I was wondering how such a small piece of cloth could hold her multitude of deposits. "I remember Martin Luther King came on the scene about then, with all of those demonstrations in the South. Then there were those bombings and such and President Kennedy was assassinated. That was a terrible time. And didn't his brother get killed right after that?"

"I think it was a few years later." I was impressed.

"And Mr. King was shot too, wasn't he?"

"Yes, ma'am, he was."

She was doing all right with pulling up ancient history. And she'd triggered something when she mentioned the assassination of John F. Kennedy. It had been my experience that everyone who was old enough to remember that sad event also remembered where they were when they heard the news. It was probably going to be fruitless, but I had to keep at it.

"Mrs. Devlin, where *were* you when President Kennedy was killed?"

She stared over my head as though she was looking for the answer. Finally she nodded and answered my question.

"Why, I was at the plant," she said, sounding surprised that she could bring up the memory. "That was a tragic thing and I remember it as though it were yesterday."

"Were you in your office?"

"Oh no, not my office as it is today. I was on the line. Things were different then. We weren't as automated, and had to rely on people more. Remember, in those days our bottles had deposits on them and were recycled. I was a bottle inspector and checked the bottles after they came out of the soaker. We were very careful about cleanliness, cracks, chipped lips, that sort of thing."

"So you were in production when you heard about President Kennedy?"

"Yes, but for the life of me I can't remember who brought in the news. Someone heard it on the radio, I suppose."

"Was Brewster there that day?"

"Oh yes. It was in the afternoon but we were let out early and on the way to my car I was walking behind Phelan and he was whistling up a storm. Happy tunes they were too. No, Phelan Brewster didn't shed any tears over John Kennedy's death."

Suddenly she jumped, as though someone had startled her.

"Oh! There is something else. And you know, I don't know if it's important or not, but I do remember a black man that day too. Goodness! How could I have forgotten that? He didn't work at the plant very long at all, really just a few months."

Goose bumps ran up my arms.

"Good grief. The police were here and everything and I couldn't for the life of me remember that man." She was agitated now, disgusted with her forgetfulness.

"Could you tell me about him?"

"I don't remember his name, but he was on the line with me that day. He was real upset when the President got killed. He never said much. But he started crying when he heard the news. I thought that was strange, seeing a grown man cry like that at work."

I waited silently, hoping her memory would continue production. My silence was rewarded.

"Yes, I remember him now. He had a number of children and he brought them in one Saturday to see where he worked. He was really tickled to get that job because he had a lot of people who depended on him."

My heart began to pound and a shiver assaulted my spine. Jesus, was this what discovery was all about?

"How many children did he have?"

"Oh, it must have been five, six. They were stair-stepped." She held out a bony hand and pantomimed walking down stairs with her fingers. "You know, something like five, four, three, two, one. No, not one, because they all walked into the plant holding hands and a one-year-old probably wouldn't have been able to do that on his own. I remember after he left that Phelan said something derogatory about Negroes breeding like rabbits."

"What became of the black man?"

"Oh, it must have been a week or so later, he just called in and quit. Said he was moving back to Georgia. We never saw him again."

"Did you tell the police this?"

She shook her head. "I didn't think of it then. But when you said 1963 and we started talking about the President, I started remembering about that man and all those children. Do you think it's important?"

"I don't know," I said, shaking my head. "But you might want to call the county attorney's office and tell them what you've told me."

"I'll do it." She sneezed again, hard enough to dislodge the dog from her side. He dropped to the floor and walked over to my chair, sniffing my ankles. I braced myself for the bite, but there was none.

"He likes you," Joanne Devlin said.

Not wanting to press my luck, I thanked her for her time and said goodbye.

On the way home I passed a Sunny Cola billboard. Unlike the old mural, this one had a black family on it.

16

I HAD JUST FINISHED FEEDING WHEN MARTÍN RODE THROUGH THE back gate.

"Out scouting?"

Fall roundup was not far off, and I figured that like me he'd been out checking where the cattle were hiding out.

"Yeah, it's gonna be fun, they're scattered all over the mountain. And I ran into Hildy Peters."

Hildy was a cowboy who worked for the B Spear outfit, which bordered part of the Vaca Grande's northern fence line.

"Four-wheelers have cut the fence again and he says there's a lot of our beef on their grass."

I groaned. It's always bad manners to feed your cattle on another rancher's pasture. Cut fences are an unfortunate fact of ranch life and they always mean work. "Well, as long as we've got to ride onto the B Spear to pull them out we might as well drive them down to the north tank pasture."

"I'll check with Diego, Memo and Ramón, see if they can help out."

All of them were cowboys who had worked for us before. Memo had worked roundup on the Vaca Grande for over twenty years. The other two were younger. Ramón we borrowed from the Oracle Ridge Ranch and, in turn, we'd send Martín up there to help them gather when their roundup came. Later in the month we'd be using more people, recruiting friends and neighbors.

"You know, I suppose I ought to thank you," Martín said.

"For what?"

"Talking to Cori Elena. I think talking with you got things going."

His cowboy hat was pulled low over his face and I didn't have a good look at his eyes.

"It's a bummer, Martín, any way you look at it. I'm sorry."

"Yeah. Well, maybe God didn't want me to have children."

"You still have a daughter."

"Do I?"

What was I hearing? Was Martín doubting Cori Elena's story?

"What are you talking about?'

"I may have flesh and blood somewhere but I've never met her. I want to."

"Do you need a couple of days?" Hermosillo was an easy day's drive from Tucson and Magdalena was on the way. The whole trip probably wouldn't take more than three, four days.

"Lousy timing, with roundup starting."

"We can move it back a week or two."

"I thought if I rode hard this week and next, then maybe I could take a break and head down there."

"You can leave tomorrow as far as I'm concerned."

He shook his head. "I've waited twenty-two years, another week or so isn't going to make any difference, and there's a lot of work to do."

"Martín, tomorrow, the day after, next week. It doesn't matter. You just go do what you have to do."

"Mil gracias, Chiquita."

He rode through the back gate.

I was just closing it when he threw his last comment over his shoulder.

"When the time comes, I'm telling Cori Elena I'm visiting a dying aunt and I'd appreciate it if this conversation never happened."

An hour later Petunia the potbellied pig was ricocheting off the seat of my truck as I tried to concentrate on the road. Already the little red bow that I had duct-taped to her head was off-kilter and the tattered ribbon now resembled a bloody tumor growing out of her right ear. At least the diaper was still on.

I had remembered the Pampers out in the tack room. I usually keep a box of them around for doctoring purposes. They make great bandages on the rare occasions when one of the horses suffers a leg wound and they can also be applied on top of a poultice as a sweat. The plastic on the outside creates warmth which, when coupled with various drawing medications, can pop unfamiliar objects—like barrel cactus thorns—right out of a horse's leg.

Since Petunia had treated Priscilla with something less than respect on her last outing, I thought the Pampers a prudent choice. While she had initially tried to remove them, the pig was now content to explore her surroundings and seemed oblivious to the fact that she was semi-clothed.

As I approached the Tucson city limits Petunia jumped up on the passenger's seat and discovered the window. She pressed her snout against the glass and began sniffing. This quickly evolved into a swinish melody of various grunts and snorts. At a stoplight a station wagon filled with kids pulled alongside of us. From the looks on their faces they were thrilled to see a pig riding shotgun in a Dodge pickup. Petunia, judging from her reaction, which sounded suspiciously like a baby dirtying his diapers, was also pleased. If the kids had known what the pig was doing, they would have been even more tickled. Kids, unlike adults, find poop mirthful.

The station wagon stayed even with me for a while as the kids laughed and pointed at the pig. She continued her singsong melody and had her tail wiggling frantically the entire time. I think she liked the attention.

I was surprised to see Top Dog's old pickup parked in his parents' driveway when I pulled in. Last I'd heard he had been in a triathlon in Hawaii.

I got out of the truck quickly and grabbed Petunia. I

really hadn't given her presentation much thought, other than the tortured red bow. Finally I decided that it would be more of a surprise if I waited to introduce her when the rest of the presents were given. Like a mother, I checked her diaper. It was a little messy, but nothing that warranted replacing it. I had had a hard enough time putting the first one on the squirming pig. As she struggled in my arms, I retied and readjusted the red bow and then carried her around to the side yard.

Uncle C and Aunt Josie's golden retriever died last summer and so far they haven't replaced him, so I knew I was safe putting the pig in the backyard. I pushed her gently through the gate, then closed it. Petunia showed no abandonment anxiety as she trotted off to investigate her new surroundings.

Then I rang the front doorbell.

Bea opened it and gave me a quick hug. If she thought it was peculiar that I was appearing without a present, she said nothing. After greeting my aunt and uncle and Top Dog we settled into a round of family catch-up, much of it centered around Shiwóyé, my grandmother.

"I was hoping she'd come down," I said, for it had been a few weeks since I had been up on the reservation.

"I tried to convince her to drive down with me, but she's working on a difficult case and didn't want to leave," Top Dog said.

I nodded. My grandmother, a full-blooded Apache, is a tribal medicine woman. Working in drug and alcohol counseling, Shiwóyé takes her doctoring very seriously, and if there was someone in need of her services she would not be eager to leave them.

Aunt Josie, as always, had fixed a wonderful dinner. Cooking had always been one of her strong suits and she pulled out all the stops for Bea's birthday feast: beef Wellington, fresh, slim-stalked asparagus cooked al dente, Waldorf salad, and potatoes Duchesse. When I finished eating, I felt like a hog in heaven, which caused me to excuse myself from the table and go to the bathroom, where I could peek out the tiny window into the backyard. It was dark, but the light from the bathroom window cast a small shadow on the ground. Softly I whistled for my pig.

As if on cue she came trotting up to the window, chewing on a mouthful of grass. So far her bow and diaper were intact, so I congratulated her and went back to the party.

"Trade, what are you working on now?" Uncle C asked. My uncle was a criminal investigator with the Pima County Sheriff's Department and while he didn't think much of my line of work, circumstances had thrown us together on my first murder case last spring. Since then, he seemed more willing to take me into the fold, so to speak.

When I mentioned the Sporting Club his eyes lit with recognition.

"Messenger's thing, it didn't pan out."

"But he admits that the body could have been there. They may have been just a few feet off."

"Can't go to court with that," he said with a huff as he lit a cigar. "It's too damn old."

"Still, if there's something to it . . . ," I mused.

"The big boys have been looking, Trade," he said gently. "They haven't uncovered squat."

"I keep thinking about those kids, though, Uncle C. I can't get them out of my mind."

"What kids?" Top Dog's question was my entrée for filling in the whole family on the gruesome details of a crime that may or may not have been committed.

"I suppose this is on the q.t.?" Bea asked.

"No Channel Four this time, I'm afraid. Messenger says it's still an open case because there's a couple of detectives that don't want to give it up."

"Who are they?" Uncle C asked.

"I don't know, he didn't say."

He nodded, and I could tell by the gesture that he would find out exactly who they were. Whether or not he would pass the information on to me remained to be seen.

"Pretty Horses"—my aunt called me by my Apache name, the one that had been given to me by my grandparents years ago—"do you think this sporting thing could be related to any of the organized hate groups?"

"I don't know. I've been reading up on the Ku Klux Klan."

"Nice guys," Top Dog said.

"But there doesn't seem to be much that happened here that related to all that stuff in the sixties."

"We weren't entirely immune," Aunt Josie said.

"There was that KKK thing last week," Bea said. "With those flyers. We covered it but it didn't amount to much."

"Hell, they sent them to the LAPD," Uncle C said.

"Sent what?" I asked.

"Those goddam flyers. Tried to recruit some of the L.A. cops."

"When?"

"Last fall. It made a few papers but it wasn't much. Far as anyone could tell, no one signed on."

"Seems odd," Top Dog mused, "that they would want to recruit cops."

"Not really," I said. "They used to have a lot of policemen on their membership roles."

"Yeah, like how many?" Top Dog asked.

"Hundreds, maybe thousands."

"No shit?" he said, earning a scowl from his mother, who was heading back to the kitchen. While she lived with Uncle C's profanity, she did not like to hear her children swear.

"They were some of the best members," I said. "Remember those COFO killings back in the sixties?" It was a loaded question and one I was not sure that I could have answered had I not done my homework on the subject.

He shook his head.

"Two white kids and a black kid named Chaney were down in Mississippi working on voter registration. They got picked up one night for speeding. The black kid was driving. Anyway, later that night the cops told them if they paid a twenty-dollar fine they could go."

"Did they?" Top Dog asked.

"Yeah. And then they disappeared."

"Not exactly," Uncle C said, for he was having no trouble remembering the story. "Turns out the sheriff and the deputy released them smack into the hands of the Klan. The FBI swarmed all over Mississippi and finally found their bodies in a dam."

"No shit?" Top Dog repeated.

Aunt Josie broke our conversation when she returned with a chocolate mousse cake adorned with less than the appropriate number of candles. She led us in singing "Happy Birthday" to Bea.

In spite of being full I managed to put away two hefty pieces of the cake.

Bea began opening her gifts after we had all finished with dessert. She started with the present from her brother. It was a beautiful book titled *The People Called Apache* by a guy named Thomas Mails. Full of history and photographs and legends and pictures, it was the most comprehensive book any of us had ever seen about the Apache. Top Dog's gift was also consistent with his dream that we would all someday return to the reservation and be a clan reunited.

Next Bea opened a box containing a turquoise silk blouse and jeweled button covers from her parents.

"Look underneath the tissue," my uncle suggested.

Bea lifted the thin paper and withdrew a small painting. It was a pen-and-India-ink watercolor by Uncle C.

My uncle, in addition to being a detective, is also an artist. He is beginning to get quite a following for his work, which is shown in a local art gallery. While most of his stuff is abstract and has to do with some of the more notorious crimes he has been involved with, this one was, thankfully, different. It was a picture of a little girl and a little boy in bathing suits, squatting and playing in the sand. In the background, their backs to the children and seated under a wide beach umbrella were two people, a man and a woman. Beyond them a sailboat drifted on a calm blue sea.

Bea stared at the picture.

"It's us," Uncle C said, obviously pleased with himself. "I painted it from a picture from that vacation in Rocky Point."

"Oh, I remember," Bea said. "That time when the boat conked out."

"Right," he said.

"Thanks, Dad. This is really special."

I smiled and wondered what our ancestors must have been thinking. In the old days our superstitions would have prevented us from posing for such a picture. Even today on the reservation there are a few old ones who will not have anything to do with a camera, for fear that part of their spirits or an essential part of themselves will be captured.

The painting was passed around and by the time it got to me I felt a strange pang. It was a wonderful family memento. Something that Bea would always treasure, and probably pass on to her children if she ever had any. A brief sorrow washed over me as I thought of my two dead parents. As an only child, all I had was this family and my grandmother. Although it was foolish and impossible, I was sorry that we had not also gone on the vacation and could have been included in the family portrait.

"Pretty Horses, are you all right?" Aunt Josie must have noticed my melancholy.

"Oh fine," I lied. "Bea, let me get your present."

I went into the kitchen and opened the back door, whistling for Petunia.

She must have been right there for she tore into the house, ducking between my legs, her diaper half on with the other half dragging on the linoleum and, not unlike Hansel and Gretel, she was leaving a little trail behind her. Only the birds, at least the self-respecting ones, would not nibble on this track as they had on the fairy-tale bread crumbs.

She was not a stupid pig, for she knew exactly where to find the party and wasted no time in getting there. As she rushed through me I noticed she had something in her mouth and that her red bow was now akimbo, trailing her as she sped into the dining room.

My first clue that she had successfully reached her destination came from Aunt Josie's shriek. By the time I ran into the room, Petunia's trailing red ribbon had entwined itself around Josie's ankle. As my aunt jumped up from her chair it fell over backward onto the floor, taking the rest of Petunia's diaper with it.

Josie jumped away from her fallen throne, dragging the pig along with her. She stopped after a few feet and began swatting at the furry thing attached to her ankle. A high piercing shriek was coming from the pig, who, in her effort to get away from the screaming woman, had only succeeded in wrapping herself tighter to the human leg. Clearly, both females were terrified.

"Wait!" I yelled, as Uncle C jumped up from the table armed with a dinner knife.

I ran to the pig and tried to comfort her. Judging from her grunts, she was happy to see me. "The knife."

Uncle C handed over the silver blade and I sawed through the tattered ribbon, finally freeing my aunt from the pig.

Petunia grunted her gratitude and trotted over to the fallen chair where she retrieved the treasure that had dropped from her mouth.

"My pansies!" Josie cried.

She was not wrong, for thus informed I could now clearly see a wilted, though still bright-eyed pansy, slowly disappearing into Petunia's bristled orifice.

"Oh shit," Top Dog said with his typical wisdom.

Unfortunately he was also right.

I reached for the pig and cradled her in my arms as I tried to comb her head with my fingers. Oblivious to this attempt at grooming, she completed her birthday party snack and wiggled in an attempt to get at the chocolate cake.

"No," I said. "Chocolate is bad for you, poison."

"What is *that?*" Bea asked, and although she was trying to be composed, I thought I caught a touch of concern in her voice.

"This is Petunia," I said proudly. "Happy Birthday."

17

It was freezing the next morning when Martín and I saddled our horses. I was grateful for the lights at the tack room, for they allowed us to see what we were doing. I watched each breath escape my mouth and my lungs complained with every intake of frigid air. Gray's and Chapo's coats were fluffed out to insulate them from the intemperate weather, and I had my long hair, which now served as a covering for my chilled ears. Martín was also bundled up and, as we saddled, neither of us said much.

Martín had the stock trailer hooked up to his pickup and it was just after seven when we loaded our horses and then picked up Sanders, my closest neighbor, and his horse, and drove north. In mid-November it's just too darned cold to go out much earlier. Early mornings in the valley hover in the low twenties. The cows are also not too keen on this cold stuff. In the winter they wait until mid-morning to go for water. The water's too cold before that. So we wait until the sun gets a little higher before starting out, shedding our layered clothing as the sun progresses across the sky.

We drove through La Cienega and then headed north above Florence Junction. Martín turned off on a dirt road and we drove for about a mile and a half before he pulled in next to a set of corrals where we unloaded the horses. While the road dead-ended here, apparently someone had thought otherwise, for the four strands of barbed wire had been cut and laid back. In the opening, a morass of cattle tracks, all headed north, could be seen on top of faint tire tracks left by the vandalizing four-wheeler.

Once we rode through the gate we were on the B Spear property. Memo, Ramón and Diego were repairing the fence and would then start a bit east and north of here and eventually, as we swept the neighbor's pasture, we'd all meet up.

Martín suggested that he would ride the middle ground, in between the area the other three cowboys were covering and the west fence line that Sanders and I would check. I suspected that he wanted to be alone, to think about his daughter.

Sanders and I rode in silence for the first few miles, our eyes scanning the landscape for cattle. We jumped a pair of coyotes hunting together and saw a lot of fresh sign, but no cows. The coyotes reminded me of us, for we were also a hunting pair.

We finally hit our first bunch of cattle down along a wash. The feed was good here, lush six-week grass nestled under the bare mesquite trees which had lost their leaves to winter. Although the creek was dry, it made a nice trail for the cows to travel up to the closest water tank, not too rocky and not too heavy with sand.

The Brahmas looked at us to see if we were just passing through or wanting something more. They know the difference. We check them often enough that seeing someone on horseback does not alarm them. And when we do move them, we do it quietly, which is the fastest way to move cattle. Billy Crystal and his pals probably couldn't hire on at this outfit.

I was happy to see that they were all wearing the 9Z brand which meant that we wouldn't have to cut them out from the B Spear stock.

We started whistling and making funny little noises like *hup, hup* and *here cow*, slapping our chaps lightly with our split reins. The cows, knowing the routine, started heading south.

That's the good thing about working cows. Many of these girls have been in this area all of their lives. They not only know the game plan, they know the territory. There are no secrets for them here. They have surveyed every gully, every water hole and every mesquite *bosque*. So when it comes time to go to the corrals they head south, albeit grudgingly, on the same route that their mother, and in some cases, their grandmother, took before them.

I'm always happy that we don't run steers up here. Those boys are on a range for a year, maybe less, and then they're shipped out to Steer Nightmare. When the steers first arrive on a new pasture they fumble around, much like adolescent boys on their first movie date, looking for everything—grass, water, places to hang out. This not only causes them some distress, but if you are unfortunate enough to have to gather these guys, you may quickly find yourself in the middle of a Chinese fire drill. The cattle scatter everywhere, having not the foggiest idea of where they are supposed to go, where the corrals are, or how to get there. It's a lot of work for everyone—cowboys, horses and steers.

There were twenty Brahma cows and a Hereford bull in this bunch. Many of the cows had young babies by their sides, the winter calves. While some outfits segregate their bulls from their cows, thus insuring a predictable delivery date for the babies, here at the Vaca Grande we keep the two sexes together year-round. It's also one of the reasons for our frequent gatherings. This keeps everyone happy and the fences in reasonably good shape—that is, unless an overzealous driver in a four-wheel drive comes along with a pair of wire cutters, like this one had.

While a lot of ranches only gather in the spring and the fall, we like to get the babies cut, ear-tagged and branded before they get too large. For one thing, it's easier on the cowboys. There are no branding tables on this outfit. We still drag them to the fire the way cowboys have been doing for a hundred years. It's also riskier for poachers if the beef's branded.

Sanders headed up the canyon and circled to the east as I pushed the group down the wash. Brahmas are funny cattle. For starters, they're survivors. While many of the British breeds—the Herefords, Angus and Shorthorns, for instance—are finicky eaters, preferring lush grass, the Brahmas will eat anything. They're browsers. Mesquite beans, desert brush, six-week grass, all of it goes into the great cow machine, is utilized and then discarded.

They have horns which help them protect their children, so our loss to predators is low, and they do well in heat and humidity. They're also quick. They can settle into an easy lope that will leave most other breeds in their dust. But they do need their space. You need to give a Brahma air if you're working her, don't crowd and don't get too close. And they're fighters. If something is threatening their children, or if they're having a bad day, they'll flat-out defend themselves and their families, so we try not to worry them too much.

These cattle, though, are like family. We've all lived out here together for so long that we understand one another. My group headed south in a ladylike manner with the Hereford bull bringing up the rear. Other than an occasional disgusted look thrown over one massive shoulder, he, too, gave me no problems.

I saw the dust from the new bunch that Sanders was bringing in long before I saw the cattle. Another forty head came trotting in to join up with my group. There were three bulls in with the newcomers. Usually when the cattle go through a cut fence, it's only a handful, but from the looks of the group we were pulling in today, they must have come into the corral for salt right after the fence had been cut. I was happy we were getting them off the B Spear, since it would have been embarrassing to have this many cattle on someone else's grass.

By one o'clock, working the canyons and hideout places, the two of us had gathered forty-three mother cows.

We drove them down the broader spread of the Sutherland and then headed south, up and down hills and canyons on the well-trod paths. As we crested the last big hill before the fence line, I saw Memo and Ramón pushing another large group toward the cut fence.

By the time I got to the corral Diego and Martín were waiting with another seven head.

"¿Dónde está Alfonso?" I asked Diego, always eager to practice my rusty Spanish.

"Está enfermo," he replied.

Not only does my Spanish leave me forever in the present tense, but my vocabulary is somewhat limited, so I wasn't exactly enthusiastic about heading into any extended conversation that would encompass medical terminology. Besides, Diego was always complimenting me on my Spanish and I didn't want to disabuse him of that. If Al was sick, that was enough for me.

"Looks like we got all of them," Martín said.

I watched our group file through the opened gate. As the last bull walked through, Ramón shut the wire fence.

I stepped off Dream, threw a stirrup up over the saddle seat, and loosened his cinch before fumbling in my cantle bag.

"Time to celebrate," I said, digging out seven packs of squished Twinkies. I handed one to each of them with one left over. I knew where the extra was going.

It's a funny thing about cowboys. You'll rarely see a cantle bag on one of their saddles. This is a nifty little contraption that fits behind the saddle seat. You can stuff it with all sorts of things in addition to the aforementioned Twinkies. A cantle bag can hold pliers, hemostats, a tally book, first-aid supplies, cellular phones and panty hose (which can be used for a bandage, for a sling, for tying things on to the saddle, for a blindfold or for emergency tack repairs). Although the cowboys don't use them, probably think they are sissy stuff, I've yet to meet one who will turn down road food when it is offered from an opened cantle bag.

"*Chiquita*, here's the keys." Martín pitched them underhand to me and I was pleased when I caught them. "We'll drive them down to the north tanks. You and Sanders go on home."

We said goodbye to the rest of the crew, loaded our horses and headed home. As I drove, the sky was turning dark with a winter storm threatening to move in.

Sanders and I hadn't seen each other in a while, so we got caught up on the ride home. Things were fine over at his place and things were fine at mine so we talked a little about the weather and swapped gossip we had picked up about various denizens of La Cienega. While I was tempted to bring up Martín's problem, his was a confidence I could not breech, so finally I turned to the other subject that had been occupying a lot of my mind this morning.

"What do you think of Dan Daglio?" I asked.

"The mayor?"

I nodded.

"Guess I haven't thought about him much."

"Have you ever heard anything about him?"

"Sure, he's in the papers all the time. I think I read something about him this mornin'."

I began talking about Victoria and her childhood. For some strange reason, I rarely talk about my cases to Juan or Martín, and nearly always do with Sanders. When I told him about the Sporting Club he didn't know any of the players.

"I've got a cousin out in Avra Valley," he said. "I could check on this Brewster fellow."

"That would be great, if he could do it kind of quietly," I said. "I don't even know if any of this is true."

He thought this over for a minute.

"There's a lot of strange people out there," he said.

"I guess important people could do something like that," I mused, feeling instantly stupid.

"Well, Trade," Sanders said, "sometimes a man just gets to thinkin' he's important. This Daglio fellow might see things a bit differently if he was to go to orderin' someone else's dog around."

18

I WAS IN MY STAGE STOP OFFICE EARLY THE NEXT MORNING WORK-
ing on Victoria Carpenter's report. Since it's my policy to
collect a healthy retainer up front, I like to send my clients
typed updates every week to show them that I'm working
on their cases. Of course I have to explain to them that my
old IBM Selectric is missing its *o*. The reports not only keep
the money and the amount of time I'm spending on each
case straight, but also bring each one into focus. By glancing through the weeklies I can get a good idea of what's
already been done and which bases I need to cover.

By ten o'clock I was in the administrative offices of the
Westside School District.

"You know, we've been over this with the police," the
tiny, efficient woman behind the counter said. "And it was
impossible. You're looking for the same thing they were, a
couple of no-name kids who may have disappeared from
school over thirty years ago."

"Well, they didn't disappear exactly from school," I
explained. "They were somewhere else, probably on the
weekend or maybe even during a vacation, but they didn't
show up again at school."

She scratched her graying head. "That's so long ago, I
have to think about this."

"Maybe there are some records somewhere by year."

"Oh, there are records," she assured me. "Cartons of
them down in the basement." Her eyes drifted downward.

"Stacks and stacks, rows and rows. They've been here longer than I have, and that's over forty years. I told the police that. And I suppose you've got the same problem they had, you don't know what school these kids went to?"

"No." I pulled out the crinkled map I had worked on. The Arizona Bottling Plant was very visible in red, as was the drawn circle around it. "I think the school may have been within this area." I tapped the paper with my capped pen, and spread a second sheet of paper next to the map. "I checked the phone book and came up with this list of possibilities."

She took the paper, adjusted her glasses and began to read. She was only partway down the list when she flattened the paper against the countertop and began moving her pencil down the list. "Too new, too new, wrong area, too new, wrong area, nope."

My list of eleven prospects had now dwindled to five.

In a bold hand she scribbled something across the bottom. Even though it was upside down, the writing was large enough that I could make out the name Millicent Springs.

"Is Millicent Springs someone who might be able to help me?" I asked.

She laughed. "No, Millicent Springs was a school that was around back then, I just happened to remember it."

"But it's not in the phone book."

She shook her head. "They found out the school was loaded with asbestos. Would have cost too much to take out and make safe so they closed it down." She scribbled something else and I could see that Washington was now keeping Millicent Springs company.

"Burned down," she explained.

Seven possible schools now fell within the circle. This was a long shot, I knew. I had guessed on the circle; it was a hope, really, that the black man and his family lived close to where he worked. While it was a great theory, and gave me something to work on, he just as easily could have lived across town and commuted. The one thing in my favor was that the bottling plant was in an area that had been, and still was, racially mixed. It was a slim idea, but the only one I had so far that might help me uncover the kids.

"Where would these records be?"

"Right here, downstairs," she said. "But we don't have the manpower to go through them, the police didn't have the manpower and you sure don't look like you've got the manpower."

"But we're only talking seven schools, if we could just get to those boxes."

"Seven schools, hundreds of boxes, thousands of pieces of paper. You're talking about thirty years of record keeping, entrance records, transfer files, aptitude tests, absentee charts, report cards, personnel files, school pictures, classroom rosters, health records, school notices. It's endless. It's easier now with computers, but you're not talking now."

Something she said stirred me. "School pictures?" Was it actually possible to get a school picture of the missing kids? Probably not likely, since I didn't even have their names, or what schools they went to, or even if they had attended school in this district. I was here hunting phantoms. That I might actually catch one would defy Jimmy the Greek's odds-making abilities.

"Oh we don't keep every kid's picture, at least not individually, but we do keep a copy of the class picture, the one with all of the kids and the teacher."

My heart began to pound. "Where would you keep those class pictures?"

"Same place." She stomped her foot to make her point.

"Downstairs," we said together.

"And there's no way that those pictures could have been in a separate file, or carton or book?"

She shook her head. "Yearbooks were high-school stuff back then." She must have seen the disappointment on my face for she offered, "The funny thing is, though, we still use the same photographer—well, not exactly the same photographer, but the same studio. Mason's has done all of our district pictures for thirty-three years now."

"Is the photographer still alive?"

"Oh I don't think so, but his daughter took over the

business, she's kept it up. I make the arrangements with her every year." The tiny woman stepped away from the counter and ran her hand along a hanging file bin, finally withdrawing a sheet and handing it to me.

Memories flooded through me as I recognized it as one of the photography sheets that I had also brought home as a child. Name. Grade. Classroom teacher. Box for the number of eight by tens, five by sevens and wallet size. Printed across the bottom was *Mason's Photography, 1010 E. Tenth, Tucson, Arizona 85716.*

"Good luck," she said, as I thanked her and left.

Mason's daughter may have taken over his business but it looked like that may have been the only change. When I pulled up to the photography studio I was guessing that it was the same building that her father had started in. Maybe even born in. It was an old mud adobe that had been stuccoed over and painted a muted pink. The stucco had eroded in spots and I could see patches of the old straw mud adobe peeking through. It was pretty in a rugged sort of way, but I knew that if the adobe wasn't stabilized soon it would eventually melt with our summer monsoons. Two windows, dressed with faded turquoise awnings, flanked the heavy wooden front door. So far the photography studio sure didn't look like what I'd been expecting.

Inside, there was a small front office with an old metal desk stacked high with papers, photographs, files, and abandoned coffee mugs housing an assortment of writing instruments. I could see still more papers, books and magazines piled into teetering towers on the floor behind the desk.

In the middle of all this desktop confusion sat a young woman. She was round, and having a bad, wild red hair day. Great silver gypsy hoop earrings framed her pleasant face, which was also set off by a blue tie-dyed rag wrapped across her forehead. She was munching half a submarine sandwich and leafing through an old issue of *Arizona Highways*. An Irish setter, whose hair color matched its owner's, lay curled at her feet, either unaware or uncaring that her territory had been invaded by a stranger.

"May I help you?" the woman said, wrapping the sandwich back up in waxed paper.

I handed her a card and introduced myself and explained what I was looking for.

"Parsley Mason," she said, licking her fingers, rubbing them on her Gap jeans and then extending her hand. "I own the joint."

My heart sank. Somehow I had expected more from Tucson's premier photographer of schoolchildren. It wasn't very logical, I guess, since most of her business would be done outside, in the schools, and there was no need for her to maintain a fancy studio. Still, I doubted whether the woman would be able to find the other half of her sandwich, much less the pictures I wanted.

I handed her the list of schools.

She studied it for a minute and then asked, "So you want negatives, prints, or what?"

"What?"

"From those schools. You want 1963, right?" She handed me back the list.

Was she kidding? Was this some kind of sick joke? She was sitting in the most cluttered office I'd ever seen, there wasn't a file cabinet in sight, and yet she was acting like she could produce them with a wave of a magic wand. I looked around for the fairy godmother, and finding none, nodded dumbly.

"So I can give you copies of negatives, prints, contact sheets, you name it. Black-and-whites, color, whatever."

"You mean you have them, you have class pictures from those schools during that time?" I couldn't believe my luck. Then I immediately held my enthusiasm in check, for she hadn't said *when* she could produce them. If she had to straighten up the office first, I'd be in for a very long wait.

"Crime-in-nently," she said, "we've got every friggin' shot we ever took of anything, anywhere."

I stared at the mess on her desk and the stacks of magazines on the floor behind her. The two windows, now that I was inside, I could tell needed a good cleaning—and I'm not all that fussy about windows.

She must have read my mind for she said, "Follow

me." She stopped to lock the door, explaining, "Everyone else is at lunch."

The building had been deceptive from the outside. I had thought that it was a small three- maybe four-room affair. As she walked me through it we passed several small rooms with dropped blackcloth backgrounds. Stuffed toys, helium-filled balloons and other make-the-baby-smile paraphernalia lay scattered about among the backdropped scenes of Sabino Canyon, Mount Lemmon and Nogales.

When we got to the end of the hallway Parsley opened a heavy metal door. As we went inside the temperature changed dramatically. While it had been warm in the outer office, the temperature in this room was at least fifteen degrees cooler. That was my first hint.

In the seconds it took my mind to figure out that I was now in a thermostatically controlled and hermetically sealed cavern, Parsley Mason punched on the overhead fluorescent lights.

I stood there in shock, finding myself in a well-thought-out repository for negatives.

The room had floor-to-ceiling sleek steel shelves. On them were stacks and stacks of gray plastic boxes which I assumed housed negatives. Each box was clearly labeled. The room was as uniform and neat as any museum curator could hope for. Given the front office, this was absolutely mind-boggling. Briefly, I wondered if Parsley Mason was a Gemini.

"The almighty archives," she whispered, brushing past me.

A computer sat against one wall on a white laminated hutch. She pulled its plastic cover off, punched a few buttons, and I listened as it came on-line. Mason sat at the chair and began feeding information into her humming electronic helpmate. "You got that list?" she asked.

I handed over the school list, still stunned at the difference between the outer and inner offices.

She began punching data into the machine and in a moment the soft whirring of the printer could be heard. A single sheet of white paper came dribbling out of its mouth.

She retrieved it and began walking up and down the

rows, pulling out a box here, a box there and handing them to me as we went along. Soon I was carrying seven boxes. While the school district may have had cartons and cartons for each school, Mason's Photography had simplified things. With their modern computerized system I was only going to have to paw through one box per school for the year 1963.

I followed Mason into an adjoining room where a large light table held center stage. She directed me to put the boxes on a low metal credenza and she began bringing them out one at a time.

"Do you know how old the kids were?" she asked.

"I don't. They were small, that's all I know." I didn't tell her how I had arrived at my school list or that I wasn't even sure that the kids had been in school at all. She was being too helpful, and I was getting too hopeful to burst either of our bubbles.

"So basically we're talking K through six, right?"

"Right."

She pulled out the first box, marked *Washington*, and started going through it, dropping negatives onto the light. "And you only want black kids?"

"Right."

Washington set the pattern that was pretty much going to dominate all of the school picture boxes. There were two kindergarten classes, two first grades, two seconds, two thirds and one each for fourth, fifth and sixth. She examined each class photo against the light, discarding most of them. When she was done with the Washington box we had two classes on the table, the only ones with any black kids in them. Most of the kids in the negatives were Hispanic, with a few Anglo faces sprinkled in.

We went through the rest of the elementary schools in the same manner. When we had finished there were seven class pictures on the table. Two of the schools, Burton and Malagueña, had no black children in their student bodies during the 1963 school year.

"Looks like that's it," Parsley said as we hovered over the negatives. "Looks like seven grades, seven teachers."

I'd started out with seven schools. Maybe that was becoming my lucky number.

"I don't suppose your computer keeps track of names?" I asked, going for the long shot.

"Not in the class pictures. We'd have them in the individuals, if you had the name."

I shook my head.

She pulled out an order form. "So, what's it gonna be?"

I ordered seven eight by tens.

In color.

19

Two o'clock found me back at the Westside School District complex. The diminutive model of efficiency was still camped behind the counter.

I pulled out my list of schools. I had lost Burton and Malagueña at Mason's Photography, for they were the two schools that had no black children in their student bodies for 1963. That left five schools, two of which only had black girls in their class pictures. Although there were seven classes with black children of both sexes, several of them were at the same schools, so my list had now dwindled to three schools: Corrales, Washington and Millicent Springs. Across from each name I had written the grades involved. Four of the class pictures had come from Millicent Springs. The paper was getting fairly wrinkled so I flattened it against the counter and ironed it with my hands.

"I'm on a new search," I said.

Diminutive rolled her eyes.

"I need the names of the teachers for these classes." I pointed to the wrinkled paper, hoping that her forty years with the school district would be helpful.

She picked it up, adjusted the glasses on her nose and studied it.

"Carlson's dead," she said.

"Carlson?"

"Third grade, Corrales. Had a heart attack years ago, I

remember it because she was only fifty and dropped dead right in class."

What if my kids had been in her class? Tracking down the teachers was really my only hope of discovering if there really had been missing children. There was nothing I could do about losing Carlson, so I had to concentrate on the teachers I could still talk to and pray that the kids had been in one of their classes, not Carlson's.

"And the others?"

"I don't think any of them are still teaching." She walked to a computer at the end of the counter and punched some data into it. After furrowing her brow and stroking several keys she returned, shaking her head. "None of them are currently employed by the district."

"Is there some way I can track them down?"

She thought for a minute. "Well, at least you're not talking hundreds of school kids. We do keep our records separate for the teachers. The current ones, of course, are in the computer. But these are too old. Let me think about it."

I wasn't feeling very hopeful but I handed her a card anyway.

I called Victoria Carpenter that afternoon when I got home. I didn't mention the pictures to her, but asked a lot of questions about her family home. Specifically I wanted to know the parameters of the property and if it was all fenced. Unfortunately it was. Four strands of barbed wire on all four sides.

I wanted to know more about Phelan Brewster's place, so on Saturday morning I loaded Gray into the horse trailer and headed out to Avra Valley. I drove through McDonald's, a tricky task with the horse trailer, and managed to kill only one curb. Once again I loaded up on Big Macs. Then it was off to Miller Lane. This time, I passed the third fork and headed west, driving along the dirt road for a couple of miles before a power line intersected it. I pulled off the dirt onto the utility line road and stopped.

After saddling Gray I retrieved a few items from the truck. The Big Macs were stuffed into my cantle bag. I had a dog whistle jammed into a front pocket of my Levi's and the small binoculars around my neck.

I rode down the power line for another mile or so and then turned back to the east. Victoria's directions were good and I soon found myself facing the four strands of barbed wire that she had described. I rode the fence line for another ten minutes and came to a Texas gate, which looks like any other section of the fence except that the barbed wire is flanked by four wooden posts, two on each side. The wooden posts attached to the opening wire are loose, not dug into the ground. The opening end of the gate has a top and bottom loop on the solid post which is set into the ground. I dismounted and struggled with it.

What Victoria had not told me was that it was such a tight gate. A lot of times a loose wooden bar, which serves as a come-along, will be attached to a taut gate. By wrapping the bar around the gate and pulling it toward you you can get better leverage on it. Working in this way, a person alone can manage the damned thing.

But I was not that lucky. Perhaps as a deterrent to anyone using this entrance, the gate had been strung as tight as possible. After a valiant struggle I was finally able to open it, knowing that I would never be able to refasten it by myself. Since Victoria had told me that there were no cattle or loose livestock on the property, I dropped the gate, leaving it lying open on the desert floor.

I rode quietly through the land, flushing coveys of quail which heralded my passing.

I stopped Gray just one side of a hill and tied him to a paloverde tree. I grabbed several of the Big Macs and stuffed them down the front of my shirt. Crouching low I approached the hill, taking care to hover in the shadow of the leafless mesquite tree on top.

The Brewster place was below me. Glassing it I could see no sign of human movement, nor did I see the dogs. Hazel's Taurus was in the driveway and the red four-wheeler was parked in front of the Quonset hut on the west side of the house. Seeing it triggered my memory of Victoria's notes. This was where she and her brother had been playing hide-and-seek when they'd found the body of a black man in a refrigerator box. What did they use the building for now? Storage? Hunting equipment? More bodies?

Through the binoculars I picked up a faint two-track jeep road heading north from the Quonset hut. It disappeared behind a hill and I picked it up again, only to have it disappear around a second hill. I wondered where it went.

I fumbled in my pocket for the whistle, finally recovered it and held it to my lips. I blew a series of three silent blasts through the stainless steel.

I untied the horse and mounted him. It was an awkward ascension as I crushed the hamburgers between my chest and the saddle, dribbling Big Mac juice down the front of my shirt. I made it up on the horse just in time.

Phelan Brewster's dogs, all three of them, came charging up the hill, barking furiously and snapping their big white teeth. They circled Gray, the ruff on their backs standing straight up as they darted in at his legs. The horse began spinning in an effort to evade them.

Gray knew about bad dogs. He'd seen more than his share of them and when his spinning alone did not discourage them, he began striking at them with his front feet. The horse became a whirling dervish, and we quickly resembled a small dust devil as clouds of the desert earth spun a fine cocoon around all of us. The dust was killing my contacts and tears ran down my face as I concentrated on staying with the twisting, spinning horse as he kicked and struck.

The German shepherd whimpered and flew ass over teakettle into a prickly pear cactus. Her misfortune was enough to deter the other two and they backed away, their courage momentarily flagging as they continued to growl and snap their wicked teeth.

Taking advantage of the lull in the attack, I groped in my shirt for a Big Mac, tore the paper from it and threw it to the ground, away from the horse's feet. This seemed to confuse the dogs even more, but after a momentary pause the Doberman darted in and grabbed the sandwich, running off with it before gulping it down. I threw a second and the rottweiler got this one.

I quickly unloaded a third and fourth. It was blissfully quiet as the dogs gulped the burgers and Gray stood, knowing he was now in no danger from the furious canines.

"Good girls," I said. "Sweet puppies."

The shepherd was back, interested in the change of fortune that had reduced her snarling friends to gourmands. I threw a hamburger her way. She limped over to it, sniffed it cautiously and then devoured it.

The dogs were back, but this time they were not snarling and ready to have my horse for lunch. The tide had turned as they realized that Gray was Meals on Wheels.

"Good girls," I repeated. I reached around to the cantle bag and brought out more Big Macs, unwrapping them and tearing them into pieces. Now that I had the dogs' attention I could afford to be more conservative with their snacks. "Here you go, pretty baby," I crooned.

I dropped a quarter of a Big Mac over the side and watched the Doberman eat it. I gave her another one and then threw chunks to the rottweiler and the shepherd.

"That's pretty good, huh?" I encouraged them. The Doberman deigned to wag her stub of a tail as I praised her gustatory skills. I threw another hunk of sandwich to encourage her friendly behavior.

Finally out of hamburgers, I sat there among the dogs for a while, talking quietly to them. The rottweiler and shepherd came up to my stirrups and sniffed the toes of my boots. I praised them and told them that they had lovely teeth, especially since they had now chosen to keep them inside the confines of their glistening lips. Whether or not they understood me, I cannot say, but they did settle down. They were quiet as they lay stretched out on the ground, away from Gray's feet.

When I finally headed the horse down the hill they tagged along with me, glancing up from time to time in hopeful anticipation. I talked constantly to them and rode at a walk. When I hit the old jeep road they fell in behind me.

I walked to the first hill, slowed the horse and cautiously peered around it. It was as I thought from up above. The hill close to the house blocked my view of it, also giving me a safe harbor. Ahead of me a single strand of old barbed wire was strung across the road. It was too low to ride under, and too ineffective to keep anything off the property. I checked it out with the binoculars and saw two other broken strands of wire lying crumpled across the old road.

As I turned back to the west, Brewster's dogs continued to follow me. I stopped when I neared the fence opening and told them to "go home." They didn't. So I had to sit on the horse for another fifteen minutes until a jackrabbit finally came darting across their path and all three of them took after it, leaving me alone in the desert with my gray Arabian horse.

I struggled with the gate but it was too tight for me to close on my own. I searched around and finally undid a fence tie and jerry-rigged it into a loop which extended the top part of the gate. It was a lot droopier now and I knew that anyone coming this way would be able to tell that someone had passed through the fence line. Without livestock to look after, I could see no reason why Phelan Brewster would be riding his fence and checking it for breaks or tears. So I did the best job I could before riding back off toward the power line.

An hour and a half later when I got home I was greeted by a blinking light on the answering machine. As I heated a bowl of *posole* I punched the Play button.

There was a message from my friend Emily Rose reminding me about the Tuesday night team-penning jackpot.

And a call from Victoria Carpenter confirming our Monday morning meeting at Rainbow's and our trip to the state mental hospital to visit her mother.

The third call was troubling.

"Trade, it's about the pig." I recognized Bea's voice immediately and knew the news was not good. She wasn't even calling Petunia by name. "You didn't tell me she knows how to open the refrigerator door. I'm going crazy and even looking up pork chops in *Joy of Cooking*. Save the pig's life and call me."

The fourth call was from the school-district lady apologizing for calling me on a Saturday. She left three names and numbers of the 1963 teachers, along with the caveat that the numbers could be old. With Carlson dead, that left three for me to find on my own.

But then, what the hell, I'm a private investigator, aren't I?

20

I WASN'T SURPRISED TO SEE MARTÍN RIDING THROUGH THE YARD early Sunday morning when I went out to feed Dream and Gray. He'd been riding hard, long hours ever since he'd told me about wanting to visit Quinta at the home in Hermosillo.

Chapo had been working hard too and today my foreman was on Shorty, a tall, race-bred quarter horse. During roundup we frequently rotate horses to give them a rest, since the work is harder on them than it is on us.

"You know, Martín, you can go any time. The work will be here when you get back," I said.

"I know, but I'll feel better leaving if that holding pasture's a little more crowded."

"I'm not worried about it."

"I told Cori Elena last night that my aunt is very sick," Martín offered with a conspiratorial smile.

"My lips are sealed."

"Thanks, *Chiquita*," he said as he rode off.

Later that evening I lit a fire, curled up in the La-Z-Boy and looked over Victoria Carpenter's file. In rereading her notes, as much as it pained me to do so, next to the two-word entry "Hitchhiker? Tags?" I penned in "foreskin? trophy? where?"

After I had finished with the notes, I reread the copies I had made of the *Arizona Daily Star* indexes. Going over them line by line, I once again checked out the various categories, ranging from Discrimination to Missing Persons. I guess maybe I thought something would speak to me now that I had a little more knowledge under my belt. Unfortunately, nothing did.

I saved Unidentified Bodies for the last and carefully looked through the headlines. Although it was after nine, I knew it was not too late to call Emily Rose Kibble.

Emily Rose, in addition to being my good friend and one of my team-penning partners, is also my conduit into the Pima County medical examiner's office. She's worked there for years and knows the ins and outs of dead bodies as well as anyone.

She answered on the third ring.

"Am I too late?" I asked.

"Nope, just folding the laundry."

We chatted for a few minutes about the jackpot team penning and local neighborhood gossip and then I got down to business.

"Em," I began. "Do all the unidentified bodies make the papers?"

"Usually the interesting ones—that's if there's someone at the lab when they come in, or if the police are involved or if the crime reporter catches it."

"What's the procedure if no one knows who it is, if you can't identify a body?"

"Well, if it's still fresh, we examine it, if not, then we might have to go outside our realm."

"Meaning?"

"It depends upon the state of decomposition."

"Maybe bones," I said.

"If it's that far gone, we'd send the remains to a forensic anthropologist to check it out, try to get a fix on sex, age, race, cause of death, that sort of thing."

"So everything stays in-house?"

"Nah, we use Samantha Trilby-Smith over at the university. She's top-drawer."

I jotted the name down on a corner of Carpenter's file and then called Charley Bell.

· · ·

The front room at Rainbow's was packed on Monday morning. Many of the patrons had dropped in on their way to work while others, the un- and marginally employed, really had nowhere else to go. The room was filled with white Anglo-Saxon males hovered over steaming coffee mugs taking long drags on their Camels while getting caught up on all the latest stories dealing with automobile accidents, local adultery, hunting reports, politics—and just generally philosophizing.

I was on my second cup of decaf when Charley Bell came into the cafe. After the usual greeting to the front-room boys he found my table, back around the corner in the No Smoking section.

"Hey, Ellis, whadya know?"

I stood and shook Charley's hand, marveling at the white fluff that ringed his domed bald head. The humidity was low today, almost nonexistent, and Charley's fluff fairly crackled with the static electricity in the air, giving him the appearance of a benevolent clown.

But I knew better. Charley is no clown. He's an information broker, able to extract data out of a myriad of computer sources. Because of this expertise he is able to sell information to clients all over the country. He lives, eats, breathes and probably even makes love to his electronic darlings and because of this, he has saved my ass on more than one occasion. Charley stays up half the night communicating with computers all over the world so for him to meet me before ten in the morning was a real sacrifice.

He ordered coffee, black, and then we got down to business.

"So, Ellis," he began, "did you hear about the convict who asks his friend, 'Say, do you want to buy a ticket for the warden's ball?' "

I shook my head, both as an admission to not having heard the joke and in perpetual amazement. Charley always has a joke, most of them dirty, and all of our conversations are punctuated by this ritual.

" 'I don't dance,' says the guy." Charley was already beginning to laugh.

" 'Dance?' says the convict, 'it's not a dance, it's a raffle!' "

It was funny, so I had no trouble laughing. Then I pulled out the copies of the *Star* indexes and handed them to Charley.

"I'm wondering if you can tap into some databases and make a kind of a time line for me," I said.

"A time line?"

"I'm looking for what happened in the civil rights area in the year 1963 specifically, and maybe in sixty-two and sixty-four." I decided to cover my bets by adding a year on each side of my target. Maybe my concentration on 1963 was wrong. Could Carpenter have been so sure that she was five when she had witnessed the beating of the black man with the two small boys?

"And you want these factored in?" Charley waved the indexes.

"Yes."

"Piece a cake. Hell, Ellis, this one's so easy you shouldn't have wasted a breakfast on it. I can have it by noon."

"I'm driving up to Phoenix so I won't be back until later."

"I'll drop it off at the ranch."

When Victoria Carpenter arrived, I introduced her to Charley.

"Pleased to meet ya, Carpenter." With Charley Bell no one has a first name.

We ordered breakfast, making small talk through it.

By a quarter after eight Vicki and I were on the road to Phoenix. It was a treat, for she was driving. The Jaguar was comfortable, and in spite of its age, still had that wonderful new-leather smell.

We took the back way, going up to Florence past the Casa Grande ruin and then heading through the Sacaton Mountains before we finally hit I-10. Along the way we talked about the case and I brought her up-to-date on my search for the black family. She was still seeing the male therapist recommended by her Chicago shrink and felt that he might be doing her some good.

I struggled to remember the line I'd read in one of the

reference books I'd looked at in the library. What was it? Something like *recovered memories often seem to emerge with increasing clarity the longer they are pursued.*

Vicki was like a bloodhound on fresh track. If she kept at it, she just might tree something.

21

Less than two hours after we left La Cienega, we pulled onto the grounds of the Arizona State Hospital.

Because she had visited her mother many times before, Victoria knew the drill and I followed her like a little puppy. We checked in and took the elevator to the second floor, walking down a long hallway with closed doors where the denizens were put away like so many un-iced cupcakes, and ended up at a nurse's station that resembled a hospital waiting lounge.

A large glass window overlooked a huge room that was furnished like a living room. There were scattered seating arrangements, a television set and a long table strewn with plastic things that appeared from the distance to be toys.

I drifted to the window while Victoria talked to the nurse on duty. Although the population of the common room was coed, the sexes had segregated themselves. A young teenage girl and two middle-aged women hovered around a television set yelling out figures as they watched *The Price Is Right*.

Two men, one Hispanic and the other Indian, were seated at the table working on a project together. Although they seemed to be taking turns pounding the plastic pegs down through the synthetic board, I noticed that when it was the Hispanic man's turn, he always began his round with a light tap of the plastic hammer to the top of his friend's head. The Indian, however, did not seem to mind.

Another man sat by himself, very still, by a barred window, looking outside. He reminded me of the live mannequins that merchants sometimes use. The ones that never move and seem to hardly ever blink. The kind that little kids and teenagers love to torture so they can say "See, he moved!" Only there were no little kids or teenagers here. I had the feeling that the man was spending the rest of his life, day in and day out, allowing his mind to escape out the window, which, on balance, was probably not a bad idea.

A woman patient came up to the observation glass and tapped on it. I smiled at her and when she smiled back I saw that she had no teeth. As she turned away, her hands went overhead in movement. I couldn't tell if she was conducting a great symphony or taking giant knit-and-purl stitches out of the air.

"Trade"—Victoria was talking to me—"we can go in now."

I was startled when the nurse opened the door into the big room. Somehow I had thought that our visit would entail more privacy and security. My concern must have shown, for the nurse said, "Oh, they're perfectly harmless. This is one of our social groups. No one will bother you."

We followed her into the room and almost immediately a fat woman with kinky white hair tugged on my sleeve.

"Let him out."

I hesitated.

"Alzheimer's," the nurse explained.

"Let him out of *there*." A fat, freckled arm pointed in the direction of a door on the far wall.

"She thinks her husband's locked in the medicine room. Suzy."

The mention of her name, whether as a greeting or in warning I could not tell, was enough for the woman to quit tugging at me. We left her standing in the center of the room staring at the distant door as the nurse led us to a corner. The nook was tucked into the same wall as the observation window, so I hadn't been able to see Dorothy Brewster.

Her years of being the perfect wife to Phelan had not taken their physical toll for she was still a strikingly attractive woman. Slim, with cropped gray hair, the shiny kind, framing a sweet blank face with haunting cold blue eyes that could not conceal what can only be called a crazed look.

"I'll be in there if you need me," the nurse said, pointing to the station behind the glass before leaving.

Dorothy Brewster looked up at us momentarily, without a glimmer of recognition for her daughter, and then returned to her task. Pushing seventy, she was nursing her baby, its bloated vinyl face showing no disappointment over the lack of milk coming from the woman's exhausted clothed breasts.

"Hello, Mother." Victoria said.

Dorothy continued to rock, although the chair was not a rocker, and whisper to her nameless infant. Brewster, a twentieth-century version of the biblical Sarah, had no idea of her child's conception and seemed unconcerned that her ward had not grown during its years of suckling.

"Mother, this is Trade Ellis."

"Do you like babies?" Dorothy Brewster asked, removing the doll from her chest long enough for me to admire it.

"Yes, she's beautiful."

"Yes!" Brewster clutched the child close to her body, which, had the doll been a real baby, would surely have put it in danger of suffocation.

"Mother, Trade wants to know about the Sporting Club."

Victoria cut straight to the chase, which I thought was a bit abrupt, but then, with her mother's state of mind, perhaps there was no need for subtlety.

Brewster stuck her finger in the doll's diaper and then held it to her nose. "Pee you," she said.

I watched in fascination as she removed the diaper and then put it back on. She did this three times.

"Mrs. Brewster, there was a group of men who used

to hunt with your husband. Do you remember any of them?"

"Husband?" she asked.

"Phelan, Dad," Victoria said.

"Phelan, Dad," Brewster repeated.

"Do you remember Robinson? Stone?"

Dorothy stared into the baby's eyes.

"Osborne? Dan Daglio?"

"Do you have babies?" Dorothy asked me in a clear voice.

I shook my head.

"Mother, the picnics we had, do you remember them?"

"The baby had croup last night. Horrible." Dorothy Brewster shivered. "Doctor says she's very, very sick."

She's not the only one, I thought.

"I hear you were quite a cook," I said.

Something different flickered in her cold blue eyes. "Oh yes. Do you like venison ragout?"

"Love it," I lied, feeling somewhat hopeful that we had gotten off the subject of the damned stupid doll. "You used to make a good ragout, didn't you?"

"Stew you know. They taste like what they've eaten."

"Yes."

I waited.

"Dan loved it."

"Dan?"

"Dan, Dan the candy man."

"Daglio used to bring her U-No candy bars when he could find them," Victoria whispered close to my ear, not eager to break the spell.

Dorothy Brewster laid the child across her thin legs, face down, and rubbed its back, much as you would a colicky baby.

"The candy man," I said softly.

Nothing.

"I hear you were a great cook," I repeated. What the hell, it had worked once. "Did you cook for the picnics?"

She gave me a cold stare. "What are you talking about?"

"The picnics, Mother, remember?" Victoria cut in.

"The ones where we used to go out in the desert and have such wonderful times."

Victoria choked a little and I looked at her. This was the closest she had come to emotion since I'd met her. Funny, since she was a romance writer, I would have thought she'd been full of it.

"Remember, Dan and Stone and Robinson. The Osbornes?"

She nodded. "Osborne and Harriet Nelson, Ricky."

Shit, she was remembering Ozzie and Harriet Nelson.

She rolled the doll over, then picked it up and slung it over a shoulder as she patted it on the back, I guess waiting for it to burp.

Victoria kept talking to her, trying to get her to remember her life with Phelan, but Dorothy's comments remained nonsensical.

"Hunting, Mother? Remember all the hunting that Dad used to do?"

Suddenly a terrified look filled Brewster's face. She crushed the doll to her bosom and began to hyperventilate, her open mouth sucking air. If there had been any sign of normalcy in the blue eyes, it had quickly evaporated.

Victoria and I exchanged glances and waited.

Dorothy's blue eyes darted around the room. Suddenly she tipped to the front edge of her chair. As she did so, her baby splatted onto the carpeted floor. Brewster pointed up to the ceiling. "He's in there!" she yelled. "I can see him. Get him out!"

We looked up to the ceiling, but of course there was nothing there.

"Who's there, Mother?"

"He is! He's watching! I see him. Get him!" Although her eyes rolled wildly in her head I knew that in her mind she was convinced that there was someone on the ceiling.

"Oh, I see him," I said.

"I told you he was there," she said petulantly.

"But I haven't met him," I continued the lie. "Will you introduce me?"

Dorothy Brewster fixed me with a disbelieving look. "No. You don't need to know him."

"Why it's Dan," Victoria said, taking a gamble to further the charade. "Dan Daglio."

"Stupid," her mother said.

I was afraid we were getting nowhere fast when she sat back in her chair and her breathing began to slow.

The fact that the word "hunting" had set her off was not lost on me. Briefly I wondered if a crazy person could be successfully hypnotized.

Dorothy Brewster took a couple of deep sighs and then returned to what, for her, was normal. When she remembered her baby she calmly reached down and retrieved the doll from the floor, as though nothing unusual had happened. She put it on her lap, bending its pudgy legs into a sitting position with its back against her torso.

She began examining it, much as a new mother does the first time she views her offspring. She appeared to count its fingers and toes and wiggled its legs and arms.

Victoria and I said nothing.

When she got to the back of the baby's head she gave it a thorough going over. The doll was bald, sporting wavy vinyl creases which gave it the appearance of hair. Brewster ran a long thin finger over the ridges, reminding me of a monkey mother looking for head lice.

"Not here," she said.

"What's not there?" I whispered.

"Perfect. No scars."

"Scars?"

"He hasn't done surgery on *this* one." She gave us a satisfied look. "It's not right, you know, doing that."

"No," I agreed, having no idea what in the hell she was talking about.

"He did it to the big one. I didn't think it would work, but it did."

"Which big one?" My mind raced. The larger of the two black children? The big black man that Victoria had written about, the one whose foreskin Phelan Brewster had saved? I knew the words had to come from her mouth.

She laughed, which really came out as a shrill, demented wail. "Danny Boy," she chortled. "Our beautiful Danny Boy had surgery."

I looked at Victoria, who shook her head.

Dorothy Brewster returned her baby to her breast and began rocking again, eyes closed. Although we continued to ask her questions, she appeared to be sleeping and would not acknowledge us.

It was time to go.

22

On the way back to La Cienega I asked Victoria, "Has your mother had any kind of surgery?"

"Only the three of us, but that probably doesn't count."

I shook my head. "I was thinking . . . since she's been in here, have they done any treatments that might make her think of operations?"

"No, at least I think I would know."

"Then you don't know what all that surgery talk was about?"

She shook her head.

"And Danny Boy?"

"God, I have no idea. She was talking about him almost like he was one of us kids. She never called Hank that, that I know of. I don't know what she meant."

"Does your brother have a middle name?"

"Wilkins, Mother's maiden name."

"Do you think Danny Boy could be Dan Daglio?"

"Dan, Dan the candy man." Carpenter slid the Jag onto I-10. "That's how she usually talks about him."

"But Danny Boy, has she referred to him before?"

Victoria kept her eyes on the road and shook her head.

Although I wrestled with it all the way to the 387 turnoff, I knew that I was going to have to talk to Dan Daglio a lot sooner than I'd planned. It was not something I was looking forward to.

We were on the homestretch when Victoria started talking about her new therapist, Michael Burns. She was pleased with the way things were going.

"This stuff is so morbid, I hate even thinking about it, but I guess that's the only way I'm going to get well."

"Whatever works," I said.

"I told you about the dog tags, didn't I?"

"What dog tags?"

"That hitchhiker, the one with the . . . uh . . ."

"Uh huh." I didn't want to say foreskin either.

"Well I remember that he was in the military and that he had dog tags around his neck."

I looked at her. "Did you see them? Did your father have them in the box?"

"I don't remember seeing them when I snuck in that night. All there was, was that leathery thing." She shuddered and I saw her hands shake against the leather-laced steering wheel.

"God, Victoria, if he kept them, if we could trace them through the military to someone who lived and disappeared, we might be able to prove something. It would be another cog in the wheel."

"I know. I just don't remember actually seeing them. I'm not even sure how I remember that they even existed, but I know that they did, that he was wearing them. Before . . ."

I was back in the office by two-thirty, checking my mail and messages. Then I started going down my teacher list.

The first number I tried was answered on the second ring.

"Mrs. Trevor?" I asked.

"No, this is her daughter."

After explaining who I was, why I was calling, and verifying that the Mrs. Trevor in question was in fact the one who had taught at Washington Elementary School in 1963, I discovered that it was also the same Mrs. Trevor who had signed on with the Peace Corps and was finishing up a stint in Uganda. I got Mrs. Trevor's address, for she had no telephone number, thanked the daughter and circled the name on my list to be dealt with later.

Cornelia Deadham was suffering with Alzheimer's and had been packed away in a nursing home.

I wasn't doing too well. My original list had now dwindled to four. If the missing children had been in Carlson's or Deadham's classes, I was sure out of luck. If I had to, I could probably track Trevor down in Uganda and somehow get the class picture to her.

Phyllis Jergensen answered on the seventh ring. She had a delightful voice and seemed genuinely happy to hear from me. Although she didn't readily remember the children from so many years before, she seemed confident that if we could get together, her memory would improve. Because she lived on the far east side, over an hour from the ranch, I set an appointment with her for the following afternoon. Since four of the seven teachers had taught at Millicent Springs, I also asked her about the three left whose numbers I did not have.

She told me that Robert Prentice had been electrocuted on his own roof while repairing his evaporative cooler in the summer of 1974. Another piece of bad news.

And then I got lucky.

"And Lily Belle Preble and Mary Jo Crest?" I asked.

"Oh yes, I have their number right here. We still have lunch from time to time," Jergensen said in a voice as soft as silk.

She gave me a telephone number.

"Is that for Mrs. Preble or Mrs. Crest?" I asked.

"Why both," she said. "The Preble girls are sisters, I thought you knew that."

Sometimes, although rarely I have to admit, the investigating business is like that. Things just flat fall into place without too much effort on my part. Since this case was getting so damned complicated in terms of personalities and time lines and faded and repressed memories, Mrs. Jergensen's gift was one I happily accepted.

I called the Preble sisters and made an appointment for the next morning.

·   ·   ·

It was after dinner that night when I finally got to take a look at the time lines that Charley Bell had left at the ranch for me.

1962 was James Meredith's year. An Air Force veteran, Meredith enrolled at the all-white University of Mississippi, an action that necessitated his being escorted onto the campus by federal marshals. A riot ensued and three thousand armed troops were called in to restore order, as well as the National Guard. Two people were killed. Meredith's enrollment also set the Ku Klux Klan into yet another organizational frenzy, which resulted in the most violent Klan ever.

Next I zeroed in on 1963, which began with President Kennedy sending the civil rights bill to Congress, where it died in committee. On the local scene, Tucson was getting involved with public housing which the home builders opposed.

Spring that year was a fiery one. By May, demonstrations and riots were commonplace. Martin Luther King Jr.'s Alabama arrest spurred demonstrations across the country as thousands converged on Birmingham in support of the black minister and the cause of civil rights. Americans were horrified as their television sets gave evidence of Birmingham police chief Eugene "Bull" Connor's decision to turn fire hoses on black protestors and sic specially trained "nigger dogs" on them. While blacks also demonstrated in Tucson, the results were less dire.

The Klan also had television sets and they were equally persistent as members throughout the country rallied in Birmingham, pledging to make the decade the "roaring sixties." A bomb demolished the home of Martin Luther King Jr.'s brother and a hotel from which Reverend King had just departed was also firebombed.

Spring of 1963 was followed by a long hot summer with Alabama governor George Wallace pledging segregation forever on the steps of the Tuscaloosa campus, Kennedy federalizing the Alabama National Guard and NAACP field secretary Medgar Evers getting assassinated.

In Arizona, blacks were hired by the Veterans Administration and labor union officials denied discrimination charges. The Phoenix Freedom March drew five thousand participants while a quarter of a million Freedom Marchers marched on Washington. Blacks held a sit-in at a Phoenix cafe that refused them service and a local grocery chain signed an anti-racist pledge.

Then things came closer to home. Blacks picketed the Pickwick Inn in Tucson. This escalated into shoving incidents, ministers fasting in protest, and the local NAACP threatening legal action to enforce an accommodations ordinance.

Klan violence ran throughout the time line. Members were arrested for possessing dynamite, and the Klan sponsored seminars, taught by a former Navy frogman, on how to rig bombs and select fuses. Four young black girls were killed in Birmingham's 16th Street Baptist Church.

I shook my head. From a bigot's standpoint, 1963 held a lot of allure.

November was a banner month, culminating in the assassination of President Kennedy, which pleased many Klan members, who were convinced that violence would halt the civil rights movement. They were furious when, four days after the slaying, President Lyndon Johnson urged the passage of the civil rights bill as a memorial to JFK. With such a threat nipping at their heels, the Klan went on an all-out crusade for new members.

November, I remembered, was also the opening of one of the most important hunting seasons in Arizona. Deer. Which required tags. If a black man had really gone hunting with Phelan Brewster, wouldn't he have gotten a hunting license?

On the edge of the time line I jotted, "Tags? License? G & F?"

I also glanced at Charley's work for the following year.

By 1964 the civil rights bill was back in Congress and race riots erupted throughout the country. Volunteers converged on Mississippi to educate blacks and help them register to vote. When Andrew Young attempted to lead a march to the old slave market in St. Augustine, Florida, it was thwarted by Klansmen assaulting the marchers with clubs, axe handles, bicycle chains and baseball bats.

Goose bumps ran through my body as I read "baseball bats." If I was to believe Victoria Carpenter, they had been the weapons of choice for the Sporting Club on at least one occasion—the picnic featuring the black father and his two young boys. Was this just a coincidence or were they tools of the hate agenda of the Ku Klux Klan?

1964 was also the year that Andrew Goodman and Mickey Schwerner, "the kids down in Mississippi," as Uncle C had referred to them, along with a black man, James Chaney, disappeared and were killed by the Klan and buried in a Mississippi dam.

By July, the Civil Rights Act was signed into law, which only increased the hate campaign of the Ku Klux Klan. Bombings and beatings escalated and more people were murdered. During the summer, over forty-four black churches were bombed or torched, many in rural areas, where the FBI had a hard time keeping track of them all. In Tucson, the university drew such divergent national speakers as Alabama Governor George Wallace and James Meredith, which added additional fuel to the local fires. Blacks marched on the capital in Phoenix, where demonstrators were thrown out of the Senate.

There was more, but none of it as inflammatory. After jotting a reminder to myself to copy the time lines for Abel Messenger, I picked up the phone and called Victoria Carpenter.

I was about to hang up when she finally answered the phone, out of breath.

"Bad time?" I asked.

"No, I just came in, I've been out."

"Do you remember anything, any specific event dealing with civil rights, or President Kennedy's assassination, anything at all that may have triggered your father?"

A false laugh came over the line. "Everything triggered my father."

"I'm looking over some historical stuff," I explained, "dates and places that were important to the civil rights movement. I just thought that they might somehow be related to the Sporting Club."

"It's probably all related," Carpenter admitted. "God, I can remember the blessings he used to say over food. They all started 'Heavenly Father, we are grateful we are white.'"

"I'll fax you this stuff and you can look it over, see if anything rings a bell or stirs a memory."

She hesitated before saying, "Okay."

I grabbed my down jacket and went outside after hanging up the phone. Mrs. Fierce and Blue danced around my feet, grateful for our unscheduled outing. Usually once I'm in for the night, that's it.

However, since hitting my forties I've found that I'm suffering from Craft disease—can't remember a friggin' thing. Serious things like, I've opened the refrigerator door, what am I looking for? and, I've gone into the den, why? or I'll be driving halfway down the highway and ask, Did I turn off the Mr. Coffee? Tonight's mystery was the horse gate. Had I put the latch on? If I hadn't, then the brilliant Dream would surely discover my oversight before breakfast and he and Gray would be loose all night, kicking up their heels and creating disasters for me to tend to the next day.

As usual, the latch was on. Just like the Mr. Coffee is usually off and I eventually remember the specific quest I'm on.

On the way back to the house an owl hooted from the creek. I answered him back and we carried on a friendly conversation for a few minutes before I finally went back inside the warm house. Somehow over the years I have been able to overcome my ancestors' superstitions about owls. Shiwóyé still says that they are bad luck, that it is an ill omen to have an owl hooting outside one's house. I think this stems from our belief that after death owls come to take the spirit away.

Later that night as I drifted off to sleep my head was spinning with the conversations I should have. I still needed to talk to Victoria's brother and sister, and the family friends, Stone, Robinson and Mayor Daglio.

Chances were good that none of our discussions would be as pleasant as the one I'd just had with the unknown owl.

23

It was just after nine on Tuesday morning when I got to Mason's Photography. A black beret perched precariously on top of Parsley Mason's wild red hair as she sat behind her cluttered desk, phone cradled against her shoulder. Besides talking on the phone, she was sorting through papers and she waved a fistful of them at me in greeting. The Irish setter didn't even open an eye.

Mason reached out to a corner of her desk and retrieved a large white envelope which she handed to me. I opened it and pulled out the seven class pictures I had ordered. Unfortunately, with Prentice and Carlson dead, Trevor in Uganda and Deadham in a nursing home with Alzheimer's, my options were now fairly limited. I put their four pictures back in the envelope and, although I wasn't optimistic, concentrated on the three I had left.

Phyllis Jergensen was blonde and pert and the kindergarten teacher at Millicent Springs in 1963. She looked about twenty-five in the picture, which would put her in her early sixties now. She had six black boys in her class.

Lily Belle Preble was the first-grade teacher at Millicent Springs. There were three black boys in her class, two of whom had gone on to second grade at the same school.

Mary Jo Crest was a long shot. Fourth grade. Really out of the loop as far as the supposed ages of the black boys who had allegedly been killed by the Sporting Club. Still, there were two kids who could have qualified in her class. Both seemed smaller than the rest of their group. Crest also taught at Millicent Springs, which probably accounted for the continuing friendship of the three women.

In the pictures, Crest and Preble both appeared older than Jergensen, somewhere in their mid-forties, I guessed, which would put them at least in their late seventies now.

My list of seven schools had narrowed to one. Millicent Springs. One school, three teachers. While I was discouraged, for I figured the odds of having the missing children identified by one of the three teachers were long, it was all I had right now. And I knew, as Abel Messenger had known, that if I could just produce a name, a face, that I might have something. Otherwise we were all grasping at air and ancient memory. A phantom case or a figment of a novelist's imagination.

After Parsley hung up her phone I asked to borrow it and placed a quick call to Abel's office. His secretary informed me that he was in court and would be all morning. I left a message asking if he could spare a few minutes at lunchtime and left instructions as to where I'd be if he could make it.

The Preble sisters lived in a town house on Fourth Street. While the complex had started on a more minor scale, it had been remodeled a few years ago; in fact, I remembered reading about the renovation in an article in the Lifestyle section of the *Arizona Daily Star*. In its present incarnation the homes were ultramodern, having survived serious gutting and facelifts.

Mary Jo Crest answered the bell. Tall and patrician-looking, with hazel eyes and blue hair, she greeted me warmly.

"Welcome, Miz Ellis," she said in a Southern accent dripping with magnolia blossoms and Southern Comfort. "Do come in."

As I entered the home I was struck by a cloying smell. I recognized the formula—too much perfume being applied to a not-too-recently washed body.

"This way," she said. "We're in the parlor." That, coupled with the accent, should have been my first clue that I had left Arizona.

"Lily Belle, our guest has arrived." Mrs. Crest announced me as we entered a sunny, glassed-in room overlooking a small rose garden. What the Realtors delight in calling the Arizona Room in their weekend ads had now transformed into "The Parlor."

Lily Belle Preble, other than being shorter and plumper, did bear a striking resemblance to her sister. "Welcome," she said, extending an arthritic hand which I shook lightly. A hint of white froth tickled the corner of her mouth. "We were just indulging in a Ramos Gin Fizz—won't you join us?"

While her accent was not as pronounced as that of her sister, it was there nonetheless.

Drinking gin fizzes at ten in the morning is not usually my idea of a good time, but then again, I was apparently on vacation, somewhere down South—Georgia, Kentucky, I wasn't sure where. Also, I wanted the Preble sisters to tell me about their classes and if it would make them feel more comfortable if I had a Ramos Gin Fizz, who was I to argue?

Lily Belle guided me to the chintz-covered, overstuffed sofa and then handed me a chilled, silver-stemmed wineglass filled with the sweet drink.

We exchanged pleasantries and then I got down to business, explaining that I was looking for two children who may have been in their classes at Millicent Springs. I made no mention of the Sporting Club or the possibility of their having been murdered, preferring to have them believe that I was dealing with a missing-persons case, nothing more.

I opened the white envelope and withdrew the two class pictures with Crest and Preble in them. Both sisters now flanked me on the sofa. I handed the first-grade shot to Preble, fourth-grade to Crest.

"Mrs. Preble," I began, pointing to three black boys, "do you remember these children?"

Preble reached for a huge magnifying glass and studied the photograph.

"Why, they're negras," she said, as though she had never realized that she had had black children in her first-grade class.

"Yes ma'am."

On the other end of the couch, I could see Mary Jo study her class picture a bit more intently.

"Oh, it's been so long," Preble said. "Sometimes it's so hard to remember things, especially children, since there were so many of them over the years." She reached for the silver pitcher and refilled her glass.

"Sister," Crest said, waving her empty silver chalice in the air.

I covered the top of my glass with my hand and prayed that their memories would hold out longer than the gin fizzes.

Crest leaned across me and looked at Preble's picture. "I don't recognize him," she said. "I did not have that child in my class." She was pretty definitive about the whole thing but her sister, who had had the child in her class, was still studying him as though he were an unusual insect.

"You would think I could remember that child. There just weren't that many negra children back then."

I wondered about the wisdom of the school district in placing the two Southern belles in a school where they would instruct "negra" children. I couldn't imagine it having been a very positive experience for either the children or the teachers.

"Do you have your class pictures?" I asked, with a faint hope that maybe they could scour through some overburdened closet and produce the duplicate with a list of names neatly printed on the back.

"Heavens no," Preble said. "When we decided to move in here, everything was so new and all, Mary Jo and I just decided to start all over again. We got all new furniture and threw almost everything out. The clutter from combining our two homes from before was just atrocious. We had to do something."

She held the picture up close to her face as though that would produce the answer to the mystery. It didn't work.

"I'm sorry, I truly am, but there were just so many children over the years, I just can't remember them all. You'd think I'd remember the ones that were different, though."

I could tell her memory loss was upsetting her more

than her embarrassment at not being able to produce for me.

"Let me see that." Mary Jo Crest reached for the picture.

She adjusted her glasses and then extended the photograph out away from her body. It was probably time to go back to the drugstore and get the next number up on the reading glasses.

"This one was Samuel and this one was William," she said. "They graduated from Millicent Springs, I do remember that."

Still, neither sister could remember the missing black boy from Lily Belle Preble's first grade.

Although I knew it was probably useless, I pulled out the other class pictures, the ones from the dead teachers' classes, along with those of Deadham and Trevor. None of the children meant anything to either Crest or Preble.

Before I left, I handed the women each a card and extracted a promise from both of them that they would call me if they should happen to remember anything. I thanked them for their time, and the gin fizz, which I left half-full on the coffee table, and said goodbye.

I'd been hoping for a miracle and I didn't get one. The list that had me so excited just a few days earlier had now been reduced to one name.

Phyllis Jergensen.

By the time I found a parking place I got to the courthouse plaza just after noon. It was filled with secretaries, lawyers, clerks, government workers, policemen, all taking advantage of the warm Arizona day to have an alfresco lunch.

I headed straight for the green-and-white Good Dogs cart and stood in line. After a few minutes I ordered two hot dogs and a couple of Diet Cokes. When they were ready I slathered them with mustard and chopped onions, managing to smear some of the mustard on one of the sleeves of my shirt. Mustard and I have never gotten along. I think it's because I know it stains clothes and I am so mesmerized by this fact that invariably I manage for it to end up on what I am wearing. Besides, yellow has never been one of my favorite colors.

I sat on a cold concrete tree well that corralled one of the huge mesquite trees and forced myself to wait for Abel to arrive before starting on my own hot dog. There was the possibility that he had gotten tied up and wouldn't make it. But, looking on the bright side, that would give me two hot dogs to eat.

"Hello, Lady Love." His deep baritonal voice pulled me out of my culinary contemplation. "How's it going?"

He looked good, as always. The sun picked up the highlights of his salt-and-pepper hair. He had that good kind of gray, the shiny silvery stuff that the foxy grandmother types have.

I handed him a hot dog and pointed to the Coke as he joined me on the tree well.

"So, how's the case going?"

I shook my head. "Crazy. Seems like I'm pumping lots of water but the bucket's got a hole in it."

He laughed. "Some of them are like that."

"Did Joanne Devlin call you?"

"That's the Sunny Cola lady?"

I nodded, my mouth full of hot dog.

"Thanks. She told us about the man. That's the first verification that we've had that a black was working there at that time."

"So have you done anything with it?"

"I sent a couple of guys back to talk to the manager and a few of the older employees, but they don't remember anything."

"Don't or won't?"

He shrugged.

"I saw the mother," I said. "In the loony bin."

"So how'd that go?"

"Pretty nonsensical. She did mention someone called Danny Boy—does that ring any bells?"

"Danny Boy," Abel repeated. "No, should it?"

"I don't know. She was talking kind of crazy and looked at the back of her doll's head and then said something about it not having scars and 'at least he hadn't done surgery on this one, the way he had on the big one.'"

"Doll's head?"

"She has a great baby, never cries. Anyway I just had the feeling that this Danny Boy might mean something, might be one of the children."

I went on to tell him about the visit to the school district and the photos that I had gotten from Mason's Photography. He was interested in them.

"I thought you might be." I handed over color photocopies of the class pictures along with copies of Charley Bell's time line.

"We didn't think of that. God, what an oversight."

He felt better when I explained that there were only three of the teachers left that could be readily interviewed. I told him about my visit to the Preble sisters and about my afternoon appointment with Phyllis Jergensen. "Maybe I'll get lucky."

"Maybe," Messenger said, polishing off the tail end of his hot dog. A tiny bit of mustard was clinging to his salt-and-pepper beard. I didn't know what to do about it. These are heavy ethical questions. When do you say anything? Where do you draw the line? A drop of mustard's pretty innocuous and will probably only be taken for what it is. But what if someone has something green and unattractive dangling from their nose? Do you speak up and risk embarrassing them or do you say nothing and let them go through the day with their little suspension amusing all who see them when you could have saved them from such silent ridicule?

After a moment of inner debate I went through a little pantomime of touching the corner of my face with my napkin several times, hoping that he would take the hint. He didn't, so I said nothing and found myself thus released from the ethical hot seat. I had given him the chance, but he had neglected to take it. Free will is a wonderful thing.

"I met with Dad," I said. "He wasn't any help."

"No."

"But at least I met my first boojum tree. I'm going to interview the other people Victoria mentioned."

He nodded and wadded up his hot-dog papers into a tight ball which he lobbed into the metal wastebasket across from the tree.

"Is there anything I should know?" I asked.

"You probably won't find much. The brother says it's all lies and sis is a little unsure of what happened."

"And the Sporting Club?"

"That one guy's dead."

"Osborne?"

"Right. The California guy won't talk and Robinson owns that miniature-golf place out on Oracle."

"Dragon Links?"

He nodded. "You can probably reach him there."

Abel had forgotten one of the players. "And Dan Daglio?"

"Go easy, Lady Love. He *is* the mayor."

"Did you go easy?" I asked.

"Very easy," was his reply.

After saying goodbye to Abel I was heading for my car when a bright idea hit me. I turned abruptly and headed back across the plaza to the city administration building. I checked the directory and then took the elevator to the ninth floor.

It was just before one when I entered the mayor's office. His secretary, probably still on her lunch hour, was applying a coat of fire-engine red nail polish to her fake fingernails.

"I'm wondering if it's possible to see the mayor?"

She looked at me as though I were a nutcase. "Now?"

"Yes."

"Why no, it's not. He's speaking to the Downtown Rotary Club so he's not even here."

"Then you'd suggest an appointment?"

She capped the nail polish. "Yes."

I fumbled in my purse for a card and handed it to her. "Maybe you could just have him call me at his convenience," I said.

"Of course," she said, studying the card. "Ms. Ellis."

I headed for the door, then turned back as though I'd forgotten something. "Oh, where does the Rotary Club meet these days?"

"Sorry, I don't know," she said in a well-trained voice.

•   •   •

The woman at the downstairs information booth was more helpful. After making a couple of calls, she gave me the name of the Holiday Inn downtown.

Since it was only a block away, I was there within minutes. I checked the marquee and found the Rotarians in the Pima Room. Stopping at the registration desk, I asked for a telephone message slip. I quickly scribbled on it, *The Sporting Club*, before entering the meeting room. Things were just breaking up as a small group of men crowded around the mayor.

I hailed a busboy who was clearing tables and handed him the slip.

"This came in for him," I said, nodding in the direction of the mayor.

The kid never questioned it as he headed up to the podium and handed the mayor the folded slip.

I hovered at the back of the room, shielding myself as much as possible with the departing Rotarians. Daglio answered a question, and then another one before he glanced at the pink slip.

A dark look came over his face as his eyes searched for his messenger of doom. I had seen enough and quickly left the room.

On the way back to my car, a thought struck me.

If the sick look on Daglio's face meant anything, if he was a dog, he'd be chewing grass about now.

24

AFTER I LEFT DOWNTOWN I DROVE STRAIGHT OUT SPEEDWAY, through the University district, and then passed by a series of strip shopping centers. At one time, back in the sixties, *Life* magazine dubbed this main artery the "ugliest street in America." Unfortunately, in spite of recent attempts to facelift the decrepit shopping centers and widen the road, it's still a contender for the title.

I headed out Tanque Verde and turned north on Sabino Canyon Road and drove for another couple of miles before finally turning off. After a few bends and turns, checking my notes along the way, which is always tricky when fumbling with sunglasses and reading glasses and a three-quarter-ton truck, I finally located Phyllis Jergensen's address.

It was an older home, located on what I guessed to be an acre, set along Tanque Verde Creek, another of our usually dry rivers. Elderly eucalyptus trees, their smooth white trunks shedding rough brown bark, towered over the tiny house. Offset to one side was a still smaller guest house. An empty carport between the two homes made me wonder if Jergensen had forgotten our appointment.

I lifted the brass quail door knocker and thumped its little metal feet hard against the wooden door twice. I could hear a shuffling from inside. I recognized Miss Jergensen's voice from our phone call.

"May I help you?" she asked pleasantly.

After I identified myself, the door opened and I was ushered in.

My guesstimates had been correct. She was in her early sixties, and still a very good-looking woman. Her hair, as near as I could tell, was still a natural blonde color, still cut in the same way she had worn it in the kindergarten picture that had been taken over thirty years ago.

Although the room was fairly light—there was a skylight over the kitchen counter at one end and a living-room lamp was on—I didn't think it was bright enough to warrant the sunglasses she was wearing.

"Would you like some coffee? I've a fresh pot."

"No thank you," I said. "I've just come from lunch." In fact, I was still having it, for the hot dog was threatening to return.

"Please, make yourself comfortable," she said, motioning to a small tweed loveseat.

She retrieved a mug of coffee from the kitchen counter and took a straight-backed wooden chair next to me. There was a side table, hosting framed photographs, between us and after seating herself she placed the mug on it. A two-tiered glass coffee table was in front of both the loveseat and chair.

"Lily Belle called me after your visit with them," she said. "So I think we can probably go right to business."

I liked that. I pulled out the picture of her Millicent Springs kindergarten class and tried to hand it to her.

She didn't take it. Instead she reached for her coffee mug and as she did so, I noticed that her hand moved slowly across the table before it caressed the lip of the mug and then dropped to its handle.

My hand was still in midair, the class photo suspended, but still she ignored it.

And then it hit me.

Phyllis Jergensen was blind.

And then it really hit me.

Phyllis Jergensen would not be able to identify any of the six black boys who had been in her kindergarten class. My last hope couldn't see. Wouldn't be able to tell which children I was pointing to, wouldn't be able to jar her memory with an old class picture, wouldn't be able to tell me their names or if they had left school unexpectedly years ago.

I hated doing it, but I had to ask, "Miss Jergensen, may I ask how long you've been without sight?"

Her face showed no regret. "An automobile accident when I was in my thirties. A young boy ran a stop sign and broadsided me. I was lucky that it wasn't worse."

She was pretty incredible, for she sounded as though she meant it. The thought of being blind has always freaked me out. Sometimes I play mental games with myself. If I had to lose a body part, what would I choose? An arm? A leg? An arm always won that one, for mobility was important to me. Deaf or blind? No contest. A silent world would still allow me to read, work and ride my horses. Yet here was this beautiful woman, seemingly at peace with herself and with the accident that had cost her her sight.

"It was very difficult for the boy," Jergensen said. She reached for a grouping of photographs nestled on the side table. Feeling along the edges of one frame, she handed it to me.

It was a picture that had been taken in warmer weather, when leaves were on the trees and the grass was green. Centered in the frame was a smiling Phyllis Jergensen and a young man wearing a graduation robe and cap.

"William Adamson Rhine," she said with obvious pride in her voice, "on the day he graduated from Brown."

"You're friends?" I asked, unable to keep the amazement out of my own voice.

"Why not? That accident brought us closer together than many people ever get."

I wondered if there had been accusations and lawsuits and settlements and such, but did not have the nerve to ask. Clearly, Phyllis Jergensen was a very special lady.

"Well, I suppose you have better things to do than admire my friends. Shall we get to business?"

Was she serious? Could she really help me in spite of being blind?

She reached under the glass-topped table to the lower tier and pulled out a photo album. There were several others resting there. Running her fingers quickly across the raised Braille lettering on the brass cover plate of the book, she handed it to me. "I'll need your help. You'll have to find the kindergarten picture you're looking for."

I leafed through the book. All of the photographs were of classes that had been taught by Jergensen. They were all neatly in order, encased in plastic cover sheets. I had no trouble finding the 1963 kindergarten class of Millicent Springs.

"I have it," I said.

"Tell me about the picture. I've had a lot of classes and sometimes it's hard."

Although I wanted to cut right to the black kids, I began by describing what she was wearing the day the picture was taken. I described the children that were flanking her, and then went through them row by row, describing each child the best I could.

She nodded.

"There were six black boys in this class," I said. "Do you remember them?"

"Probably only by name."

Inwardly I groaned.

"Pull the sheet out of its folder," she instructed.

This miraculous blind woman had produced what the full-sighted Preble sisters had not. Printed neatly in block letters on the reverse of the photograph were the names of all of the children pictured. The nomenclature was very precise, with row numbers and the names, beginning from the left of each row. The last row was marked, "Standing, from L to R."

"You'll have to go to the front of the picture and check out the children you are interested in and then give me their names."

I was grateful she had not said the word *negra*. To Jergensen they were all children; color did not come into her equation. I knew then that had I been in Millicent Springs in 1963 I would have wanted to be in Phyllis Jergensen's class.

She remembered the first two boys—George James and Willie Smith. One was now in prison, the other a chemist.

"Clinton Brown," I said, describing a skinny little kid who had lost his front teeth prematurely.

She chuckled. "The class clown, that one. Very bright. His folks moved out on the east side after his first year with us. They gave me a dictionary as a thank-you for having him in class."

We were down to three. Two of them shared the same last name. I gave her the odd one next.

"Billy Norman."

"Billy Norman," she repeated, running her fingers over the raised lettering on the photograph album, as though that would stimulate her memory. "Billy Norman."

He was a dark chunky kid who wasn't smiling in the picture. In fact he looked pretty grumpy for a five-year-old. I described him as best as I could, but Billy Norman still rang no bells with his kindergarten teacher. I moved on, trying to hide my disappointment that she had not remembered him.

"Matthew and Mark Johnson," I said, trying not to hold my breath. While Johnson was a common last name, could these two be brothers?

"Oh yes," Jergensen said. "I remember them. One's quite a bit taller than the other, right?"

"Yes."

"And the bigger one is kind of hiding his left side behind the student next to him."

I studied the picture more carefully. "Yes."

"His arm was shorter on that side. They came from Georgia and he'd been in a farming accident of some sort. He was always very careful to guard that, to keep his shorter arm out of sight. Sometimes the rest of the children teased him about it." Although the teasing incident had occurred years before, there was still pain in Jergensen's voice.

My heart went into overdrive. What was it that Joanne Devlin had said when I'd asked her about the black man at the bottling plant? Something about when he'd quit he said he was moving back to Georgia, and now Phyllis Jergensen was remembering two black children from the same state. Could that mean something?

"They were brothers?"

"Yes. They were in the same grade, even though Matthew was a year older. He lost time because of his accident so they were both placed in K when they came to Tucson."

"But they didn't stay at Millicent Springs," I said, hoping it was true.

"No. They didn't even complete kindergarten. It was very unusual."

The accelerator in my heart headed toward full throttle. "Unusual in what way?"

"They just quit coming one day. It was right before Thanksgiving. I remember that because Matthew was going to be in our play. We were doing *Pocahontas* and he was to play Captain John Smith. Becky in the office tried to reach their home, but couldn't. And then a few days later, the mother came and withdrew them. Said the father had taken them back to Georgia."

"But she didn't go with them?"

"I don't know. I just know that he took them. I remember thinking that it was fortunate that they had decided to go back while the boys were so young. Sometimes those midyear school adjustments can be very difficult for children."

"You don't happen to remember the parents' names, do you?"

She placed a finger to her lips and tapped it for a minute. "Hmmm, she had an unusual name. Brenda? Bridget? Brisha? Brisha! That was it. Brisha Johnson. Her husband was Rodney."

I sat there dumbstruck. How had this incredible woman been able to come up with that? Had her loss of sight somehow enhanced her memory or was she just one of those people with amazing recall? I'd probably never know. But I did know one thing. I was back in the miracle business.

Maybe, just maybe, I had hit pay dirt. I had two black boys who had disappeared abruptly from school. I had their pictures and I had their names, along with those of their parents. My phantoms had materialized.

Now all I had to do was prove that they had been unfortunate guests of the Sporting Club.

25

WHEN I ARRIVED HOME I FOUND MARTÍN TOWING THE TRACTOR with his pickup truck. Definitely not a good sign.

When he pulled in next to the hay barn I was waiting for him. He climbed out of his pickup.

"Another rod bearing." He unhitched the tractor from the towing chain. "I knew I should have replaced them all. This time *despacio voy porque de prisa estoy.*"

I bit. "Cough it up."

"This time," he grinned at me, "I'm going slowly because I'm in a hurry."

"Makes sense to me."

"I'll start on it tomorrow."

A quartet of blinking red lights greeted me when I came in the kitchen. I dug a pack of Twinkies out of the pantry. My Levi's had been getting a little tight, so my concession to this recent corpulence was a box of Light Twinkies. I unwrapped the cellophane and examined them carefully. They didn't seem quite as golden as usual. I broke one in half and studied the interior. It was white, like the real thing. I squeezed it and as the gooey stuff oozed out I started licking. They'd do in a pinch, but they weren't the real thing.

I punched the Play button on the machine and returned to the pantry to get another pack. One Twinkie was not going to cut it.

The first message was from Emily Rose, reminding me about tonight's team penning. In a momentary panic I checked the stove clock. Four-thirty. I had an hour.

"Trade," the second one started, "I'm serious about this. Everyone thinks she's adorable but she's got to go."

I recognized Cousin Bea's voice.

"You didn't tell me that they like the water." Her tone dropped into an accusatory whine. "She went swimming this afternoon. And you also didn't tell me that even though they go swimming they don't go swimming. They don't even know how to swim."

I was worried about Petunia's welfare for a minute and relieved when Bea continued.

"So guess who had to jump in the pool and get her out? In forty-degree water? Not my idea of a good time, Trade. I had my hair done today and now I'm going to look awful for the five o'clock. Call me or the Humane Society gets her. I mean it."

The machine whirred before heading into message number three.

"Hi, Trade, this is Julie, from the hardware store. A fax came in for you. We've got it."

I didn't have time to retrieve the fax, which was probably from Victoria, and get ready for penning. The fax could wait until tomorrow.

The final call was from Dan Daglio's office. It wasn't the man himself, but his secretary, who said that Mr. Daglio would be leaving town in the morning for a mayors' conference but would be in next Monday and I could try him then. Quickly I dialed the telephone only to discover that he had left for the day.

By the time I did chores, hooked up the horse trailer and brushed Gray it was well after five. As I went back in the house for my down jacket and wallet, I remembered to turn on the TV.

Channel 4's five o'clock news was in full swing. Cousin Bea sat to the left of Jimmy Douglas, her co-anchor. They were in the middle of a story about food poisoning and Jimmy was talking, so I waited until it was Bea's turn. The camera zoomed in on her as she talked about the latest heart transplant at University Hospital. I didn't need to bury my face in the television screen to see that she was right. Her hair did look like shit.

I walked into the kitchen and called her number, even though I knew that she was in the television set in my living room. At least it was an effort. I love answering machines. For starters, they protect you from people who call you who you don't want to talk to. Then, if you return calls from people who you really don't want to talk to but know that you have to call and they're out and you get their machine you're protected from talking to them once again. And your ass is covered because you get credit for returning their call.

I left a message on Bea's machine saying that Petunia could have R & R at my house for a while.

I was right on schedule when I pulled into Sanders's spread. After loading his gelding into the trailer we headed out for the penning, which was in Avra Valley. As we exited the freeway it seemed strange not to stop at the McDonald's for doggie burgers.

When we pulled into the arena, Emily Rose was already there, her big palomino gelding standing by her trailer. Sanders and I quickly saddled and the three of us rode into the arena to warm the horses up. Now that the sun was down it was getting cold. I had on three layers, including my down jacket, and was sorry that I hadn't thrown tights on under my jeans.

An old cowboy wearing chinks and a battered felt hat rode up on a stout buckskin horse. Sanders grinned at him.

"Trade, Emily Rose, this is my cousin Stink," he said.

Stink thankfully didn't.

"Ma'am," he said, tipping his hat in that endearing old cowboy way.

"Stink knows Brewster," Sanders said softly. "He lives out here too."

In my haste to interview the school teachers, I had forgotten that Sanders had offered to ask his cousin about Phelan Brewster.

Stink spit a long stream of brown tobacco off one side of the buckskin.

"He used to hunt a lot," he volunteered.

I looked at Sanders but couldn't tell just how much of the story he had shared with his cousin.

"He worked at that bottling plant in Tucson," Stink said, trying to be helpful. "Retired from there a while ago."

"Does he still hunt?" I asked.

"Oh I hear a little bit, not like he used to though. He's got a lot of trophy stuff, just about every danged thing in the book."

And some not in the book, I thought.

"I know," I said. "I've been to his house."

"It's like a danged museum," Stink explained to Sanders. "Heads all over the danged place."

I shuddered, remembering the glassy-eyed creatures I had seen.

"You know he does 'em," Stink said.

"Does who?" I asked.

"Them heads, he makes them. He's a tax-i-der-mist." Stink drew out every syllable. "Has a little workshop right there on the place."

Was that what he did in the Quonset hut? Taxidermy?

"You sound like you know him pretty well."

"Nah." Another brown stream sailed over the horse's side. "We howdy now and then but that's about it. He pretty much sticks to hisself."

The announcer asked for us to clear the arena.

We sat on our horses along the fence line and watched the first team try to cut out their three assigned cows and pen them in ninety seconds. The cows were fresh, they'd never been penned before. Although they'd been run into the pen a few times to show them the pattern, they really were not in a cooperative mood.

The first team out in a team penning always has the disadvantage. Especially with fresh cattle. Since the cattle are changed after every ten teams, everyone wants the Number Ten position. Not only have the cattle had nine previous teams work them and you can see how they are doing, but if you pay attention to the numbers drawn, you can figure out which group you'll have before you ever enter the arena.

We ran seventh. Like our predecessors, our run turned into a glorious game of tag with everyone "it." Cattle and riders scurried everywhere. At the thirty-second call, signifying that we had only thirty humiliating seconds remaining, we decided to go with the single calf that we had been able to cut out.

It didn't work out. It rarely does, running only one calf. They're herd animals and they like to hang out together. Part of the team-penning strategy is if you can get that second calf out quickly, then that leaves two of them outside the herd to kind of hang out together. If you've just got one out there, he gets lonely and wants to rejoin his play group.

Even armed with this knowledge, we gave it a valiant effort, running the calf down to the pen. He stopped abruptly, eyed me on the wing and then looked at Sanders—who was trying to drive him—and then darted between the two of us like a hot knife through butter.

"That's time," said the announcer.

During the second go-round we had a little excitement. Dick Smith, a chronic complainer who was always grumbling about the cattle or the surface of the arena or the weather, or just about anything, went down. His horse cut a sharp turn, slipped and crashed into the ground on top of Dick. Unfortunately, on the way to the dirt, Dick's head collided with that of a calf, which not only knocked his cowboy hat and glasses off, but also took along his toupee, which, of course, none of us knew he wore. Now the little Brahma had the hairpiece dangling down from one long ear, blocking a brown eye.

Dick floundered on the ground, his hands groping madly in the dirt in an effort to collect what his eyes could not see. The lost toupee, of course, was not resting on the earth, but still adorning the Brahma calf.

He finally connected with his glasses—and his hat, which he quickly placed on his bald pate—and stood up, brushing dirt off his Wranglers. We were trying hard not to laugh, so we clapped to cover our embarrassment at his loss; and, although he was a jerk, we were pleased he wasn't hurt. Besides wishing him no harm, hurt penners have a tendency to remind us of our own mortality. And, accidents slow down the penning.

Although we were able to pen three our second time

out, we didn't have the lead time so after a cup of hot cider—it was too cold for beer—we left empty-handed.

On the drive home I prattled on to Sanders about my visits to Dorothy Brewster and to the schoolteachers. As we drove down the lane, I told him about passing the cryptic note to Mayor Daglio at the Holiday Inn.

We unloaded his horse, said goodnight, and I was just getting back into Priscilla when Sanders called out. I turned back.

"Trade," he said, "if you're gonna ride on this thing, then ride like hell."

"Thanks, I appreciate that."

"But if you're not," he cautioned, "then you might not want to spur ahead of the shoulder."

26

I WAITED UNTIL AFTER EIGHT THE NEXT MORNING BEFORE COLLECT-
ing my fax from Darrell's Hardware Store.

"Hey, Trade," Darrell himself greeted me. "I've got
something for you."

"Julie called about the fax."

"Oh, I've got the fax too. I've got something else to
show you."

I followed him as he walked back to the little alcove
that housed his office, along with the Xerox and fax machines. Pulling his office chair easily away from the big
steel desk that he used, he said, "I'm a daddy."

Belle, one of Darrell's hounds, the same ones that he
chases mountain lions with, an enthusiasm of his with
which I wholly disagree, lay nestled in the kneehole of the
desk, a slew of long-eared black-and-tan hound pups attached to her belly.

What could I do? The fax was momentarily forgotten
as I dropped to my knees, praising the dog for doing such a
fine job of producing little lion chasers. There were ten of
them, all squirming and sucking and making those little
puppy slurpy sounds. Belle took my praise in stride as she
attended to her motherly tasks, flipping one round-bellied
little pup on his back so she could clean him up.

When Darrell reached down and picked up another, its
mother did not seem to mind. In spite of his pledge of

paternity, I couldn't help but notice that there really wasn't much family resemblance, but said nothing.

"Aren't they something?" he said, with pride in his voice. He handed me the pup.

I nuzzled my nose in its soft baby fur, drinking in that wonderful puppy smell. There really is nothing on earth like it. Fresh and sweet and innocent. I've gotten into arguments with people over baby smells before. Some folks actually think that babies, human babies, smell good. Yuk. Not to me. They just smell like sour milk. Give me good old-fashioned steer manure or skunk any day, as long as it's not too strong. And puppies? My all-time favorite.

"Go ahead, pick one out," Darrell urged. "Of course you can't take him today, he's too young."

Quickly I handed back the sleepy pup. "Can't do, Darrell, Mrs. Fierce would never forgive me."

"She'd love a friend," he said hopefully.

"Nope, she's got a friend, we've got Blue." Blue, an Australian cattle dog, had come into the ranch a couple of months ago. In spite of my running ads, no one had come forward to claim her. She was now an official resident of the Vaca Grande and the number two woman dog in charge of Ranch Security, the number one position being something that Mrs. Fierce would never willingly forfeit.

I collected my fax and left, congratulating myself on the resolve to turn down the puppy. I also made a mental note to stay the hell out of Darrell's Hardware until Belle and her brood were out of there. I mean, a person is only just so strong.

Two Brahma cows were blocking the turn into the stage stop. I waited for them to amble across the road before I turned in. I'd stopped at the office before going to the hardware store and turned on the coffee and heater so the building was now toasty. After pouring a cup of decaf I settled in at the rolltop.

I was right. The fax was from Victoria Carpenter. I began to read.

I tried to reach you today, and then thought maybe it would be better if you had a record. I had a good session with the doctor this morning. I'm remembering more and he thinks we're making progress. He says that repressing these memories is normal for a child, that I couldn't handle what happened back then so I just shut it all down. He says it's a case of "lost memory." As my ego gets stronger, he says, then I'll be able to handle more and my memory will improve.

She's on the book racks of every major grocery chain in the country, has been on Oprah and Donahue, has written God knows how many books and she needs a stronger ego?

Spellbound, I continued reading. Carpenter vaguely remembered an outing concerning a black man in some kind of uniform and a Hispanic woman. This was new information, but the details were vague. She remembered the pair as being the center of attention at one of the Sporting Club picnics. The site this time, she recalled, was somewhere south of Tucson, in the Santa Rita Mountains.

Victoria had written even fewer details with the star-crossed lovers. She remembered that a car had driven into the meadow where they were gathered. Three white men had gotten out and had pulled a black man and a Hispanic woman from the vehicle. She wrote,

I remember thinking that the people were not happy to be there. The lady was very sad and I asked mommy, "Why is she crying?" Mommy told me curiosity killed the cat and then took my hand and we went for a walk. I'm not sure, but I think Jerri Osborne was with us. She was a little older than me and had a great collection of plastic horses with little cowboys that fit on them. You could take the cowboys on or off. She also had plastic Indians that you could put on the horses. Anyway, we went to a wash and looked for sand rubies. When we got back to the meadow, the man and the woman were gone.

I rubbed my eyes. This account was not as full as the one about the father with his two small children. There was no baseball bat, or threat of violence. I made a note to call Michael Burns, Victoria's therapist, and then continued reading.

I had lunch today with Jerri Osborne to talk about the Sporting Club. She won't remember any of it. That's right. Won't. I saw it in her eyes, the fear. She remembers, I know she does, but she doesn't want to, just like I don't want to. But at least I'm making the effort. She won't. Did I tell you she's with the ACLU?

Inwardly I groaned. A bleeding heart employed by a liberal organization admitting to picnics where minority groups were killed? No wonder she didn't want to remember.

She's in denial, Trade, just like I was for so many years. The problem is that even when you tell yourself that something isn't true, your heart knows the difference.

Anyway, I was driving home and thinking about when I was a kid, about Jerri and her plastic horses and cowboys and Indians and about the picnics. And I remembered something else about that day, the day when the kids and their father were killed. When I went back for Jerri's Barbie doll and ended up at the clearing and the black man was hit with the baseball bat, one of the kids screamed, "Oz!"

Oz? Could it be a reference to Osborne in some way? A perversion of the name? Did the kids know Osborne, maybe trust him and then realize that he was not their friend? Maybe Osborne was the one with the baseball bat.

Anyway I don't know what this means, or if it's even important. Somehow I think it's all important. I'm tired, Trade, really tired. The nightmares are back, every night now, terrible visions but the faces are still all blurred and mushy. And I keep hearing people scream, Trade, sometimes even when I'm awake. I'm really scared and I just want it to be over with. Help me, please.

That was it. A few more bits and pieces of Victoria's shattered memories. A little information, another piece to a puzzle that I did not yet understand and Victoria Carpenter's plea for help. Was there a critical memory cell that she would eventually recall? Would the pieces fall in place? Only time would tell.

For now, though, my search for Rodney Johnson was on.

I dialed Victoria's number and apparently awakened her. By the time she fumbled with her clock, stalled to get her mind working and we exchanged banalities, her voice finally began warming up.

"Does the name Rodney Johnson ring any bells?" I asked.

"Rodney Johnson," she rolled it over her thick tongue. "No, should it?"

"I don't know." I hesitated, unsure that I wanted to

divulge the information I had. "It's just one of the leads I'm working on."

"Thank God you've got leads. Did you get my fax?"

"Uh huh. Do you think 'Oz' might have something to do with Osborne?"

"I don't know. I keep thinking about it, keep hearing that little kid yell."

"You were a little kid too," I said.

"I know."

I could see a cloud of dust coming up the ranch lane.

"I'll stop in and talk to the Osborne woman this week."

"I hope you do better than I did," Carpenter said. "She won't admit any of it."

Looking out the window, I saw Jake Hatcher's white pickup drive by. Although he could have easily spotted Priscilla outside the old stage stop, he kept on driving. I wondered if he had business with Martin, although he hadn't said anything about the brand inspector coming by.

After hanging up from talking to Victoria, I reached for the telephone book and my reading glasses. Metropolitan Tucson has a population right around 750,000. I quickly found out that 1,059 of them were named Johnson. And that didn't even include the Johnsens or the Jonsens or the Jonsons.

There was one Rod Johnson listed. I dialed the number, only to find it disconnected.

No Brisha appeared in the book, although there were twelve with just the initial B or the B along with another initial. I jotted these down with their telephone numbers, starting with the ones who had just Tucson listed as their address, knowing that single women often preferred this listing.

Next I checked Matthew and Mark. There were two Matthews, a Matthew R and a Matthew B; and six listings for plain Mark Johnson. There were thirty initial M's.

I looked at my list. Fifty telephone numbers to check out.

I called Information and asked for a listing for a Rodney Johnson and was rewarded with old Rod's disconnected number.

There was no Brisha Johnson on record.

Since I do a few skip traces from time to time I knew there was no sense calling U.S. West. They just have telephone directories for the last couple of years on hand and their record archives only go back ten years. And they're stingy about sharing information.

When Charley Bell answered on the second ring I knew that he'd had time for his morning coffee, as he was sounding somewhat fluent. Quickly I explained what I wanted.

"I'll check Fast Track," he said. "But I don't know if they'll go that far back, sixty-three right?"

"That's what I'm going on."

"Dang, Phonefiche only goes back to 1976." Phonefiche, I knew from past experience, carries thousands of telephone directories.

"Can you check DMV for me?" Charley pays a subscription fee to the Department of Motor Vehicles, which gives him on-line access to part of their database.

"Righto, Ellis. Say, did you hear about the guy who had prostate surgery and his doctor says, 'I've got good news and bad news for you'?"

"No." Charley had definitely had his morning hit of caffeine.

"The guy says, 'You better give me the good news first.' So the doctor says, 'We were able to save your testicles.'"

"So what's the bad news?" I asked.

"The doc says, 'They're under your pillow!'" Charley laughed uproariously, as he always did at his own jokes. Sometimes I think he laughs loud just to cover up the silence if his punch line doesn't achieve its desired effect. So far, he had nothing to worry about, for I always found his jokes funny.

I didn't bother telling him that he was on a testicle kick. That was the second joke in a row with the same subject matter.

"Oh, Charley, one more thing . . ."

"I know, I know, Ellis, you need this stuff ASAP."

My finger flicked the hang-up button and I started down my list. An hour later I had touched base with fifteen assorted Johnsons. None of them knew either Rodney or Brisha, although Bertilde Johnson on Fourteenth Street allowed as to how that must have been a slave name and she thought that maybe her great-grandmother's name might have been something like Brisha. Or was it Brighty? Or maybe Bridget?

My left ear was hot from all the telephone work so I took a break and started a sheet on Rodney Johnson. I put everything on it that I knew about him. Under a big fat question mark, halfway down the legal pad, I wrote, *Arizona Bottling Plant? Hunter?*

I called the Arizona Game and Fish Department. While they were as cooperative as they could be, all their records were in their main office. I called the Phoenix number and discovered that they only kept files for the past three years, so I was again out of luck.

After trying a few more Johnsons, I grabbed my keys and purse, set the answering machine and was out the door.

As I climbed in the truck, the thought occurred to me that I hadn't seen Jake drive back by. Instead of turning to town I headed back to the ranch to make sure everything was all right.

I found Jake Hatcher out near the hay barn, sipping on a mug of coffee. Cori Elena was standing across from Hatcher, with the tractor in between them. Martín was under it, working on the rod bearings.

"Everything all right?" I asked.

"*Sí, claro,*" said Cori Elena.

"I'm finishing up the last one now," Martín offered.

"Did we have some inspections?" I asked.

Jake smiled and shook his head. "Nah, I was just in the neighborhood and thought I'd stop in."

When had he ever done that before? While Jake Hatcher frequently stopped in the house for a beer or coffee, depending upon the time of day, he never went out of his way to come to the ranch unless he had business here.

"Five-eighths," Martín said.

Cori Elena leaned over and handed a wrench to Martín. She was wearing a low-cut V-neck knit sweater and as she did so, she gave Jake and I a clear view of her bare brown breasts.

I glanced at Jake, who had not missed it. He blushed when he caught me catching him.

What in the hell was going on here? Was Cori Elena trolling for Jake Hatcher?

"Trade, are you going to town?" Cori Elena flashed me one of her perfect smiles.

"Uh, yeah, I have to go in on business."

"Did you hear about Martín's Tía Maria?" she asked, a sad look coming over her face.

"She's sick?" I played along.

"Very, very sick," Cori Elena said. *"Pobrecita."*

"Martín, I'm sorry to hear that," I continued the charade.

"Gracias."

I waited a few more minutes making small talk with Jake and Cori Elena before finally getting back in the pickup and driving off. I noticed that Jake Hatcher did not follow me out.

Cori Elena had always been cute and a flirt, but flashing the brand inspector was really going above and beyond. What had that been all about? He was almost old enough to be her father. Maybe I had misread things. She could be pretty ditzy on occasion and she probably hadn't even been aware of what she was doing. Hell, maybe she'd even forgotten that she owned a bra. After all, she had Martín, what would she want with Hatcher?

To take my mind off my uncharitable thoughts I started surfing through radio stations. When the poignant strands of "Danny Boy" came over the air, I remembered Dorothy Brewster's talk about her Danny Boy. Danny who? Victoria had assured me that it was not a name her mother had used for Dan Daglio. My mind raced with the possibilities. I started with the actors Danny Thomas and Daniel Day-Lewis and then drifted to the political with Dan Quayle. Finally I settled on the historical Daniel Webster and Daniel Boone.

It had to mean something. But what?

27

THE PIMA COUNTY RECORDER'S OFFICE IS LOCATED IN THE OLD county courthouse, a grande dame of a building draped around a central courtyard and crowned with a huge Moorish dome of yellow, blue, red and brown tile.

The Good Dogs hot-dog stand was located west of the building in the modern brick patio that harbors city and county employees during lunchtime. As I walked through the portico I could see the green-and-white cart in the newer section. If I'd had Rodney Johnson's name yesterday I could have saved both time and fuel.

Although the Recorder's office has all sorts of good information, not all of it is accessible to the public. Arizona birth and death certificates, for instance, are not a matter of public record. You need a legal reason or a relationship to the person involved to be able to get them. Guess it's too easy to paper-trip, to fabricate an identity on a deceased's documents.

Legal records, marriage licenses, divorce documents, civil and domestic suits as well as criminal records are a matter of public record, but they are only available at the clerk's office of the Superior Court, which is located in another building.

From past experience I've found that the most productive avenues for finding someone are the Department of Motor Vehicles, which Charley was checking, and Voter Registration, whose records date back to 1936.

The voter registration office is dark and dismal with an overhead bank of fluorescent lighting. I stood behind a man who was requesting information and waited my turn.

"May I help you?" A young Hispanic woman with shiny black hair that hung to her waist straightened a stack of forms on the counter with long, graceful hands.

"I'd like to see the voter registration microfilm from 1963," I said. Getting this information is so easy, no forms to fill out, no identification required, just ask and it is delivered. Of course if you want copies of the actual files, then that's trickier, because you need a political reason for those.

She went to the cabinet in the middle of the office behind the counter and returned with a tray of microfilm.

"Instructions are on the machine," she said pleasantly.

There was one viewer in the public access area, along with two terminals to check current registrations. Luckily the viewer was empty.

I fumbled with the microfilm, attempted to follow the directions and fed it from one spool to the other. Even armed with a college degree I got the damned thing in upside down and had to pull it back out, think things over thoroughly before finally flipping it right side up and getting it in right. I pulled a pen and a piece of paper out of my purse. As I did so, I made a hasty but fervent prayer that Rodney Johnson had registered to vote.

The records were in alphabetical order. As I zipped through the first part of the alphabet, names blurred by me as the machine took on the tone of an insistent whispering rattlesnake. I started slowing when I got to the H's sped up too much and found myself in the L's, and then backtracked to the J's. My eyes were stinging with the effort.

Rolling the knob slowly I came into the Johnsons. It was terrible. It felt like Christmas when I was a kid and opening up the big present, where your mind races before you get the wrapping off, thinking this has got to be it, the big thing I asked for and what if it isn't how can I hide my disappointment from them and pretend that this other thing is what I really wanted instead of what I asked for?

I held my breath as I rolled into the Johnson, R category. Checked all the initials, then hit the Ralphs and

Randys and Raymonds. Started breathing again through the Richards and Roberts and finally landed on the Rodneys. One Rodney actually. Rodney Herbert Johnson, 115 E. Kingston, Tucson, Arizona.

I sat and stared at the name. Rodney Herbert Johnson, I found myself mumbling. I scribbled it on the piece of paper and rolled the knob back up through the Johnsons, settling in at the B's. Going backward now I rushed past the Byrons, Burtons, Bufords, Bryans and Bruces before hitting on Brisha. Brisha Louise Johnson, 115 E. Kingston, Tucson, Arizona.

Bingo.

I stopped at the pay telephone in the courtyard and called Charley Bell.

"Bell here," he answered.

"Charley, it's Trade."

"DMV shows one Rodney Johnson for sixty-three."

"One-fifteen East Kingston."

"Righto, Ellis." He sounded hurt that I had unearthed the same information. "Say did you hear about . . ."

"Gotta run, Charley, later."

A momentary guilt pang hit on the way to Priscilla. Usually I never cut Charley off from telling a joke, but I was hot on a trail now, albeit a thirty-plus-year-old trail, and I wanted to get to the end of the road as soon as possible.

I unlocked the toolbox of my truck and retrieved my city map. I checked the location of Kingston and found it about a mile and a half from the Arizona Bottling Plant in the south part of Tucson, not far from downtown.

I headed for the closest intersection that I was familiar with and then consulted the map again, intentionally trying to miss every stoplight so that I could read without interruption. After making a few turns I found myself driving past the boarded-up Millicent Springs Elementary School.

Kingston was the third cross street down from Millicent Springs. I went another couple of blocks before I got to the 100 block.

115 Kingston was just off the corner, a faded pink stucco house with wooden trim that looked as though it

had been tacked on as an afterthought. A huge prickly pear cactus, almost as tall as the house, threatened to take over one side of it. A chain-link fence, rusty and dipping in places, guarded the barren front yard. An ancient over-stuffed chair, its arms leaking horsehair, sat in the middle of the front porch with a thin gray cat curled up on its seat. The pale tin mailbox carried no name or address. The house number had been painted on the curb, an effort I'm sure by either the police or fire department to make their calls easier.

Since I could see where the chain-link was attached to the sides of the house, I knew there was no hidden dog waiting to surprise me. I opened the gate and walked to the porch. The cat opened one yellow eye before returning to sleep.

There was no bell or door knocker, just a sagging torn screened door. I opened it and knocked on the weathered wooden front door, carefully, to keep splinters out of my knuckles.

It took forever but finally a wizened little gray-haired woman opened it. She was Hispanic and judging from the width of the opened door, fearless.

"¿Sí? Bueno?"

"Buenos días, señora," I began. In less than perfect Spanish, I gave her my name and explained that I was looking for an old friend, Rodney Johnson.

"¿Mande?"

I repeated the name. *"Es un negro,"* I said, *"con familia—con muchos niños y una esposa que se llama Brisha."* I pulled out the school photo of Matthew and Mark Johnson.

She studied it. *"No se."*

"¿Cuántos años lleva aquí?" I asked, trying to get a line on how long she had lived in the house.

"Veinte, veinte-cinco."

Twenty, twenty-five years, but it sounded like she'd never heard of the Johnsons. I gave her a card and asked her, in what I hoped was intelligible Spanish, to call me if she ran across anyone who had known them.

I tried the houses on each side. There was no one home on the west so I left a card in the door with a scribbled note on it.

The house to the east held a harried young mother with a passel of kids hanging off of her. She reminded me a bit of Belle, Darrell's hound dog. Same sad eyes and drooping breasts. She was friendly but no help. Had lived in the neighborhood for three years and didn't know a soul.

I crossed the street and knocked on yet another door. This one was opened by a huge black man with gray hair.

I went through my spiel.

"Praise the Lord," he said, arms to the heavens. "Let His glory reign down upon you."

"Uh, Rodney Johnson, does that name mean anything to you?" I asked.

"In a lowly mangy our King was born," he continued, in a not unpleasant voice.

I thought he probably meant manger, but did not correct him.

"He lived across the street, years ago, in that house." I pointed to the faded pink structure. "Maybe you were here then?"

"Thou shalt not commit adultery," the old man cautioned. "For it is a sin."

I had about decided this one was hopeless when he came to life.

"Son-of-a-bitch! Hell! shit!" He screamed as he began dancing in circles, and unbuttoning the cotton trousers he wore.

I started backing away from his door. He pulled down his zipper and let his pants fall to the ground, but made no effort to start after me. Stunned, I saw that he wore no undershorts.

"Fart!" he yelled at the top of his lungs. "Turd!"

"Daddy!" A slim black woman appeared at the door, a dish towel draped over one dark arm. She stood on his fallen pants as she gently clasped his elbow and steered him into the house. "Who are you?" she asked over her shoulder.

"I'm looking for a man called Rodney Johnson," I yelled to her back, unsure of whether or not I should follow her.

She was back in the doorway, without her father, and she retrieved his pants, folding them as we spoke.

"Rodney Johnson," she repeated. "Sorry."

"He lived over there"—another toss of my head toward 115—"thirty years ago."

"Well Daddy was here then. The Church of Christ Apostle over on Portal was his church."

"His church?"

"He was a minister."

Some church. Fart? Turd?

"He has Alzheimer's," she explained. "It does funny things with his head. Those words, he never used them before, wouldn't think of it."

I made a mental note to tell Bea the diagnosis if she ever heard me say "goodness gracious" and "mercy me" when I stubbed my toe.

"Did you live here in 1963?"

She shook her head. "Overseas. My husband was in the service. We've only been back for a year."

"Then you wouldn't have known the Johnsons?"

She shook her head. "There may still be people here who might remember him though. You might check the church."

She gave me directions to the Church of Christ Apostle and I thanked her.

Disappointed at the dead end I had found, I drove down Kingston to Beverly and over to Portal. I was thinking about the church and not paying much attention when it dawned on me that I had just passed a drugstore. An old drugstore. Esquina Pharmacy. I slammed Priscilla into reverse.

I parked at the curb and pretended not to notice a middle-aged man sprawled against the side of a building with a paper bag clutched in one of his hands. He returned the favor by pretending not to see me.

The building was an old adobe, stuccoed over with chipping plaster. I wondered how long it had housed Esquina's.

Inside it had that old-time drugstore feeling. Worn wooden floors with wide aisles flanked with tan metal tiered shelves housing very few items: three or four faded boxes of tampons, a few tubes of toothpaste, half a dozen rolls of paper towels, that kind of thing. Whenever I'm in one of these neighborhood jobs, I always think they're going out of business and thus reducing their inventory. Of course that's not the case, they just do less volume than their larger, more contemporary counterparts.

Things were clean and well dusted. The front counter was empty, as was the rest of the store. I walked back to the arced neon PHARMACY sign and spotted a tall, thin, gray-haired Hispanic man behind a counter which was a step above the pharmacy counter.

"Be right with you," he volunteered as he scooped up a pile of pills and dribbled them into a plastic bottle. He cleaned his glasses before stepping down.

I handed him a card.

"I'm looking for someone who might remember the Rodney Johnson family. They lived here thirty years ago."

"Well that would fit," he said. "We've been here for forty-two years. My father had it before that."

"The mother's name was Brisha and they had several children," I explained. "The two oldest boys were called Matthew and Mark."

"I don't know, Johnson's a pretty common name. We've always filled a lot of Johnson prescriptions here."

I pulled out the class picture and my finger tapped the two boys in the face. "Here are the kids. They were in the same grade because this one, Matthew"—my finger lingered on his shirt—"was in some kind of accident in Georgia that left his left arm kind of funny. I think it was shorter than the right one."

The pharmacist removed his glasses again, held them up to the light as though trying to identify the offending speck on the lens, breathed on them and rubbed them again with his sweater.

"The blue lady," he said. "That's who you want to talk to, the blue lady over on Chambray." He reached under the counter and retrieved an old metal file box. The letters across the top said "G–L." He withdrew a card and began writing on a prescription slip.

"Sara Lincoln, that's who can help you. One Twenty-five Chambray. She lived on the street behind them and was good friends with Mrs. Johnson."

"Then you remember them?"

He nodded. "The boy with the crippled arm was on medication. Nice family. But I'm sorry, they've been gone for years and I don't have any idea how you could find them."

"But you think Mrs. Lincoln may have kept in touch?"

"Don't know. But she'd be your best bet."

I was halfway across the store before I remembered something and turned around. He was back filling prescriptions.

"You called her the blue lady? Why?"

"She had a terrible reaction to a drug years ago and it turned her blue. She never has been able to reverse it."

I wondered on the way out if he had prescribed the drug, but he wasn't talking and I wasn't asking.

I drove past Kingston, passed an alley and then hit Chambray. One Twenty-five was the third house in, which made it kitty-corner across the alley from the old Johnson house.

Although I'd been warned, when Sara Lincoln answered my knock I was struck by the color of her skin. It *was* blue. Kind of that faded gray/blue color that New Mexicans paint around their doors and windows for luck. I had never seen the color on a human being before and tried hard not to stare. I doubted whether it had been a lucky color for her.

"Mrs. Lincoln?"

"Yes?" she said, in a voice that held a core of suspicion.

"My name is Trade Ellis and I'd like to talk to you about Rodney and Brisha Johnson."

"What about them?" Her voice was very soft and I found myself straining to hear it.

"I'm trying to find them, to see if they're all right."

She laughed softly.

"Do you know how I can reach them?"

"I don't know nothin'."

"I mean them no harm, in fact, I'm trying to find out if someone did indeed harm them years ago. I need to know what happened to Matthew and Mark. If their father took them from school that day."

Her eyes narrowed. "Who are you?"

There was no other way to cut through the suspicion. "I've been hired by someone who thinks that a black man and his two small boys were murdered years ago. There's a chance that that man could have been Rodney Johnson. Please, Mrs. Lincoln."

She hesitated, as though she was mulling things over. "You best come in," she said finally.

The house was hot and stuffy. She led me through a tiny living room to a Formica table in the spotless kitchen. In addition to being blue, which gave her an ancient cast, she was bent over, either with arthritis or osteoporosis or both. It was impossible to judge her age.

"Tea?"

"No thanks."

"Sit."

"I've been trying to track down a family that would fit the description that I was given," I explained. "The Rodney Johnson family fits. The pharmacist at Esquina's told me that you might know where to find them."

"After all these years," she said, a faraway look creeping into her tired eyes. "After all these years."

"You knew them well," I prodded.

"Brisha and I was friends."

"Do you know where I can find her?"

"I don't know," she said, but her eyes told me she did.

"Mrs. Lincoln, this is difficult, I know, after all of these years. It's hard for me to even talk about what may have happened because it also may not have happened. I may be stirring things up that don't need to be."

She reached for the salt and pepper shakers and began moving them slowly around one another with her gnarled hands. "Murder, you said."

"Possible murder. I talked to the boys' teacher and she said that their father pulled them out of school and returned to Georgia. Do you know about that?"

When she raised her eyes I could see the mist gathering in them.

"Brisha said he'd run off, run off with another woman and the boys."

"She told you that after they left?"

"Why would she lie?"

"I don't know, Mrs. Lincoln. Maybe he did run off."

"No. It's in my bones now. Now that you come and said there may have been murder, I can feel it in my bones. My bones don't lie. Feels so right, feels so wrong."

"I need to talk to Brisha Johnson," I said softly, for her blue hands were twitching as she still played with the shakers. "I need to find out what happened that day."

Sara Lincoln reached across to a Kleenex box, knocking over the salt shaker. She quickly grabbed a pinch of it, threw it over her left shoulder and then blotted her eyes with a tissue. "How'd they die, Miz Ellis?"

I took a deep breath. "I'm afraid not well, Mrs. Lincoln, not well at all."

She digested this and then continued.

"She left the week after he did. Packed up and left in the middle of the night and never said a word to no one. Not to me, not to no one. I didn't hear from her for years, then I got a Christmas card."

"Did you get one this year?"

She nodded. "We been writin' back and forth, at Christmas time."

"May I see it?"

She shook her head emphatically. "No. She made me promise to never tell no one where she is."

"If her family was killed wouldn't she want the person who did it punished?"

"Lordy, Lordy, I don' know, I just don' know what has happened. But I know I can't give you her address. I can't do that. I can't break that promise."

"Do you have a telephone number for her?"

She shook her head.

I reached in my purse for a card and laid it on the table. "Could you write her and ask her to contact me right away?"

"I do it today," she said wearily. "Today."

"I don't want to hurt her," I said. "I just want to help."

"No, she been hurt enough," Sara Lincoln agreed as she walked me out.

28

I WAS BACK RUMMAGING IN THE TRUCK BOX BEFORE I FINALLY RE-
trieved the Tucson phone book. Ran down the A's until I
found the American Civil Liberties Union. As long as I was
in town, I figured I might as well call on Jerri Osborne.

The ACLU was located on south Sixth Avenue, just off
Broadway. It was a flat-faced building of tan slump block
sandwiched between Planned Parenthood and the Plasma
Center. A person could hit this one block and solve a lot of
problems, maybe even make a little money.

A young man with a shaved head sat hunched over a
computer terminal when I walked in.

"May I help you?" he asked without looking up from
his keyboard, which he was still typing on.

"I'm looking for Jerri Osborne, is she in?"

"Sure. Jer?" he hollered, still working madly. If I'd
been a murderer there was no way he could have given
even an elementary description to the police. For all he
knew I looked like qwerty.

A tall, rawboned woman with a badly bleached buzz
cut filled the doorway behind the man.

"Yes?" she asked, in a small voice that did not begin to
match her oversized body.

I stepped around the desk and extended my hand.
"Trade Ellis."

"Oh," she said, not surprised. She returned my handshake with a soft fishy thing. "Come in." She looked nervously at the young man before closing her office door.

In spite of her hair, she was dressed conservatively, in a navy suit with a beige silk blouse and a patterned scarf tied in a loose Windsor knot, giving the illusion of a tie. She was wearing mascara and maybe a tiny bit of blush. Briefly I wondered if maybe she'd been undergoing chemotherapy and had lost her hair, but didn't think it prudent to ask.

"I'm here about the Sporting Club," I said.

"Don't know anything about it." She moved the stack of papers she had been working on to an upper corner of her desk.

"Not even from Victoria Carpenter?"

"Of course from Vicki. She's trying to convince me that I know about it, but I don't," she snapped. "Her imagination's running wild. I told the police just that."

"Yes, it might be," I agreed. "But if it isn't, if what she says happened, happened, then we've got a hell of a problem on our hands, don't we?"

"It's not my problem, I don't know anything about it."

"You weren't at the picnics, didn't bring your plastic men and horses and dolls to them?" I studied her carefully.

"Of course I did." She fumbled in her desk drawer, bringing out a pack of Marlboros. She started to withdraw one, changed her mind and replaced the pack in the desk. "Our families were friends, we did a lot of things together. Including a few picnics."

"But you don't remember any black people being killed?"

"God no."

"Maybe a black man and his two small boys?"

She shook her head. "Look, I don't know what Vicki's trying to prove with all of this, maybe she needs the publicity for her books, I don't know, but I'm telling you that nothing like that happened at any time when I was with Vicki or her parents, or when I was with my parents. It just didn't happen."

"She's beginning to remember more."

"Remember? Or make up?"

"Have you ever been in therapy?" It was none of my

business and a question that I would have been offended at if someone had asked it of me.

"That's a pretty personal question."

"Murder's pretty personal too."

"Well, I see no need to answer a question like that," she said, unaware that she just had.

"If, let's just say hypothetically, Victoria Carpenter's accusations proved true, would that jeopardize your position here?"

A cold naked look invaded her eyes. "I can't see where it would have any bearing on my job. I didn't witness any murders. Besides, I was a child, how could that possibly affect me?"

"Vicki tells me your father was a member of the Sporting Club."

"My father's dead and isn't here to defend himself. I resent the hell out of Vicki's implications."

"Do you remember Dan Daglio at the picnics?" I asked, trying a different tack.

"I don't remember, it was too long ago. I can't tell you who was there or wasn't." She was tugging on tufts of her peroxided hair. "Sorry."

I pulled the Millicent Springs class picture out of the envelope and placed it on her desk. I pointed to Matthew and Mark Johnson. "These are the children that may have been killed," I said.

Her eyes never dropped. There was no way she was going to look at the photograph.

"Could you at least look at it?"

"I've told you I don't know anything about that." Her eyes flickered to the picture, but did not stay there.

She was holding back. I could feel it, almost tangibly see it. But there was nothing I could do, nothing I could say that would make her more forthcoming.

"Does the name Danny Boy mean anything to you?"

"Sure, it's a song."

"Did anyone ever call your father Oz?"

"What?"

I repeated it.

"I never heard him called that."

I retrieved my picture from the desktop and stood. "Well, thanks for seeing me."

She reached across the desk and laid another fishy shake on me. "Any time. I'd like to give you a little free legal advice though."

"What's that?"

"If you're going to throw around charges of murder at people like Phelan Brewster and Dan Daglio, then you'd better be very very sure that you can support them."

"I know, I know," I said as I walked out. "Or my ass is grass."

It was just after three when I headed out to Avra Valley, making my obligatory stop at McDonald's. I drove down Miller Lane, turning south at the third fork and after two miles was at the metal farm gate with the NO TRESPASSING and BEWARE OF DOG signs.

As I crested the hill before getting to the house, I spotted the old jeep road nestled between the two hills to the north. Maybe I was lucky that the old barbed-wire fence, or at least a strand of it, was still stretched across the road. Otherwise I might have gotten too bold on the horse, gotten too close to the house and been caught by Brewster.

As I drove in, Hazel's white Taurus was sitting in the drive with one of its back doors open. I could see that the front door to the house was also open.

The three dogs came running out and as they did so, Phelan's wife came through the opened front door. I reached for the bag of hamburgers and stuffed them in Priscilla's console.

Hazel Brewster grabbed the rottweiler's collar and shepherded all of the dogs back into the side yard. She returned without her canine companions.

"Phelan's in the shop," she said, pointing to the metal Quonset hut west of the house. It was cold enough that her words came out in fog puffs.

I thought it curious that she would automatically assume my business was with her husband, but said nothing, leaving her to retrieve groceries from the back of her car. Besides, I was thrilled to finally get a peek inside the legendary Quonset hut.

The wide steel door was open and I could see Brewster inside, standing over a workbench.

"Hello."

He looked up from his work and grunted, a stubby hand motioning for me to come in.

The back end of the building was set up for Brewster's taxidermy. The long wooden workbench, covered with tools, ran along the metal wall of the building. Among the things that I could easily recognize were a couple of claw hammers, pliers, assorted saws, twine, needles and thread, cotton batting, excelsior, plaster of paris, artist's brushes and various mixtures of turpentine and linseed oil. There was a whole lot of other interesting stuff on the bench, most of it, I'm sure, vital to the taxidermist, but I had no idea what I was looking at.

Brewster was bent over a deer head form anchored in his vise. Antlers were secured to the model with screws, and one glass eye was in place.

"Be with you in a minute," he said, placing the second eye and securing it with pins. He reached for a three-pound coffee can of papier-mâché and began slopping this around the antlers and the eyes, modeling it as he went.

A wooden stove in the center of the hut was putting out quite a bit of heat and I noticed that a red plaid flannel shirt, probably the same one he'd been wearing the first time I'd met him, was draped over a chair. He was working in a white scoop-necked T-shirt. I stared at his huge hairy forearms and wondered if they were attributable to genetics or to his years of work at the bottling plant. They were also hosting a couple of tattoos, an eagle in flight with a snake in its talons on one, and a funny-looking tower thing on the other. I was disappointed not to find any swastikas.

"Interesting," I offered, stepping closer to the vise so I could get a better look at the tattooed tower.

He grunted and continued applying the papier-mâché. "Want to get this on before it dries."

"Take your time," I said. Now I could see that the tower sprouted wings. I squinted in an effort to make out the details, all the while pretending to be fascinated with the mount.

Jesus. The tower was a penis. A fuzzy penis outlined

in blue tattoo ink with wings. In flowery script below it, I read "Dickie-Bird." I never would have pegged Brewster as a member of the Audubon Society and he didn't look like a man who would have something worth advertising.

I shifted my picture envelope under my other arm and decided to start the conversation rather than wait for Brewster's invitation. I stared at his hands patting the papier-mâché as I began talking.

"I, uh, got some information from the school district," I began. "About some children who disappeared abruptly back in 1963."

The stubby hands never faltered as he applied thin strips of paper to the deer mount.

"And I was able to talk to their kindergarten teacher. Both of the boys were in the same grade." I reached into the envelope and withdrew the class picture.

He glanced at it.

"Not too surprising for niggers," he grunted.

I tried not to wince.

"She also had their names." I paused, scrutinizing him, his body language, hands, the slump of his shoulders, trying to determine some clue as I dropped my bomb. "Matthew and Mark Johnson. Their father was Rodney Johnson. Does that name mean anything to you?"

He dipped into the coffee can again. "Nope." He turned his churning sea eyes on me. "Should it?"

"They lived on Kingston Street, not far from Arizona Bottling."

"So what? A lot of people lived near the plant."

"I think he worked there. There was a black man who was working there the day President Kennedy was assassinated. I think it was Rodney Johnson."

"That's bullshit. I don't remember any black people working there then. Not one."

"Well, someone does."

"Who's that?"

I hesitated. "I'd rather not say."

"Sure," he said as he walked to a utility sink and began washing the paste off of his hands. "Come on in, I've got something I want you to see."

We were almost at the open steel door when a brick

shithouse of a man stepped into the entrance, blocking our exit.

While he wasn't particularly tall, he had the body stance of a professional weightlifter.

And he was aiming a gun at my chest.

I'm not an expert on guns, but it was the weirdest one I'd ever seen. It looked like something out of a B-grade science fiction movie with its huge bore and a bottle-shaped thing hovering over the barrel.

I froze.

Phelan Brewster laughed.

"Hank, you're scaring her to death."

This had to be Vicki's brother.

The man lowered the weapon and backed out of the threshold. "Sorry," he said, not sounding like he meant it.

He was a larger version of Phelan Brewster, but where Dad was short and stocky, Henry Brewster was more defined. He was also wearing a T-shirt and I could identify huge muscles corded just under his skin. He stood in that bowlegged stance that guys who work out have, where they chafe themselves if their thighs rub together. His body was so absurd I wondered if he was on steroids. His head looked about two sizes too small for his frame, and on this precarious perch sat a black baseball cap with TULSA WELDING SCHOOL in red letters.

"One of the guys picked it up for me," Henry said to his father as he raised the gun again, only this time the barrel with its oversized mouth was pointed at the late-afternoon sky. "So I'll have it this weekend for the game."

I wondered what kind of games he was playing, but kept my mouth shut.

"This is that woman I told you about, the one Vic hired," Phelan Brewster said, not bothering with my name.

"Vic's a liar," Henry offered.

"Then you don't remember anything about the Sporting Club?"

"Not what she remembers," he said, slinging the gun over his steroidal shoulders.

"That certainly seems to be the party line," I admitted. "No bodies buried in the yard?"

"Vic's crazy," her brother said. "She always was a squirrel."

I thought about asking about Danny Boy and Oz but decided to keep them close to my chest a while longer.

We were walking toward the house when suddenly Henry lifted his gun again and fired at Priscilla's tailgate.

Immediately a red burst landed between the *d* and *g* in Dodge. It had the pattern of a shattered window as rivulets resembling blood dribbled down the white paint.

Shit. I'd been assaulted with a paint-ball gun.

Inside, the house was as I remembered it, although the heavy dining-room table was now covered with grocery bags. Hazel Brewster was washing the canned goods she had just bought and placing them in her pantry. I got a glimmer into Hazel's exotic reading tastes as I spotted a tabloid balanced on top of a couple of rolls of paper towels offering the headline, "Woman Eaten By Her Own Fur Coat."

The sun was low in the west and coming in through the bank of windows. In the intense light, the eyes of the huge stuffed mule deer shone like crystals. Mentally I compared him to the giant lame one-antlered buck I had seen in the park, but there was no comparison. This one was truly a trophy deer. It saddened me to think of his hanging on a wall instead of out in the desert where he could sire a string of handsome young children.

"Harrison called," Hazel said to her husband. "He found his dog dead in one of the mine shafts."

The Avra Valley abandoned mines had taken their toll again.

Brewster grunted and rummaged through the pile of papers on the table. Hank went to the refrigerator and helped himself to a Budweiser.

"Have you seen this?" Phelan Brewster handed me a sliver of a newspaper clipping.

The American Medical Association has adopted a resolution, I read, *saying the memory-enhancement techniques in the area of childhood sexual abuse are fraught with problems of potential misapplication.*

"Sexual abuse?" I asked.

"If we were killing people and letting our kids watch, don't you think that's a form of abuse? We're talking to a lawyer next week about this thing with Vic. I've had about all I can stand of this."

"Damn straight," Hank Brewster agreed as he drained the Bud.

I didn't know what to say. Clearly I was going to get nowhere with either Phelan Brewster or his son.

"I don't suppose you knew Rodney Johnson?" I asked Hank.

He was seated in a recliner, his hands clasped behind his head, I'm sure in an effort to show me the bulging biceps. They were fascinating. And they were ugly. He shook his head, his arms moving with it. "Can't say that I do." He reached for the remote television control and began channel surfing.

"Just think about this," Phelan Brewster said, removing the clipping from my fingers. "Please don't be so gullible to believe what Vic is telling you. She's a mental case and she needs help, not encouragement with her sick fantasies."

"I'll consider that," I said as I saw myself out.

The door closed behind me. When I walked around Priscilla I was pissed at the red paint on the tailgate. I hoped Hank Brewster was right about the stuff washing off.

As I drove slowly out, I spotted Phelan releasing the dogs from the side yard.

After I crested the first hill, which placed me out of sight of the Brewster homestead, I put the truck in neutral and reached for the dog whistle. I blew three short blasts, the sound inaudible to my own ear.

As I fumbled with the McDonald's bag and wrappers, the Doberman was the first one to top the crest.

"Here, girl," I said through the half-opened window, taking care to stay inside the truck. I threw a hamburger onto the dirt and she quickly gulped it down.

The German shepherd and rottweiler had now arrived and were looking for their share of the bounty. I gave each of them a hamburger, again thrown from the confines of the vehicle.

In one reckless moment I hit the power button and let the window all the way down. I then dropped the fourth hamburger out the driver's window and watched the Doberman eat it. All three dogs were now wagging their tails and begging for more food.

"Good girls," I said, "great puppies."

They seemed pleased as they milled around the truck. Although the window was open, none of them tried to jump in, or even stand on their hind legs to lunge at me. We were quickly becoming pals.

I was already cheating on our new friendship for I had two cold hamburgers left. But then I remembered Mrs. Fierce and Blue, who I hoped were doing a better job on ranch security than Brewster's dogs.

With a final "Good girls," I slipped Priscilla into Drive and headed out.

As I hit the farm gate, a silly Groucho Marx quote came to me.

"Outside of a dog, a book is a man's best friend. Inside of a dog, it's too dark to read."

I was glad that it didn't look as though I'd have that opportunity.

Driving to the freeway I thought about what Phelan Brewster had said about Victoria's having mental problems. Michael Burns was just the latest in her string of shrinks. Were they really helping her unravel blocked memories, or was her father right? Was she, like her mother, suffering from a serious mental illness?

29

THE SUN WAS JUST SINKING INTO THE TUCSON MOUNTAINS AS I pulled into Bea's town house development. I wound slowly around the narrow streets, none of which were configured for the mass of a three-quarter-ton Dodge pickup. Priscilla's healthy diesel purr caused a few curious looks in our direction, so out of place was she among all of the Japanese imports and BMWs.

I parked behind Bea's Honda and grabbed a dog leash from the floor.

From the moment I entered her small front courtyard I could hear shrieking coming from inside.

I rang the bell.

Bea yanked the door open.

"Your fairy godmother has arrived," I said.

"You!"

A popping crash sounded from the confines of the house as we both ran inside.

Petunia was having a party in the kitchen. What looked like four or five eggs lay broken on the floor with a splintered Knotts Berry jelly jar mixed in and a shattered bottle of mayonnaise on top of that. Crowning this epicurean delight was a head of iceburg lettuce which the pig was happily devouring, oblivious to the shards of glass which she was also probably ingesting, which would or would not cut her innards to smithereens, thus insuring that my veterinarian would be even richer than she already is. The pig seemed relatively unconcerned about the mess she had made.

"Hello, darling," I said.

She grunted a greeting and returned to her greens.

"Now do you see what I mean?" Cousin Bea demanded. "She knows how to open the refrigerator, and she knows what she wants, and then she just gets it."

Coming from the ranch, where a slew of creatures depended on me to feed them, I must admit that I found this self-feeding idea fascinating, but I said nothing, reaching for the paper towels instead.

"Where's her diaper?"

"Oh she's housebroken," Bea said. "She's just not refrigerator-broken."

She lifted the pig and put her out on the back patio, then returned to help me clean up the mess.

As we worked, we talked some about the Brewster thing. Bea had no new angles for me to work, but once again made me promise that I'd give her the scoop, if and when one came.

"Will you go with me to the art show?" she suddenly asked.

"The Mountain Oyster show?"

"Right. I've got an extra ticket."

Every November the Mountain Oyster Club puts on a Western Art show. It's a grand affair, with hordes of people threatening to implode the building as they vie for the chance to bid on Western art. The attendance of the contributing artists is a bonus that adds fuel to the bidding fires. Although the club is a private one, whose membership is limited to those who have some connection with the ranching industry (admittedly as the years have gone by those connections have become somewhat tenuous), for this one day of the year it is opened to the public. Sometimes the media is comped for the show and these were the tickets that Bea had referred to. This year, although I am a member thanks to my father's legacy, I hadn't planned on attending the show.

"I thought you were going with that real-estate guy," I said.

"No, not now."

I opened the left side of Bea's refrigerator. There on the top shelf of the freezer, just below the icemaker, next to the Weight Watchers lasagna, sat a row of glass vials. I reached for the one closest to the refrigerator side, for I knew Bea's system.

I twirled it in the light until I could read the piece of paper frozen inside.

"Peter Langley," I read. I looked at Bea. "So old Pete's hit the dust?"

"I don't want to talk about it."

Langley was in real estate. He'd gone to high school with both of us and Bea had been dating him for months. Now he was consigned to Siberia, destined to live out the rest of his life frozen in a glass vial in Bea's freezer.

He was in good company. Jordan Perrelli, Cruiser Bronson, George Dispen, Mickey Jordan and Andrew Clark were all similarly preserved. Although Bea said that it was her way of dealing with her broken heart, truthfully, she had broken up with most of them. In psychobabble I think it just gave her a sense of closure to chill them out.

I put Peter Langley back in the freezer to join his frozen brethren.

"You know, sometimes I think it'd be easier if you were a prairie dog," I offered.

"A prairie dog?"

"Yeah, they're only in heat three to four hours a year."

She considered this for a moment.

"Is that all at one time or spread out over the year?"

"All at one time."

She wrinkled her nose, a nose I'd always envied. "What if the prairie dog's boyfriend has car trouble?"

"S.O.L."

"So what about the show?"

"Sure, I'll go." What the heck, normally I'd have to spend thirty bucks for the privilege of getting crushed by hundreds of people and clawing my way to a few hors d'oeuvres. Sunday, at least, would be a freebie.

Bea handed me a bag of pig chow. "She'll eat this when she can't find anything else."

It was a twenty-pound bag, barely opened. Somehow I

didn't think that Bea was envisioning this as a respite, but more as a permanent solution.

"I thought you'd like her," I said.

"Oh I do," she said, "I just can't stand having her around."

I retrieved Petunia from the backyard and put her in the truck.

On the way home I discovered that although she was housebroken, she was not truck-broken. By the time I picked up the mail, "we" had had two accidents in Priscilla.

It was dark by the time I got home and my late arrival made for a joyous homecoming since no one had been fed dinner. The bunkhouse was dark, so I assumed Martín and Cori Elena were out for the evening.

Mrs. Fierce and Blue greeted me and Petunia enthusiastically and were pleased with their stone-cold hamburgers. Dream and Gray came running up nickering a horsey chatter to me as I dumped flakes of alfalfa hay in their feed bins and the chickens, already roosted for the evening, deigned to flutter down from lofty heights to peck at the lay pellets I scattered across the dirt. As I passed the pond, I dribbled scratch along its banks and even the ducks pulled their heads out from under their wings in order to assault the grains in the earth.

After all the animals were fed, I went to work on the tailgate of the truck. With soap and water and a lot of elbow grease I was finally able to scrub the oily paint off Priscilla. The close-range shot had left a dent in the tailgate and I found myself cursing Hank Brewster anew.

Finally done, I stopped in the winter garden and pinched off a few leaves of romaine and iceburg lettuce.

It was after seven by the time I got into the house. A single blinking light greeted me from the answering machine. I punched the Play button.

"Trade, it's Abel." Messenger's deep baritone filled the kitchen. "I sent a couple of detectives over to see Joanne Devlin at her home last night. She can't give us a positive on the kids, but thinks that they may be the ones the man brought to the plant. I'll let you know if anything else turns up."

In all of my excitement of finding Rodney Johnson, I had neglected to call Abel and tell him of my discovery. Was it forgetfulness or did a little part of me want to play Nancy Drew? Did I want to solve this thing on my own? I decided that another day or two of not telling Abel about Johnson probably wouldn't make any difference in his investigation or the ultimate result, if indeed there was going to be any result at all. No, I'd wait a few days in case the blue lady got in touch with Brisha Johnson and she called me.

I called Victoria Carpenter and brought her up to date on the investigation.

"You've found them, Trade! God, I can't believe you've actually got their names."

Although I was also pleased with identifying Matthew and Mark Johnson, Victoria sounded so surprised that I wondered what she thought she'd been paying me for.

"Do you remember if one of the children had a deformed arm?"

There was a long silence before she replied. "No, I'm sorry, it just isn't there. Is it important?"

"Frankly, I don't know. No one's going to be prosecuted unless we come up with hard evidence. We need bodies, Vicki."

"I was just a little kid." She sounded defensive.

"I know you're doing the best you can. Keep up the good work," I said before hanging up.

I washed the fresh lettuce leaves and wrapped them in a towel to crisp in the refrigerator for a few minutes while I chopped a Granny Smith apple into neat little chunks. Since the pecan trees had just gifted us with an ample supply of nuts last month, I reached in the freezer and grabbed a handful of shelled pecans out of a plastic bag and threw them into my salad bowl. After tearing up the lettuce and tossing it with the apples, pecans and some crumbled Feta cheese, I topped it with red wine vinegar and olive oil. I sprinkled some fresh Parmesan cheese on an English muffin and threw it under the broiler until it was all soft and bubbly. A glass of merlot topped off my meal.

Although it was the end of the day, I was finally sitting down with the morning newspaper. Since I was tired, I skimmed through it quickly, reading only the lead paragraphs. One story caught my eye, though. A white supremacist, on trial for murdering a prostitute in Florida, filed a motion asking that he be allowed to wear his Ku Klux Klan robe in the courtroom. He also requested a name change on all of the documents relative to his case, stating his preferred substitution, "the honorable and respected name of Hi Hitler."

Sounded sort of like that game we used to play where we sat in a circle and someone whispered in our ear and then we in turn whispered in the kid's ear next to us and so on all the way around the circle. What eventually came out had little or no resemblance to what went in the first ear. Only with this dumb shit, "Heil Hitler" had evolved into "Hi Hitler." But then I never thought guys who dressed up in bedsheets and terrorized people were particularly brilliant anyway.

While I did the dinner dishes, the virtue of my light dinner hit me so I headed straight for another Twinkie, but this time I had the real thing.

I smiled halfway through it. Not because it was so good, which it was, but because I remembered the Twinkie Defense. A defense psychiatrist in a murder trial in San Francisco years ago had argued that his client had become violent after pigging out on junk food, like Twinkies.

As I got ready for bed, I remembered the book that Victoria Carpenter had given me. I retrieved it from the living room and went to bed armed with *Love's Finest Hour*.

Right before I fell asleep, my thoughts drifted back to the unfortunate pairing of Phelan Brewster and Rodney Johnson. If we did nail him, I prayed that there would be no Twinkie Defense to save his sorry ass.

I was jarred awake in the middle of the night by the telephone ringing. When I answered it there was no one there, just a static crackling on the line.

Half-asleep, I offered two "hello's." The crackling continued. It didn't sound like a true telephone-line problem, more like a technique I use when I'm trying to track down someone at home but don't want to talk to them. Cellophane crunched up in front of the mouthpiece does a fine job of mimicking a legitimate line dysfunction. Was someone checking to see if I was home? And why?

As I fumbled in the dark to replace the handset, the breathing and moaning began.

"Hello," I repeated in a futile effort to try to identify my caller.

A high-pitched scream, not unlike that of a rabbit being caught by a coyote, came over the line. Although I couldn't tell if it was made by a human, or an animal, it was enough to make my stomach cartwheel.

"Bitch!"

I was wide awake now, for the single word was strung out, dripping with venom from a muffled voice.

"Blood-red on white looks good on you."

"Hank?" I was remembering the paint on Priscilla's tailgate. Was that the reference? "Hank, is that you?"

"Your blood will beat you to hell."

I clutched the phone to my ear, straining to try to identify the low whisper, but I couldn't even tell if it was a man or a woman.

"Curiosity killed the cat."

That phrase again. Victoria had said that her mother used it. Could this somehow be Dorothy Brewster? Did they let them get near phones in the state mental hospital?

The heavy breathing returned.

"Who in the hell is this?" I asked.

"Come say hello, bitch, I'm on a cellular phone in front of your house."

I slammed the receiver down and fumbled in my bedside drawer for my .38. Grabbing my glasses, for there was no time to put on contacts, I dashed to the living-room window and stood to one side, carefully peeling back the drape. Blue and Mrs. Fierce were silently on my heels. If someone was really there, why weren't they barking?

This case was really getting to me. Not only was I obsessed with it, but now someone was becoming obsessed with me. Obsessed enough to kill? I had to be getting close to something, but what? Just because I'd found the Johnson boys didn't mean I knew where they were buried. Or who had killed them. But something I was doing made my midnight caller nervous. Very nervous.

What was that reflection in the orchard? I squinted to make out what it was. Could someone have driven a car out there? I could hear my heart beat in my ears. Was this a ruse to divert my attention to the front of the house so someone could break in the back? And then I remembered. It was a ladder we'd left in the orchard when we'd been picking pecans. There wasn't a car there after all.

I ran to the kitchen and looked out to the screened porch. Petunia licked the glass door, the pond shimmered beyond, and as near as I could tell, there was nothing unusual happening in the yard.

Quickly, I checked the rest of the house.

Nothing.

30

ALTHOUGH THERE WERE NO MORE CRANK CALLS I HAD TROUBLE sleeping the rest of the night. The few times I did drift off, nightmares assaulted me. I jumped out of bed after one such dream and checked every window and every door in the house. When I was sure that sleep had indeed deserted me, I rolled out of bed. The clock read four-thirty.

The outside thermometer hovered at twenty, so I bundled up in my down jacket and set out to do the morning chores.

My lighting isn't terrific, although there are floodlights anchored above the screened porch in the back, one of which almost reaches the pond. And there are lights at the barn, but in between is dead man's land, where a flashlight is definitely in order. Of course on moonlit nights, one isn't required. Luckily, by the time the rattlesnakes wake up from their winter nap the days are longer and the sun rises earlier, also eliminating the need for artificial light.

But this was no moonlit or spring morning so I fumbled with the Mag-Lite and stumbled into the darkness.

When the light hit the chicken coop, Dudley Do-Right, rooster son of Phyllis the Polish hen and the itinerant Romeo who drifted into the ranch one Mother's Day, began crowing. He's silly that way. Not too sure about what constitutes a sunrise and what does not, but will happily accommodate any flashlight beam or headlights slicing through the dark of night. Honest daylight is definitely not a prerequisite for his performance.

When I finally got back inside the house, I had worked up a healthy appetite, spurred by my light dinner the night before. I scrambled a couple of fresh eggs, slathered them with salsa, sprinkled cheese on top and dumped the whole creation into a flour tortilla.

I'm one of those people who, if I'm eating alone, likes to read something. I think this stems from my childhood when I would sit and read the back of the milk carton or the cereal box. Of course cereal boxes back then were a lot more interesting. You could send away for secret decoder rings and a free deed to an inch of Alaskan real estate.

Lacking a milk carton or cereal box I tried reading *Love's Finest Hour* while I ate, but I was having a hard time getting into the sixteenth-century Celtic novel. Maybe Victoria Carpenter was like Jean Auel, I'd like her if I'd started in the beginning.

The two Ku Klux Klan books were sitting on the table ready to be returned to the library so I thumbed through the Kennedy book, pausing to reread the Superman section. In Kennedy's role as an undercover Klansman he hit upon the idea of having Superman take on the Klan. At that time the popular superhero was on the radio every day. Feeding the scriptwriters all of the Klan's private roles and rituals, a set of programs was written and updated constantly as the secret passwords changed.

Klansmen throughout America were coming home to find their children dressed in ersatz Superman costumes playing "Superman against the Klan" and mocking that which they held so dear. The caped crusader took on this particular enemy for a month as the secrets of the hate group were broadcast throughout America. The radio program culminated in a dual result: KKK membership fell off, and throughout the country children were exposed to the evils of the Klan.

Martín was getting into his pickup when I headed out the door. When he saw me, he closed the truck door and walked over.

"The tractor's a hundred percent," he offered.

"When are you leaving?"

"I've got a few things to finish up here so probably day after tomorrow."

"How's Tía Maria?"

He grinned. "Pretty damned sick. She's getting sicker every day."

"Has Cori Elena suggested going with you?"

He shook his head. "I already told her it would be hard, since she's still married."

"I thought she was divorcing him."

"She is. She just hasn't gotten around to it yet. You know Cori Elena."

Hadn't gotten around to it or didn't want to until something better than Martín came along? Jake Hatcher sure didn't fit that bill, in my opinion.

"So when did you and Jake Hatcher become such good *amigos?*" I asked, feeling like a bitch. But Martín was no dummy and I figured he'd be wondering about Jake's hanging around too.

"It's not me. He's here to see Cori Elena."

I raised an eyebrow.

"Not what you think, *Chiquita*. He used to date her aunt a long time ago."

"Yeah?"

"They talk a lot about her. Cori Elena likes that, since she was a little kid when she left. When Jake talks about her aunt it makes her feel better."

Yeah. And I bet seeing Cori Elena's little brown *chi chis* made Jake Hatcher feel a ton better too, I thought, but said nothing.

It sounded to me like a great way to cover up an affair. Was history repeating itself? Cori Elena had already broken Martín's heart once, when she ran off with Lazaro Orantez. Was she about to do it again with Jake Hatcher?

I finally reached the old stage stop at eight, which meant ten o'clock Chicago time. I called the Art Institute of Chicago and asked for Jessica McKinnon, Victoria's younger sister. She worked in the art library and I was put right through.

Jessica knew who I was, for she and Vicki had been in contact with one another.

"Then you know about the Sporting Club?" I asked.

"I know that's what Dad called his hunting buddies."

"Victoria's told you about what she's remembering, about the murders?"

"Sure, we've talked about it at length. My telephone bills are going to show it, too."

"Has she sent you the journals she's been keeping?"

"Yes, hold a minute, please."

Muzak assaulted my ears while she caught another line. My eyes watched the second hand sweep by on the office wall clock.

"Sorry, where were we? The journals, you mean the stuff about the killings?"

"Yes. Does any of that ring a bell?"

"God, I don't know. Truthfully, I probably don't want to know. This thing's wrecking all of us. Vicki's not talking to Dad or Hank and they're pressuring me that she's out of her mind. Of course, that runs in the family."

I said nothing, remembering Dorothy Brewster at the Arizona State Hospital.

"Vicki keeps saying that seeing Jasmine brought it on, she's my daughter. But I would have been just a little younger than Jasmine's age now when all of this happened and I'm not remembering the kind of stuff Vicki is."

"Do you have memories from that age?" I asked.

"Sure, doesn't everyone? But they're fragmented. God, I have trouble remembering anything up until about junior high."

"The picnics?"

"Yes, I remember some picnics. And I remember Dad's friends around all the time."

"Dan Daglio?"

"Doesn't ring a bell."

"Trevor Osborne? Robinson? Stone?"

"Osborne and Robinson were Dad's best friends. They've been around all of my life."

"But you don't remember any of the things that your sister has written?"

There was a long pause on the other end of the line.

"Not in the detail that she's written, no."

"But you remember some things?"

"Look, I'm not sure about anything. I don't have awful nightmares the way Vicki does. Nothing is haunting me."

"If you did remember something similar to what your sister has written about, would you think that it was a memory or chalk it up to imagination?"

"Mine or hers?" She laughed.

"It doesn't matter."

She got serious again. "I don't know."

There was another long pause. I said nothing, for I had the feeling that this was a bit like being in an automobile accident where the shards of glass were slowly oozing out.

"Okay, I do remember a little, but it's not much and it's not like what Victoria has written."

I waited.

"I remember a picnic where there was a really big black man. I think he was a friend of my dad's. He was like a giant. He was just there, that's all."

"Did he have two little boys with him?"

"I don't remember any."

"What did this black man do at the picnic?"

"Do? What do you mean?"

"Well, did he play ball, or talk to your mother or the other women? Did he eat?"

"Eat? No I don't remember him eating. I don't know, maybe he left before we had the picnic."

"That's it?" I asked, trying to keep the disappointment out of my voice. "You remember one black man one time at a Sporting Club picnic?"

"Yes," she said in a small voice.

"Well, do you remember what you did that day?"

"I went for a walk with my mother and the other women and children. We were looking for pottery shards in the desert, I guess, we used to do that a lot."

"Did Victoria or Hank ever tell you about a body they found in a shed?"

"Not then, but I was the youngest one, maybe they didn't want me to know."

"Maybe not."

"Look, I'd tell if I could remember. I mean I'm not one

of these Pollyanna types that thinks the family should be preserved at all costs. I just don't remember, that's all."

"Do the names Danny Boy or Oz mean anything to you?"

"No."

She promised to call me if she remembered anything else.

After hanging up, I called Samantha Trilby-Smith at the university. She sounded very friendly on the telephone and we agreed on an appointment the next afternoon.

Eight-thirty our time was an hour earlier in California. I tried Charley Stone anyway, only to reach a house sitter who told me that Stone and the Missus had loaded their Airstream and headed to Baja for the winter. There was no telephone number for them, although she did have a number at the General Popo tire outlet in Santa Rosalia, did I want that? I declined.

My last call was to Michael Burns, Victoria Carpenter's Tucson therapist. When I was finally put through to him, he wasn't very helpful.

"I can't possibly discuss one of my patients with you," he said. "That would be unethical."

"How about if you had the patient's permission?"

"I highly discourage you from seeking even a hypothetical patient's acquiescence on this."

"Is that true of all your patients, or just the ones with repressed memory problems?"

"If you have a specific general question, I may be able to help you," he sniffed. "If not, then our conversation is over."

"Hypothetically then, what can you tell me about recovering childhood memories?"

There was a long silence on the other end of the phone before he answered. "Recovered memories often emerge with increasing clarity the longer one pursues them. If someone is in treatment for such a condition, it would be helpful for the patient to stay focused and not be distracted."

"In your opinion, is your hypothetical patient mentally ill?" It was a wild shot and one I knew would probably not be rewarded. I was right.

"I'm not at liberty to discuss the mental health of any of my patients with you, Miss Ellis."

I gritted my teeth, thanked him for his time and hung up the phone.

I pulled into Dragon Links Miniature Golf around eleven. Its hideous landscape has made it a notorious local landmark easily visible from Oracle Road. Truly tasteless in design, it sports grotesque gargoyles perched on gloomy castles, manticores hosting a man's face, lion's body and scorpion's tail, a seven-headed multicolored hydra and a huge red griffin with an eagle's head and wings on top of a lion's body and tail. Miscegenation is rife at Dragon Links.

Its signature piece was a great winged purple dragon with formidable horns and long, sharp fangs dripping blood. During operating hours the dragon's red eyes flash with the intensity of a strobe light, while its mouth slowly opens and quickly shuts, exposing a brace of three-foot-long teeth and a rubbery pink tongue. Every hour on the hour a stream of smoke pours out of the dragon's nostrils, a feat that infuriates the county fathers and local tree huggers, as they explore yet another ordinance to still the fire breather's offensive breath. So far, Robinson's attorneys have been able to thwart these efforts.

I found Dave Robinson, or at least his rear end, deep in the dragon's mouth, perched on the back part of the great dragon's tongue. He held a wrench over his head and was twisting something with it. I leaned around the huge yellow teeth of the beast.

"Mr. Robinson?"

At the sound of my voice he jumped, dropping the tool.

"Sorry, I didn't mean to startle you."

He sat on the tongue, facing me.

"Well you sure as hell did. Who are you?"

"Trade Ellis," I said, unsure of whether I should crawl in the mouth and shake his hand or just stand my ground. I opted for the latter. "I'm a private investigator."

"Oh shit," he said, "is this another personal injury deal? You better talk to my lawyer."

"Oh no, nothing like that," I attempted to reassure

him, although I was not sure at all that what I had to say would be reassuring. "I've been retained by Victoria Carpenter."

I watched him carefully, but he seemed oblivious to her name, as he wiped the grease from the wrench on his drawstring cotton pants and then retrieved the tool. He scooted across the dragon's tongue on his bottom, got to the top of it, rolled to one side, ducked the dragon's teeth and stood up. Obviously, this was a feat he had performed many times before.

"Pleased to meet ya," he said, extending his hand.

He looked about eighty, very fit, with white hair peeking out from under a black Colorado Rockies baseball cap. His long sleeves were rolled up and like Brewster he was sporting a tattoo on one forearm. This one, however, read *Semper Fi*.

"Damn thing won't smoke," he said, pointing his wrench back at the dragon. "Left nostril's gone haywire."

I chalked it up as a small victory for the tree huggers.

"Victoria Carpenter," I repeated, "has hired me to look into the Sporting Club."

"What about it?"

"Then you remember it?"

"Well, sure. Hell, I used to hunt with her daddy all the time. In fact, I still see a lot of him. What's this all about?"

"Phelan hasn't mentioned it to you, then?"

He shook his head.

"Do you have children, Mr. Robinson?"

His eyes narrowed. "What's that got to do with anything?"

"I just wondered if you had any children who might have been members of the club?"

"My kids were grown by the time we moved here. Now what's this all about?"

"Victoria remembers some picnics that the club had, picnics where black people were guests."

"We never had black people at our doings."

"Do you remember a man named Rodney Johnson?"

"No."

"A black man with two little kids?"

He shook his head again.

"Or maybe a really big black man who had been hitchhiking?"

Robinson played with the wrench. "I told you, there weren't any black people in the Sporting Club."

"Not in it, just attending the picnics."

"Did Victoria tell you that?"

"Uh huh."

"She's a writer, you know, writes those books that women like to read."

"I know."

"Sounds to me like she's making this all up."

"Well, she's got a good imagination. She says they were killed, beaten to death with baseball bats by members of the Sporting Club."

"Balderdash! Sure we killed things. We killed a lot of deer, pig, antelope, you name it. But killing people's against the law. If it hadn't been, maybe we would have tried that too, I don't know, but we didn't."

I shuddered at his admission that he would kill if it weren't against the law.

"But we didn't," he repeated. "Now if that's all you want to know, you'll have to excuse me, I've got to get back to my dragon." He dropped to his knees and began climbing down the huge pink tongue.

I was walking back to Priscilla when I remembered I'd forgotten to ask about Daglio. I headed back down the concrete path to the fire-breathing dragon. Robinson was still inside, sitting at the back of the tongue, only now instead of a wrench, he held a cellular telephone to his ear. When he saw me he covered the mouthpiece.

"What?"

"Was Dan Daglio in the Sporting Club?"

"I don't remember, you'll have to ask him."

These guys were neck and neck with the Cosa Nostra in terms of their vows of *omerta*.

As I pulled back onto Oracle Road I wondered if the Sporting Club had played poker in addition to hunting.

So far, even their faces were not talking.

31

ALTHOUGH IT WOULD HOLD NO SURPRISES FOR HER, I FAXED MY second weekly report to Victoria Carpenter early Friday afternoon and then headed into Tucson.

Parking is always tricky around the university area, but Friday afternoons are better than most as the college kids head out to greener pastures. I managed to find a pay parking lot within a couple of blocks of the Anthropology building.

After taking an interminable trip in an old freight elevator, I finally surfaced on the fourth floor. A few bad turns later and I found the Human Identification Laboratory.

An eager grad student greeted me.

"You must be the private investigator." His deduction led me to believe that lab visitors were few.

"Yes."

"Then you want Sam," he said, leading me to a cubbyhole created by a bank of filing cabinets conjoined with the walls of the building.

Dr. Trilby-Smith was a tiny little thing—I doubted whether she'd even hit five feet—with a head full of permed gray curls, and granny glasses hanging off the tip of her stubby nose. With her aristocratic-sounding name I'd expected someone cool and regal, or even expected, since she was a forensic anthropologist, a mad-scientist cast about her. Instead, she looked like she belonged in a Betty Crocker test kitchen.

"Let's go in here," she said, leading me into an adjoining room. Although she'd been with the university for years, she still carried a hint of a British accent.

Where the front room had resembled a typical office, this one dropped all pretense of being ordinary. My first clue was the anatomically correct skeleton dangling from the coatrack, along with assorted white lab coats and a red cardigan sweater. Glassed cases held vials, beakers, slides, cover slips and boxes of autopsy gloves, while photographs of burned bones adorned the walls.

Slides were clipped on a rail above a kitchen sink and a corner of a chalkboard was marked:

Save:
Cauc ♀ 24–28 yrs(rib)
p113 20–24
5'7 ½" + or − 2.5".

It was mind-boggling as I tried to take it all in while also concentrating on talking to the pathologist.

"Here, let me clear this off for you," Trilby-Smith said, moving to the gray work table. She gently pushed the little piles of bones that were resting there off to one side. The rest of the table was covered with gray plastic bins filled with bones and stapled paper bags marked with things like "verts" and "scaps."

"Are those," I hesitated, pointing to the small bones, "someone?"

"Oh yes." She held one of the bones up. "These particular bones represent a body that has been burned in a somewhat clandestine manner."

There weren't many bones in the piles.

"This is the whole thing?"

"Oh no. Only about one-twentieth, actually. There, you see, is the pile of hands." She pointed to a few small bones. "That's the clavicle pile and the larger ones there are the ribs."

"And you'll be able to figure out who this was?" I asked, trying to keep skepticism out of my voice.

"Well, perhaps not precisely," she said. "We've been able to determine, first of all, that there is actually not more than one individual involved. We have determined that it was a Caucasian female and we are currently working on our other identifications. Cause of death though, I'm afraid, may be difficult on this one unless we find knife or tool marks." She tried to hand me the piece of bone.

I hesitated. This was against all of my ancestral teachings. Apaches are very careful about dead people. We don't say their names after they are dead for fear of bringing their ghost back. We don't touch bodies. Yet Trilby-Smith was trying to hand me a piece of a body, even if it was old dried-up bone.

I swallowed hard and took her offering.

It was deceptively light. As I turned it over, I could see tidy tiny black writing marking a case number. I quickly returned it to the table and rubbed my hands on my Levi's.

"Please sit." Trilby-Smith pointed to a chair. If she'd noticed my discomfort at handling the chunk of bone, she chose to ignore it. "Coffee? I'm having one."

I accepted, and the graduate student reappeared with a steaming mug.

From my seated vantage point I now noticed a row of ceramic skull coffee mugs lined up across the top of the case. They were flanked on one end by a resin sculpture of a puzzled primate pondering a human skull.

I quickly explained about Victoria Carpenter and the murders that may or may not have occurred over thirty years ago.

Trilby-Smith nodded at the mention of Abel Messenger's name.

"Yes, I'm familiar with the case. Did he share the water witcher with you?"

I shook my head.

"Apparently a dowser was called in, a gentleman with a curious wooden stick and an overabundance of confidence. He knew the exact location of where the bodies were buried and the depth of the graves. On his recommendation the police went out into the Santa Rita Mountains and started digging. Unfortunately it was a fruitless effort."

That sly old Abel hadn't shared the witcher with me.

"Dr. Trilby-Smith," I began.

"Sam, please. Call me Sam, everyone does."

"Okay, Sam, I guess I'm wondering if those murders

did in fact take place, and if there were unidentified bones found years ago, where would they be?"

"We don't have them. I've already been over that with the police. We have very little in the way of black bones, maybe four to five in the last ten years. Children are also in short supply."

"Is there a reason for that?"

"Oh yes. Someone usually cares about them and instigates a search. The people we have here are being stored for evidence. None of them are black juveniles."

"If you had the bones of these children, would you be able to determine their ages, say if they were five or six years old?"

"Oh, indeed. Children are fairly easy to identify, through their dental maturation, their long bones, their growth plates and so on. Sex, however, is more difficult to determine on the young."

My eyes roamed the room as I weighed the good and the bad news. If the kids were here, they could tell they were black and the right ages. The bad news was, of course, that the kids weren't here.

"Then they probably haven't been found, if they existed at all." I was careful here for I had the distinct impression that Trilby-Smith did not believe that the Sporting Club murders had taken place.

"Not necessarily. They may have been buried."

"Buried?"

"In potter's field. We don't keep all unidentified bodies here, just the ones that are important to a case, or that indicate evidence of foul play."

"Who determines that?"

"The medical examiner, oh no, let's see, how long ago?"

"Thirty years."

"Hmm, let me think." She took off the granny glasses and rubbed the red line marching across the bridge of her nose. "No, no, that's not right, thirty years ago we were under the coroner system. The coroner would have made the decision for the postmortem examination of the remains. He would have decided whether or not there was a case."

"And if he decided there was?"

"If there was evidence of foul play then an investigation would have been called for, and the coroner would then determine whether or not the body was posted."

"Posted?"

"Autopsied, for evidence of murder. He would then have hired a pathologist, who would have been either an M.D. or a hospital pathologist, to look at the remains to determine the cause of death. If that was the case, then the coroner would call for an inquest and would impanel a jury."

"And if not?"

"If there was no evidence of foul play, either by the pathologist, or by the coroner not ordering an investigation, then the bodies would be buried in potter's field."

I thought about this for a long moment.

"I wonder how I would check those records."

"Hmmm, that may be problematic. Thirty years ago we didn't have the computerization we have now. There would have been at least three sets of files—the Tucson Police Department, the South Tucson Police Department, and the Sheriff's Office."

A difficult thought was beginning to form in my head.

"How are they buried in potter's field?"

"Wooden boxes with plastic waterproof covers."

I remembered the chalky stuff that Victoria had told me about on the body she had seen in the refrigerator box in the shed.

"What kind of an effect would tossing lime on a body have?"

"Well, lye has a tendency to inhibit oxidation, just the opposite of what you'd expect. In fact, there used to be a substance called 'quicklime' that was supposed to speed up decomposition. It actually had the opposite effect, acting as an inhibitor."

"So if lime were thrown on a body, it might actually slow the decomposition?"

"Yes."

I couldn't think of any more questions to ask the forensic anthropologist, but I knew that I'd have many more after I'd had a chance to digest what I'd learned. In the meantime, a big machine in one corner of the room had caught my curiosity.

"That machine?" I pointed to it. Fronted with glass and topped with a solid metal vent it looked as though there were a couple of cooking pots perched on metal stands inside. A line of valves ran down each side of the glass front.

"That's a fume hood," Trilby-Smith explained. "We use it to achieve a clean-bone situation, because it rids the bones of grease, tissue, bugs and so on."

My stomach twitched a bit. If I caught her drift, the thing was used for kind of like cooking up human soup where all the stuff falls off the bones. Yuk.

I now noticed the kitchen utensils hanging above the sink. Bottle brushes, spatulas, basters, strainers and funnels. All used, I was sure, for the cooking of the dismal brew.

"Those are Bunsen burners"—she pointed to two tripod-looking things—"the pots are old pressure cookers where we place the material. We use a high-enzyme detergent to help knock it down, along with sodium carbonate."

I could imagine the smell that would result from such a recipe and now knew why the front was glassed.

"The fumes are then all vented to the roof." She pointed overhead.

"Does it smell?" I asked a stupid question.

"Oh it can be dreadful, depending upon the decomposition, but the venting takes care of most of it. Before we got the fume hood it was ghastly. We opened the doors and windows and still the people on the street were complaining, to say nothing of the anthropology classes. In those days the flies would come pouring in the minute the windows were open. They have wonderful instincts, you know."

"What do you do with the stuff that comes off?" Why, oh why, do I have this sick sense to know everything?

"It goes in those." She pointed to some red plastic biowaste garbage bags. "Then we put it in the freezer."

Her Betty Crocker test kitchen even had a refrigerator/ freezer. I assumed the med-waste stuff went in the top door.

"And you keep your lunches and Cokes in the bottom?"

"Oh no," she laughed. "In fact, we never eat in this room."

"I'm not surprised."

"Oh, not for the reasons you'd imagine. No, we don't want to chance ingesting some long-lived virus."

I wondered about the coffee I had just consumed.

"No, we use the bottom part for X-ray film and some of our more volatile solutions, the thirty-percent concentrated hydrogen peroxide, chloroform and amyl alcohol. It's a special explosion-proof refrigerator, specially wired so that it cannot ignite volatile gases by exploding."

I glanced at the wall clock. The time was pushing five, the busy second hand sweeping around a skull face, actually a photograph of a skull plastered across the face of the clock.

My look did not go unnoticed by Trilby-Smith.

"That was a young woman found five or six years ago by a hunter up on a ridge. He put the body in a beer box and went on with his hunt, turning it in a few days later to the S.O."

"Do you know who she is?"

"We think we know who she is, but we can't prove it."

On the way out, I stopped to look at six skulls perched on one of the filing cabinets.

"Those are models?" I asked, with an unusual degree of perception.

"Yes. Done by six different artists."

"How interesting."

"Quite, when you realize they are all supposed to be the same person."

I gave her an incredulous look. The six models were all totally different.

"And it becomes even more amusing when you compare each model to the artist who crafted it. They all resemble their creators."

We laughed about that as she walked me to the front door of her office.

"Sam, about the coroner," I said.

"Remember now, we don't have one anymore. Everything goes through the M.E. these days."

"But back then, who appointed him, I mean how did he get his job?"

"Why, he was elected, of course. Let me think." She tapped a tiny foot against the gray linoleum. "Thirty years ago. Hmm, I think it was Louis Shriber."

"Louis Shriber," I repeated. The name didn't mean a thing to me.

On the drive back to the ranch I kept thinking about potter's field. Could the Johnson children be in so obvious a place?

Perhaps.

But how in the hell was I going to convince anyone to go looking for them there?

32

I AWAKENED IN THE MIDDLE OF THE NIGHT IN A COLD SWEAT. I HAD been digging a hole in the desert, madly searching for something. It was one of those disturbing, fuzzy nightmares that I tried to analyze upon awakening even as it was floating away from my mental grasp.

What did it mean? I usually don't pay a lot of attention to my dreams, although I know that a lot of people are interested in their subtle meanings. I go for the quick hit. What was I searching for?

And of course the only answer I could come up with was Matthew and Mark Johnson.

After breakfast the next morning I was saddling Gray when Martín came out to the tack room.

"¡Buenos días, Chiquita!"

I noticed his crisply ironed shirt. He was wearing Levi's with a sharp crease down the front, and his good Stetson, so I wasn't surprised when he said, "I'm heading out for Mexico."

"Good for you."

"I, uh, don't have much experience with this sort of thing."

"No, I guess not."

"So I really don't know what to expect," he said.

"Love."

Even as I said it, I wasn't sure what I meant. According

to Cori Elena, there was nothing for Martín to know of Quinta.

"I'll try to be back Monday or Tuesday," he said. "And then we'll get serious about gathering cattle."

"A day or two really won't make much difference," I said. "Take as much time as you need."

There were tears in his brown eyes as we hugged and I could feel him shake within my grasp. I said a silent prayer that things would go well with him in Mexico.

"Vaya con Dios, mí hermano," I bid him farewell.

After he left, I bridled Gray and headed out for the mountains. I'd spent so much time on the Sporting Club this week that I needed the balm of the desert and the fresh air to clear the cobwebs gathering in my head. I was thinking clearly enough to throw on an orange vest over my jacket, as deer season had opened yesterday. There was no way I wanted some eager hunter to mistake either Gray or me for a mule deer.

Although it was late November, by mid-morning I had shed my jacket. I stopped at the cottonwoods and let the horse drink his fill from the creek which was now running, thanks to the snowmelt from the Catalina Mountains.

I headed up Dynamite Canyon, a rugged crevasse that owes its name to the cowboys having dynamited it long ago so the cattle could have passage through it up to the grass above. A sliver of a creek ran through here also, and we crisscrossed it working our way up the gorge.

When I came to an old scattered pile of bleached cow bones I found myself again thinking of the Johnson family. If I ever did find the bodies, would there be anything left? Would the coyotes have dug them up and chewed on their bones to the point where even Matthew's deformed arm would not be recognizable? If lime had been thrown on them, would the lye really inhibit decomposition or would it speed things along?

A coyote sat under a mesquite tree, watching my passage. I stopped and we stared at each other for a long moment before he took one rear leg and scratched his ear with it. I wondered if the fleas were stirring. Having satisfied his itch, the coyote took a last look at me and then trotted away, his leisurely amble a far cry from the twenty-five-miles-an-hour pace he was capable of.

As I crossed onto the Coronado National Forest I ran into a cow baby-sitting several large calves. The calves had all been branded and ear-notched, the heifers ear-tagged. The cow's horns were turning inward, threatening to grow into her face. I jockeyed the horse around her until I was able to read her number, 172. Groping in my cantle bag I retrieved my tally book, a leather-covered notepad, and recorded her number in it. When we brought this bunch in, we'd look her up and take a saw to her horns.

That's not always the reason we saw off horns, though. Sometimes we'll have a wicked cow, although the really hurtful ones usually get shipped off the ranch, for none of us is eager to fool with them. But the ones that get a little chargey—that's chargier than what our parameters allow—meet the horn-tipping saw. We take off about six inches of horn, leaving a blunted tip. This causes the cow no real distress other than the temporary inconvenience of her travel plans.

While the process does not hurt the cow, it may save a cowboy or his horse, for when we see an animal whose horns have been tipped, we realize that the cow may have less than a sunny disposition.

The horse was blowing pretty good by the time I topped out on the lower ridge. I stopped and let him catch his breath. From there I grabbed a fairly bright cattle trail up to Fanning Tank.

The stock pond, named after a local cowboy who years ago had overseen its construction, lay nestled below a small hill. Snowmelt dribbled off the mountain, down a creek into the small pond which was now overfilled and draining to the *bajada* below.

I hobbled Gray, loosened his cinch and let him nibble on the dried grass around the pond while I ate lunch. Closing my eyes for a minute, I was lulled to sleep by the warm Arizona sun against my face.

I awakened slowly, with the eerie feeling that I was not alone. Sitting as still as I could, my eyes swept the landscape before me. Just out of my left eye, I spied a bushy golden something. I held my breath while I debated about turning my head.

The suspense was killing me and when I finally succumbed, I caught a troop of *chulos*, or coatimundis, trotting away. The funny-looking creatures, with their bushy, raccoon-type bodies, anteater-looking noses and two-foot-long tails had been after the remnants of my lunch. I watched the pack of thieves disappear into the thick brush.

Seeing the coatis drifted me back to thoughts of the Sporting Club. How many people were involved? Robinson? Daglio? Their wives? Being a party to murder, no matter how reluctant one might be, could certainly drive you over the edge. Dorothy Brewster was in a mental institution and Libby Osborne had committed suicide. Jerri Osborne looked as though she might be trying to survive cancer. As for the rest of the children, there was no telling what kind of emotional baggage they might be carrying thirty years later. With all of the people involved, how on earth would I ever be able to pull any of it together? And if the murders had really happened, why was Victoria Carpenter the only one talking?

As I tightened Gray's cinch, I decided that I couldn't torment myself with the logistics of the thing. Phelan Brewster was in my sights and it was enough for me to keep him there. If I nailed him, then maybe it would be like playing dominoes, where the rest of the pieces would fall into place.

I circled around the ridge, climbing a bit higher before dropping down onto the Deer Camp trail. Briefly I considered heading back up the mountain to Deer Camp but then recalled the half-heart I had scratched on the old picnic table. Remembering my promise to complete it once the case was over, I sadly turned the horse back down the mountain.

The Speed Tanks on Sutherland Flats were so named because of the old highway speed-limit sign that someone had swiped years ago and ditched in the desert. We'd found it and now it covered the float, protecting it from the depravations of the cattle, who find it one of their singular amusements to seek out and destroy anything connected with a watering system.

As Gray played with the water in the steel tank, I watched a group of cows and calves. They were mostly bedded down, taking it easy during the warmest part of the day, although November's warmth cannot hold a candle to that found in June.

As the momma Brahmas chewed their cuds with sleepy eyes, their babies, for the most part, stretched out and slept. Spotting a couple of unbranded, slick-eared calves, I jotted the numbers of what I thought to be their mothers, in the tally book.

During calving the "drys"—those cows who are either not with calf, or have not yet birthed—hang out together in their own group, and the new mothers do likewise. I don't really know what the cow etiquette is that covers this, but this self-segregation is readily apparent to anyone who has worked cattle.

We settled into an easy lope on the way home. The breeze created from the horse's quick forward motion blew against my face and, for a brief moment, I felt as though I was transported back in time.

If I'd known then what lay ahead of me, maybe I would have cantered the horse a lot longer.

33

Late Sunday afternoon I met Cousin Bea at the Toys R Us parking lot on Oracle Road. I locked Priscilla and left her there and climbed into Bea's Honda Civic for our jaunt to the Mountain Oyster Club.

Parking, never one of the long suits of the club, for it has a fairly small walled parking lot that can become tricky when littered with long-bedded pickup trucks, is a disaster during the Western Art Show. The lot next to the railroad tracks was full, the streets were bulging with nary an empty space, and the Western Tire Center lot across the street was also replete with the vehicles of the art-loving public.

We got lucky. On our second approach to the Western Tire Center an elderly couple was getting into their El Dorado. We waited patiently while the driver took his time maneuvering the huge vehicle out of its space.

The parking situation was a mere prelude to pandemonium. People were backed up onto the sidewalk, awaiting their turn to hand over their tickets and thus gain entrance to probably the niftiest private club in the United States, if not the world.

Every major city in the country has private clubs. They're all pretty much the same. Sterile affairs, frequently perched on the top floor of one of the highest buildings in town affording a view of said city, tables graced with crisp white linen tablecloths and fresh flowers, obsequious help genuflecting all over the member diners and a clientele sporting white long-sleeved Oxford shirts and ties and sport coats or suits. Sneaking a peek under the tables in such clubs will find a predictable assortment of well-polished Bally shoes and nylon-clad female legs slippered in designer pumps.

There is a general feel of gentility that runs among these clubs. And one of familiarity. Having been in one, you can generally assume, with some clarity, the atmosphere you will find in the next.

Not so with the M.O. Club.

Founded by a group of real, honest-to-God cowboys who were tired of the denizens of Tucson's "other" downtown club looking askance when they came in for lunch in their manure-clad cowboy boots and Levi's stained with blood, guts and assorted fluids they earned from riding the range and greasing tractor parts and fixing fence and branding and all the other investitures of their myriad cowboy duties, they decided they wanted a place of their own.

Thus the birth of the Mountain Oyster Club. The first rule was that there would be no rules. And certainly no dress code. A hat rack was moved in to accommodate the cowboys' Stetsons and no one complained if a piece of dried manure fell off a member's boots and onto the floor.

Although the club's membership, once strictly restricted to those with some intimate connection to the cattle industry, has now spawned into somewhat tenuous links—such as a lawyer representing a cattleman—the club is still a casual, cheery place with cowboys littering the bar and dining rooms.

And, judging from today's attendance, everyone in Tucson wanted a glimpse of this private bastion of cowboy culture.

After a long wait, Bea and I finally moved through the foyer and into the bowels of the club. While a mid-afternoon art seminar is always part of the program, we had decided to forgo any edification in this regard.

I felt a little like I was in a stampede, as people milled and pushed all around, trying to get close to the artwork that hung on the crowded walls. Underneath each painting, or sculpture—for there were a few of these strewn about—was a slip with the title of the piece, the artist's name and the price. Underneath this information were numbered lines where prospective purchasers put their names.

This was no simple art show. If more than one person was willing to pay the artist's asking price for the work, then a lottery was held. The drawing would start at five o'clock and we had arrived just under that deadline, so there was the mad rush of people scurrying around to place, or in some cases, scratch out, their names below the prized paintings.

"Toilet-paper painting," Bea said, nodding to a Mary Schaefer work.

Schaefer's paintings always were. With her masterful use of light and shadow, the list with ten lines on it was already full and then another one was Scotch-taped below that and once filled, yet another list was added. The resulting paper trail resembled nothing so much as toilet paper. Bea and I counted the names. Forty-three people were eager to part with four thousand dollars for the privilege of taking the beautiful bougainvillea-draped Mexican hacienda home with them.

We finally squeezed into the bar, and were able to belly up to it. After a few minutes we each held a drink in our hands.

"Why look at you all." Lolly MacKenzie, of the ranching MacKenzie fortune, was hugging both Bea and me. We had known her since we were children. "You girls look just great."

We made small, mad cocktail-party chatter with Lolly and a few other friends before exiting the bar, which was the smallest and most crowded room in the club.

A ringing bell signified the start of the drawing, so I shunned the entrance foyer where I knew it would begin, and made my way to the Horn Room, aptly named after the large heads of dead animals that reside there. From this vantage point, I could stay away from the crowds that were centering around the bell ringer, and still have some hope of seeing the show.

I was studying a Howard Terpning painting of a group

of Indian shamans when I heard a familiar voice behind me.

"Trade, is that you?"

I turned to see Victoria Carpenter, dressed in a long fawn-colored suede skirt, chambray shirt and silk scarf. She was wearing beautiful hand-tooled boots. Briefly I wondered if Paul Bond in Nogales had made them for her.

"Vicki, you look great," I said, not lying this time. She looked a lot spiffier than the first day I had met her in the Mexican restaurant. Maybe Arizona was having a good effect on her sense of style.

"I'm so glad to see you," she gushed. "There's someone I want you to meet."

A woman with overdone ebony hair stood off her elbow. Although ferret-nosed and beady-eyed, she was not unpleasant-looking, in a New York sort of way. Reading glasses, attached to a faux pearl chain, dangled on top of her ample bosom.

"Adele Leaman," Carpenter said. "Adele's my agent, from New York."

"Oh, right. You said something about her coming out." I turned to Leaman. "Welcome to Tucson."

"Oh, it's wonderful," she said. "Is this normal weather for winter here?"

I hesitated. Damn, I'm torn. I hate to lie because that makes Arizona seem less than nirvana, but God, when you tell the truth then all of the damned snowbirds start coming for a week in the winter. The next thing you know, they extend their visits, eventually retire, sell their homes in the East, buy goofy polyester wardrobes and settle out here. Then, to compound matters, they send Christmas cards to all the family and friends they've left behind, showing themselves playing golf in shirtsleeves in December, and then *those* folks get the bright idea to come out. It's a vicious circle.

"No, it's warmer than usual." I chose the lie. Hell, anyone with an ounce of a brain can turn on a television set and see the Tucson Open Golf Tournament in the middle of winter and see green grass, sunny skies and seventy-degree weather. Every year when they run the tournament, the Chamber of Commerce and local resort switchboards are overloaded as Easterners book space. Add to that the world-class Gem and Mineral Show, also a winter event, and the word-of-mouth extolling of Arizona's virtues becomes endless.

So far, this winter has been the most unbearable one we've had, in terms of winter visitors. Why we even bother spending a nickel on advertising for tourists is beyond me. The Open, the Gem and Mineral people and the hordes that have already discovered our blissful state are doing a pretty good job of screwing things up already.

"Mountain oyster?" Belinda, a pretty young thing who had recently been hired by the club, was passing a tray of the signature hors d'oeuvres.

I helped myself to two of the frilly-toothpick-punctured treasures, and dipped them into the cocktail sauce. Victoria and Adele followed my lead.

"Mmmm," sighed Adele, polishing off her first one. "Delicious."

"They are great," Vicki concurred. "I didn't think you had that much water out here. Do they come from a lake or a river?"

"Are they freshwater oysters?" Adele asked.

"Not exactly," I said, popping the second one into my mouth. "They're bulls' balls."

A sick look passed over the ferret's face.

"Bulls?"

"Balls, testicles," I said cheerily. "They castrate them. This is what makes the difference between a bull and a steer."

"Testicles," Vicki repeated in a small voice that told me that in spite of all the game she had eaten as a child, mountain oysters had probably not been a staple in her family menu.

"Uh huh. Taste a lot like chicken, don't you think?"

The two women exchanged glances and I could tell that they probably didn't think they tasted anything at all like chicken.

"The . . . Mountain . . . Oyster . . . Club," the newly educated Adele said slowly.

"Right." I pointed to the red and white carpeting below our feet. Their eyes followed my index finger to the club's logo resting beneath us, two crossed bottles above a bull's full scrotum.

"Excuse me," Vicki said, hand over her mouth as she headed for the ladies' room.

"You're a heifer," I yelled to her retreating back, afraid that in her haste she would not make the distinction that the club had carved into its rest room doors.

"Well, this certainly is unique," the literary agent said.

"The club goes through about two tons a year," I offered, now on my educational high horse.

"Two tons?" Amazement crept into her voice. "How many animals is that?"

"Oh, hard to say, you didn't really have a whole one."

"Oh?"

"They're bigger than that." I used my hands to give her an idea of how big a calf's testicle would actually be. She looked impressed so I continued. "They're cut up in smaller pieces, dipped in batter, then fried. It's kind of like escargot. No one would probably eat them if not for the cocktail sauce."

"Well, it's a first, I assure you."

My mouth was full, so it was a moment before I could ask, "You're here for Vicki's new book?"

"Yes. That and a mini-vacation."

"I'm reading *Love's Finest Hour*." It was a tiny lie. After all, I had started it, hadn't finished it, so wouldn't it still qualify as being in the "still reading" category?

"Lovely book," she said. "We've just sold the foreign rights to the U.K."

"She must research a lot," I said. "I mean all of that sixteenth-century Celtic stuff and all."

"Oh yes, she's very thorough. That's one of the reasons her books are so popular."

"Is she sticking with the same era in her new one?"

"Oh no, no. This one's a departure, a total departure for her. She's been wanting to go mainstream and get out of the romance genre. It's a gamble, in fact I tried to talk her out of it, but her heart's set on trying something new."

"So what's it about?" I asked.

"Murder, mayhem, the usual."

A gnawing feeling was beginning to settle into my stomach.

"Well murder sells," I said lamely.

"Sure, suspense, women in jeopardy, that sort of thing, but I'm not all that confident about this one."

"Why not?"

"She's bringing in a lot of difficult elements. Racism, child abuse, the Ku Klux Klan."

Shit.

I remembered my visit to the Rock Ranch and how Vicki had kicked the books under the table. They had been reference books, all right, but they must have been books about the KKK. They didn't have a thing to do with the romance book she had led me to believe she was writing. No wonder she didn't want me to see them.

My client was writing about the stuff she was paying me to investigate. Was it all a farce? Was she just looking for a way to flesh out her stories and using me to help her do that? James Michener had had paid research assistants, was that what I was doing for Victoria? Everyone was in agreement that she had a good imagination. In fact, most of the people involved who had denied the Sporting Club murders, were attributing all the hysteria to Vicki's fantasies.

Had I been had by a romance writer?

Furious, I left Adele Leaman with a mountain oyster halfway to her mouth. I caught Vicki just as she was leaving the ladies' room.

"We've got to talk," I said, but it probably came out more like a hiss.

"What's happened?"

I propelled her through the Bull Ring room and out onto the patio, which, like the interior of the club, was thick with people. I finally found a quiet spot near Buck McCain's huge cowboy bronze.

"You want to tell me about your book again, the one you're working on?"

She looked confused. "Well, I already told you, it's the usual stuff, woman meets man—"

"Wrong, Vicki. How about woman meets Ku Klux Klan?"

Her face fell and she leaned into the sculpture.

"Your agent's very keen on you. In fact, so keen that she's concerned about the new book you're working on, the one that isn't a romance."

She stared at her boots while I waited.

Finally she whispered, "I'm sorry, I should have told you."

"You're damned right you should have told me! What's going on here, Vicki? Am I your gofer? It can't be cheaper to pay a private eye than a researcher."

"I should have told you," she repeated. "But I was afraid that if I did, you wouldn't have taken my case."

"Well I sure as hell should have known about it. It's a little too close for my tastes. Art mimics life? Or is it just art mimics art?"

"Those things really happened, Trade, I swear." She was crying and black streams of mascara made rivulets down her cheeks.

"Gosh, Vicki, why am I having trouble believing you? I just can't imagine." And with that I spun on my heel and walked off, leaving her with the lifeless cowboy.

As I stumbled through the crowd, I could hear Abel Messenger's earlier caveat ringing in my ears: *Victoria Carpenter's elevator may not go all the way to the top floor.*

34

BEA DROPPED ME OFF AT PRISCILLA AND I HEADED HOME. SINCE the radio was off and I wasn't listening to Books on Tape, tonight was one of the quiet drives. I had a lot to think about.

I thought of all sorts of things I should have said to Victoria Carpenter, and didn't. Isn't it always like that? The quick comebacks and put-downs only come after the opportunity to use them is long gone.

I was still trying to digest what I had learned and frankly, my ego was bruised. Why hadn't I, the great hotshot private detective, been able to uncover the truth about Vicki's book? Instead I'd had to rely on the chance comment of her New York agent to discover that I was being lied to.

Thinking back to the beginning, I'd always doubted her veracity. I remember then that I'd thought her story was too far-fetched to be true. Hell, maybe it was too far-fetched to even make good fiction.

I should have known. She was a writer, a *fiction* writer. And what did fiction writers do? They made things up.

I felt like a sucker just thinking about it. I wondered if the Johnson children were finding their way into her latest book, and the thought of all I'd gone through made me furious. Who were the Johnsons anyway? There was little doubt that the black man Joanne Devlin had remembered was Rodney Johnson and that Matthew and Mark, who had been recalled by their kindergarten teacher, were his children. But so what? They were all probably happy and well, living with their father and his new wife in Georgia.

And Phelan Brewster? Maybe he was just a jerk, but not a liar or a killer.

I kept coming back to writers paying researchers. Still, if Victoria was looking for juicy stuff to add to her already fertile imagination, she was overpaying me. I hadn't given her much in the way of new information. Mostly I had just asked questions and tried to dog an ancient make-believe trail.

While I was furious, I had to admit to some relief that a family had not had to suffer the terrible cruelties and losses that Victoria Carpenter had detailed in her notes to me.

In an effort to derail my ill humor I found myself humming "Danny Boy" again. I was doing that more frequently now. I guess it must have been my subconscious trying to make some sense of the gobbledygook that Dorothy Brewster had graced me with.

In spite of my doubts, I ran through my litany of Daniels. Webster, Quayle, Dapper Dan, Day-Lewis, Boone. My memory seemed to be stuck and I had a hard time coming up with any new Danny Boys.

I thought back to the Brewsters' place. Were there any clues to Danny Boy there? And then I remembered the wooden cross with the suffering Jesus and I finally landed on a new one. Daniel in the Lions' Den. What was that story? My religious education was somewhat short-shrifted. While many Lutheran and Catholic churches were on the reservation and had been for years, many Apaches blended the Apache religion with that proselytized by the Christians. Somehow in the process my family had fallen through the cracks and I now found myself in kind of a made-up religion of my own. I believed in God, talked to plants and animals and felt I had a pretty good sense of right and wrong. But Bible studies had somehow eluded me.

Still, I vaguely remembered the story of Daniel. He had been a dream interpreter for a king and was pretty good pals with him. Then the king was murdered and a new ruler came on board. The new king's advisors were pissed about Daniel's influence so they came up with a scheme whereby anyone who did not worship the king would be in big time *caca*.

They tattled on Daniel, and told the king that he was actually worshiping God instead of him. Naturally this didn't set well with the new king so he tossed old Dan into a lions' pit and sealed the entrance with a huge rock.

The next morning the king was surprised that his dream interpreter had made it through the night unscathed. When he asked Daniel about it, he said that God had sent his angel to shut the lions' mouths.

The story was reminding me of the one I was working on. All those shut mouths, although I doubted whether an angel was involved. Then I cheered up, remembering the ending. The king was pretty impressed with Daniel's survival and so he ended up throwing all the bad guys into the pit and the lions totally ate them, including their bones.

Maybe there was justice in this world, after all.

I was almost to the turnoff to the Vaca Grande when I remembered I was out of dog food. Curly's wasn't open so I had to drive to the Circle K in La Cienega.

Ginny Eske's Blazer was in the lot and as I was walking in, her son, five-year-old Tanner, still dressed in his soccer finery—including socks that threatened to suffocate his knees—came running up to me, hand extended. I held my own out, prepared for the worst.

He gave it to me, a hard high five. "All right!" he hollered. He left me with a stinging right hand as he ran off to catch up with his mother and sisters.

Suddenly a sadness enveloped me. I was drawn into a vision of two other little boys, long ago, who had been cheated out of their childhoods. Knowing what I now knew—that Victoria was writing about the Ku Klux Klan and had probably made up the entire Johnson story—why was I tormenting myself? And then it hit me. I had so much invested emotionally in this case that I had to see it through to the end. Even if it was all an elaborate smoke screen strewn by an overzealous novelist.

"Wait for me." Madison Eske, Ginny's three-year-old, was running after her brother, who refused to slow down. "Key key head!"

"Madison," Ginny warned.

Both kids disappeared into the store.

"Key key head?" I asked.

"She's not allowed to say 'pee pee head,' which is what she really wants to say, so she says 'key key head' instead, although everyone knows that what she really means is 'pee pee head.'"

I bought a small bag of dog food, enough to last Mrs. Fierce and Blue until I got to the feed store, and was just getting back into my car when Tanner ran out of the store.

"Trade! Look what I got!" He unwrapped a flat package of gum, stuffed the pink rectangle into his mouth and fanned out a grouping of baseball cards. "They're for my collection, aren't they cool?"

I don't know much about baseball but I told Tanner that they were indeed cool.

I was almost to the turnoff to the lane when I passed Jake Hatcher's white pickup truck going the opposite direction. I waved at him, but he didn't see me. I glanced down at Priscilla's digital clock and read 8:37. Pretty late to be doing his job, I thought. Most of the time he was inspecting animals, their brands and identifying characteristics, which was pretty hard to do in the dark.

Jake lived in Tucson, so he was also a long way from home. Was there any chance he'd been visiting Cori Elena while Martín was away? What in the hell was going on? But I was jumping to conclusions here. After all, all I'd seen was Jake's pickup on the road not far from the ranch turnoff. That certainly didn't mean he'd even been to the Vaca Grande.

As I turned onto the dirt lane my thoughts returned to "key key head" and the trading cards and Tanner's collection.

Phelan Brewster was also a collector. He had those heads on his walls. He was a hunter. He loved his trophies. And wouldn't Rodney Johnson and the other black people be the ultimate trophies? Trophies so rare because they were so illegal.

Did Brewster have a secret treasure trove stashed somewhere? His own version of trading cards? Victoria told me about the black foreskin she had seen years ago. Was that what Phelan Brewster had kept from the black hitchhiking giant? If Rodney Johnson thought he was going deer hunting, wouldn't he have gotten a hunting license and deer tag? How about the Hispanic serviceman Vicki remembered, and his dog tags? Were those trophies?

But once again I was getting ahead of myself. After what I'd just learned about Vicki's book, why was I even thinking about Phelan Brewster? Sure, he was into his trophies. Maybe he'd even love to have stuffed black heads on his living-room walls. And a secret box of loot? He seemed like the type. But I still had no proof that there was any truth to the wild story that Victoria had told me.

I was almost to the ranch and still thinking about the Johnson family. Damn Victoria Carpenter. And damn her storytelling skills. This case had become a personal nightmare for me, whether it was fact or fiction.

I was only sure of one thing.

I had to ride it out. And I had to do it quickly if I was ever going to have peaceful dreams again.

35

My headlights hit Sanders's Ford, parked just outside my front gate. He's a lot like the chickens, he has a tendency to roost at dusk and not come out again, so I was surprised not only to see his truck, but to see him leaning on a shovel next to it. Mrs. Fierce, Blue and Petunia were running around in ecstasy at my arrival.

I pulled up and turned off my engine so we could hear each other.

"What's up?"

He pointed to a charred mess on the ground, partially covered with dirt.

"I heard the dogs raisin' Cain and thought I should check it out."

I walked over to the remains of the fire. In the middle I could see what looked like two two-by-fours nailed together.

"What was it?"

"It was still burning when I got here. Looked like a cross, some of that Klan-type stuff."

Chills ran up my spine.

"The Sporting Club," I said.

"Well they ain't too sportin' to go sneakin' around at night startin' fires. That thing could have spread." Sanders threw the shovel in the bed of his truck. "Do you want me to check out the ranch with you?"

"No, I'll be fine," I said, with a bravado I did not feel.

Was it a coincidence that Martín was away and I was now staring at a smoldering hate symbol? Could someone have been watching the ranch? And was the cross burner the same person who had called me in the middle of the night, threatening to spill my blood at the gates of hell?

What really confused me was, what did all this mean if Victoria's story was just a story? Could she have hired someone to scare me so I'd believe her? But why? What was in it for her?

"Are you going to call the sheriff?" Sanders's voice was filled with concern.

"Probably not." I tried to keep my voice steady. "After all, what can they do about it?"

Once safely inside my house I checked the answering machine. There was one call from Victoria apologizing for not telling me the truth about the book she was working on.

"Trade, I know you're upset and I should have told you," she said. "But everything else I've told you is true, I swear. Please keep working on this." She left her number—as though I didn't have it—and asked me to call, no matter what time I came in.

I didn't.

My sleep that night was punctuated with nightmares of being chased. I wasn't sure who was chasing me, but they were intent on killing me and I was desperately trying to escape.

Upon awakening, I thought briefly about the burning cross. Someone wanted me to leave the case alone, but who? Was the Sporting Club still in existence? And if it was, who were the current players? Was Dan Daglio involved?

After considering this for some time I began playing mental teeter-totter with myself, going back and forth from thinking about the Johnsons as victims to believing that Victoria Carpenter had made the whole thing up. But if it was all make-believe, then why had someone set a cross on fire in front of the ranch last night?

The fact that Brisha Johnson hadn't contacted me didn't help.

Thoroughly confused about whether I had a real case or not, I pulled out Carpenter's notes and started rereading them.

Her family recollections offered no new surprises. Then I began reading about the murders.

When Daddy drove up with the black people I remember that his friends, the other men, were very angry with him, I read. *He took the black people to the back of a truck where the food was on the tailgate and told them to eat. Then he came over to where the men were, near our car. I was playing in the dirt with Jerri Osborne's new Barbie doll on the other side of our station wagon. I had taken it from her chair and later she was real mad when she found out I had it. Anyway I was pretending that Barbie was baby-sitting and I remember she came with a little baby.*

The baby-sitting Barbie? Was there such a thing?

I picked up the phone and got the toll-free number for the Mattel Corporation.

After going through various voices I finally connected with Darwin Rich in Public Relations. After introducing myself, I launched into my spiel.

"Mr. Rich, I'm doing a research project here in Tucson on the evolution of the Barbie doll."

His bored "uh huh" told me that much of his day was spent fielding such calls.

"And I've heard that there was a Barbie doll that baby-sat, that even came with a little baby."

"Barbie Baby Sits."

"Yes."

"No. That was the name of the doll. Barbie Roberts came with a soft vinyl baby so she'd have something to baby-sit."

Barbie had a last name? I was impressed. The guy was good, there had been no hesitation on recalling that particular doll.

"I'm wondering if you could tell me when Barbie Baby Sits first came out?"

"Hold on." I could hear the keyboard of his computer. "That would be 1963," he said.

I felt like the air had been knocked out of me. Victoria Carpenter had not made up her doll. And somehow, in knowing that, I suspected that regardless of the book she was currently writing, she might not have made up the rest of it either.

That phone call, coupled with the burning cross, had me back on track.

I called Dan Daglio's office and talked to the red-nailed, officious receptionist. She gave me fifteen minutes with the mayor at one o'clock.

I was just walking out the door when the phone rang. It was Vicki.

"Trade, I'm glad I caught you," she said.

She must have been calling from a public telephone. I could hear people and machinery in the background.

"I just put Adele on the plane and I wanted to call you as soon as I could. I'm really sorry about last night and I hope you'll forgive me."

Still mad, I stayed quiet.

"I know now that it was a mistake, that I really should have told you the truth, but I was afraid that you'd think it was just a big novel in progress. That you wouldn't take the case, that you'd think it had to do with the book." It was the same song she'd sung last night.

"Doesn't it?" I was feeling bitchy, but even as I said it, I knew that Victoria Carpenter had been somewhat redeemed by the baby-sitting Barbie.

"Sort of. It's all entangled. But the book is fiction, Trade, this isn't. This really happened."

I wasn't in the mood to argue.

"Look, I'm finally seeing my father."

"Well I guess that's good, that you two are talking again."

"No, I mean I'm seeing him in my dreams. His face is there now."

I waited.

"He's hitting them, Trade. So is Hank."

"With the baseball bats?" She sucked me right in.

I thought I heard a sob, I wasn't sure.

"Yes," she said in a small voice.

I wondered if this would hold up in court and thought that it probably would not.

"Are there any others that you're seeing?"

"No, not yet. There's another face, but it's blank, sort of like those De Grazia things."

The artist Ted De Grazia had lived in Tucson. His faceless Indian paintings were legion.

"Just one face, that's all that's left?"

"Yes. But that person is hitting them too."

One face. Dave Robinson? Dan Daglio? The deceased Trevor Osborne? But this was only one incident that Vicki was remembering. All of them could have been involved at one time or another.

"I'm seeing the therapist later today," Vicki said.

"Good," I said before hanging up.

I grabbed my keys and headed into town.

Frederick Payne of the Evergreen Cemetery was dressed in a black suit and looked rather like a stiff himself. I think that's a job requirement for this kind of work. You have to be extraordinarily dull, drab, and you get demerits if you smile at all. Also you must have some kind of discreet handkerchief, in his case a burgundy-looking silk thing, dangling out of your jacket pocket. Your hands must be soft and well manicured and your voice must always be kept low and well modulated.

Payne fit the bill. And he couldn't have been nicer, even after his disappointment that I was not there on burying business. He gently corrected my reference to "potter's field," calling it the "county section."

"Although the county section is within the cemetery boundaries, we have nothing to do with it, either recordwise or carewise."

"Who does?" I asked.

"The public fiduciary would be the guardian of those records."

The county cemetery was back in the northwest corner of Evergreen. We drove past the carefully tended graves, clipped grass and neat monuments onto a dirt road, parking next to a bleak red field hosting a couple of spare eucalyptus trees, a few scattered pines and one desolate Italian cypress. A faded, tattered American flag, one that surely would have been retired years ago in the tonier part of Evergreen, stood sentinel over the lonely ground.

Payne escorted me through the graves. The older ones were marked with flat gray granite markers, while the newer residents were identified with steel and glass temporary plates, placed by the mortuary. On many of them the glass was broken, the statistics covered with dry dirt, making their visibility impossible.

We talked as we walked among the dead.

"Two to a grave, here," Payne explained. "One on top of the other." There seemed to be little rhyme or reason to the housing arrangements, no visible sign of kinship, with strangers bunking together.

"Are there three in there?" I pointed to three stones lined up in a row.

"Unfortunately," he said in a disapproving tone.

"Would the children I'm looking for have been buried together in the same grave back then?"

"That would be difficult to ascertain," he said. I mentally added that words like "ascertain" must also be in the potential mortuary applicant's vocabulary. "That would depend upon how many the county mortuary was interring on that particular day. If they had just buried someone else and the earth was fresh, then they would most certainly have placed someone else on top."

"The mortuary?"

"The county has an annual contract with a local mortuary that is responsible for this area. They handle the arrangements and the details of the interment. They usually wait until they have several people before they bury them."

We were among the children now. Infant Boy Murray and Infant Girl Vallela and the Infant Twins Sandoval. All of the graves bore names and a single year on their headstone. They were adorned with faded plastic flowers, baby pictures and toys including a faded fur-covered rabbit, similar to those given as prizes at the county fair when one successfully pitches a dime into the glass saucer. Battered Santas and a faded Easter egg with a broken pop-up chick were among the seasonal decorations.

"Here are the Does," Payne said.

They were a large clan judging from the several rows of Jane and John Does. Many of them had the approximate date of birth and approximate date of death on their markers. While I spotted a few children, I did not find two double-stacked nor even a five- and six-year-old.

I thanked Mr. Payne for his time and headed downtown.

Luck was with me and I found a parking spot on Pennington Street close to the Public Fiduciary's office.

I explained my mission to Alma, the young woman behind the counter.

"So, Alma," I said, "how would I go about finding out about any Jane or John Doe children you may have had from 1963 on?" I couldn't be exact in my year, for even if the Johnson children's bodies had been found, there was no telling that it would have been in 1963, 1964 or even 1984.

Alma excused herself to check with her supervisor to see if she could cooperate with me. Apparently it was not a problem, for she came back with a box of files.

"This is 1963," she explained, pulling one off the stack. "If they're not identified, then we get them as John Doe and Jane Doe. If the medical examiner's office was able to tell race, approximate age, approximate date of death and where they were found, then this information will also be on the records."

"It was a coroner back then."

She handed the box to me.

"You can just start through it. Finding children will be a little bit easier."

Especially black children, I thought.

I pulled my reading glasses out of my purse and began riffling through the Jane and John Does. It was hard to keep on task, for my eyes kept drifting to the brief information on all of the unknown people. It seemed like damned little to account for a life.

There was nothing that fit in 1963. Alma returned with two more boxes.

In February of 1964, a javelina hunter had found two Hispanic kids out near Three Points. The approximate dates of birth were close to those of Matthew and Mark Johnson and the unknown children had been buried together in plot number 405 of the county section of Evergreen. Cause of both deaths was listed as exposure. No one had claimed the kids and a penciled notation on the card read "illegal immigrants?" This wasn't so unusual, since a lot of people die of dehydration crossing the desert every summer to come into the country through Arizona. I made a note of it on my pad, along with the case number, and kept looking.

Three hours later I had gone through every box. Through every Jane and John Doe found and buried in Pima County since 1963. Nothing fit.

Except the two Hispanic kids in 405.

But Samantha Trilby-Smith had told me that determining race was one of the easy things, easier than determining sex on children. How could they screw that up?

I'd have to find the coroner from back then. Louis Shriber, or whoever it was.

I thanked Alma and walked over to the County Recorder's office.

"I'd like to find out who the coroner was back in 1964," I said to the young man behind the counter.

"Okey doke," he said, reaching for a bound volume.

"I think it may have been Louis Shriber," I said, offering my barter.

"Yup," he said as his finger ran down the fine print. "Nope."

"Nope?"

"Yup and nope." He gave me a silly grin. "Shriber was the coroner until January that year. This doesn't tell me why, but he left office and another guy was appointed to fill out his term."

He turned the book so I could read it.

"Some guy named Daglio. Hey, isn't he the mayor?"

36

I WAS WAITING IN DAN DAGLIO'S OFFICE WHEN HE CAME IN FROM lunch. His secretary had not yet returned from hers, and the mayor greeted me warmly, as though we were long-lost friends.

"Come on in, Miss Ellis," he said, shepherding me into his spacious corner office, its spotless windows offering a substantial view of the city below and the mountains beyond.

"Now then, what can I do for you?" His eyes alternated between looking at me and trying to check the stack of telephone messages that had been left on his desk. I didn't feel that either one of us was getting the attention we deserved. While I was having trouble seeing the mayor as Dorothy Brewster's Dan, Dan the Candy Man, could he be Danny Boy?

"I'd like to ask you about the Sporting Club," I said.

"Uh huh." He didn't bother looking up.

"You know what that is?"

He glanced up quickly. "The Sporting Club?"

"It was a club started by Phelan Brewster, back in the sixties."

"That thing again? I've told the county attorney everything I know, which is nothing."

"I've been told you were a member." It was a baby lie, and not one I was likely to get caught in.

"Your information is wrong." He smiled broadly, as

though he could charm me out of any suppositions I might be making.

"It was a hunting club, all men. They hunted game, deer, elk, javelina, that sort of thing."

"Well, I used to hunt. And I knew Phelan Brewster, although I never see him anymore. But until the county attorney's office contacted me, I'd never heard of anything called a Sporting Club."

I found it curious that he wasn't asking more questions. He sat patiently, like a cat waiting for a hibernating gopher to emerge in the spring.

"Phelan's daughter, Victoria, has hired me to investigate this club. She's been in therapy and she's remembering some bad things that happened on some picnics back then."

Daglio had a ballpoint pen in his hands, rotating it end over end. This was probably the closest I was going to come to getting his full attention.

"In particular, she remembers a father and his two small children being beaten to death with baseball bats. They were buried out in the desert someplace. I think I may have found them."

A shadow passed across his eyes. He was good, but the shadow had still passed and I had seen it.

"If you've found dead bodies, Miss Ellis, then you should certainly report that to the proper authorities. I believe Miss Carpenter has already done that."

"I'll be contacting the county attorney's office shortly. But in the meantime I thought you might be interested in them, in the children I've found. Their names were Matthew and Mark Johnson, and they were five and six years old." I handed him the school photograph and pointed to the brothers. "Their daddy worked with Phelan Brewster at the Arizona Bottling Plant."

He glanced at the photo before handing it back.

"Miss Ellis, it sounds to me as though this is an issue for law enforcement, not for the mayor's office."

"I think it concerns both. The bodies of the children were found in 1964." I waited, but he was good. He sat there in silence.

"Do you remember who was the coroner back then?"

He gave me a hard stare but said nothing.

"You were." It was a gamble, but I wanted to bait him. "You determined whether or not the bodies were posted, whether there was an inquest. Is any of this familiar to you?"

"Miss Ellis, I posted a lot of bodies in the short time I was the coroner. If you're asking me if I remember those two particular ones, the answer is no."

"Let me refresh your memory, Your Honor, there was no inquest." I don't know what made me go for broke. Maybe I wanted to show off, I don't know. I hate it when I do that. If those kids in 405 weren't the Johnsons, then Daglio would probably see to it that my license was pulled and I'd be out of work. Thank God for the ranch.

Daglio's face turned to rock, any semblance of charm had evaporated from it, and a muscle just below his left eye was twitching slightly.

"Miss Ellis, are you accusing me of covering up something?"

"There are two murdered children, there wasn't an autopsy. You were the coroner. I just want to know if you remember them."

He shook his head. "I was appointed and didn't run again. That was over thirty years ago."

"So you don't remember these kids." I waved the photograph in the air.

"No, I don't. Now, if you'll excuse me, I have other appointments."

I saw myself out and practically ran to the county attorney's office. I didn't know what kind of influence the mayor had in county quarters, but now that I had stupidly let all of my marbles out of the bag, I needed to cover my ass before Daglio figured out a way to snatch the occupants of county plot 405.

I raced to the ninth floor of the county building only to be told that Abel Messenger was in court. I ran over to Superior Court, checked the calendar there and finally found him in Division 12.

It was a drug case and the jurors, judge and lawyers all sat with headphones on, listening to an incriminating wire that had been worn by a police snitch. I sat quietly in the back of the courtroom, praying for a recess.

Messenger saw me and gave me a couple of smiles and a wink in the hour and a half I sat there. Finally, the judge called for a break and Abel greeted me.

"Lady Love, what brings you down here?"

"I've got to talk to you about the Sporting Club."

He took my arm and led me out of the courtroom and into an empty jury room.

"I think I've found them, Abel. I think I've found the kids!"

He stared at me in disbelief.

"I think they're buried as Hispanics in the county section of Evergreen."

"Jesus," he said, "how'd you come by that?"

"It's a long story. Bodies of two kids, the same ages as the Johnsons, were found in 1964 by a hunter."

"So who are the Johnsons?"

Shit. I had gotten so wrapped up in finding someone who knew them, and then with the forensic anthropologist, that I had neglected to fill him in. I quickly brought him up to date.

"Has the mother contacted you?"

"No, not yet," I admitted. "Abel, do you know who the coroner was back in 1964?"

He shook his head.

"Dan Daglio."

"Christ."

"It was an elective office and he was appointed to fill in some guy's term. No experience required, no formal education, forget forensics. So in this case there was no autopsy, no inquest, *nada*. I think he passed them off as a couple of wetback kids that died of exposure on their way into the States. I've just come from his office."

He gave me an incredulous look.

"Of course he denies everything, but I'm worried that if we don't dig them up, they'll disappear."

He thought about this for a minute.

"Yeah, that could probably happen," he said.

"Can you get an exhumation order?"

"Disinterment order."

"Whatever, can you get one¿"

He rubbed his forehead with his hand while he considered my request.

"You're sure about all of this¿"

"That's why I'm here. I think it's important, real important."

"Digging up people is expensive. We had one about six months ago and it cost us nine hundred bucks. Out of our budget."

I waited.

"Yeah, I can request one. It'll take some time." He didn't sound all that committed, but then I had given him a lot to think about.

"Abel, if those kids in 405 are black, you may make this case."

"We'll go for it, Lady Love." He looked at his watch. "I've got to get back. I'll let you know how it turns out."

I practically danced all the way back to the car. Finally, I felt like I was getting somewhere.

Since I rarely go to town, when I do get there I have a long list of errands. By the time I finished running them it was late.

When I pulled into the ranch I spotted Jake Hatcher's pickup in front of the bunkhouse. With Martín in Mexico, there was no reason for Jake to drop in, unless he was there to see me. My antennae were definitely up now. What was going on with Cori Elena¿ Was she thinking about trading Martín in for a man old enough to be her father¿ If that was the case, it sure seemed risky since Martín had said he'd be home today or tomorrow.

I drove around to the tack room, dropped the tailgate and backed as close to the door as I could get. When I got out of the truck I could hear Cori Elena's loud Mexican music drifting through the air.

I unloaded the eighty-pound sacks of pellets, the horses' vitamins, the dog food and the chicken scratch. Since Martín had turned the ranch horses out to graze, I fed my two. After wrestling a fifty-pound salt block into the pasture for Dream and Gray, I sat on the tailgate congratulating myself.

Unloading feed, while a pain to do, can also be exhilarating. Something about manhandling all of those pounds and being able to dump all of that stuff precisely where you want it. I guess it's my equivalent of a Nautilus machine or StairMaster. At any rate, I'm always pleased when the job is done properly, without bags breaking and feed spilling all over the floor, and without my body complaining too passionately.

As I unloaded the last bag I saw Jake's pickup head out the drive.

While I sat on the truck congratulating myself for my Wonder Woman act, I watched the two dogs and the pig play tag. They were tearing around after one another, taking turns with being "it." Finally tiring of the game, they turned to their favorite pastime, Hump Dog. This one is fairly self-explanatory, only where there had previously been two players, they had now initiated Petunia into their fun and were having a fairly spirited *ménage à trois*.

The pig, however, took a dim view of being the object of Mrs. Fierce's affections and was grunting her objections. Since she hadn't gone into her piggish scream, I figured she had things under control as I watched her squirm out of the dog's persistent embrace.

Finally done with chores, I headed over to the bunkhouse. It was time to have a chat with Cori Elena.

37

Cori Elena opened the door holding a glass of beer with a lime floating in it. There was another half-filled glass on the kitchen table, sitting next to an empty bottle of Corona. It didn't take a brain trust to figure out who had been using the second glass.

"*Hola*, Trade." She was dressed in Levi's and a low-cut peasant blouse. As she greeted me, she crossed her arms in front of her chest. While it was a defensive posture, I also suspected that she was doing it so I couldn't see that she wasn't wearing a bra.

My eyes drifted to the opened bedroom door. The sheets and spread of the rumpled bed were in disarray. Had she been bouncing Jake's bones? Cori Elena in the months she'd been at the ranch had not seemed a likely candidate for a housekeeping merit badge, so it was hard to really tell. Maybe she just hadn't made the bed.

She closed the front door.

"You want a beer?"

"Nope."

"Did you hear from Martín?"

"No."

"Oh, you think something's going on, don't you?" She wrinkled her nose, whether in distaste of the thought of bedding down the brand inspector or of my own disgust, I couldn't tell.

"Is it?"

"I think you better sit down, Trade." She motioned to the table.

I sat.

"So why's Jake hanging out so much?" I asked.

"He was my friend years ago, you know he used to go out with my Tía Consuela. He was her boyfriend for a while."

"Okay." I was all ears.

"But then she broke his heart and started going out with a guy from the base."

I didn't have to be told which base. Davis-Monthan Air Force Base had been one of Tucson's premier employers for years.

"So what's this have to do with you?"

"He's been telling me what she was like. She disappeared when I was little."

Something she just said struck a nerve.

"What do you mean, disappeared?"

She drained the glass of beer. "She left home one Saturday morning to go on a picnic and we never saw her again."

I struggled to remember what I'd seen in Victoria Carpenter's notes. Hadn't there been a reference about a black man and a Hispanic woman being at one of the Sporting Club picnics?

"Cori Elena, this is very important," I said. "Was your aunt's boyfriend, the airman, a black man?"

She shrugged and put her glass in the sink. "That's what Jake says, but I never met him."

As she walked back to the table, I could clearly see that she was once again braless. If Jake Hatcher was giving Cori Elena solace, he in turn was getting an eyeful of her.

"Was your aunt's disappearance reported?"

"*Seguro*. But they never found anything. No one listened to poor Mexicans in those days."

I'd come to the bunkhouse looking for answers and I'd found them for questions I'd never even asked.

When I finally got inside my house I found that the answering machine had gone crazy, as a long line of blinking red dots marched across its face. Obviously someone was trying to reach me.

I hit the Play button and listened to four hang-ups in a row.

"I had a hard time convincing Randy," Abel's bold voice came over the machine, "but he's going to stick his neck out on this one. The paperwork for the court order will be done this afternoon and we'll get it to Superior Court first thing in the morning. Then it's up to the judge whether or not he'll grant the disinterment order. I'll keep in touch."

I was thrilled. And scared. The county attorney wasn't the only one at risk on this thing. I might as well have been a giraffe for as much neck as I had hanging out.

There was another long stream of hang-up calls.

Someone was trying hard to reach me but didn't want to leave a message.

Could it be Brisha Johnson?

There was also a call from Sanders telling me that a woman had picked up one of my calves and we needed to find its mother. I called him back and arranged to meet him.

We rode out at eight the next morning when it was still cold enough for our breath to catch on the brisk air. I blew puffs of frost out my mouth, briefly pretending that I still smoked.

We had just topped the mesa when Sanders started talking.

"Some foolish woman picked up a calf yesterday afternoon," Sanders began. "Said she was ridin' down on the flats and it jumped up and followed her. She figured it was an orphan."

I groaned. Invariably some well-intentioned but misinformed do-gooder would come across a calf without its momma and would "rescue" it. So far this was the third such rescue we'd had this fall. It's worse in the spring, when the babies are smaller. What people don't realize is that cows like to hide their babies. They'll stash them in a pile of brush and then wander off to catch a bite to eat, go shopping, or read a book or something, and everything is fine. Momma knows where her kid is and the kid is usually content to stay put. If you go looking for such a calf, you're probably not going to find it. We've followed cows for a mile and a half and they've never given us a clue as to where they've stashed their babies.

But if someone rides close to the hideout, the calf—and it's usually the young ones that are hidden—may think that Mom has returned and may jump up. And what does he see? A red or brown hairy belly that looks like Momma's, so he figures he should follow it.

The rider should leave well enough alone and gallop off and leave the baby where his mother left him. In this case, the woman unfortunately had a lariat on her saddle so she dropped it around the calf's neck and took it home with her.

Now Momma Brahma was out here somewhere looking for her child. Her bag would be full and hurting and her heart wouldn't be far behind.

We checked the feeder canyons into the Sutherland, then doubled back up on the power line ridge before dropping back into the canyon. By ten o'clock, a line of cows was heading to the Speed Tank so we followed them in. We sat and watched them for a while as they mothered up.

Since we had nothing better to do, I told Sanders about my call from Messenger and our effort to disinter the bodies.

"Well, Trade, timin' has everything to do with the outcome of a rain dance," he said with characteristic wisdom.

We were there for thirty minutes or so when a gray Brahma came trotting in, a worried look across her face. She was bawling as she trotted from group to group and her swollen bag told us what we needed to know.

A slow smile spread across Sanders's face. I knew he was pleased that I would not be saddled with a dogie calf, who never do as well as they do when they are with their mothers.

We couldn't have found her in a better place. A dirt road led into the tank and was used to drop off salt blocks for the cattle. We opened the wire gate to the old corral and herded in the forlorn mother, along with a couple of other cows and their calves for company, then closed the gate.

Then we rode home, put the horses up and loaded the calf in the back of Sanders's Ford. I drove and he baby-sat the calf on the rough road to the tank.

After a joyous family reunion our work was done. It was after two.

As I walked to the house I noticed that Martín's pickup was not at the bunkhouse. Since he'd said he'd be home Monday *or* Tuesday, I wasn't too worried. Yet. But I'd seen what Lazaro Orantez had done to his bride, so there was the possibility that he and Martín could get into it. Still, I decided not to worry. There was still a lot of Tuesday left.

The telephone was ringing as I came in the kitchen door.

"He went for it, Lady Love." I could hear the excitement in Messenger's voice. "Judge LeRoy signed the disinterment order this afternoon."

"Great. How soon will they dig them up?"

"We're hand-carrying it to the mortuary. They'll take care of it."

"How soon?"

"Depends upon their equipment schedule, plus I've got to squeeze the money out of here."

"I guess the cemetery won't take credit?" I asked.

"Funny lady."

"Will you be there when it happens?"

"I don't know. Since we're talking a possible homicide investigation, someone from law enforcement will have to be there to establish the chain of evidence. The M.E. usually covers it."

"Abel, I want to come."

There was silence on his end before he finally answered.

"You sure?"

I wasn't, but I said "yes" anyway.

I'd seen too many movies where it looked easy. Little did I know that it wouldn't be.

38

MARTÍN'S TRUCK WAS STILL MISSING WHEN I AWAKENED WEDNES-
day morning. I waited until seven before checking in with
Cori Elena, who hadn't heard from him either. Frequently,
when one or the other Ortiz headed down to Mexico, they
missed their return date by a day or two, so logically I
knew I shouldn't be concerned. Still, there was a little thing
tickling the back of my brain. What was going on? What
had Martín found in Mexico? His daughter? Trouble?

Abel called me at nine the next morning to say that the
disinterment of county plot 405 was set for eleven o'clock.
I left the ranch with time to spare, for this was one appointment I did not want to miss.

The high-pressure system that had been sitting over
Arizona all week had moved off, leaving a windy, chilly
day in its wake. Poetically, it was probably the perfect day
to go around digging up dead bodies. Besides, the weather
forecasters were predicting a winter storm to start moving
into the state by tomorrow, which could have delayed the
disinterment if it had been scheduled any later.

I had no trouble finding the grave, as a huge backhoe
was perched over it, the machine's cavernous metal mouth
scooping great jawsful of soil from the earth. Already a
substantial mound of dirt was beginning to pile up. A tent

had been set up next to the grave and I could see tables and chairs inside.

A small group of people stood off to one side, watching the giant machine do its work. I recognized Samantha Trilby-Smith, Abel and Mr. Payne from the mortuary. A couple of young people, who looked like students, stood next to Sam and there was another official-looking type and two guys in work shirts leaning against shovels.

"Morning, Lady." Abel yelled over the sound of the diesel engine, dropping the "Love," I'm sure, because we were in company.

Trilby-Smith also said hello and introduced me to Fuzzy Baker from the Pima County Medical Examiner's office.

"We're called in on the older graves," Trilby-Smith explained. "We'll be doing the initial examinations here." She nodded in the direction of the tent. "We're all set up."

Two sleek-faced granite headstones sat beside the grave. I walked over to them and stared. They both read *John Doe, 1964.* That was it. Whoever had buried the kids hadn't put any other dates on the stones so there was no indication that the grave's occupants were children.

The backhoe was taking out less dirt now, as it burrowed deeper into the earth.

The drone of the engine changed.

"That's about it, Mr. Payne. Six inches or so, if there's a liner."

Frederick Payne nodded as the man on the backhoe put it into reverse and backed away from the grave.

The two men in work shirts dropped into the hole and began scooping out shovelsful of earth. They worked for ten minutes or so before hitting the concrete liner that theoretically was supposed to keep moisture out of the coffins. They then wrapped chains around the liner, and lifted the heavy concrete cap out with yet another machine.

As much as I wanted to go over and peer into the grave, I stayed put, following the lead of those around me. This was my first disinterment and I wasn't sure of the etiquette involved.

Fuzzy Baker took a white body bag and placed it at the edge of the grave.

One of the grave diggers dropped back into the black hole and began handing pieces of pressed board up to the man on top. The plastic waterproof covers that Samantha Trilby-Smith had mentioned were missing. Was that intentional, so the bodies would decompose more rapidly?

"I was afraid of that," Payne said. "Coffin's rotted. Those pressed-board things don't last any better than wood."

My stomach took a turn. It had never occurred to me that the bodies would not still be neatly encased in their coffins. Idiotically, I remembered a verse from a childhood ditty: *They wrap you up in a big white sheet, and drop you down about six feet deep, then all goes well for a couple of weeks, and then your coffin starts to leak.*

I tried to push the rest of the verse from my nervous brain.

In spite of the chill of the day, beads of sweat pelleted the inside man's forehead as he continued handing pieces of the rotten board up to his partner, who in turn handed them off to one of Trilby-Smith's grad students, who disappeared into the tent with them.

"Okay, I think I can get one now," he said as he bent over in the hole.

Fuzzy Baker eagerly went to the edge and peered in.

The worms go in, the worms go out, the worms play pinochle on your snout. God, I hate it when my head does this.

Without fanfare, the gravedigger put a small skeleton on the plastic sheet. It was draped in dirt and shreds of a red shirt were sticking to the bones, along with a tiny pair of jeans. There was no flesh on the skeleton, as far as I could tell, and it was impossible for me to determine whether or not it was black or Hispanic, although I knew this question would soon be answered by either the medical examiner's office or by Trilby-Smith.

Baker began snapping pictures of the small skeleton, the white body bag giving it a perfect backdrop. Once this was done, the two students descended upon it with sifters and brushes and trowels, much in the same way as an archaeologist treats his find, as they collected evidence from the long-interred body.

The digger placed a small pair of worn tennis shoes next to the opened grave. Baker quickly returned and smoothed a second fresh body bag on the earth.

The gravedigger continued his work, bringing up more pieces of particle board to the surface, where they were handed off to his partner. These seemed to be in better shape than the first set; perhaps they had been protected by the coffin on top.

"Shit," the gravedigger said as he pulled up a headless second skeleton. This one seemed cleaner than the first. It too had pieces of clothing, a white shirt, abraded with dirt and debris, and what looked like denim stuck to the long leg bones, but it was missing its head. After depositing the bones on the plastic, the man ducked back into the grave and retrieved the cranium.

I stared at the small headless skeleton. Although the shirt was pocked with dirt and holes I recognized the cartoon characters on the front of it. Rocky the flying squirrel and his pal, Bullwinkle the Moose.

Tears threatened my eyes, and they were not from the wind. Abel's arm was steady on my shoulder and I leaned against him, trying hard not to cry.

"Easy, Lady Love," he whispered. "It's going to be okay."

I kept remembering the two smiling kids in Phyllis Jergensen's kindergarten class. What had they done to deserve this? And how on earth could we possibly ever make it okay?

Abel walked me back to my truck where I found a box of Kleenex and gave my nose a hearty blow.

"I'll call you when we know anything," he said.

"How soon will that be?" I asked, trying not to break down. Any pretense I may have had about being objective and this just being a case had evaporated with the Rocky and Bullwinkle shirt.

"They'll work on it here, weather permitting. It might take a couple of days. We'll post a guard tonight."

We said goodbye and I slowly drove out of the cemetery. As I did so, I remembered a funeral of an old Apache I had attended. His people had lived in Fort Sill, Oklahoma, and they had brushed sage branches over their bodies to protect them from danger. From time to time one of them spat on the ground to further dispel evil. Would that it was that easy.

On the way back to the ranch it was like there was a movie camera running in my head. The scene was the same, playing over and over again. A horrid vision of a black man trying to protect his two small children from evil, one of them wearing a Rocky the flying squirrel T-shirt. In my head I saw the black man crumbling beneath the blows of the baseball bats and the terror on the faces of the children as one of them screamed "Oz!"

Tears streamed down my face and when I stopped at the stoplight on Oracle and Magee I saw a couple of construction workers in a battered pickup next to me, pointing at me and laughing. Briefly I thought about flipping them off, and then remembered that throwing kisses usually pisses people off more. So I made the ugliest face I could, not a real stretch since my face was blotchy and red from crying anyway, crossed my eyes and blew them a kiss. The light changed before the confrontation went deeper.

When the mental movie of the dead children threatened to play yet again, I pushed it from my mind. There was no sense torturing myself with what had happened. It was in the past and the only way I could make any of it right was to do what I could to find out the truth about the Sporting Club.

By the time I pulled into the Vaca Grande I was completely drained. Crying does that to me, just washes me out. While sometimes it's fun to wallow in grief and despair and really indulge in the tears, for the most part it's pretty unproductive. All it does is make me tired. In a way it's like drinking too much. There's no real percentage in it when the smoke clears and the hangover sets in or in this case, the exhaustion, so why do it?

Seeing that Martín had not returned home only depressed me more. He was now more than a day late. As much as I wanted to check in with Cori Elena, I didn't. The subjects I wanted to explore—Orantez and Quinta—were precisely the two things I couldn't ask her about. After all, Martín had gone to visit his sick aunt in Mexico, hadn't he?

Briefly, I thought about riding, but the wind had picked up into an even stiffer cadence so I dismissed the thought, opting for the book-and-chocolate-bonbons routine, hoping they would cheer me up.

I gathered kindling from the woodpile and began building a fire. After twisting newspaper and laying it beneath the wood I draped the pile with a broken candle and lit it.

When I checked the answering machine, again there was a steady stream of blinking red lights, but no messages. Maybe if I stayed home I could find out who was trying so desperately to reach me, but afraid, or unwilling, to leave their name.

In between fixing a late lunch, chile verde in a hamburger bun, I peeked out to watch the fire, praying that it would take. It's always chancy with me. Some of them do and some don't. And the ones that don't, piss me off as I go through the whole dreary twisting newspaper process all over again, including smearing my hands with the printer's ink. I like instant gratification. If I've made the fire, then I want the damned thing to be cooperative and start.

This was one of my lucky days, as my effort blossomed into a full-fledged inferno.

I had just taken my first bite of the chile verde when the phone rang. I jumped up, eager to catch it in case it was my mystery caller. But the bite was too big to swallow quickly before catching the phone and too good to spit out in the sink, so I shoved it to one side of my mouth and said "hello" in a tone that I hoped could pass for normal instead of someone talking with their mouth full.

There was nothing. No dial tone. No breathing. Nothing.

"Hello," I repeated.

And waited.

Finally I heard a sigh.

"Miss Trade Ellis, please," said a soft voice on the other end of the line.

"This is Trade, may I help you?" I knew who I had, but I wanted to hear it from her.

"You looking for Brisha Johnson?" The voice was very quiet and soft and I found myself straining to hear it.

"Yes, that's right. I need to talk to her. It's very important."

Silence. Suddenly I was afraid that if I didn't convince her of how important it was that I talk to her, she could quickly hang up and I would never hear from her again.

"I may have information on her children, on her husband," I said.

"She got no husband. He left."

My heart sank, but I went on.

"Well, if he really left her, then maybe I don't need to talk to her. But if he didn't, if something terrible happened in 1963, then that needs to be made right. And I think I can help make that happen, if I can talk to Mrs. Johnson."

This was all bullshit. I knew I was already talking to Brisha Johnson.

"What make you think that?" The voice was getting no stronger. It was almost a monotone, a soft, quiet monotone.

"A woman I'm working for remembers things from long ago. Bad things. She wants to remember everything."

"What woman?"

"Victoria Carpenter, she's Phelan Brewster's daughter."

A gasp came over the line.

"Leave it be."

"Well, I'm afraid I can't do that. It's a case I'm working on and if someone was murdered, even long ago, then the people responsible need to be brought to justice."

I waited. Nothing.

"I need to talk to Mrs. Johnson. I need to ask her about Matthew and Mark and what happened to them."

She was breathing heavy now and I couldn't tell if she was crying, asthmatic or scared.

"Florence," she finally said. "You come to Florence tomorrow. Alone. Miz Johnson meet you there, in the park by the library."

I looked out the kitchen window. The cottonwoods were bowing in the wind and I'd heard the weather predic-

tions. By tomorrow evening a storm was due in. In all
likelihood, tomorrow was not a good park day.

"There's a good Mexican restaurant next to the museum," I offered, "if the weather's bad."

"The park. Alone. Eleven o'clock," she said.

And then the line went dead.

39

THE SCREAMING AWAKENED ME AT 5:17 A.M.

It sounded like someone was being killed, and yet the dogs were curiously quiet. I jumped out of bed and grabbed my .38 from the bedside table drawer. Throwing my down jacket on I ran out the kitchen door onto the screened porch, Petunia looked up from her bed there and quickly went back to sleep. Mrs. Fierce and Blue, who accompanied me, were still quiet.

From the porch, I could see the bunkhouse lit up like a Christmas tree. I was instantly relieved to see Martín's old pickup parked in front of it. In spite of the cold, the front door was open and I could hear Cori Elena yelling.

What in the hell was going on? While I didn't see the brand inspector's pickup, had Martín walked in on Jake Hatcher and Cori Elena? Had something happened to Martín in Mexico?

I stood in the dark and listened for a few minutes, but I could not make out any of the conversation. Martín was also raising his voice and the two of them were clearly going at it. So far, there was no audio sign of Jake.

In all of my years of living with the Ortiz family, I'd never had this problem before. While we'd seen each other through death, injury, disappointment and assorted victories, I'd never had one of them, not one, get into a visible domestic fight before. One thing was sure, I didn't want to get involved in this one.

I had about decided that I could delay feeding the horses until things settled down in the bunkhouse and was headed back into the kitchen to put the coffee on, when something recaptured my interest.

Another voice.

There were three of them in the bunkhouse.

But the third player was not Jake Hatcher. It was another woman.

All thought of staying out of it evaporated as I put my .38 on top of the outside freezer and trotted across the yard to Martín's house.

Since the door was open, I didn't bother knocking. As I stood in the threshold, Martín waved a piece of paper in front of Cori Elena's face. I noticed he was sporting a healthy-looking black eye and a cut lip.

"Mentirosa!" he yelled.

What had she been lying about? And what was in that paper?

Cori Elena, her black-lace teddy displaying her considerable charms, broke into another stream of Spanish expletives, *pendejo* and *cabrón* among her favorites.

But I wasn't listening too closely, for my eyes were riveted on the other woman.

She was young and short and plump with a very pleasant face, her brown eyes opened wide at the exchange that was going on between Martín and Cori Elena.

Although I'd never laid eyes on her before, I instantly knew who she was.

"Chiquita." Martín finally noticed my presence.

"Trade." Cori Elena came out of her invective to also acknowledge me.

"This is . . ." Martín began.

"The brain-dead daughter," I said. I turned to the other woman and extended my hand. "Quinta, I'm Trade. Welcome to the Vaca Grande."

The young woman gave me a nice firm shake. "My father's been telling me about you on the drive up from Magdalena."

My father. While the words hit me in the gut, if she had said nothing, I still would have known, for the face looking at me was clearly an Ortiz. This apple had not fallen far from the tree. She had Martín's eyes, brown with flecks of gold, the quick smile and the flawless white white teeth, a trademark of the Ortiz's. None of them had ever been to a dentist, as far as I knew.

Cori Elena stood with her arms folded across her chest. Even without her heavy eye makeup, a defiant look punctuated her black eyes.

Although I was dying to know the story, I stayed quiet. I knew it would eventually come out.

"Nice meeting you. I was just on my way to feed," I lied as I backed out the door and closed it behind me.

When the sun came up, I could see that dark clouds had moved in, scudding across the atmosphere in an effort to take over the blue Arizona sky. The wind, killed by the onset of dusk last night, barely stirred and the cloud cover had raised the morning temperature by a good ten degrees.

When I heard Martín's truck start up around eight-thirty, I purposefully stayed inside. I figured he had a lot to think about and when he needed to talk to me, he would.

I finally left La Cienega at ten o'clock, knowing the drive to Florence on the two-lane road would only take about forty-five minutes.

From the minute I turned onto the main highway I kept glancing in my rearview mirror. I couldn't overlook that burning cross from Sunday night or get over the feeling that someone had been watching the ranch, waiting for Martín to leave. Someone didn't want me meddling in this case. Was it just an accident that the cross had been burned less than twenty-four hours before I'd talked to the mayor? If that someone had been able to watch the ranch, couldn't he also follow me to Florence and to Brisha Johnson?

I pulled into the Circle K and drove around to the back of the building, where I waited for a couple of minutes. When I pulled back onto the highway, I saw no sign of anyone following me. It was a procedure that I repeated twice more on the way to Florence, including a stop at the Tom Mix memorial, a roadside statue of Tom on his horse commemorating the popular Western movie star's fatal car wreck here in 1940.

Florence's main claim to fame is the Arizona State

Prison. When I hit the junction, I turned off, heading in to the main part of town. Still, the razor-topped fence, guard towers and monolithic structure were easily identifiable off to my right.

The library was on a quiet side street. It was a small prefab building surrounded by patches of dead grass, chain-link and a couple of concrete picnic tables and benches.

I parked Priscilla on the dirt shoulder of the road next to an old green Buick. It was one of those monster-size cars, probably dating from the sixties, in need of a paint job and new tires.

No one was in the yard and since the wind was beginning to pick up, I grabbed my down jacket and put it on.

I had just come through the chain-link when I spotted a frail black woman leaving the library. She looked at me and then went to the closest picnic table. I approached.

"Brisha Johnson?"

The woman looked up at me with scared red rabbit eyes. She just as quickly averted them from my gaze as she nodded.

"Trade Ellis." I thought about extending my hand and thought better of it, for such a gesture would probably scare her even more. I sat down. "Thank you for meeting me."

She said nothing. Instead, her slender black hands gripped the rolled edge of the concrete table. Her fingernails and angry red cuticles were gnawed down and I noticed she was wearing a dull gold wedding ring. Curious, I thought, for someone whose husband had run off with another woman. But then, maybe she had remarried.

"As I said on the phone, I have a client who has been in therapy and who is remembering some terrible things. I think some of it may have to do with your children, Matthew and Mark."

She stole a glance at me again, her lower lip trembling.

"My boys," she said softly.

"Mrs. Johnson, where are they now?" I felt as though I had a cottontail in a snare and I wasn't really sure how to proceed.

She grabbed a big white handbag and pulled out a handkerchief and blew her nose.

"They gone a long time ago."

"And Rodney Johnson?"

A tear fell from one bloodshot eye, again not the response I'd expect from someone whose husband had run off with another woman and taken two of her children with him.

"He gone too."

"The same day?" I asked, although it really wasn't a question.

She nodded.

"But they didn't go to Georgia, did they?"

She gnawed on her lower lip and twisted a corner of the handkerchief. "Miz Ellis, it's all in the past. They ain't nothin' you can do."

I reached over and patted her thin arm.

"You're wrong, Mrs. Johnson. We've been investigating this, the county attorney's involved, and I think we can do something about it."

"It won't bring 'em back, will it?" she asked in a barely audible voice.

I had no answer.

"Will it bring my babies home? Will it bring my husband home?"

"No," I admitted, "but it might bring someone to justice. And you can help us accomplish that."

She was crying softly. "Nothin' I can do. I have other children to think of." She fumbled in her handbag and withdrew a photograph. It was taken of the family long ago and I recognized Matthew and Mark. It was as Joanne Devlin had said, the children were standing next to their parents and they were stair-stepped down. Her finger ran across the bodies, identifying Rodney, Matthew and Mark.

"Micah," she said, pointing to a little boy a head shorter than Mark. "He does physical therapy at the prison."

The last two children were the same size.

"Esther and Ruth, my twins," she said. "Esther's a secretary and Ruth does X-rays."

All Old Testament names, I thought.

"They've done well."

"And they're still alive," Mrs. Johnson said softly as she returned the aged photograph to the huge purse. She fumbled in it for a minute and pulled out a tattered manila envelope and handed it to me.

I opened it and withdrew a stack of papers. Some were yellowed with age, but they all carried the same word, the letters cut out from different magazines and newspapers. My heart raced as I thumbed through them.

REMEMBER.

REMEMBER.

REMEMBER.

REMEMBER.

REMEMBER.

"There's a pile of these things," I said in awe.

Johnson stared at the ground. "I got one every year on the anniversary. I moved a lot, so they wouldn't find me. Finally, three years ago, they stopped coming after my last move. Maybe I fooled 'em this time, I just don' know."

"Who?"

She shook her head.

"Mrs. Johnson, can you tell me about that day?"

She stared at a pile of leaves that the wind was playing with. They skittered across the yard.

"One of the men that RJ worked with axed him to go hunting. He was so pleased, Miz Ellis, so happy that a white man thought enough of him to include him in such a thing. He took the two oldest boys with him, thought it would be good. We'd just moved to Arizona from Georgia, and in Georgia back then you didn't get too many chances to be social with white folks."

I stared at the moving leaves behind her.

"They never come home. Then about midnight two men came to my door. They had hood things over their heads."

"The Klan?"

"No, but like that. I seen the Klan one time in Georgia and that's somethin' you never ferget once you see them night riders. But this was just two men, with pillowcases or somethin' like that over their heads. Maybe *pretending* to be

Klan. They told me RJ had taken off with a woman from the plant and that he wuzn't comin' back."

Tears were streaming down her tired black face.

"He wouldn't do that, I knew that. But then they told me that if I wanted to keep my other babies then I'd never say a word to no one, that I was to say that my husband left me and took the boys with him."

"And you never said otherwise?"

"No ma'am. I lost my husband and I lost Oz and Markie and I didn't want to lose the rest of them."

"Oz?" Goose bumps marched up my spine.

"Matthew. When Mark was beginnin' to talk he couldn't say 'Matthew' so for some reason he started calling him Oz. We started callin' him that."

Victoria's memory of Oz had nothing at all to do with Osborne. It was Mark's terrified advice to his older brother, "Oz, run!"

I felt sick to my stomach.

"The children know none of this. I never said a word to them, figured they be safer that way."

"The men at your home that night, did you recognize them?"

She shook her head.

"Could one of them have been Phelan Brewster?"

"I don't know, I never met him, although RJ mention his name before."

"If we can make a case against Brewster, will you testify for us?"

She chewed on her cuticles.

"I don' know."

"Mrs. Johnson, it could be important, very important to our case."

"It won't bring 'em back," she repeated.

"No."

"Today's the anniversary."

"Of the day they disappeared?"

She nodded. "That's why I chose it to meet you. Thirty-seven years ago today they disappeared."

I felt numb and it wasn't from the weather, which was getting increasingly nasty.

"I'd give anything to have 'em back, but they're in the

hands of the good Lord now and there's nothin' I can do about that."

They weren't, of course. They were, I hoped, in the hands of the county medical examiner and Samantha Trilby-Smith.

"Mrs. Johnson, there's a chance that I may know where your children are, where their bodies are," I said.

Hope flooded her dark brown eyes.

"My boys?"

God, I hoped I was right.

"We'll know in a few days. Is there a number where I can reach you?"

The scared rabbit took over and she shook her head.

"I call you," she said, retrieving her handbag from the table and bunching her worn wool coat around her frail body. "I call you."

She was bent over, with either the fatigue of the doomed or osteoporosis, I could not tell, and I watched her slowly walk to the Buick. She never looked back.

I felt bad telling her about the kids. What if the occupants of 405 proved to be Hispanic?

But I had to have something to trade with or I knew I'd probably never see her again.

Sometimes this is a shitty business.

40

ON THE DRIVE BACK TO LA CIENEGA I HAD A LOT TO THINK about. The mystery of "Oz" had finally been solved and its grim solution was haunting, to say the least. It also validated much of what Victoria Carpenter was remembering through therapy. There was no way she could have made up the oldest Johnson boy's nickname.

With the "Oz" puzzle behind me, my thoughts drifted back to Dorothy Brewster's cryptic "Danny Boy" comments. As I usually did when I was thinking about it, I ran through the Daniels—Webster, Dapper, Quayle, Day-Lewis, biblical and Boone being my prime contenders. Still, I could not make out a connection to Phelan Brewster with any of them.

While most of my drive time was concentrated on what I had learned from Brisha Johnson, my thoughts occasionally drifted back to the little drama that was playing out in the Vaca Grande bunkhouse. Why had Cori Elena so blatantly lied about her daughter? How had Martín found Quinta and where did he get that black eye and cut lip? Had he had a run-in with the abusive Señor Orantez?

By the time I hit Oracle Junction it was after one. My stomach, never shy about complaining, was letting me know that it was time to eat. I passed up the small restaurants at the junction, opting for Rainbow's instead.

The sky was getting darker and the wind had turned mean, so when I pulled into the crowded parking lot, I wasn't surprised. The cafe always does a booming business on cold, blustery days. I pulled a free *Tucson Weekly* newspaper out of one of the vending machines.

Inside, a blue haze filled the smoking room, where two full tables of good old boys sat swapping tall tales of the Old West. Although the no-smoking room was busy, I was pleased to find my favorite table, the one that faces the front door, empty. It was a four-person table, but I took it, feeling no guilt since my regular status affords me some privileges.

"Hey, Trade," Rainbow yelled as she ran through, plates filled with hamburgers and french fries running up her arm.

I ordered the Cienega Special—turkey, bacon and jack cheese melted on rye—and began thumbing through the *Weekly*, grateful for something to do besides staring at the other patrons.

The other thing I like about "my" table is that it is far enough away from the smokers that secondhand smoke is not a problem, but close enough for eavesdropping.

The talk this afternoon centered on some fugitive that had been shot to death up north in the Verde Valley. Since I wasn't familiar with the story, it was a fairly easy task to read the paper, eat my sandwich and only half-listen to the other room.

Soon the good-old-boys drifted into making an atom bomb, and the Philosopher held center court while he revealed the secret formula.

"Got chocolate pie," Rainbow said on one of her runs through. I gave her a thumbs-up sign. Cold weather always makes me feel like a bear about to go into hibernation, and instinct tells me to fuel myself for the long onslaught of winter.

Halfway through the pie the conversation in the other room took yet another turn.

"Elkins got one," the Philosopher informed the rest of his court. "Great big sumbitch. Four point. Bet it'll go Boone and Crockett."

There it was again, the hunter's reference guide. The Boone and Crockett guides were never far away from any hunting conversation, for every serious hunter wanted to get in one.

While the men all speculated on the size of Bud Elkins's mule deer buck, something teased the back of my brain.

"Got enough points to get in?"

"You sure that's Boone and Crockett?" another male voice asked.

Then it hit.

Boone.

Daniel Boone.

Danny Boy.

Only Dorothy Brewster wasn't talking about the frontier woodsman. Her husband was a hunter. She'd know about the Boone and Crockett records. And judging from the size of the monster deer on Phelan Brewster's living-room wall, I wouldn't be surprised if he was in the record book.

Danny Boy. Super deer.

And suddenly I knew where Phelan Brewster was stashing his illegal hunting trophies.

I quickly paid my bill and headed back to the Vaca Grande.

I wasn't too surprised to find Martín waiting for me when I got home. He didn't look much happier than he had that morning. He followed me into the house and declined my offer of coffee or a beer. We both shed our coats and Martín sat at the scarred wooden table as I poured us each a glass of water.

"You're probably wondering what's happening," he began.

"That thought did occur to me."

'Jesus, *Chiquita*, what a mess.' His eyes were bloodshot, whether from the all-night driving or his dilemma, I couldn't tell. His black eye and swollen, bloody split lip did little to enhance his good looks.

"You want to talk about it?"

He nodded. "But I need to know that it won't go any further."

I was crushed. How could Martín even say that, after all we'd shared over the years? If there was one thing we could each count on, it was that our secrets were safe with one another. Hell, he knew things about me that I had never even shared with my cousin Bea or Emily Rose.

"It's that serious," he said.

"I guess it's gotta be, for Cori Elena to have told the whopper she did."

"She's going to talk to you," he said. "When she calms down."

I wasn't holding my breath.

"I don't know where to start on this thing." Martín took a long drink of water, and as his hands grasped the glass I could see that his knuckles were raw, the wounded flesh just starting to scab over. He caught me looking.

"I'll get to that."

I nodded and sipped my water.

"When I left here, I drove to Magdalena and asked a few questions. I figured that was the way I was going to find exactly where my daughter was in Hermosillo, but I wasn't going to talk to Orantez."

"But she wasn't in Hermosillo," I said, remembering that Quinta had told me that morning that they had driven in from Magdalena.

"No."

"So you found Orantez and got into a fight with him," I said, pointing to Martín's battered knuckles.

He held up a hand.

"I'm afraid it's not that easy. I didn't find Orantez."

"Then how'd you get to Quinta?"

"That part wasn't hard. I just kept asking questions. You know how that works. One thing leads to another and eventually you get to where you're going."

I thought of Brisha's children and all of the information I'd gleaned this morning and nodded.

"So I found out where she was staying."

"Did you know then that she was, you know, all right?"

"The first person I asked told me that. I felt like such a fool, but I never told anyone why I was looking for her or who I was. And finding her, after all those questions, was easy."

"Did she know about you?"

He shook his head. "That was the hard part, why I had to stay there longer than I thought I would. Cori Elena had told her nothing. It took some time for her to consider it."

"She didn't have a mirror?"

Martín chuckled. "She does look like an Ortiz, doesn't she?" he said with obvious pride. "I don't think she really believed it until this morning when her mother said so."

"And the face?" I pointed to his.

"In a town like Magdalena, the word gets around quickly. There was a person who didn't want her to come with me."

"Orantez," I repeated, although he'd already told me he hadn't found him.

"No, someone else. It's a long story."

I waited, but instead of continuing, he got up, went to the kitchen sink and refilled his glass.

"She hasn't had an easy life, *Chiquita*."

"Quinta?"

He was pacing the kitchen now. "Her mother."

The knock at the door startled both of us. I could see Quinta through the glass and I beckoned for her to come in.

"I'm sorry, am I interrupting anything?" Unlike her mother, Quinta wore no eye makeup and her brown eyes, like her father's, were bloodshot and rimmed in red.

"You might as well join the party," I said. "It's a wild one, we're drinking water. Want a glass?"

"No thanks."

"Your"—I hesitated, not sure what to call Martín in front of his newfound daughter—"uh, Martín was just telling me about his trip."

"Did you tell her?" Quinta asked.

He shook his head. "No, *mí hijita*."

"Tell me what?" Suddenly I had a chilling feeling. "Where does Lazaro Orantez fit in?"

"Orantez is dead," Martín said flatly.

Jesus, had Martín killed him in a fistfight? Was that what this was all about?

"It's not what you think," Martín continued. "He was dead before I ever got to Magdalena, before Cori Elena ever left."

"What'd he die of?" I was praying of old age, but I knew better.

"Well, that's the problem. He was killed. His throat was slit."

"He broke her leg," I said, remembering Cori Elena's broken leg when she had first arrived at the Vaca Grande.

"He pushed her down some stairs," Quinta said.

"Jesus."

Quinta dabbed at her eyes. "He caught her in bed with one of his bartenders."

A mental image of Jake Hatcher's truck flashed through my head. Still, in my opinion, infidelity didn't warrant a broken leg.

"So why the lies about you?" I asked her.

"I know too much."

"How can you ever know too much about your own mother?" The whole idea was ludicrous to me. I'd have given anything to have known my mother longer, but her brain aneurysm had interrupted that chance.

"The Mexican authorities are looking for Cori Elena, Trade," Martín offered. "They want to question her in Orantez's death."

"Did she kill him?"

There was a long silence between the two of them.

"I'm going to take a walk," Quinta said, heading for the kitchen door. "You might as well tell her the rest of it."

We watched her walk out through the screened porch and she was almost to the pond before Martín began speaking again.

"This is pretty tough on her. Her whole world has been turned upside down and I'm the one doing it."

"Not exactly. I think Cori Elena has to take some responsibility for this, too. I still don't get the big lie," I confessed. "So, did she kill him?"

"No. She told me she wanted to get back to this life, to me. And she was afraid that if Quinta told me what she knew that I wouldn't take her in. She wasn't going to tell me about her at all, but then I found that letter."

"And what does Quinta know?"

"Just what she told you. Orantez is dead and the authorities want to talk to her mother."

"There was something about the 'rest of it,'" I prodded.

Martín drained his second glass of water.

"Orantez had some business associates that were a little shaky."

"A little shaky or Mexican Mafia?"

"Both. He was a laundry for them. The *federales* aren't the only ones looking for Cori Elena." His index finger rubbed his lip self-consciously. I wasn't going to ask again, but I was beginning to get a mental picture of the someone who didn't want Martín taking Quinta. She'd probably been bait for Cori Elena.

Although I loved Martín, the idea of harboring a possible murderer, even if she was his girlfriend, didn't set well with me. The fact that thugs were trying to track her down didn't help. Although I can't say I was particularly fond of her, I didn't want to turn my back either, especially since she was the mother of an Ortiz. But I also didn't want to put those I loved in jeopardy. And there was that little matter of my private investigator's license. Briefly, I wondered what would happen to it if I was discovered harboring a Mexican fugitive.

"Martín, we've got to go to the authorities on this."

"We can't. You know how they are, they'll lock her up forever, if she lives that long. Guilty until proven innocent," he said.

"I was talking about our authorities."

His face was as haggard-looking and as tortured as the day he'd first told me about his daughter. "If you ever owed me one, I'd like to use it now."

Owed him one? We never thought in those terms. What in the hell was this new development going to do to our relationship? With my relationship with the whole Ortiz family, for that matter.

"Do you love her?" I asked.

"She's the mother of my daughter."

"Martín . . ."

"Give me time to try to fix this, please, *Chiquita*, just a little time."

It was the least I could do for someone I loved as much as I loved him.

41

WHEN I FINALLY GOT AROUND TO CHECKING MY ANSWERING MA-
chine, there was only one message on it, but it was the one
I'd been waiting for. Quickly I returned Samantha Trilby-
Smith's call.

"I thought you'd want to know that with the storm
moving in, we've had to move everything over here,"
Trilby-Smith said. "However, I do have some information
for you."

"I'm all ears."

"The M.E. didn't have much to go on, since they were
a little old for them," she chuckled. I knew she was talking
about the skeletons. "But of course that means they were
precisely our cup of tea. And we got fortunate. You were
right, it looks like quicklime was placed on the bodies,
which helped preserve them by inhibiting oxidation. Of
course, there are other tests to be run."

I was pacing the kitchen floor, phone tucked into my
shoulder as I unwrapped a Twinkie and took a big bite.
Although I'd eaten not long ago, I have a tendency to turn
to them in times of stress.

"Your John Does were inaccurate. The children are
black."

I threw the rest of the Twinkie in the trash and emitted
a big sigh.

"Sex is going to be difficult, if not impossible. From the

long bones and growth plates it looks like they're around five or six years old. We're working on the dental now."

"How about cause of death?"

"Hmm, that might be tricky. However, there is some evidence of blunt-force injury on some of the bones. Again, I cannot commit until our tests are finalized."

"Thanks, Sam, I appreciate the call."

"Oh, one last thing," she added before hanging up. "One of them has a left arm that appears to have suffered some sort of trauma some time before death. If we can locate any X-rays taken before, then we might make a match."

While Matthew's crippled arm had caused him grief in life, it might be his salvation in death. It was the definitive that could identify the bodies in county plot 405 as the Johnson boys.

Dan Daglio was going to have a tough time talking his way out of this one.

I had just hung up the telephone when it rang again. I caught it on the first ring.

"Lady Love, I've been trying to reach you."

"Abel, I've just talked to Samantha Trilby-Smith, guess what?"

"You were right, that's why I'm calling."

"I can't believe it."

"McIntyre's thrilled. I haven't even heard about the nine hundred bucks today."

Briefly I debated about telling him my hunch about the deer, but decided not to. A hunch was not enough to justify a request for a search warrant, especially when it was *my* hunch. Instead, I filled him in on my visit with Brisha Johnson.

"How can I get hold of her?"

"I'm afraid that's a problem. She's scared to death for her other children. They've been sending her notes, Abel, one a year on the anniversary of the murders."

"Son-of-a-bitch."

"They look like those ransom things you see in old movies, all cut out of newspapers and magazines. They just say REMEMBER."

"As if she could ever forget."

"Right. She's terrified. I told her I might know where her children are, so I think she'll call again."

"We're going to need her."

"I know, I'm working on it."

"There's something else about this whole thing. When we dug up the kids there was a lot of dirt encrusted on the bones."

"I know, I was there, remember?" I shuddered, remembering the dirty Rocky and Bullwinkle T-shirt.

"Well, the M.E. extracted a leaf, one tiny little leaf from the debris. It went to the forensics lab and they rushed it over to the university."

"Sam didn't say anything about a leaf," I said.

"It didn't go to Sam. It went to Brayden Forester over in Plant Sciences. Do you remember him?"

I had to confess that I didn't.

"Big in the papers here last year. Remember that Basalt case up in Maricopa County?"

While I knew that Messenger kept up on all the interesting murder cases in the state, it was a passion I did not share, so again, I confessed my ignorance.

"Guy murders a prostitute out near the old Caterpillar plant. They find a leaf in his truck, run a DNA on it and find that it matches, exactly, a paloverde tree at the scene of the crime. That convicted him. First time it's been done here. So we're having him run a DNA on our leaf."

"Great, Abel." I wasn't real hopeful that a leaf would connect any of the Sporting Club to the Johnson boys' bodies.

"You must be tired, Lady Love, you're not going to ask?" he sounded disappointed.

"Ask what?"

" 'What kind of leaf is it?' "

"Okay, what kind of leaf is it?"

"Boojum, Lady Love. Very unusual. Not many of them here, but it seems to me that I remember your mentioning a boojum tree out at Brewster's."

"I love you, Abel," I said before hanging up.

Now I was playing a waiting game. There wasn't much for me to do but let events take their course. With the county attorney involved, I knew that it was just a matter of time before they'd nail Dan Daglio and, I hoped, he'd pull Phelan Brewster down with him.

While I was curious if my hunch about his secret stash was correct, I couldn't see any feasible way for me to go snooping around Brewster's living room, looking for the hunting trophies. No, I'd have to wait this one out.

When I called Victoria Carpenter I reached an answering machine and left a message for her to call me when she got in.

Then I laid a fire. The wind was really brisk now, howling through the cottonwood trees as the huge eucalyptus danced to its tune. Black clouds moved quickly across the gray sky, a prelude to the impending storm.

From the kitchen, I could see the ducks still floating across the pond, not minding the nasty weather at all. If anything, they seemed to prefer it.

The lights were on in the bunkhouse and I suspected that Martín, Cori Elena and Quinta were trying to sort out their lives.

In the pasture, Dream and Gray had turned their backs to the wind, tucking their tails flat against their rear ends. Blue and Mrs. Fierce were curled up together on the biggest dog bed in the bedroom and Petunia was in residence on her blanket on the screened porch.

With everyone so cozy, I decided to curl up and read. I started with the quarterly, *Journal of Arizona History*, and found my attention flagging, so I reached for Richard Shelton's *Going Back to Bisbee* instead.

I had been reading for ten minutes or so when the telephone rang.

"Trade, I'm glad I caught you." I recognized Victoria's voice on the other end of the line. She sounded like she was under a lot of stress.

"Are you all right?"

The line was quiet for a minute before she answered, "Oh, fine."

"Some interesting developments have come up on the case," I volunteered, all suspicion of her having made things up gone. "We should—"

"Everything's come back. I found some things you need to see," Victoria interrupted me.

"What things?"

"I really can't go into it on the phone, can you meet me?"

"Sure, where?"

"I'm out in Avra Valley, at my father's house."

Shit. She had no idea of how much jeopardy she was in. "Victoria, listen to me very carefully. Get out of there. Now."

"No, it's okay."

"It is very definitely not okay. You could be in serious danger." With one phone call, Dan Daglio could have told Brewster what I was up to with the kids in plot 405.

"No, no, he's gone." She hesitated, as though searching for the right words. "To the White Mountains, hunting elk. He won't be back until Sunday night."

If she was so sure of that, why was her voice so broken and nervous? She must have found something pretty good, I thought, because she sure didn't sound like she was happy being in her father's house.

"Where's Hazel?"

She faltered again before answering. "Visiting her sister in Awatukee. Hank's at work."

I looked at the kitchen clock. It was three-fifteen. I wondered when Hank got off and if he had any plans to visit Brewster's place. Someone probably had to go out and feed the dogs, was it Hank? A neighbor?

"This won't take long. It's important."

"You need to get out of there," I said. "The police are coming into this."

My pleas for her to leave had no effect, as she kept insisting she had something to show me at her father's house. Finally frustrated, I told her that it would take me an hour or so, but that I'd be there as soon as I could.

I called Abel Messenger back and told him about Victoria's call. While he was insistent that I not go out to Brewster's, I knew that that was exactly where I was headed.

"The paperwork's going to take time, we can't just go pick him up," he cautioned.

"Brewster's out of town. Victoria won't leave the

house until she's shown me what she's found. I suspect that she's uncovered his trophies in that big deer head he's got hanging on the wall."

"I'd rather you not go. We'll be getting a search warrant. Let us handle it. Don't tamper with the evidence, Trade."

Huh? Messenger had all but given up on this case until I found the Johnson kids, and now he was asking *me* to butt out? While there was no way I'd walk out with any evidence that Victoria had uncovered, there was also no way that I wasn't heading out to Avra Valley.

"I'm heading out there, Abel. I'm not expecting any problems, and I don't want you to come to my rescue . . ."

"I know, I know. I'm your insurance policy, right?"

"I'll call you tonight," I promised before hanging up the phone.

I pulled my holstered .38 out of the bedside table and checked the cylinder. There were five hollow points in it, just like always. Although the day was overcast and gray, it was still daylight and I was probably being overly cautious. As stupid as it seems, I always feel safer during the daylight hours, even on rainy days.

I reached for a belt and threaded it through the loops on my Levi's and through the holster. Then I threw on a long denim jacket that, when buttoned, would conceal the weapon.

I was glad I hadn't yet lit the fire as I hate leaving home with a fire behind me. Grabbing an umbrella from the closet and my keys from the table, I headed out the door.

When I exited the freeway I detoured through McDonald's, thinking of Brewster's dogs. Cocky with my new friendships, this time I only bought three Big Macs, one for each of them. As I pulled out of the parking lot, I checked my rearview mirror to make sure that I hadn't been followed. While Brewster was out of town and Hank was at work, I couldn't dismiss either Dave Robinson or Dan Daglio. So far, there was no sign of either one of them.

In other parts of Tucson green signs dotting the roadways brag, "This section of highway adopted by the 20/30

Club" and so on. Out in Avra Valley, the roads were orphans and their neglect was obvious as the wind whipped debris from the cotton fields and other paper litter into a mad frenzy across the two-lane road.

I turned off on Miller Lane and drove to the third fork, where I turned south. They'd had more rain out here than we'd had and the road was slick with mud. After slipping and sliding along the two miles I ended up at Brewster's closed gate. As I got out of the truck to open it, I grabbed my steel dog whistle and gave three hearty short blows on it and waited. The wind was to my back so I had some hope that the dogs would hear it and come running, but they didn't. Had Brewster locked them up in his absence?

I closed the gate and slowly made my way up to the house, briefly wondering how bad the creeks I was crossing would run if we got a good storm. I figured that my visit with Vicki wouldn't take more than an hour and that really wasn't enough time, even in a bad storm, for the walls of water to gather enough steam to make it to this point. One thing was certain, I sure didn't want to be stranded at Brewster's house any longer than I had to.

When I pulled into the front driveway I saw Victoria's white Jaguar with the Illinois plates. There was no sign of Hazel's Taurus or any other car.

After I shut Priscilla down, I could hear the dogs' ferocious barking, but they still didn't appear. Where in the hell were they? Around the side of the house, where Hazel had stashed them that day?

I took two of the hamburgers and stuffed them into my jacket pockets. Maybe the opportunity would arise where I could slip them to the dogs. If not, I'd try again on the way out or, worst-case scenario, take them home and Mrs. Fierce and Blue would get a surprise treat. They were also beginning to develop a taste for fast food.

I knocked on the door and waited a minute. Thinking maybe she was in the bathroom, I knocked again.

When Victoria opened the door she did so slowly and then only held it open about a foot.

"Hi there," I said stupidly.

Although it had only been four days since I'd seen Vicki, the stress was obviously taking its toll. She looked awful. Her eyes, bloodshot as though she'd been crying, were rolling madly around in her head. She kept flitting them up and to the left and her eyebrows were doing a crazy dance in cadence to her jittery eyes.

I got her subtle message too late and was reaching for my gun when the door was jerked open and Phelan Brewster knocked her away.

Suddenly I found myself staring at a sleek black lethal-looking handgun.

42

His hands were rough on my body, and after checking my shoulders he was at my waist in no time, pulling the .38 out of its holster. He snapped it open and collected the cartridges, which he pocketed, and then stashed my gun in his hip pocket.

He pushed Victoria ahead of us and pulled me past the couch with its needlepoint pillows and huge wooden cross with the suffering Jesus, past the curio cabinet with the Hummel figurines, past the gun case, until we finally stopped at the dining end of the living room, where he threw my empty gun on the table.

"We've just been talking, trying to work a few things out," Brewster said, his gun pointing to an empty chair at the table. "Why don't you sit down. You too," he said to Victoria.

"God, Trade, I'm sorry," Victoria said. "He made me call you."

"I know."

"My daughter's just been telling me what she remembers and I've been trying to explain again how they're finding people all over the country that are remembering things that happened to them when they were children that really didn't happen to them."

"Well, that gun sure helps us see your viewpoint," I said.

He ignored me and pointed to a pile of brochures on

the table. "Some therapists are being sued. Do you realize that with some of them, every single client they have re-members something terrible happening in his childhood?"

"I've been to more than one therapist, Dad, and I still remember bad things about the Sporting Club," Victoria said in her own defense.

I sat down in my designated chair, which was in full view of the massive mule deer buck on Brewster's living-room wall. Today the eyes were flat and black. With the lack of sunlight streaming in through the west windows, the shining orbs were gone. I stared at the mount, wonder-ing if it was even possible to stash things inside of it.

He sat down at the end of the table, flanked by his daughter and me, and pushed a pamphlet my way.

"I think you've been had," he said. "Vic's been had, too, by her therapists. They've got her so crazy that she doesn't know what she's saying anymore. She needs help."

Victoria reached for a Kleenex from the box that sat on the table and dabbed at her eyes. I could hear her take a deep breath.

"I didn't make it up, Dad, and you know it. I've been having these nightmares forever, ever since I was a little girl, they've been recurring. I remember that day with the black children."

Brewster stared at his daughter, but it was impossible to read what he was thinking.

"Before when I had the dreams, the faces were all blurred, I couldn't see who they were. But I've been seeing them, Dad, and you know what? They're your face, and Hank's."

Jesus, why did Victoria take this moment to bare her soul? Couldn't she just pretend that she didn't remember anything, just this once? There wasn't much percentage in goading a man with a gun aimed at us.

"Vic, Vic." He shook his massive head. "Why do you want to do this to your family?"

"Victoria, I think your dad has a point," I said, trying to give her a subtle hint to shut up.

But she was having none of it. Her hysteria had over-taken reason. "Why did you do it to that family, Dad?"

"Will you at least talk to these people?" Brewster

asked, tapping one of the pamphlets with a fat blunt fore-finger.

She shook her head. "I don't need to, I'm talking to the right people. I know what I'm doing."

"No, Vic, I don't think that you do." He looked at me. "I suppose you're in this for the long haul?"

What the hell. He'd forced her into calling me, and the gun told me that he was very, very serious about what was happening. Besides, Daglio had probably already called him about the Johnson boys.

"I have a client that I'm working for," I said, nodding at Carpenter. "I'm in it until she decides she's through with it." I lied. Things were progressing so quickly that we were definitely in the homestretch, but I didn't want him knowing that. My eyes glanced over at the huge deer again as I wondered how I could get to it.

Suddenly Brewster stood up. "I'm sorry it has to be like this."

I looked at Vicki. Her eyes were wide with fear.

"There's no reason for this, Phelan," I said. "It's too late."

"You're wrong, it's never too late."

"I guess this means Vicki didn't make all of this up?" I asked stupidly.

He laughed.

"Vic, you were my precious little doll baby. I loved you," he said.

"No you didn't, Dad. You took me to those awful picnics, did terrible things that have screwed me up all of my life. You didn't love me. Look what you did to Mother. To Hank. You made him a killer too."

"Shut up," he said.

"You were pretty clever, weren't you? Picking black people who disappeared and no one would look too hard for them."

"You don't know squat."

"1963 was a very good year, Brewster," I chimed in. "That was the link that pulled this whole thing together. A body here, a missing hiker, a soldier disappears from Fort Huachuca and no one really notices. The news stories were scattered, no one put together the link. But Victoria remembered a black man and his two children when she was five. That gave me 1963 to work on."

"So what?" he sneered.

"They found the Johnson boys' bodies," I said, in an effort to divert him from whatever plan he had. "They know about Daglio's coroner's report, about his burying them as Hispanics."

"That's Daglio, not me."

"He was working for the Sporting Club, wasn't he? Covering up for all of you?"

"Daglio was a chickenshit," he said. "Lost all of his balls. The club fell apart after that. Not that it matters. They can't tie any of it to me," he said. He waved the gun at Vicki. "Not without her."

A pasty lump congealed in my stomach, settling in on top of the chocolate pie and half-eaten Twinkie. Now instead of hibernating, I felt like barfing.

Victoria gave her father a look filled with overwhelming sadness.

I was already planning our defense. There were two of us. If we could somehow divert his attention, maybe we could jump him. My eyes scanned the table, still littered with assorted newspapers, food coupons and stray pieces of paper. Other than my gun, which was too close to him for me to get, there was nothing heavy on the table to fling at him or knock him on the head with.

"This isn't going to work," I said. "I talked to the county attorney this afternoon. They're on to you."

"So what?" he sneered. "On to me and proving something are two different things."

"It's going to be difficult explaining our murders," I said.

"Difficult, but not impossible. Besides, you're not going to be murdered, you're going to have an accident."

"An accident," Vicki repeated dully.

"In one of the mine shafts up there." He flung his head in the direction of the hills that ran behind his house. "She"—he pointed the barrel at his daughter—"asked you"—now it was back to me—"to go hiking, to check out one of the scenes from her stupid dreams. Unfortunately you ran across an open pit and fell in. It's been known to happen. Besides, this is great weather. The earth gets saturated and breaks away."

I had to give him credit for creativity. Without Messenger's involvement, it was credible enough, given Victoria's story and my role as her private investigator, that it might have washed.

"It won't work."

"Maybe not." He shrugged, as I struggled to remember which arm held the Flying Dickie-Bird. Why I cared at this point was beyond me, except I hoped it wasn't his gun arm. Somehow that didn't seem right, being shot by an arm with a winged penis on it. "But it's better than having my own daughter testify against me, better than those damned dreams."

I was glad I'd told Abel about my suspicions about the deer head. A search warrant would uncover the incriminating evidence, if it was there. That, coupled with the boojum tree DNA, would probably be enough to convict Phelan Brewster of murder. This was a small consolation, however, considering his plans for us.

It was as though he read my mind. He sidled over to the wall that held the massive head. Shifting the black automatic to his left hand, he fumbled with the huge mount. Lifting it from the nail that held it, he pressed it against the wall for support, for the weight and bulk were difficult to manage with one hand, and slid it down the wall. Pulling it up by one of its four-point antlers, he flung the thing on the table.

"I'll bet he's Boone and Crockett," I said.

"Very good." Brewster rolled the deer on its nose, exposing the flat part of the mount opposite the buck's neck. A hinged door was now visible.

He reached in and pulled out a velvet pouch, one of the kind that comes with classy whiskey. This one had *Crown Royal* on it.

He fumbled with the drawstring and dumped the contents out on the table.

"Dreams, Vic, you want dreams?" he said, his free hand spreading out his treasures. "Here you go."

Victoria looked as though she was going to vomit.

I stared at the black tanned thing in the middle of the table, instantly knowing what it was.

A deer tag was in the mess, along with a set of dog tags and an engagement ring, a tiny diamond surrounded by diamond chips. Had that belonged to Cori Elena's Tía Consuela? There were a few old quarters and a black-and-white feather.

Brewster picked up the tanned foreskin and waved it in his daughter's face. "Your friend from the shed. He's still out there in the yard. They didn't look in the right place."

She shuddered.

I picked up the deer tag. "Rodney Johnson's?"

Brewster nodded.

"But no trophy from the Johnson boys?" I taunted.

A clouded look came into Brewster's sea eyes. It was the closest thing to remorse that he could muster. "That was a mistake, a stupid mistake. He never should have brought them, they weren't invited."

In my book, none of them should have been invited to the Sporting Club picnics, but I said nothing. Unfortunately, it was the children that had motivated all of us. If we hadn't found their bodies, Messenger probably wouldn't have been as close to making the case as he was.

"But you planned on killing their father," I said.

"Damned right. We didn't mind killing niggers, that's what it was all about. But kids." He wiped his face with the back of his hand, although he was nowhere near crying. "Robinson did them, he didn't mind."

"And Daglio helped?"

"Not that day," Brewster said. "He wasn't even there. After we'd taken care of the family, we decided that we couldn't leave all three bodies in one place so I took the kids home and then called Daglio. That's when we came up with the idea of stashing them at Three Points. It was easy. We had Stone 'find' them the next year. From there Daglio doctored the reports and buried them as a couple of greaser kids."

"And Hank?"

"Hank got his licks in," Brewster admitted.

So they were all involved.

"Put them back," he said to Victoria.

She averted her eyes as she gathered the things and placed them back in the Crown Royal bag.

He grabbed the sack from the table and stuffed it into his back pocket.

"And you've been sending Brisha Johnson the anniversary letter every year."

He smirked.

Far away, as though it was in a dream, I thought I heard a police siren. Perhaps it was the Avra Valley cops on a car chase, although the optimist in me wanted to think it was the cavalry coming to our rescue. I said nothing, not wanting to alert Brewster to our possible salvation. Besides, it might just inspire him to kill us sooner than he had planned.

But he was cocking one ear. He, too, had heard it.

He backed away from the table and opened the back door. The Doberman, rottweiler and German shepherd all came running into the kitchen. They circled Victoria, uttering low growls. She froze. Obviously these were not dogs that she had grown up with.

Brewster pulled his chair away from the table and pointed to the spot where it had stood.

"Pass auf," he demanded, in what sounded like German. *"Bleib."*

Thus instructed, the dogs sat and looked at us, deep low growls punctuating their throats. The Doberman sat between Vicki and me, her eyes staring straight ahead. She could have been a ceramic dog but for her sides, which were heaving in and out in anticipation of eating us. There was not a wagging tail in the bunch. It was lousy timing to discover I'd been wrong. The dogs, in spite of their gluttonous hamburger-eating ways, had obviously had some professional protection training.

Brewster backed away from the table, still listening for the siren, which was now quiet. Damn! I wondered if the policeman had pulled the car over and was not coming to save us.

"I have a little chore to do, before I deal with the two of you," Brewster said, pulling a yellow rain slicker off a hook near the kitchen door.

I thought it was pretty stupid. If it had been me I

would have gotten rid of us first, but decided against offering this suggestion. Besides, he'd been spooked by the sirens.

"If you move, the dogs will attack," he said, confident with his four-legged weapons.

The Doberman, as though Brewster spoke her language, snarled, showing brilliant white teeth. From all indications she had forgotten that we were ever friends.

Brewster walked out the kitchen door.

"We've got to do something," I whispered.

"But what about them?" Vic said, afraid to move, her eyes rolling in her head to look at the dogs.

"Don't look them in the eyes," I cautioned.

My hands were frozen on the top of the table and I flicked one finger. The Doberman went apeshit, snarling and barking like crazy. The German shepherd, apparently having already forgotten Brewster's command, was now lying down. The rottweiler, closer to Vicki than to me, was still in the sitting position, watching both of us intently. But it was the Doberman, as always, who was the leader of this pack.

I knew better than to look at the dog, so I directed my conversation to Vicki. "Good girls, pretty girls," I said in my singsong let's-be-friends dog voice. "What smart puppies."

The Doberman closed her mouth and watched me.

"Such good girls," I crooned.

It was as if the dog had not recognized me, which I knew was not true, until I had settled into my silly vocal pattern with her. She immediately dropped down and began licking one of her front paws. The German shepherd, taking her cue from the lead dog, began sniffing under the table, looking hopefully for a tidbit that someone might have dropped.

"Pretty girls," I continued my spiel. This time when I moved one finger, none of the dogs paid any attention. Slowly I dropped my hand from the table and into my lap. I held it there for a minute. "Are my babies hungry?" I crooned.

Still, no aggression from the pack. I slowly inched my

hand from my lap up to my jacket pocket and retrieved one
of the cold Big Macs and slowly unwrapped it. This caught
the dogs' attention and all three came to my side, wagging
their tails.

"Good girls."

Over the fierce wind I could hear a motor being
started. It sounded like a four-wheeler and I remembered
the one I had seen at Brewster's on earlier visits.

Quickly I split the hamburger into three unequal parts
and threw them around the living room. The dogs went on
a frenzied chase to retrieve the treats.

"Get up slowly," I said to Vicki, "very slowly. If they
come at you, just freeze." My eyes drifted to the gun case.
"Are the guns locked up?"

"Probably."

Mentally I calculated the odds of getting into the gun
case without a key in time to not get eaten by the dogs. It
was not a risk I could afford to take.

The dogs had gobbled up the hamburger and were
back for more. Their attitudes had completely changed as
they circled me, wagging their tails, putting on happy faces
in the hope that this would earn them more of the cher-
ished burgers.

Victoria edged toward the back door as I unwrapped
the second Big Mac.

"What good watchdogs," I said, tearing the hamburger
into lots of little pieces. With a great flourish I pitched the
mess in my hands into the living room. "Go get it!"

But the dogs didn't need my encouragement as they
dashed after the meat.

I grabbed my empty .38 from the table and Vicki and I
ran out the back door.

43

THE MINUTE WE WERE OUT THE DOOR WE WERE HIT WITH RAIN-drops. Great giant splatters that dappled our faces and clothing. We were in the backyard, which was surrounded by a chain-link fence, too high to jump over. I followed Vicki to the corner gate.

The wind was howling. Dusk was not far away and the sky was dark and foreboding. That, and the increasing tempo of the rain, made it difficult to see very far ahead of us.

Victoria opened the gate and we raced through and ran around to the front of the house.

Over the roar of the rain, I could hear the engine of the four-wheeler. It sounded as though it was idling.

"Shit!" I screamed, in an effort to be heard.

But Vicki had also heard the motor. She sprinted along the side of the house with me at her heels.

"In here," she said, pulling open a door to a furnace room.

We squeezed in and I pulled the wooden door almost shut, leaving it cracked an inch so I could tell when Brewster passed by, if, in fact, that was his plan. The last thing we needed at this point was for him to discover our escape. Thick cobwebs brushed my hair and briefly I wondered if there were any sleeping black widows in them. While the thought of being bitten by a spider spooked me, it was a damned sight better than being taken out by Phelan Brewster. I fumbled with my holster, replacing the bulletless .38.

I could hear the dogs' uproar from inside the house. They were clearly unhappy, confused perhaps. Between the drone of the four-wheeler and the concert of the storm, I didn't think Brewster would be able to pick up their clamor.

We waited for what seemed like an eternity. Finally, the sound of the four-wheeler changed slightly as it was put into gear. My face was glued to the slim opening, the rain pouring in through the crack, drenching me and stinging my eyes. I squinted, in an effort to keep my contacts in place. I didn't need for the rain to pop them out or dislocate them.

The sound of the engine was louder as Brewster came around the corner on the four-wheeler, moving slowly. He was shrouded in the yellow rain slicker, the hood pulled up. I held my breath as he putted by the furnace-room door and past the house.

He was passing the Quonset hut when we edged out of the tiny room.

"Let's get my truck," I said, fumbling in my Levi's for Priscilla's keys. In the rain, the truck would be able to better navigate the road out, and more quickly, than Victoria's foreign-made job. She didn't argue.

We were running for Priscilla when suddenly we were caught up in a set of headlights. The lights were soft and blurry with the rain, and low to the ground. Although visibility was poor, it looked like a red truck, a small imported job. And familiar. Victoria and I hesitated for a split second, but it was enough. The truck charged forward, heading straight for us.

It was between us and the Jaguar and my Dodge pickup. In the rain and the darkness, it was impossible to tell who was driving. Could it be Hank Brewster, called to the scene by his father, his murder mentor?

We jumped to the side, into the center cactus cactus, and the miniature truck turned sharply to the right, trying to clip us. I fumbled in my wet Levi's for my keys. But the truck had pulled back and was skirting the cactus garden on the far side as it settled between Priscilla and the cactus.

Vicki's Jag was parked in front of my truck so there was no way we were going to get to our vehicles as long as the small truck was blocking us.

The passenger's window was rolled down and although the light was dim, I could make out the outline of a huge man in the passenger seat and I knew what was coming.

"Run!" I yelled, just before the first shot was fired.

Vicki ducked and ran out of the cactus garden, with me on her heels.

Suddenly we were caught in yet another set of headlights as a second car roared full-speed into the drive.

Shit. The cavalry was here all right, but they were the wrong troops.

Although we were caught flush in the lights of the car for a long second, it made no move to run us down, lumbering to the right side of the driveway. The driver of the red pickup realized too late the car's intent and even as it was dropped into reverse, the heavy green Buick plowed into the front end of the smaller vehicle, pushing it easily aside. More shots were fired from the imported truck as it tried to spin away from the larger car but it got mired in the mud. The Buick took advantage of this opportunity, and slammed into reverse to get a running start. Without letting up, it smashed into the driver's side of the import, flipping it over and onto its roof in the mud, as its tires spun against the downpour.

The driver of the Buick laid on the horn.

I didn't need the encouragement. I knew the car. An old sixties green Buick. And Brisha Johnson was at the wheel.

She leaned across the front seat, pushing open the heavy passenger door.

"Get in!" she yelled over the rain and wind. I didn't know that her voice could go that loud.

We leapt into the old car.

"We need to get out of here," I said.

But Johnson, having thus captured us, was having none of it. As we passed the overturned truck, I could see a magnetic sign featuring a fire-breathing dragon on its crumpled door. I suspected Dave Robinson was driving his Dragon Links truck.

Brisha floored the old car and it bucked and lurched through the mud toward the Quonset hut.

"No, the other way!" I yelled, remembering Brewster's nasty black automatic. Even though we were in a big heavy car and he was on a little four-wheeler, I knew that it was not an even match. His possession of the gun more than evened the score. In fact, I'd have to give him at least four points. And Robinson and the other armed passenger in the overturned truck might not have been hurt, only delayed.

Johnson ignored me as the Buick careened around the Quonset hut, taking the seldom-used jeep road. In the impending darkness, I could barely make out the yellow slicker bouncing and bobbing ahead of us.

"That's him, isn't it?" Brisha asked softly.

Although Brewster disappeared around a hill, I suspected that he was still on the jeep road.

"Yes," I admitted. "But he's got a gun. We need to get out of here and call the police."

Although her voice had dropped back to her normal quiet cadence, there was a reckless look in her tired brown eyes. When I saw it, I knew there was no dissuading her.

I glanced at the speedometer. We were hitting thirty, not a monstrous speed, but unsafe for the old rutted jeep road which had now turned to mush. The heavy rear end of the Buick was fishtailing in the slush, but we were around the hill now, on a straightaway and gaining on Brewster.

He was caught on the front edge of our headlights as the Buick bore down on him. He glanced back and then hunched back over his machine. Cocooned as we were within the confines of the car, where visibility was still a problem, I wondered how he could see to drive, since he was out in the open with nothing protecting his face.

"Brisha, don't," I cautioned, knowing that she had it in her head to run him down. Although that was a possibility, I knew that Brewster would have more maneuverability with the four-wheeler than we would have in the ancient car. If he could get it off the road and into the desert, he would be long gone. And, he still had the gun.

He was clearly in our headlights now and, sensing impending danger, he gave another last look over his shoulder.

And then the most amazing thing happened.

It was as though the hand of God reached down from the sky and plucked Phelan Brewster from the four-wheeler like a rag doll. He was thrown up and over the vehicle, landing spread-eagled into the thick slime in front of us.

Johnson slammed on her brakes as the Buick squirmed all over the road, trenching through the mud. Finally we stopped inches away from the man sprawled out in front of us.

On the horizon of Brisha's headlights was a single strand of rusted barbed wire. It was sagging, but still strung across the old jeep road, evidence of a bad choice on Brewster's part. He had taken the wrong moment to look back at his pursuers, for in that split second, he had forgotten about the wire, which then gripped him around the neck and catapulted him from the four-wheeler.

Johnson opened the car door.

"Careful," I warned, scrambling for the door handle on my side, "he's got a gun."

Considering this, she dropped the car into reverse and backed it away from Brewster. The headlights kept him on center stage, and he lay unmoving in the mud with his arms outstretched.

I unholstered my gun, although it held no bullets. Was it like in the movies? Was my gun heavy enough to knock someone out if I hit him on the head with it? He was a hunter, would the thought occur to him that I had a speed loader? I glanced in the backseat, hoping for something more that we could hit him with, should that become necessary. There was nothing.

Victoria, although it was her father who lay like a dead man in front of the car, sat as though in a trance and said nothing.

"Get behind the wheel," I said, "in case we need to get out of here."

Brisha Johnson and I slowly advanced from opposite sides of the car.

It was as though Brewster was a rattlesnake. Neither of us wanted to get close to him. I was afraid that he might be faking it in an effort to suck us into a range where he could grab us. Certainly we were already within shooting range, but as far as I could tell, he was making no effort to go for his gun, wherever he had it stashed.

He lay face up in the mud as though crucified, and both of his hands were imbedded in the slime. A necklace of red blood dripped from his neck, pooling onto the yellow slicker. It was an oozing sort of thing, not an arterial splash, and I didn't think he was in any immediate danger of bleeding to death.

We were standing over him now, although a couple of feet away.

"Stand on his hand," I instructed Brisha, who did just that. I braced my foot against his right hand, hoping that would be enough if he went for his gun.

I leaned over him. Although his eyes were open and somewhat glassy, even in the rain I could still make out the faint rise and fall of the yellow slicker. He was not dead, just wounded. And he might not even be that, just stunned.

I patted his raincoat and found the .357 in the front right pocket. As I extricated it, Brewster made no effort to stop me. Aiming the gun at him, I continued patting him down. I didn't want to be surprised by a second gun.

"Okay, you can get off his hand," I said, the gun now firmly in my possession and pointing at the fallen villain.

The slap slap of someone running through mud caught our attention.

"Vicki!" I yelled. "Get down!"

Still she sat in her trancelike state, only now she was behind the wheel.

I pushed Brisha Johnson in front of the cover of the car as I made out a shithouse of a man running through the rain. So far he had not fired a shot.

"Stop right there or I'll shoot," I warned, bracing Brewster's automatic against the Buick's hood.

Still the man kept coming.

"I mean it."

He slowed to a walk. A weightlifter's walk, with thighs apart. The rain was really pelting us, but I still recognized the silhouette of Hank Brewster.

I fired a shot into the sky. He stopped.

"That's far enough."

He was standing beside the Buick, the splayed body of his father clearly visible in the car's headlights.

"Put your hands up or I'll shoot you in the leg." That seemed like a reasonable request to me.

Remarkably, he did as instructed.

"Dad?"

I stood aside and let him pass by. He dropped to his knees in the mud and shook his father's shoulder. "Dad? Dad?" There was a catch in his voice as he looked in his father's eyes. "Oh God, Dad." An eery, high-pitched keening, incongruous with his massive body, filled the air as he rocked back and forth with his father in his arms.

"Phelan, can you hear me?" I asked.

Nothing came from the man in the mud.

"Brewster, if you can hear me, blink your eyes."

The rain pelted his face and I stared at it intently.

I repeated my instructions.

Brewster's eyelids fluttered.

"Again."

They opened and shut again. He was conscious.

"Can you move your hand?" I asked.

The eyelids closed again, but I had no idea if that was a yes or no. Nothing on him moved.

And that was our first clue that he had broken his lousy red neck.

Epilogue

WHILE IT WOULD HAVE MADE A NICE STORY IF THE SIRENS WE HAD heard in the night had been the cavalry coming to save us, that wasn't the case. Turns out that a cattle truck had turned over out near the cotton gin and the rescue vehicles had gone out there. It was just a nice coincidence that sent Brewster on a somewhat different course of action, that, in all probability, saved our lives.

The quiet, unassuming Brisha Johnson had followed me home from Florence after our meeting that morning. Me, the hotshot private investigator, and I never even noticed the old green Buick on my tail. It never occurred to me that she would follow me. Of course she did admit to hanging back a few cars.

Brisha was fueled not by revenge so much, although that certainly had a play in how things turned out, but by her craving to find her boys. Since I had bragged that I might know where they were, she said there was no way she was going to let me out of her sight until she found out what was going on. It was a good lesson for me, and now I'm using my rearview mirror more.

That wasn't the only thing I learned from this case. Getting stuck with a gun without bullets wasn't a lot of fun, so I'm now carrying a speed loader in addition to the five rounds in my .38.

I knew when I saw the fire-breathing dragon on the truck that had tried to run down Vicki and me that it was from Dragon Links. Dave Robinson was behind the wheel. Thanks to Brisha's driving, Robinson broke both of his legs, fractured his left arm, lost a kidney and his spleen. And that can't hold a candle to his legal problems. Hank, in the passenger seat, came out of the rollover unscathed.

Abel Messenger finally had his case. The muddy Crown Royal pouch was found in Brewster's back pocket. While there was no way of proving who took out the deer tag, or where the quarters, engagement ring and feather came from, the dog tags were traceable. They belonged to Spec. 4 Lipton Shield of the U.S. Army, who was declared AWOL on February 13, 1962.

But the most incriminating thing in all of it, the one item that cinched the case, was the tiny boojum leaf found in the coffin debris of Matthew Johnson. Samples of boojum leaves were gathered in an effort to determine how complex each one was. It turned out that they were as complicated as the paloverde leaves used in the Basalt murder trial, and that individuality made the case.

For the second time in Arizona history, a plant lineup was held. A boojum leaf taken from the tree in Brewster's yard, along with eight other boojum samples, were presented to Dr. Brayden Forester, who was not told which leaf came from the suspect tree. He matched it easily to the coffin leaf.

Because he was paralyzed, and no longer deemed a threat to society, it was questionable for a while as to whether or not Phelan Brewster would be charged. After his medical condition stabilized, he was finally arrested and charged with the murders of Matthew and Mark Johnson.

After some haggling, a plea bargain was struck, and in return for turning state's evidence against Robinson, Daglio and Stone, Brewster avoided the maximum sentence and was remanded to the Arizona State Prison in Florence. He refused to implicate his son, Henry, although investigators are still examining his involvement with the Sporting Club.

In a quirky twist of fate, Brewster's therapist at the prison turned out to be Micah Johnson, the third son of Rodney and Brisha. Until the publicity, Micah had no idea that his father and brothers were murdered, or that the murderer would come under his care.

So today, Phelan Brewster is a prisoner not only in the Arizona state penal system, but within his own body. His custodian is the brother and son of the children and man he murdered over thirty years ago. What goes through each of their minds from day to day as they interact, is anyone's guess, although I imagine that a certain amount of terror invades Brewster's head every time he sees Micah Johnson.

Victoria Carpenter finished her book, and contrary to her agent's dire predictions, it made a very respectable showing and earned her a contract for doing more serious books. Vicki was thrilled to be catapulted out of the romance genre and into mainstream fiction.

As for me, I was happy that I was able to exorcise some of the old ghosts.

On the home front, Petunia is still living with us. While Bea comes out and plays with her from time to time, she hasn't asked to take her back home, and, I must confess, I haven't offered to return her. The porcine princess has definitely carved a niche in all of our hearts and Blue and Mrs. Fierce would probably never forgive me if she went back to Bea's town house.

So far, neither the Mexican Mafia or our authorities have shown up on my doorstep looking for Corazon Elena Figueroa de la Fuente Orantez. Since I really don't know what happened down in Mexico, I've gotten reasonably comfortable with keeping my mouth shut, although I suspect the last chapter on this little drama is yet to be written. Quinta is living with her grandfather and I've found her to be as charming and helpful as the rest of her family. Jake Hatcher's still hanging around the Vaca Grande a lot more than he ever used to, but it doesn't seem to bother Martín.

Right before Christmas, after the charges had been filed, I saddled Gray one afternoon and headed up the Deer Camp trail. It was a clear, sunny, winter Arizona day and as I rode, I did not bother looking back at the traces of civilization behind me.

Once I hit Deer Camp I tied Gray to a tree and pulled out my Buck knife. With the sun on my face, I carved the second half of the heart on the weathered table, taking care to place the jagged edge of the new half as close to the old one as possible. It was a Humpty Dumpty heart, broken, never to be the same again, but as complete as I could make it. I debated for a while about what names to put in the heart, finally settling on Rodney and Brisha.

As I carved on the old, scarred table, I noticed that two new names had been added since my last visit. *JB loves Abby*. I knew the players. Abigail Van Thiesen, heiress to a vast candy fortune, was the talk of La Cienega, for she'd begun dating a penniless bull rider named J. B. Calendar, who was half her age.

When I rode back down the trail I thought of all the names on the old battered picnic table. Would J. B.'s and Abby's love story turn out any better than Rodney and Brisha Johnson's?

Little did I know then, how soon I would find out.

About the Author

Sinclair Browning is a "dirty shirt cowgirl" whose family ranched for years. Having lived in, and ridden, the Sonoran desert for most of her life, she still breaks her own horses, rounds up cattle and team pens. The license plate on her pickup reads "Wrider," a term she coined that describes her two loves—writing and riding.

sinclairbrowning.com